1945 - 46
SEASON

Theatre WORLD

EDITED BY
DANIEL BLUM

ABOUT
THEATRE WORLD

•

This is the Second Volume of *Theatre World*, the complete pictorial and statistical record of the 1945-46 New York theatrical season.

Theatre World is published annually.

Readers will find that this vastly illustrated book will afford great enjoyment as well as prove to be a ready reference.

We believe that *Theatre World* will be a welcome volume on any booklover's shelf.

THE EDITORS

Theatre WORLD

DANIEL BLUM, Editor and Publisher
NORMAN MACDONALD, Associate Editor
JOHN ATKIN, Art Editor
GEORGE FREEDLEY, WILLIAM LEONARD
—Feature Writers
LOUIS MELANCON, CONSTANTINE
—Staff Photographers

᧞

CONTENTS

———

The editors wish to thank the Broadway Theatrical Press Representatives, the Theatre Collection of the New York Public Library and Celebrity Service, Inc., for valuable assistance.

———

Alfred Lunt and Lynn Fontanne in "O Mistress Mine"

THE NEW YORK SEASON

Compared to last season, the theatrical season of 1945-1946 was disappointing from both a quality and quantity standpoint. Then, too, it was not as good from a financial point of view. The hits were far between and fewer.

Not excluding experimental productions or City Center revivals or return engagements, Broadway produced seventy-five attractions as against eighty-seven the year before. There were forty-six straight plays, thirteen musicals, two reviews, thirteen revivals and one vaudeville show. Twelve plays that opened last year achieved runs of over a year. This season only seven seem destined for that honor. These include "State of the Union", "Born Yesterday", "O Mistress Mine", "Annie Get Your Gun", "Call Me Mister", and revivals of "The Red Mill" and "Show Boat".

The past season can be remembered as one of many successful revivals and many unsuccessful racial problem plays. The revivals included "The Red Mill", "Pygmalion", "Show Boat", "Hamlet", "The Would-Be Gentleman", "He Who Gets Slapped", "The Winter's Tale", "Candida", and the Old Vic Company's repertory of "Henry IV, Parts 1 and 2", "Uncle Vanya", "Oedipus", and "The Critic". Of these only two, "He Who Gets Slapped", and "The Would-Be Gentleman" were failures. "The Red Mill", "Pygmalion", "Show Boat" and "The Winter's Tale" passed the runs of their original productions and Maurice Evans' G. I. version of "Hamlet" missed by one performance matching the record run of John Gielgud's "Hamlet".

The problem plays produced were "Deep Are the Roots", "Home of the Brave", "Strange Fruit", "This, Too, Shall Pass", "On Whitman Avenue", "Jeb", and "Walk Hard". Only "Deep Are the Roots" achieved real success.

This season can also be remembered as "the battle against the critics". Irwin Shaw started the *barrage* in protest against their treatment of his "The Assassin"; Maxwell Anderson and The Playwrights' Company followed through upholding their "Truckline Cafe"; Messrs. Hecht and MacArthur continued the fight by forcing a run of their "Swan Song", and Orson Welles brought up the rear guard attack by "hexing" a very famous critic who calls himself Robert Garland. To add insult to insult and further dent the prestige of that thankless critical profession, the Critics Circle failed to reach an agreement as to the best play of the season. The Pulitzer Prize Committee had no trouble awarding its prize to "State of the Union".

Broadway Calendar

JUNE 1, 1945 TO JUNE 1, 1946

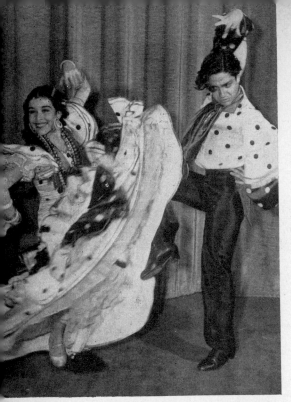

Rosario & Antonio

ZIEGFELD THEATRE

Opened Friday, June 1, 1945*
Billy Rose presents:

CONCERT VARIETIES

Orchestra conducted by Pembroke Davenport; Technical direction by Carlton Winckler.

Featuring

Katherine Dunham	Zero Mostel
Deems Taylor	Jerome Robbins
Rosario & Antonio	Imogene Coca
Eddie Mayehoff	Salici Puppets
William Archibald	Nestor Chayres
Ammons, Johnson & Sidney Catlett	

Including

"INTERPLAY"

A ballet by Jerome Robbins; Music by Morton Gould; Decor and Costumes by Carl Kent.

Danced by:

Jerome Robbins	Janet Reed
John Kriza	Muriel Bentley
Michael Kidd	Rozsika Sabo
Erik Kristen	Bettina Rosay

Katherine Dunham Company: Vancye Aikens, Talley Beatty, Eddy Clay, La Verne French, Tommy Gomez, Lenwood Morris, Roger Ohardieno, Lucille Ellis, Sylvilla Fort, Dolores Harper, Richardson Jackson, Ora Leak, Gloria Mitchell.

A Variety Show.

Company Manager, John Tuerk
Publicity, Tom Van Dycke
General Stage Manager, Frank Hall
Stage Manager, George Hunter

*Closed June 28, 1945   (36 performances)

Imogene Coca and William Archibald in a burlesque of "The Afternoon of a Faun"

Lyle Bettger—Jutta Wolfe—Gloria Stroock, kneeling—
Arleen Whelan—Hugh Herbert—Susana Garnett—Forrest Orr

Hugh Herbert   Arleen Whelan

Gloria Stroock—Arleen Whelan—
Lyle Bettger—Jutta Wolfe

ROYALE THEATRE

Opened Tuesday, June 19, 1945*
Maximilian Becker and Peter Warren present:

OH, BROTHER!

By Jacques Deval; Directed by Bretaigne
Windust; Setting by Samuel Leve.

Cast of Characters
(In order of appearance)

Allen Kilmer.............. ....Don Gibson
Sue Atkins....................................Susana Garnett
Charles Craddock.........................Hugh Herbert
Ethel Shores................................Eva Condon
Rose...Sally Archdeacon
Larry...Kendall Bryson
Marion Cosgrove.........................Arleen Whelan
Amelia Broadwell ....Catharine Doucet
Steve Foley.................................Lyle Bettger
Julian Trumbull...........................Forrest Orr
Connie Rowland...........................Jutta Wolfe
Joan Massuber.............................Gloria Stroock

A comedy in three acts. The action takes
place in the Study of the Cosgrove Home, Daytona Beach, Florida.

General Manager, Charles Stewart
Company Manager, Allan Attwater
Press, Frank Goodman
Stage Manager, James Gelb

*Closed July 7, 1945   (23 performances)

7

BOOTH THEATRE

Opened Thursday, June 21, 1945*

The Messrs. Shubert in association with Albert De Courville present:

THE WIND IS NINETY

By Ralph Nelson; Directed by Mr. De Courville; Setting by Frederick Fox; Lighting by John Davis.

Cast of Characters
(In order of appearance)

Nana	Blanche Yurka
Joan	Joyce Van Patten
Tommy	Roy Sterling
Jimmy	Kevin Mathews**
Chris	Donald Devlin
Bert	Teddy Rose
Doc Ritchie	Bert Lytell
Mr. Wheeler	Scott Moore
Jean	Frances Reid
Ernie Sheffield	Dickie Van Patten
Dan	Wendell Corey
Soldier	Kirk Douglas***
Boy	Marty Miller
Youth	James Dobson
Young Man	Henry Barnard
2nd Lieutenant	Gordon McDonald

A play in three acts, one set. The Front Lawn of an American Home.

Company Manager, George Oshrin
Press, C. P. Greneker, Stanley Seiden, Ben Kornzweig
Stage Manager, John Holden

*Closed September 22, 1945
(108 performances)
**Replaced by Victor Vraz
***Replaced by Bob Stevenson

Wendell Corey and Kirk Douglas

Bert Lytell—Blanche Yurka—Frances Reid

Luba Malina as Countess Landovska sings "Czardas" for the officers in the Red Room of the Sacher Restaurant

WINTER GARDEN

(Moved to BARRYMORE THEATRE, October 1, 1945)
Opened Wednesday, July 18, 1945*
Jules J. Leventhal and Harry Howard present:

MARINKA

Book by George Marion Jr. and Karl Farkas; Lyrics by Mr. Marion; Music by Emmerich Kalman; Dances and Ballet by Albertina Rasch; Settings by Howard Bay; Costumes by Mary Grant; Staged by Hassard Short; Conductor, Ray Kavanaugh.

Cast of Characters
(In order of appearance)

Nadine ....Ruth Webb**1
Countess Van Diefendorfer....Elline Walther**2
Bratfisch ....Romo Vincent
Crown Prince Rudolph.........Harry Stockwell**3
Count Lobkowitz.........................Taylor Holmes
Naval Lieutenant...........................Noel Gordon
Count Hoyos.................................Paul Campbell
Francis ....Leonard Elliott**4
Tilly ....Ronnie Cunningham
Marinka ....Joan Roberts**5
Madame Sacher...................................Ethel Levey
Countess Landovska..........................Luba Malina
Waiter ....Jack Leslie
Lieutenant Baltatzy.........................Bob Douglas
Emperor Franz Josef........Reinhold Schunzel**6
Countess Huebner.................Adrienne Gray**7
Sergeant Negulegul....................Michael Barrett
Lieutenant Palafy.....................Jack Gansert**8

Musical Numbers: "One Touch of Vienna," "The Cab Song," "My Prince Came Riding," "If I Never Waltz Again," "Turn On The Charm," "One Last Love Song," "Old Man Danube," Hungarian Dance, "Czardas," "Sigh by Night," "Paletas," "Treat A Woman Like A Drum," "I Auditioned For The Shah," "Young Man Danube."

A Musical Comedy in two acts with a Prologue and Epilogue. Time: The Present and 1888-89. Scenes: An Open Air Movie Theatre in Connecticut, Gardens of the Imperial Palace, Schoenbrunn, Lodge at Mayerling, Street in Vienna, Red Room of the Sacher Restaurant, Austro-Hungarian Border, Parade Grounds in Budapest.

General Manager, Charles Mulligan
Press, James D. Proctor, Frank Goodman
Stage Manager, Robert Barre

*Closed December 8, 1945 (165 performances)
**Replacements: 1. Ethel Madsen, 2. Helene Arthur, 3. Jerry Wayne, 4. "Doodles" Weaver, 5. Edith Fellows, 6. Taylor Holmes, then John McKee, 7. Elline Walther, 8. Charles Laskey.

Harry Stockwell and Joan Roberts

Edith Fellows and Jerry Wayne

Virginia MacWatters and George Rigaud

CENTURY THEATRE

Opened Thursday, September 6, 1945***
Felix Brentano presents:

MR. STRAUSS GOES TO BOSTON**

Music by Robert Stolz; Lyrics by Robert Sour; Book by Leonard L. Levinson, based on an original story by Alfred Gruenwald and Geza Herczeg; Choreography by George Balanchine; Designed by Stewart Chaney; Costumes by Walter Florell; Musical arrangements by George Lessner; Conductor, Robert Stolz; Directed by Mr. Brentano.

Cast of Characters
(In order of appearance)

Dapper Dan Pepper	Ralph Dumke
Policeman McGillicudy	Brian O'Mara
Inspector Gogarty	Don Fiser
1st Reporter	Dennis Dengate
2nd Reporter	Larry Gilbert
3rd Reporter	Joseph Monte
Pepi	Florence Sundstrom
Bellhop	Frank Finn
Johann Strauss	George Rigaud
Elmo Tilt	Edward J. Lambert
Hotel Manager	Lee Edwards
Brook Whitney	Virginia MacWatters
A Waiter	Paul Mario
Mrs. Dexter	Lailye Tenen
Mrs. Blakely	Rose Perfect
Mr. Whitney	Sydney Grant
Mrs. Taylor	Arlene Dahl
Mrs. Hastings	Selma Felton
Mrs. Iverson	Marie Barova
Mrs. Byrd	Cecile Sherman
Butler	John Oliver
Tom Avery	Jay Martin
A Photographer	John Harrold
Earl	Brian O'Mara
Hetty Strauss	Ruth Matteson
Man In Overalls	Paul Mario
Aide To President	Lee Edwards
President Grant	Norman Roland
Solo Dancers	Harold Lang / Babs Heath / Margit Dekova

Musical Numbers: "Can Anyone See?" *"Radetsky March-Fantasie," "For The Sake of Art," *"Laughing-Waltz," "Mr. Strauss Goes To Boston," "Down With Sin," "Who Knows?," *"Midnight Waltz," "Into The Night," *"Coloratura Waltz," *"The Gossip Polka," "Going Back Home," "You Never Know What Comes Next," "What's a Girl Supposed To Do?" "The Grand And Glorious Fourth," *"Waltz Finale."

A Romantic Comedy with music. Time: 1872. Scenes: Lobby, Corridor and Sitting-room of the Grand Palace Hotel, New York City; Drawing-room of the Whitney Home in Boston; Bedroom and Balcony of the Governor Winthrop House; and along the Charles River.

General Manager, Milton Baron
Company Manager, Joseph Moss
Press, James D. Proctor, Frank Goodman
Stage Manager, R. O. Brooks

*Musical arrangements of Johann Strauss' melodies.

**Any similarity to actual history is coincidental.

***Closed September 16, 1945 (12 performances)

Ruth Matteson, as Mrs. Strauss, has breakfast at the Governor Winthrop House

BILTMORE THEATRE

Opened Tuesday, September 11, 1945*
Hall Shelton** presents:

A BOY WHO LIVED TWICE

By Leslie Floyd Egbert and Gertrude Ogden Tubby; Staged by Paul Foley; Setting by John Root, the song "Forgotten Roads" by Carlos and Sanders.

Cast of Characters
(In order of appearance)

Ellen Blake............................Cecil Elliott
Braxton..................................Stapleton Kent
Jeane Hastings.........................Anne Sargent
Randall Hastings......................Grandon Rhodes
Martha Hastings......................Claire Windsor
Dr. Cecil Blake (Dockaby) W. O. McWatters
Philip Hastings........................John Heath
Anne Cunningham....................Strelsa Leeds
Dr. Broulette ....Vaughan Glaser
Mother ....Nellie Burt

A Psychological Play in three acts. The Scene is the living-room of the Hastings' Home—Long Island, New York. Time: The Present.

General Manager, Louis Cline
Press, Larry Anhalt
Stage Manager, George Zorn

*Closed September 22, 1945 (15 performances)

**Mr. Shelton spent seven years preparing this script for production.

Claire Windsor and Vaughan Glaser

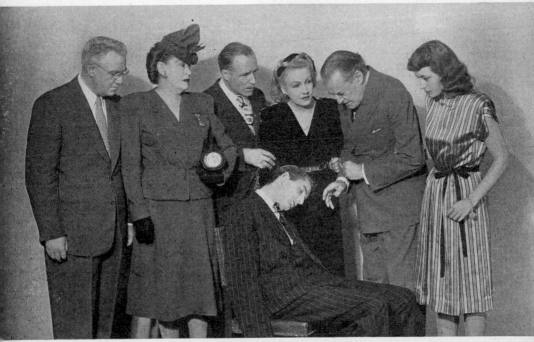

W. O. McWatters—Cecil Elliott—Grandon Rhodes—Claire Windsor—Vaughan Glaser—
Anne Sargent—John Heath (sitting)

11

ROYALE THEATRE

Opened Wednesday, September 12, 1945***
William Cahn presents:

DEVILS GALORE**

By Eugene Vale; Staged by Robert Perry;
Setting by Howard Bay; Costumes by Peggy
Clark.

Cast of Characters
(In order of appearance)

Effie Thurston	Tony Eden
Bernie Grant	Michael King*1
Dr. Aguirra	Harry Sothern
Cecil Brock	George Baxter
Miss Pierce	Betty Kelley
Mrs. Isabel Goodwyn	Jean Cleveland
A Devil	Ernest Cossart
Larry	Paul Byron*2
Bobbie	John (Red) Kullers
Inspector Brandon	Malcolm Lee Beggs
Atamar	Rex O'Malley
Packey "The Flash" Gurney	Solen Burry

A Comedy of the Supernatural in three acts.
The Time is the Present. The Place is Cecil
Brock's Office on the 34th Floor of a Fifth
Avenue Skyscraper.

General Manager, Irving Cooper
Company Manager, Harold C. Jacoby
Press, Ivan Black, Maurice Turet
Stage Manager, John Effrat

*Played by 1. James Elliott, 2. John Effrat
during out of town try-out.
**This play was put into rehearsals last season
by John Clein with Gene Lockhart in the
lead but the production failed to materialize.
***Closed September 15, 1945 (5 perform-
ances).

Jean Cleveland—Rex O'Malley—
Harry Sothern—-Betty Kelley

Ernest Cossart—Betty Kelley—Rex O'Malley—Tony Eden

Bonnie Nolan—Donald McClelland—Loy Nilson—Gray Stafford—Philip Huston—
Bernadene Hayes—Robert Noe

BARRYMORE THEATRE

Opened Thursday, September 13, 1945*
Albert N. Chaperau and Johnnie Walker
present:

MAKE YOURSELF AT HOME

By Vera Mathews; Directed by Mr. Walker;
Scenery by William Noel Saulter; Costumes by
Janice Wallace.

Cast of Characters
(In order of appearance)

Luther Quinn ....Donald McClelland
Honeybelle Collins ....Bonnie Nolan
Vic Arnold ....Philip Huston
Ray Gilbert ....Donald White
Porter ....Charles Carol
Dwight Waring ....William Valentine
Mona Gilbert ....Bernadene Hayes**
(Mama) Gilbert ....Suzanne Jackson
Ivy ....Elizabeth Brew
Ferris Delmar ....Robert Carleton
Barney (Reporter) ....Grey Stafford
Bob (Reporter) ....Robert Noe
Sammy (Photographer) ....Loy Nilson

A Comedy in two acts. Action takes place in
the Living-room of Mona Gilbert's New York
Apartment.

Manager, William Brennan
Press, Zac Freedman
Stage Manager, Paul E. Porter

*Closed September 15, 1945 (4 performances)
**Sally Eilers played this role during the out of
town try-out.

Bernadene Hayes and Philip Huston

13

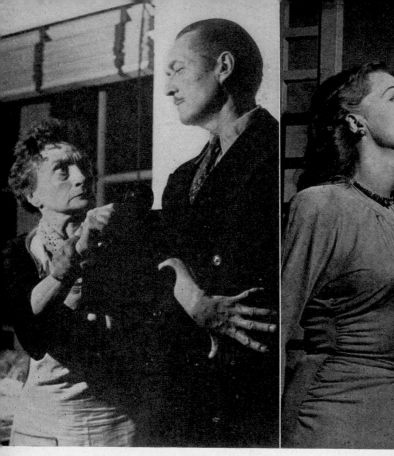

Una O'Connor   Edmund Lowe   June Havoc   Edmund Lowe

Doris Dalton—Edmund Lowe—June Havoc

PLYMOUTH THEATRE

Opened Monday, September 24, 1945*
The Messrs. Shubert in association with
Albert De Courville present:

THE RYAN GIRL

By Edmund Goulding; Setting designed by
Raymond Sovey; Staged by Mr. Goulding.

Cast of Characters
(In order of appearance)

Weavy Hicks ....Una O'Connor
Miley Gaylon ....Edmund Lowe
Venetia Ryan ....June Havoc
Harold Tyler ....Curtis Cooksey
Lt. George Clark ....John Compton
2nd Lt. Victor Sellers ....Richard Gibbs
Jane Clark ....Doris Dalton
Edwin Rourke ....Calvin Thomas

A Drama in three acts. The Action takes place
in Venetia Ryan's Apartment, New York City,
a Sunday afternoon in September, 1944.

Company Manager, Eddie Lewis
Press, Leo Freedman
Stage Managers, Stuart Fox and
Richard A. Martin

*Closed November 3, 1945 (48 performances)

14

BOOTH THEATRE

Opened Tuesday, September 25, 1945*
Guthrie McClintic in association with Lee
Shubert presents:

YOU TOUCHED ME!

By Tennessee Williams and Donald Windham,
Suggested by a Short Story of D. H. Lawrence's
of the same name; Setting by Motley; Staged
by Mr. McClintic.

Cast of Characters
(In order of appearance)

Matilda Rockley	Marianne Stewart
Emmie Rockley	Catherine Willard
Phoebe	Norah Howard
Hadrian	Montgomery Clift
Cornelius Rockley	Edmund Gwenn
The Reverend Guildford Melton	Neil Fitzgerald
A Policeman	Freeman Hammond

A Romantic Comedy in three acts. The Action takes place in a house in rural England in
the Spring of 1943.

General Manager, Stanley Gilkey
Company Manager, William Tisdale
Press, Francis Robinson, Lorella Val-Mery
Stage Manager, Freeman Hammond

*Closed January 5, 1946   (109 performances)

Neil Fitzgerald and Edmund Gwenn

Catherine Willard—Marianne Stewart—
Montgomery Clift—Edmund Gwenn

Montgomery Clift—Edmund Gwenn—
Catherine Willard

Carol Goodner and Barbara Bel Geddes

FULTON THEATRE

Opening Wednesday, September 26, 1945
Kermit Bloomgarden and George Heller
present:

DEEP ARE THE ROOTS

By Arnaud d'Usseau and James Gow; Staged
by Elia Kazan; Setting by Howard Bay; Costumes by Emeline Roche.

Cast of Characters
(In order of appearance)

Honey Turner ....Helen Martin
Bella Charles ....Evelyn Ellis
Senator Ellsworth Langdon....Charles Waldron*1
Genevra Langdon ....Barbara Bel Geddes
Alice Langdon ....Carol Goodner*2
Roy Maxwell ....Harold Vermilyea**
Howard Merrick ....Lloyd Gough
Brett Charles ....Gordon Heath
Sheriff Serkin ....Andrew Leigh
Chuck Warren ....George Dice
Bob Izay ....Douglas Rutherford

A Drama on Racial Prejudice in three acts;
Scene: the Living-room of the Langdon Home
on the outskirts of a small town in the Deep
South; Spring, 1945.

Production Assistant, Coby Ruskin
Company Manager, Max Allentuck
Press, James D. Proctor and Frank Goodman
Stage Manager, Esther Snowden

*Replaced by 1. Edwin Jerome; 2. Barbara
O'Neil.

**During Mr. Vermilyea's two-months' absence,
Donald Macdonald substituted.

Carol Goodner—Lloyd Gough—Gordon Heath—Barbara Bel Geddes—Charles Waldron

Charles Waldron and Gordon Heath

Carol Goodner—Charles Waldron—
Barbara Bel Geddes

Gordon Heath and Barbara Bel Geddes

17

Katherine Dunham and Her Dancers

ADELPHI THEATRE

Opened Thursday, September 27, 1945*
George Stanton presents:

CARIB SONG

By William Archibald; Music by Baldwin
Bergersen; Lyrics by Mr. Archibald; Book di-
rected by Mary Hunter; Choreography by Kath-
erine Dunham; Scenery designed and lighted by
Jo Mielziner; Costumes by Motley; Musical
Direction, Pembroke Davenport; Orchestrations,
Ted Royal.

Cast of Characters
(In order of appearance)

The Singer ....Harriet Jackson
The Friends............Eulabel Riley and Mary Lewis
The Fat Woman ....Mable Sanford Lewis
The Tall Woman ....Mercedes Gilbert
The Husband ....William Franklin
The Fisherman ....Avon Long
The Woman ....Katherine Dunham
The Fishwoman ....Elsie Benjamin
The Madras Seller ....Byron Cuttler
The Shango Priest ....La Rosa Estrada
The Boy Possessed by a Snake......Tommy Gomez
Leaders of the Shango Dancers....Vanoye Aikens
and Lucille Ellis
The Village Friends: Roxie Foster, Lauwanne
Ingram, Richardena Jackson, Eartha Kitt,
Ora Leak, Gloria Mitchell, Priscilla Stevens,
Enid Williams, James Alexander, Eddy Clay,
Norman Coker, John Diggs, Jesse Hawkins,
Julio Mendez, Lenwood Morris, Eugene Lee
Robinson, William C. Smith, Charles Welch.
Musical Numbers: "Go Sit By The Body," Legba,
"This Woman," "Water Movin' Slow," "Basket,
Make A Basket," Congo Paillette, "Woman Is A
Rascal," "A Girl She Can't Remain," Shango**
Market Song, "Sleep, Baby, Don't Cry," "Things
Remembered," "Today I Is So Happy," "Can't
Stop The Sea," "Forest At Night," "You Know,
Oh Lord," "Go To Church Sunday," "Go Down
To The River," Washerwomen Dance, "Oh,
Lonely One."

A Musical Play of the West Indies in two
acts. The Action takes place in a West Indian
Village, on the Road to the Shango, in the
Forest, and down by the River.

General Manager, Jesse Long
Press, Karl Bernstein and Martha Dreiblatt
Stage Manager, William Lilling

*Closed October 27, 1945 (36 performances)
**A Ritual which is based on West African re-
ligious practices in combination with Catholic
elements.

Katherine Dunham   Avon Long

Mary Rolfe—Donald Buka

BELASCO THEATRE

Opened Saturday, September 29, 1945*
S. S. Krellberg presents:

LIVE LIFE AGAIN

By Dan Totheroh; Directed by Sawyer Falk;
Settings and Lighting by Albert Johnson; Costumes by Grace Houston.

Cast of Characters
(In order of speaking)

Preacher Hill	Edward Bushman
Mrs. Jones	Kay MacDonald
Mrs. Smith	Isabelle Bishop
Mrs. Brown	Ruth Saville
Mrs. White	Phoebe Mackay
Mrs. Black	Mathilda Barling
Mrs. Green	Florence Beresford
Mr. Smith	Lester Lonergan, Jr.
Mr. Jones	Bruce Halsey
Mr. Brown	Pat Smith
Mr. White	Robert Gardet
Mr. Black	Ken Bowles
Mr. Green	James Coyle
Spiers	Parker Fennelly
Nathan Spiers	Zachary A. Charles
Judith Spiers	Mary Rolfe
Greer, the Gravedigger	John O. Hewitt
Mark Orme	Donald Buka
Saul Orme	Thomas Chalmers
Joe	Ken Bowles
Hilda Paulson	Beatrice de Neergaard
Doctor Bush	Harold McGee
Rose	Mary Boylan
Mrs. Hansen	Grace Mills

A Poetic Drama in three acts and six sets.
The Action takes place near the prairie village
of Bison Run, Nebraska, at Saul Orme's House,
the Graveyard, Pleasant Grove, Judith Spier's
Bedroom, a Cornfield, and Orme's Bedroom.
Soon after the turn of this century.

General Manager, Nicholas Holde
Press, Bernard Simon
Stage Manager, Al West

*Closed October 1, 1945   (2 performances)

Mary Rolfe as "Judith" and Donald Buka
as "Mark"

Donald Buka

19

ALVIN THEATRE

(Moved to ADELPHI THEATRE December 3, 1945)
Opened Saturday, October 6, 1945***
W. Horace Schmidlapp** in association with Harry Bloomfield presents:

POLONAISE

By Gottfried Reinhardt and Anthony Veiller; Music by Frederic Chopin, Adaptations and Original Numbers by Bronislaw Kaper; Lyrics by John Latouche; Choreography by David Lichine; Book directed by Stella Adler; Settings by Howard Bay; Costumes by Mary Grant; Orchestrations by Don Walker; Musical Director, Max Goberman; Choral Director, Irving London.

Cast of Characters
(In order of appearance)

Captain Adams	John V. Schmidt
General Washington	Josef Draper
Colonel Hale	Martin Lewis
General Thaddeus Kosciusko	Jan Kiepura
Sergeant Wacek Zapolski	Curt Bois
Private Tompkins	Sidney Lawson
Private Skinner	Arthur Lincoln
Private Motherwell	Martin Cooke
Marisha	Marta Eggerth
Vladek	Rem Olmsted
Tecla	Tania Riabouchinska*1
General Boris Volkoff	Harry Bannister
Count Casimir Zaleski	Josef Draper
Peniatowski	Lewis Appleton
Kollontaj	Andrew Thurston
Potocki	Gary Green
Countess Ludwika Zaleski	Rose Inghram
Blacksmith	Martin Cooke
Butcher	Larry Beck
Priest	Larry O'Dell
Pianist	Zadel Skolovsky
King Stanislaus Augustus	James MacColl
Count Gronski	Walter Appler*2
Princess Margarita	Candy Jones*3
Princess Lydia	Leta Mauree*4
Princess Lania	Sherry Shadburne
Princess Anna	Martha Emma Watson
Peasant Girl	Betty Durrence

"EXCHANGE OF LOVERS"

The Princess	Ruth Riekman
The Prince	Shawn O'Brien
The Highwayman	Sergei Ismaeloff
The Page	Amelia Valez

The Ballerinas — Jean Harris, Virginia Barnes, Adele Bodroghy, Joan Collenette.

Musical Numbers: Autumn Songs, "Laughing Bells," "O Heart of My Country" (From Nocturne in E Flat), "Stranger," "Au Revoir, Soldier," "Meadowlark" (from Mazurka in B Flat), Mazurka (from various themes), "Hay, Hay, Hay," "Moonlight Soliloquy" (Nocture in F Sharp Major), "Just For Tonight" (from Etude in E), Finale (from Polonaise in A Flat and Revolutionary Etude), Gavotte (Variations on a French Air), "Exchange of Lovers" (from various themes), "An Imperial Conference" (from Chopin Theme), Polonaise (Polonaise in A Flat), "Now I Know Your Face By Heart" (from Waltz in D Flat), "Next Time I Care," Tecla's Mood (from various themes), "I Wonder As I Wander," Battle of Macijowice Ballet (Four Etudes), "Wait For Tomorrow" (from various themes).

A Musical in two acts. Time, 1783. Scenes: West Point Ramparts, New York Waterfront, Hayfield and Manor House near Cracow, Poland, Royal Palace and Street in Warsaw, and Philadelphia Waterfront.

General Manager, Ralph R. Kravatte
Press, Karl Bernstein and Martha Dreiblatt
General Stage Manager, Murray Queen
Stage Manager, Walter E. Munroe

*Replaced by 1. Jean Harris, 2. Martin Cooke, 3. Mary McQuade, 4. Ann Dennis.
**In November, Mr. Schmidlapp relinquished his managerial rights, leaving Harry Bloomfield the soie producer thereafter.
***Closed January 12, 1946 (113 performances)

Jan Kiepura and Marta Eggerth

Jan Kiepura as "Kosciusko"

Dame May Whitty

Eva LeGallienne as "Therese Raquin"

BILTMORE THEATRE

Opened Tuesday, October 9, 1945*
Victor Payne-Jennings and Bernard Klawans present:

THERESE**

By Thomas Job; Staged by Margaret Webster; Setting and Costumes by Raymond Sovey.

Cast of Characters
(In order of appearance)

Camille ....Berry Kroeger
Madame Raquin ....Dame May Whitty
Therese ....Eva LeGallienne
Laurent ....Victor Jory
Madame Louise ....Doris Patston
Mr. Grivet ....John F. Hamilton
Inspector Michaud ....Averell Harris
Suzanne ....Annette Sorell

A Drama in three acts. The scene is a Living-room above a milliner's shop in the Pont Neuf district in Paris, 1875-1876.

Company Manager, Charles G. Strakosch
Press, Richard Maney and Anne Woll
Stage Managers, John Lynds, Cavada Humphrey

*Closed December 31, 1945 (96 performances)
**Based on Emile Zola's "Therese Raquin."

John F. Hamilton—Eva LeGallienne—
Victor Jory—Dame May Whitty

Eddie Foy, Jr., Robert Hughes and Michael O'Shea tell the Dutch girls how things are
"In Old New York"

Eddie Foy, Jr.—Odette Myrtil—Michael O'Shea

Michael O'Shea and Eddie Foy, Jr.

ZIEGFELD THEATRE

(Moved to the 46TH STREET THEATRE
December 24, 1945)
Opening Tuesday, October 16, 1945
Paula Stone and Hunt Stromberg, Jr., present:

THE RED MILL

Music by Victor Herbert; Original Book and Lyrics by Henry Blossom; New Orchestrations and Dance Arrangements by Edward Ward; Stage Direction by Billy Gilbert; Scenic and Lighting Supervision by Adrian Awan; Dances staged by Aida Broadbent; Costumes by Walter Israel; Orchestra under the direction of Edward Ward.

Cast of Characters
(In order of appearance)

Town Crier	Billy Griffith*1
Willem	Hal Price
Franz	George Meader
Tina	Dorothy Stone
Bill-Poster	Tom Halligan*2
Flora	Hope O'Brady
Lena	Lois Potter
Dora	Mardi Bayne*3
The Burgomaster	Frank Jaquet
A Sailor	Thomas Spengler*4
Juliana	Lorna Byron*5
Con Kidder	Michael O'Shea*6
Kid Conner	Eddie Foy, Jr.
Gretchen	Ann Andre
Hendrik Van Damn	Robert Hughes
Gaston	Charles Collins
Pennyfeather	Billy Griffith
Madame La Fleur	Odette Myrtil
Georgette	Phyllis Bateman*7
Suzette	Nony Franklin*8
Fleurette	Kathleen Ellis*9
Nanette	Jacqueline Ellis
Lucette	Patricia Gardner *10
Yvette	Joan Johnston
The Governor	Edward Dew

Musical Numbers: "Mignonette," "Whistle It," "Isle of Our Dreams," "The Dancing Lesson," "In Old New York," "When You're Pretty and the World Is Fair," "Moonbeams," "Why the Silence?" "Legend of the Mill," "Every Day Is Ladies' Day With Me," "I Want You to Marry Me," "Al Fresco," "Because You're You," Romanza, "Wedding Bells."

An Operetta in two acts. Time: About 1900. The Inn at the Red Mill, a Neighborhood Street, and the House of the Burgomaster, Katwyk-ann-Zee, Holland.

General Manager, Irving Cooper
Company Manager, John Tuerk
Press, Bernard Simon and Lewis Harmon
Stage Managers, Leslie Thomas, Marvin Kline

*Replacements: 1. Earle Waltman, 2. Leland Ledford, 3. Gloria Sullivan, 4. Calvin Lowell, 5. Marthe Errolle, 6. Jack Whiting, 7. Rosalynd Lowe, 8. Betty Galavan, 9. Betty Fadden, 10. Rosemary O'Shea.

Charles Collins   Odette Myrtil

Dorothy Stone   Frank Jaquet

Frank Jaquet, George Meader, Charles Collins, Dorothy Stone, Michael O'Shea, Eddie Foy, Jr., Odette Myrtil, Robert Hughes, Ann Andre, Edward Dew, Billy Griffith and Company

23

A Cafe in Algiers, Christmas Eve, 1942

Frank Sundstrom as "Robert De Mauny"

Lesley Woods and Frank Sundstrom

NATIONAL THEATRE

Opened Wednesday, October 17, 1945*
Carly Wharton and Martin Gabel in association with Alfred Bloomingdale present:

THE ASSASSIN

By Irwin Shaw; Staged by Mr. Gabel; Settings by Boris Aronson.

Cast of Characters
(In order of appearance)

Monsieur Popinot ....William Hansen
Gustav Boubard ....Alfred White
Lucien Gerard ....Guy Sorel
Christine Theodore ....Frances Chaney
Charles Gannerac ....Ralph Stantley
Helene Mariotte ....Lesley Woods
Sophie Vauquin ....Elena Karam
Robert De Mauny ....Frank Sundstrom
Victor Mallasis ....Harold Huber
David Stein ....Henry Sharp
Ida Stein ....Carmen Mathews
Andre Vauquin ....Karl Malden
Steingel ....Peter Gregg
General Roucheau ....Richard Keith
General Mousset ....Clay Clement
General Kley ....Robert Ober
Colonel Von Kohl ....William Malten
Admiral Marcel Vespery ....Roger De Koven
Haynes ....Harrison Dowd
A Captain ....Alan Dreeben
Lieutenant Crane ....Stuart Nedd
Sergeant .... Frank DeLangton
A Lieutenant ....Bill Weyse
Monsieur Jacques ....Booth Colman
A Woman ....Florence Robinson
Guard ....Alan Dreeben
Priest ....William Marceau
Soldiers ....Booth Colman, Ralph Smiley,
Bill Weyse, William Marceau

A Drama in three acts. Time: November, 1942. Scenes: A Cafe in Algiers, Room in French Army Headquarters, a small Villa and a Cell in a Military Jail.

General Manager, Philip Ad'er
Press, Richard Maney, Anne Woll
Stage Managers, Burton Shevelove,
Helen B. Harvey

*Closed October 27, 1945   (13 performances)

CORONET THEATRE*
Opened Saturday, October 27, 1945**
Oscar Serlin presents:

BEGGARS ARE COMING TO TOWN
By Theodore Reeves; Directed by Harold Clurman; Designed and Lighted by Jo Mielziner; Costumes by Ralph Alswang; Miss Comingore's and Miss Ames' dresses by Charles James.

Cast of Characters
(In order of appearance)

Maurice	Herbert Berghof
Felix	Alfred Linder
Emile	Julius Bing
Dave	E. G. Marshall
Pasqual	Joseph Rosso
Noll Turner	Luther Adler
Lou	Harry Kadison
Frankie Madison	Paul Kelly
F.orrie Dushaye	Dorothy Comingore
Jonathan Webley	Harold Young
Mrs. Bennett Richardson	Adrienne Ames
Bennett Richardson	Austin Fairman
Ziggie	Louis Gilbert
Wilson's Wastrels	Cedric Wallace Trio
Nick Palestro	George Mathews
Heinz	Tom Pedi
Skinner	Arthur Hunnicutt
Goldie	Harry M. Cooke

A Comedy Drama in three acts. The Action takes place in the office of the Avignon, a New York Supper Club.

General Manager, Walter Fried
Company Manager, Harry Kline
Press, Harry Forwood, Reginald Denenholz
Stage Manager, Ben Ross Berenberg

*Formerly the FORREST THEATRE. Property was taken over by the City Playhouses Inc. and remodeled.
**Closed November 17, 1945 (25 performances)

Dorothy Comingore   Paul Kelly

Paul Kelly—Adrienne Ames—Herbert Berghof—Austin Fairman—Luther Adler

25

Fay Bainter and Conrad Janis

EMPIRE THEATRE
Opened Monday, October 29, 1945*
Max Gordon presents:

THE NEXT HALF HOUR

By Mary Chase; Staged by George S. Kaufman; Setting by Edward Gilbert; Costumes by Mary Percy Schenck.

Cast of Characters
(In order of appearance)

Barney Brennan ....Conrad Janis
Margaret Brennan ....Fay Bainter
Pat Brennan ....Jack Ruth
Frances Brennan ....Pamela Rivers
Peter O'Neill ....Francis Compton
James O'Neill ....Art Smith
Rosie Higgins ....Elizabeth Malone
Jessie Shoemaker ....Thelma Schnee
Bridget O'Neill ....Jean Adair
McCracken ....Larry Oliver

A Drama in three acts. The Scene is the Living-room of the Home of Margaret Brennan, on a night in early April, 1913, in an American City.

General Manager, Ben A. Boyar
Company Manager, John Henry Mears
Press, Nat Dorfman
Stage Manager, William McFadden

*Closed November 3, 1945 (8 performances)

Jack Ruth—Frances Compton—Pamela Rivers—Elizabeth Malone—Fay Bainter—
Jean Adair—Art Smith

Eleonora Mendelssohn with Fuzzy McQuade and Jane Earle

ROYALE THEATRE

Opened Wednesday, November 7, 1945*
Joseph M. Hyman and Bernard Hart in
association with Haila Stoddard present:

THE SECRET ROOM

By Robert Turney; Directed by Moss Hart;
Setting by Carolyn Hancock; Lighted by Frederick Fox.

Cast of Characters
(In order of appearance)

Noonie Beverly ....Jane Earle
Susan Beverly ....Frances Dee
Sister ....Fuzzy McQuade
Dr. John Beverly ....Reed Brown, Jr.
Mrs. Smilkin ....Juanita Hall
Margaret Beverly (Mog) ....Grace Coppin
Dr. Jackson ....Ivan Simpson
Leda Ferroni ....Eleonora Mendelssohn
Colonel Hammond ....Albert Bergh
Samuels, an Interne ....Charles S. Dubin

A Murder Melo-drama in three acts. The
Action takes place in the Living-room of the
Beverly House in the country, 1944.

General Manager, Al Goldin
Company Manager, Michael Goldreyer
Press, Michel Mok, Mary Ward
Stage Manager, Don Hershey

*Closed November 24, 1945 (21 performances)

Eleonora Mendelssohn and Frances Dee

Jane Kean

ADELPHI THEATRE

Opened Thursday, November 8, 1945*
Henry Adrian presents:

THE GIRL FROM NANTUCKET

Music by Jacques Belasco; Lyrics by Kay
Twomey; Book by Paul Stanford and Harold
Sherman, Based on a story by Fred Thompson
and Berne Giler; Additional Lyrics and Music
by Hughie Prince and Dick Rogers; Additional
Dialogue by Hy Cooper; Monologue by Mary
Carroll; Book directed by Edward Clarke Lilley;
Staged by Henry Adrian; Choreography by Val
Raset; Settings and Lighting by Albert Johnson;
Costumes by Lou Eisele; Production Assistant,
Harry Howell; Musical Director, Harry Levant.

Jack Durant and Jane Kean

Cast of Characters
(In order of appearance)

Michael Nicolson ....Bob Kennedy
Betty Ellis........... { (Eves.) Adelaide Bishop**1
{ (Mats.)   Pat McClarney
Tom Andrews ....George L. Headley
Ann Ellis ....Marion Niles
Dodey Ellis ....Jane Kean
Keziah Getchel ....Helen Raymond
Judge Peleg ....John Robb
Captain Matthew Ellis.................Billy Lynn**2
Dick Oliver ....Jack Durant
Enrico Nicoletti ....Richard Clemens
The Corporation—
The Four Buccaneers.....................Paul Shiers,
John Panter, Don Cortez, Joseph Cunneff
Roy, Caleb and Several Other
Fellows ....Johnny Eager
Mary ....Connie Sheldon
Dance Specialists............Kim and Kathy Gaynes,
Rapps and Tapps
Solo Dancer ....Tom Ladd

Musical Numbers: "I Want to See More of You,"
"Take the Steamer to Nantucket," "What's He
Like?" "What's a Sailor Got?" "Magnificent
Failure," "Hurray for Nicoletti," "When a
Hick Chick Meets a City Slicker," "Your Fatal
Fascination," "Let's Do and Say We Didn't,"
"Nothing Matters," "Sons of the Sea," Whalers'
Ballet—A Page From Old Nantucket, "Isn't It
a Lovely View?" "From Morning Till Night," "I
Love That Boy," "Hammock in the Blue," "The
Captain and His Lady," "Boukra Fill Mish
Mish."

A Musical Comedy in two acts and a prologue.
Scenes: Apartment House in New York City,
Office of the Nantucket Steamship Company,
Nantucket Pier, Mike and Dick's Apartment in
New York City, Whalers' Bar, Outside and In-
side the Museum, Old Nantucket, Mike and
Chick's Bungalow, Keziah's Beach, and the
Nantucket Square.

Company Manager, George Zorn
Business Manager, Joseph L. Gibson
Press, Marjorie Barkentin
General Stage Manager, R. O. Brooks
Stage Manager, Tony Ferreria

*Closed November 17, 1945 (12 performances)
**Played during tryout tour by, 1. Evelyn
Wyckoff, 2. James Barton.

Bob Kennedy

Ann Shoemaker   Judith Evelyn

GOLDEN THEATRE

Opened Friday, November 9, 1945*
Gilbert Miller presents:

THE RICH FULL LIFE

By Vina Delmar; Setting by Raymond Sovey;
Staged by Mr. Miller.

Cast of Characters
(In order of appearance)

Lou Fenwick ....Judith Evelyn
Mother Fenwick ....Jessie Busley
Carrie ....Edith Meiser
Cynthia ....Virginia Weidler
Fredonia ....Sandra Holman
Lawrence ....Frederic Tozere
Fred ....Frank M. Thomas
Ricky Latham ....Jonathan Braman
Miss McQuillen ....Ann Shoemaker

A Comedy Drama in three acts. The action
takes place in the Living-room of the Fenwick
Home.

General Manager, Harry Fleischman
Company Manager, Edgar Runkle
Press, Richard Maney, Ted Goldsmith
Stage Manager, Richard Bender

*Closed December 1, 1945 (27 performances)

Judith Evelyn   Virginia Weidler

Judith Evelyn   Virginia Weidler   Frederic Tozere

29

CENTURY THEATRE

(Moved to SHUBERT THEATRE, April 30, 1946)

Opened Saturday, November 10, 1945**

Richard Kollmar and James W. Gardiner present:

ARE YOU WITH IT?

Book by Sam Perrin and George Balzer; Adapted from the novel, "Slightly Perfect," by George Malcolm-Smith; Music by Harry Revel; Lyrics by Arnold B. Horwitt; Musical Number Staged by Jack Donohue; Directed by Edward Reveaux; Designed and Lighted by George Jenkins; Costumes by Willa Kim from sketches by Raoul Pene Du Bois; Musical Director, Will Irwin; Vocalizations Supervised and Arranged by H. Clay Warnick.

Cast of Characters
(In order of speaking)

Marge Keller	Jane Dulo
Mr. Bixby	Sydney Boyd
Mr. Mapleton	Johnny Stearns
Wilbur Haskins	Johnny Downs
Vivian Reilly	Joan Roberts
Policeman	Duke McHale
"Goldie"	Lew Parker
Bartender	Lou Wills, Jr.
Carter	Lew Eckels
Snake Charmer's Daughter	Jane Deering*1
Cicero	Bunny Briggs
Cleo	June Richmond
A Barker	Johnny Stearns
Balloon Seller	Mildred Jocelyn
Bunny La Fleur	Dolores Gray
Sally Swivelhips	Diane Adrian*2
Georgetta	Buster Shaver
Olive	Olive
George	George
Richard	Richard
Strong Man	William Lundy*3
Aerialist	Jane Deering*1
Office Boy	Hal Hunter
1st Musician	Lou Hurst
2nd Musician	David Lambert
3rd Musician	Jerry Duane
4th Musician	Jerry Packer
Loren	Loren Welch

Quartette: Jerry Duane, Lou Hurst, David Lambert and Jerry Packer.

Musical Numbers: "Five More Minutes in Bed," "Nutmeg Insurance," "Slightly Perfect," "When A Good Man Takes A Drink," "Poor Little Me," "Are You With It?," "This Is My Beloved," "Slightly Slightly," "Vivian's Reverie," "Send Us Back to the Kitchen," "Here I Go Again," "You Gotta Keep Saying 'No'." "Just Beyond The Rainbow," "In Our Cozy Little Cottage of Tomorrow."

A Musical Comedy in two acts, nineteen scenes. Action takes place in a Boarding House in Hartford, Conn., Bushnell Park, Office of the Nutmeg Insurance Company, Joe's Barroom, Behind the Tent of the "Plantation Minstrels," Midway—"Acres of Fun," Two Train Compartments, Carter's Office on the Train, and inside the Midway Frolics Tent.

General Manager, Leo Rose
Press, Bernard Simon, Dorothy Ross
Stage Managers, Frank Coletti, George Hunter
*Replacements: 1. Kathryn Lee, 2. Gretchen Houser, 3. Ray Arnett.
**Closed June 29, 1946 (264 performances)

Dolores Gray—Lew Parker
Joan Roberts—Johnny Downs

June Richmond—Lew Parker

Center, Joan Roberts, surrounded by clowns, Jimmy Allen, Lou Wills, Jr., Bill Julian, John Laverty and at the right, Johnny Downs and Kathryn Lee

The Midway of "Acres of Fun," center, Johnny Downs and Dolores Gray

Martha Sleeper   Spencer Tracy

PLYMOUTH THEATRE

Opened Saturday, November 10, 1945†
The Playwrights' Company presents:

THE RUGGED PATH

By Robert E. Sherwood; Directed by Garson Kanin; Settings and Lighting by Jo Mielziner; Gowns by Valentina.

Cast of Characters

Jamieson ....Emory Richardson
Hazel ....Kay Loring
Major General MacGlorn ....Ernest Woodward
Morey Vinion ....Spencer Tracy**
Harriet Vinion ....Martha Sleeper
George Bowsmith ....Clinton Sundberg
Leggatt Burt ....Lawrence Fletcher
Charlie ....Henry Lascoe
Pete Kenneally ....Ralph Cullinan
Fred ....Nick Dennis
Gil Hartnick............................Rex Williams*1
Edith Bowsmith.........................Jan Sterling*2
Firth ....Theodore Leavitt
Albok ....Paul Alberts
Dix ....Sandy Campbell
Stapler ....Lynn Shubert
Kavanagh ....Sam Sweet
Ship's Doctor ....Howard Ferguson
Costanzo ....William Sands
Guffey ....David Stone
Hal Fleury ....Gordon Nelson
Colonel Rainsford ....Clay Clement***
Gregorio Felizardo ....Vito Christi
Doctor Querin ....Edward Raquello

A Drama in two acts, twelve scenes. Time: 1940 to 1945. Action takes place in a Room at the White House, the Vinion's Home, Kenneally's Downtown Bar and Grill, George Bowsmith's Office, Mess Compartment on the Destroyer, "Townsend," Colonel Rainsford's Headquarters, and a Philippine Jungle Outpost.

Business Manager, Victor Samrock
Press, William Fields, Walter Alford
Stage Manager, B. D. Kranz

*Replacements: 1. Efrem Zimbalist Jr., 2. Margot Stevenson

**Mr. Tracy's only appearance in New York since he left the role of "Killer" Mears in "The Last Mile" in 1930, to go to Hollywood.

***Played during tryout tour by Robert Keith

†Closed January 19, 1946   (81 performances)

Lawrence Fletcher   Spencer Tracy

Olive Deering   Arthur Keegan

Alfred Ryder   Elsbeth Hofmann

BELASCO THEATRE

Opened Tuesday, November 13, 1945*
Rita Hassan presents:

SKYDRIFT

By Harry Kleiner; Staged by Roy Hargrave;
Settings and Costumes by Motley.

Cast of Characters
(In order of appearance)

Private Paul Rennard ....Paul Crabtree
Corporal Kenneth Brody ....Elliot Sullivan
Private Fitzroy Donovan ....Arthur Keegan
Private Mario Bucelli ....Zachary A. Charles
Private Edward Freling ....William Chambers
Co-Pilot ....Sid Martoff
Private Nichie Bucelli ....Carl Specht
Crew Chief ....Eli Wallach
Sergeant Robert A. Kane ....Alfred Ryder
Francey ....Olive Deering
Danny ....Marty Miller
Mrs. Bucelli ....Lili Valenty
Mr. Bucelli ....Wolfe Barzell
Angelina ....Rosita Cosio
Audra ....Elsbeth Hofmann

A Phantasy Drama in three acts, with a real-
istic prologue. The Action takes place in the
interior of a Transport Plane, the front steps
of Francey's Home, Danny's Bedroom, the Bucelli Home, and a Booth in a Night Club.

General Manager, Lodewick Vroom
Company Manager, Lew Wood
Press, Dick Weaver
Stage Manager, William G. Johnson

*Closed November 17, 1945 (7 performances)

HUDSON THEATRE

Opening Wednesday, November 14, 1945
Leland Hayward presents:

STATE OF THE UNION

By Howard Lindsay and Russel Crouse;
Staged by Bretaigne Windust; Settings by Raymond Sovey; Costumes by Emeline Roche;
Gowns by Hattie Carnegie.

Cast of Characters
(In order of speaking)

James Conover ....Minor Watson
Spike McManus ....Myron McCormick
Kay Thorndyke ....Kay Johnson*
Grant Matthews ....Ralph Bellamy
Norah ....Helen Ray
Mary Matthews ....Ruth Hussey
Stevens ....John Rowe
Bellboy ....Howard Graham
Waiter ....Robert Toms
Sam Parrish ....Herbert Heyes
Swenson ....Fred Ayres Cotton
Judge Jefferson Davis Alexander
                                        G. Albert Smith
Mrs. Alexander ....Maidel Turner
Jennie ....Madeline King
Mrs. Draper ....Aline McDermott
William Hardy ....Victor Sutherland
Senator Lauterback ....George Lessey

A Political Comedy about the present presidential race, in three acts. Scenes: Study and Bedroom in James Conover's Home, Washington, D. C., Living-room of a Suite in the Book-Cadillac Hotel, Detroit, and the Living-room of the Matthews' Apartment in New York.

General Manager, Herman Bernstein
Press, Richard Maney, Ted Goldsmith
General Stage Director, Walter Wagner
Stage Manager, Victor Sutherland

*Replaced by Margalo Gillmore.

Ralph Bellamy   Ruth Hussey   Ralph Bellamy   Ruth Hussey

Myron McCormick—Kay Johnson—Ralph Bellamy—Minor Watson—Ruth Hussey

Ruth Hussey—Fred Ayres Cotton—
Maidel Turner

Myron McCormick—Ruth Hussey—
Ralph Bellamy

LYCEUM THEATRE

Opened Tuesday, November 20, 1945*
Irving L. Jacobs presents:

A SOUND OF HUNTING

By Harry Brown**; Directed by Anthony
Brown; Setting by Samuel Leve.

Cast of Characters
(In order of speaking)

Pfc. Charles Coke ....Frank Lovejoy
Pfc. John Hunter ....James McGrew
Pvt. Dino Collucci ....Sam Levene
T/5 Frank Daggert ....William Beal
Lt. Allan Crane ....Charles J. Flynn
S/Sgt. Joseph Mooney ....Burton Lancaster
Pfc. Paul Shapiro ....George Tyne
Pfc. Karl Muller ....Kenneth Brauer
Sgt. Thomas Carter ....Carl Frank
Pfc. Morris Ferguson ....Ralph Brooke
Capt. John Trelawny ....Stacy Harris
Frederick Finley ....Bruce Evans

A War Drama in three acts. The Action takes
place on a January day, 1944, in a War-ruined
House in the town of Cassino, Italy.

General Manager, Philip Adler
Press, Tom Van Dycke
Stage Manager, Peter A. Xantho

*Closed December 8, 1945 (23 performances)
**Mr. Brown is the author of the novel, "Walk
In The Sun."

Sam Levene and Burton Lancaster

Sam Levene—Kenneth Brauer—George Tyne

A war-ruined house in the town of Cassino, Italy, on a January day, 1944

CORT THEATRE

Opened Wednesday, November 21, 1945*
Ruth Holden and Virginia Kronberg present:

MARRIAGE IS FOR SINGLE PEOPLE

By Stanley Richards; Staged by Stanley
Logan; Setting by Frederick Fox.

Cast of Characters
(In order of speaking)

Mrs. Sibyl Hecuba ....Nana Bryant
Lily Packer ....Florence Sundstrom
Reena Rowe ....Anne Francine
Cynthia Murdock ....Marguerite Lewis
Dudley Packer ....Frank Otto
Kenneth Hecuba ....Joel Marston
Una, a maid ....Nancie Hobbes
Lottie Disenhower ....Gertrude Beach
Spencer Shilling ....Robert Sully
An Expressman ....Sherman Lazarus
Reginald Hecuba ....Nicholas Saunders
A Young Lady ....Vivian Mallah

A Comedy in three acts. The entire action
takes place in Reginald Hecuba's Penthouse
Apartment in New York City.

Company Manager, Lars Jorgensen
Press, Vince McKnight
Stage Manager, Louis Cruger

*Closed November 24, 1945 (6 performances)

Nana Bryant—Gertrude Beach—Joel Marston

Nana Bryant

Marguerite Lewis and Gertrude Beach

NATIONAL THEATRE

Opened Thursday, November 22, 1945.*
John C. Wilson presents:

THE DAY BEFORE SPRING

Book and lyrics by Alan Jay Lerner; Music by Frederick Loewe; Book Directed by Edward Padula; Orchestration by Harold Byrns; Vocal arrangements by Mr. Loewe; Maurice Abravanel, Musical Director; Sets by Robert Davison; Costumes by Miles White; Ballets and Musical Ensembles by Antony Tudor; Staged by Mr. Wilson.

Cast of Characters
(In order of appearance)

Katherine Townsend ....Irene Manning
Peter Townsend ....John Archer
Bill Tompkins ....Bert Freed
May Tompkins ....Lucille Benson
Alex Maitland ....Bill Johnson
Marie ....Karol Loraine
Lucille ....Bette Anderson
Leonore ....Lucille Floetman
Marjorie ....Estelle Loring
Susan ....Arlouine Goodjohn
Anne ....Betty Jean Smythe
Horn-rimmed Hortense ....Mattlyn Gevurtz
Gerald Barker ....Tom Helmore
Joe McDonald ....Don Mayo
Harry Scott ....Robert Field
Eddie Warren ....Dwight Marfield
Christopher Randolph ....Patricia Marshall
Katherine (in the book)......Mary Ellen Moylan
Alex (in the book) ....Hugh Laing
Voltaire ....Paul Best
Plato ....Ralph Glover
Freud ....Hermann Leopoldi

Musical Numbers: "The Day Before Spring," "The Invitation," "God's Green World," "You Haven't Changed At All," "My Love Is A Married Man," Ballet of the Book according to Alex, Katherine receives advice, "Friends To The End," "A Jug of Wine," "I Love You This Morning," "Where's My Wife?", "This Is My Holiday," Ballet of the Book according to Gerald.

A Musical Comedy in two acts, nine scenes. The Action takes place within twenty-four hours on a day in June. The scenes: The Townsends' Apartment, New York City, Harrison College Campus, a Path near Harrison, Rotunda of Harrison Library, in a Corridor, a Harrison Resident House, and on the Roadside.

General Manager, C. Edwin Knill
Press, Willard Keefe, David Tebet
Stage Managers, Ward Bishop, John Sola
*Closed April 14, 1946 (167 performances).

Tom Helmore—Patricia Marshall

Bill Johnson—Hermann Leopoldi—Irene Manning

John Archer—Irene Manning

Beatrice Pearson—Walter Starkey—Walter Abel

EMPIRE THEATRE

Opened Wednesday, November 28, 1945*
Alfred de Liagre Jr. presents:

THE MERMAIDS SINGING

By John Van Druten; Setting by Raymond Sovey; Staged by the Author.

Cast of Characters
(In order of appearance)

Clement Waterlow ....Walter Abel
George ....Arthur Griffin
Bertha Corrigan ....Lois Wilson
Thad Greelis ....Walter Starkey
Dee Matthews ....Beatrice Pearson
Mrs. James ....Jane Hoffman
Mrs Matthews ....Frieda Inescort
Professor James ....Harry Irvine
Luther Cudworth ....Jack Manning
An Elderly Gentleman........Wallace Widdecombe
A Waiter ....Leon Forbes
A Drunk ....Frank Lyon
A Girl ....Dina Merrill
A Man ....David Van Winkle

A Comedy of Modern Morals in three acts and five scenes. The action passes in the Living-room of a Suite and the Corner of the Bar in the best hotel, the Home of the Matthews, and the Park—all in any large American City other than New York.

General Manager, Samuel H. Schwartz
Company Manager, Edward Choate
Press, Jean Dalrymple, Anthony Buttitta
Stage Manager, Henri Caubisens

*Closed January 12, 1946   (53 performances)

Beatrice Pearson—Lois Wilson

ROYALE THEATRE

Opened Thursday, November 29, 1945*
Jose Ferrer presents:

STRANGE FRUIT

By Lillian Smith with the assistance of Esther Smith** from Miss Smith's novel of the same title; Staged by Mr. Ferrer; Designed and Lighted by George Jenkins; Costumes by Patricia Montgomery; Under the Supervision of Arthur S. Friend.

Cast of Characters
(In order of speaking)

A Mill Hand	Murray Hamilton
Another Mill Hand	Robert Daggett
Ed Anderson	George B. Oliver
Little Miss Nobody	Doris Block
Preacher Dunwoodie	Stephen Chase
Tom Harris	Ralph Theadore
Dee Cassidy	Ted Yaryan
Gabe	Alonzo Bosan
Doug	Jay Norris
Harriet Harris	Eugenia Rawls
Charlie Harris	Francis Letton
Tracy Deen	Melchor Ferrer
Crazy Carl	Robinson Stone
Alma Deen	Vera Allen
Sam Perry	Juano Hernandez
Laura Deen	Charlotte Keane
Tut Deen	Frank Tweddell
Corporal	Herbert Junior
Nonnie Anderson	Jane White
Bess Anderson	Dorothy Carter
Jackie (Bess' Child)	Juan Jose Hernandez
Henry McIntosh	Earl Jones
Salamander	Hanson W. Elkins
Chuck	Ralph Meeker
Miss Sadie	Mary Fletcher
Miss Belle	Esther Smith
Mamie McIntosh	Edna Thomas
Tracy Deen (as a child)	Peter Griffith
Henry McIntosh (as a child)	Richard W. Williams
A Little Girl	Phyllis De Bus
Laura Deen (as a child)	Betty Lou Keim
Ten McIntosh	Ken Renard
A Colored Man	Ellsworth Wright
A Maid	Doris Block

A Drama on Racial Prejudice in twelve scenes. The action takes place in Maxwell, Georgia; Deen's Drug Store, Sunporch and Yard; the Andersons' Home and Front Gate; on a Ridge; Salamander's Cafe; and Tom Harris' Mill Office.

Company Manager, Joseph R. Williams
Press, Fred Spooner, Howard Hutchison
Stage Manager, Murray Hamilton

*Closed January 19, 1945 (60 performances)
**Lillian Smith's sister.

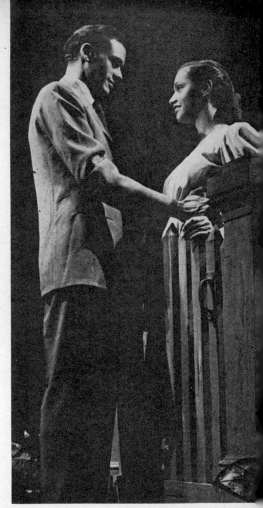

Melchor Ferrer and Jane White

Esther Smith   Jay Norris

Jane White

Jacqueline Dalya—Jerome Thor—Brian Aherne—Arlene Francis—Madeleine Le Beau

CORT THEATRE

Opened Saturday, December 8, 1945*
Herbert H. Harris presents:

THE FRENCH TOUCH

By Joseph Fields and Jerome Chodorov; Directed by Rene Clair; Designed and Lighted by George Jenkins.

Cast of Characters
(In order of appearance)

Patard ....John Regan
Roublard ....Brian Aherne
Giselle Roublard ....Jacqueline Dalya
Schwartz ....William Malten
Felix Von Brenner ....John Wengraf
Jacqueline Carlier ....Arlene Francis
Boucot ....Ralph Simone
Henri ....Jerome Thor
Georgette ....Louise Kelley
Toto ....Richard Bengali
Nanette ....Mary Cooper
Madeleine ....Sara Strengell
Robert ....Stewart Stern
Paulette ....Libby Linn
Marcel ....John Graham
Odette Renoux ....Madeleine Le Beau
Reiner ....Dave Hyatt

A Comedy in two acts. The Scene is the Theatre Roublard in Paris in the Spring of 1943, during the Nazi Occupation.

General Manager, Edward Choate
Company Manager, Joe Moss
Press, Mary March
Stage Manager, Joseph Olney

*Closed January 5, 1946   (33 performances)

Arlene Francis—Brian Aherne—John Regan

41

George Petrie—Charles Butterworth—Lenore Lonergan

LYCEUM THEATRE

Opened Wednesday, December 12, 1945*
Jean Dalrymple presents:

BRIGHTEN THE CORNER

By John Cecil Holm; Directed by Arthur
O'Connell; Setting by Willis Knighton.

Cast of Characters
(In order of appearance)

Opal Harris	Dulcie Cooper
Jeri Carson	Phyllis Avery
Neil Carson	George Petrie
Dell Marshall	Lenore Lonergan
Jeffrey Q. Talbot	Charles Butterworth
Townsend Marshall, Lt. U.S.N.	Gene Blakely
Delivery Boy	Paul Stanley
Officer Robertson	Robert Simon

A Comedy in three acts. Scene: The Living-
room and Outer Hall of the Carsons' Upper East
Side Apartment in New York City. Time: the
Present.

Business Manager, Dorothy Sealy
Company Manager, Edward O'Keefe
Press, Jean Dalrymple, June Greenwall
Stage Manager, Elbert A. Gruver

*Closed January 5, 1946   (29 performances)

Above, Lenore Lonergan—George Petrie—Charles
Butterworth. Below, Lenore Lonergan — Gene
Blakely — Phyllis Avery — George Petrie — Charles
Butterworth—Robert Simon.

Maurice Evans as "Hamlet"

COLUMBUS CIRCLE THEATRE†

Opened Thursday, December 13, 1945***
Michael Todd presents:

HAMLET**

By William Shakespeare; Staged by George Schaefer; Scenery by Frederick Stover; Costumes by Irene Sharaff; Music by Roger Adams.

Cast of Characters
(In order of appearance)

Officers of the Guard—
Bernardo ....William Weber
Francisco ....John Bryant*1
Marcellus ....Alexander Lockwood
Horatio ....Walter Coy
Ghost of Hamlet's Father.............Victor Thorley
Claudius, King of Denmark ....Thomas Gomez
Hamlet, Prince of Denmark ....Maurice Evans
Gertrude, Queen of Denmark.............Lili Darvas
Polonius, Principal Secy. of State
....Thomas Chalmers
Laertes, son of Polonius..............Emmett Rogers
Ophelia, daughter of Polonius........Frances Reid
Reynaldo ....Franz Bendtsen*2
Former Students with Hamlet—
Rosencrantz ....Howard Morris
Guildenstern ....Booth Colman
Player King ....Nelson Leigh
Player Queen ....Blanche Collins
Player Villain ....Alan Dreeben
Player Prologue ....Alan Masters
Fortinbras, Prince of Norway..............Leon Shaw
Norwegian Captain ....Nelson Leigh
Osric ....Morton Da Costa
Lords, Ladies, Soldiers and Attendants: Nan Mc-Farland, Jane Flynn, Janet Slausen, Robert Berger, John Bryant, Alan Dreeben, Charles Goff, Robert Hartung, Bill Levitt, Robert Pastene, Frank Rooney, Ray Walston, William Weber.

A Tragedy in two acts, fifteen scenes. The action takes place in Denmark—the Battlements, the Main Hall, the Apartment of Polonius, the Chapel, the Open Court, the Queen's Apartment, a Cellar Room and a Hall at the Castle at Elsinore, also a Street leading to the Port.

Frances Reid and Maurice Evans

General Manager, James Colligan
Company Manager, William G. Norton
Production Manager, Walter Williams
Press, Bill Doll, Mort Nathanson
General Stage Manager, Sammy Lambert
Stage Manager, George Cotton

†Known the past two years as the International Theatre and before that as the Park and the Cosmopolitan.

*Replaced by 1. Robert Berger; 2. Victor Rendina.

**This production was cut along the experimental lines followed by Mr. Evans for his G.I. audiences. The Church-yard scene was eliminated and the grave diggers were not in the play. The costumes were of a timeless period, based on Nineteenth Century details. Some of the members of this company served with Major Evans in the Pacific and over twenty were ex-service men.

***Closed April 6, 1946 (131 performances) This production failed by one performance to overtake the long run record of John Gielgud's "Hamlet," produced by Guthrie McClintic, which ran 132 consecutive performances.

Maurice Evans—Lili Darvas   Thomas Gomez—Emmett Rogers

Betty Field in the "Portia Scene" from "Dream Girl"

CORONET THEATRE

Opening Friday, December 14, 1945.
The Playwrights' Company presents:

DREAM GIRL

By Elmer Rice; Designed and Lighted by Jo Mielziner; Miss Fields' Costumes by Mainbocher; Staged by the author.

Cast of Characters
(In order of appearance)

Georgina Allerton ....Betty Field*1
Lucy Allerton ....Evelyn Varden
Radio Announcer ....Keene Crockett
Dr. J. Gilmore Percival ....William A. Lee
George Allerton ....William A. Lee
Miriam Allerton Lucas ....Sonya Stokowski*2
The Obstetrician ....William A. Lee
The Nurse ....Evelyn Varden
Jim Lucas ....Kevin O'Shea
Claire Blakeley ....Helen Marcy
A Stout Woman ....Philippa Bevans
The Doctor ....Don Stevens
Clark Redfield ....Wendell Corey
A Policeman ....James Gregory
The Judge ....William A. Lee
The District Attorney ....Keene Crockett
George Hand ....Edmon Ryan
Bert ....Don Stevens
A Mexican ....Wendell Corey
Two Other Mexicans .... { David Pressman
                                                 { James Gergory
A Waiter ....Stuart Nedd
Arabella ....Sonya Stokowski*2
Luigi, a Waiter ....David Pressman
An Usher ....Gaynelle Nixon*3
Miss Delehanty ....Helen Bennett
Antonio ....Don Stevens
Salarino ....Robert Fletcher
A Theatre Manager ....William A. Lee
A Head-waiter ....Keene Crocket
A Waiter ....Robert Fletcher
Justice of the Peace Billings........William A. Lee
A Chauffeur ....Stuart Nedd

A Comedy in two acts. The action takes place between 8:00 of a spring morning and 4:00 the following morning in the natural and dream life of Georgina Allerton; her bedroom, her shower and dressing room, room of a Maternity hospital, the breakfast room, the book shop, the hospital corridor, Mrs. Allerton's sitting room, a newspaper office, a courtroom, Canari Rouge Lunch Club, Tasco, Mexico, a street corner, a telephone booth, Mr. Hand's office, Amelio's Italian Restaurant, the orchestra of a theatre, Portia scene on stage, a Justice of the Peace, a Supper Club, the Allerton bedroom, a hotel room in Greenwich.

Business Manager, Victor Samrock
Company Manager, Edgar Runkle
Press, William Fields, Reginald Denenholz
Stage Manager, Elmer Brown
*Replacements: 1. Haila Stoddard, 2. Gaynelle Nixon, 3. Jean Aubuchon.

Betty Field and Wendell Corey

Betty Field and Edmon Ryan

Betty Field and Edmon Ryan

Evelyn Varden—William A. Lee—Betty Field

Edmon Ryan—Helen Bennett—Betty Field—Wendell Corey

ALVIN THEATRE

Opened Friday, December 21, 1945***
Paul Feigay and Oliver Smith present:

BILLION DOLLAR BABY

Book and Lyrics by Betty Comden and Adolph
Green; Music by Morton Gould; Choreography
and Musical Numbers staged by Jerome Robbins; Settings by Oliver Smith; Costumes by
Irene Sharaff; Musical Director: Max Goberman; Directed by George Abbott.

Cast of Characters

Ma Jones	Emily Ross
Pa Jones	William David
Esma	Shirley Van
Neighbors	Maria Harriton, Edward Hodge, Howard Lenters, Douglas Deane, Helen Gallagher, Beverly Hosier
Champ Watson	Danny Daniels
Photographer	Anthony Reed
Reporter	Alan Gilbert
Maribelle Jones	Joan McCracken
Newsboys	Douglas Jones,*1 Richard Thomas
Master of Ceremonies	Richard Sanford*2
Miss Texas	Althea Elder*3
Miss California	Virginia Gorski
Miss Florida	Peggy Ellis
Miss Oklahoma	Beth Shea
Miss Virginia	Beverly Hosier
Miss Indiana	Joan Mann
Miss Louisiana	Future Fulton
Miss Massachusetts	Doris Hollingsworth
Miss Vermont	Thelma Stevens
Miss South Dakota	Lyn Gammon
Miss Kentucky	Betty Saunders
Georgia Motley	Mitzi Green
Dream Heroes	Jim Mitchell, Fred Hearne, Bill Skipper
Violin Player	Tony Gardell
Jerry Bonanza	Don De Leo**
Cop	Arthur Partington
3 Flappers	Virginia Gorski, Helen Gallagher, Lorraine Todd
Rich Girl	Joan Mann
Playboy	Fred Hearne
A Timid Girl	Ann Hutchinson
Good Time Charlie	Bill Skipper
Collegiates	Virginia Poe, Douglas Deane
Younger Generation	Bill Sumner, Maria Harriton
Older Generation	Jacqueline Dodge, Joe Landis
2 Gangsters	Lucas Aco, Allan Waine
2 Bootleggers	Anthony Reed, Allan Gilbert
Dapper Welch	David Burns
Rocky Barton	William Tabbert
Cigarette Girl	Jeri Archer
Waiter	David Thomas
M. M. Montague	Robert Chisholm
Marathon M. C.	Allan Gilbert
Chorines	Joan Mann, Lorraine Todd, Virginia Gorski, Virginia Poe, Helen Gallagher, Maria Harriton
Comic	Douglas Deane
Danny	Tony Gardell
J. C. Creasy	Horace Cooper
Art Leffenbush	Eddie Hodge
Rodney Gender	Richard Sanford *4
Watchman	Robert Edwin
Rocky (who dances)	James Mitchell
Policeman	Howard Lenters

Musical Numbers: "Million Dollar Smile,"
"Who's Gonna Be the Winner?" Dreams Come
True, Charleston, "Broadway Blossom," "Speak-
ing of Pals," "There I'd Be," "One Track
Mind," "Bad Timing," The Marathoners, "A
Lovely Girl," Funeral Procession, "Havin' a
Time," Marathon Dance, "Faithless," "I'm Sure
of Your Love," A Life with Rocky, The Wed-
ing.

Joan McCracken and William Tabbert

A Musical Play of the terrific twenties in two
acts, twenty-two scenes: A Staten Island Living-
room, Atlantic City Boardwalk, Staten Island
Ferry, Front of a Speakeasy, Chez Georgia,
Georgia's Dressing Room, A Street, Dapper's
Apartment, The Marathon, Backstage of the
Jollities, On Stage Jollities, Porch of the Palm
Beach Plaza Hotel, Entrance to Marathon, Mari-
belle's Bedroom, Church Vestry.

General Manager, Charles Harris
Press, Karl Bernstein, Thomas Barrows
Stage Manager, Robert Griffith

*Replacements: 1. Stefan Gierasch, 2. David
Thomas, 3. Jacqueline Dodge, 4. Stuart
Langley.
**Alternate: Harry Gary.
***Closed June 29, 1946   (219 performances)

Joan McCracken and Bill Skipper dance "Dreams Come True"

Murder at the Jollities during "A Lovely Girl" number.
On rear level, David Burns and Mitzi Green. Front center, Joan McCracken and William Tabbert.

Richard Widmark—Dennis King—Jan Sterling

June Havoc   Dennis King

June Havoc   Dennis King

GOLDEN THEATRE

Opened Wednesday, December 26, 1945**
The Theatre Guild presents:

DUNNIGAN'S DAUGHTER

By S. N. Behrman; Staged by Elia Kazan;
Designed by Stewart Chaney; Supervised by
Theresa Helburn and Lawrence Langner.

Cast of Characters
(In order of appearance)

Jim Baird .... Ricard Widmark*1
Robert .... Hale Norcross
Zelda Rainier .... Jan Sterling*2
Miguel Riachi .... Luther Adler *3
Ferne Rainer .... June Havoc *4
Clay Rainier .... Dennis King
Jesus Y Blasco Hernandez........... Arthur Gondra

A Drama in three acts. The action takes
place in Clay Rainier's Residence outside a small
mining town in Mexico.

Company Manager, Allan Attwater
Press, Joseph Heidt, Peggy Phillips
Stage Manager, James Gelb

*Played during the tryout by 1. Arthur Franz,
2. Ann Jackson, 3. Glenn Anders, 4. Virginia
Gilmore.

**Closed January 26, 1946   (38 performances)

Gertrude Lawrence as Eliza Doolittle in "Pygmalion"

Katherine Emmet—Raymond Massey—Cecil Humphreys—Myrtle Tannehill—Gertrude Lawrence—
John Cromwell—Wendy Atkin

Gertrude Lawrence and Raymond Massey
Below, Portico of Saint Paul's Church, Covent Garden

BARRYMORE THEATRE

Opened Wednesday, December 26, 1946**
Theatre Incorporated presents:

PYGMALION

By Bernard Shaw; Staged by Cedric Hardwicke, Settings by Donlad Oenslager; Costumes
by Motley; Managing Director, Richard Aldrich.

Cast of Characters

Clara Eynsford-Hill ....Wendy Atkin
Mrs. Eynsford-Hill ....Myrtle Tannehill
Bystander ....J. P. Wilson
Freddy Enysford-Hill ....John Cromwell
Eliza Doolittle ....Gertrude Lawrence
Colonel Pickering ....Cecil Humphreys
Henry Higgins.....................Raymond Massey*1
Sarcastic Bystander.........................Jay Black*2
Taxicab Driver........................Rudolph Watson*3
Mrs. Pearce.................................Anita Bolster*4
Alfred Doolittle ....Melville Cooper
Mrs. Higgins ....Katherine Emmet
Parlourmaid ....Hazel Jones
Pedestrians and Bystanders: Lucy Storm, Barbara
    Pond, Walter Kapp, Janet Dowd, Ralph
    Edington.

A Revival of the Romantic Comedy in three
acts and a prologue. The action of the play
takes place in London in the year 1908—a
Portico of Saint Paul's Church, Covent Garden; Henry Higgins' Laboratory, Wimpole Street;
and Mrs. Higgins' Drawing-room, Chelsea Em-
bankment.

Company Manager, Chandos Sweet
Production Manager, Robert Woods
Press, William Fields, Walter Alford
Stage Manager, Alfred Boylen

*Replaced by 1. John Williams, 2. Leslie
Austin, 3. Walter Kapp, 4. Dorrit Kelton.
**Closed June 1, 1946 (181 performances.
World's record-breaking run)

Melville Cooper   Anita Bolster— Gertrude Lawrence   Raymond Massey

Raymond Massey—Melville Cooper—Gertrude Lawrence—Cecil Humphreys   53

BELASCO THEATRE

Opened Thursday, December 27, 1945.*
Lee Sabinson in association with William
R. Katzell presents:

HOME OF THE BRAVE

By Arthur Laurents; Directed by Michael
Gordon; Designed and Lighted by Ralph Alswang.

Cast of Characters
(In order of appearance)

Capt. Harold Bitterger	Eduard Franz
Major Dennis Robinson, Jr.	Kendall Clark
T. J.	Russell Hardie
Coney	Joseph Pevney
Finch	Henry Barnard
Mingo	Alan Baxter

A Psychological War Drama in three acts,
eight scenes. The Action takes place in A
Hospital Room, An Office, The Jungle, and A
Clearing, all on a Pacific Island.

General Manager, Philip Adler
Press, Samuel Friedman, James Davis
Stage Manager, James Russo

*Closed February 23, 1946 (69 performances).

Alan Baxter

Russell Hardie—Henry Barnard—Alan Baxter—Kendall Clark—Joseph Pevney

Russell Hardie and Alan Baxter

Alan Baxter—Henry Barnard—
Joseph Pevney

Joseph Pevney and Eduard Franz

Russell Hardie—Joseph Pevney—
Alan Baxter

55

ZIEGFELD THEATRE

Opening Saturday, January 5, 1946
Kern and Hammerstein present:

SHOW BOAT†

Music by Jerome Kern; Book and lyrics by Oscar Hammerstein 2nd, Based on the novel by Edna Ferber; Staged by Hassard Short; Dances by Helen Tamiris; Settings by Howard Bay; Costumes by Lucinda Ballard; Musical Director, Edwin McArthur; Orchestrations by Robert Russell Bennett; Book directed by Mr. Hammerstein.

Cast of Characters
(In order of appearance)

Windy	Scott Moore
Steve	Robert Allen
Pete	Seldon Bennett
Queenie	Helen Dowdy
Parthy Ann Hawks	Ethel Owen
Captain Andy	Ralph Dumke
Ellie	Colette Lyons
Frank	Buddy Ebsen
Rubber Face	Francis Mahoney
Julie	Carol Bruce
Gaylord Ravenal	Charles Fredericks
Vallon	Ralph Chambers
Magnolia	Jan Clayton*1
Joe	Kenneth Spencer
Backswoodsman	Howard Frank
Jeb	Duncan Scott
Sal	Pearl Primus
Sam	Laverne French
Barker	Hayes Gordon
Fatima	Jeanne Reeves
Old Sport	Willie Torpey
Strong Woman	Paula Kaye

Congress of Beauties:

Spanish	Andrea Downing
Italian	Vivian Cherry
French	Janice Bodenhoff
Scotch	Elana Keller
Greek	Audrey Keane
English	Marta Becket
Russian	Olga Lunick
Indian	Eleanor Boleyn
Dahomey Queen	Pearl Primus
Ata	Alma Sutton
Mala	Claude Marchant
Bora	Talley Beatty
Landlady	Sara Floyd
Ethel	Assota Marshall
Sister	Sheila Hogan
Mother Superior	Iris Manley
Kim (Child)	Alyce Mace
Jake	Max Showalter
Jim	Jack Daley
Man with Guitar	Tom Bowman
Doorman at Trocadero	William C. Smith
Drunk	Paul Shiers
Lottie	Nancy Kenyon*2
Dolly	Lydia Fredericks
Sally	Bettina Thayer
Kim (In Her Twenties)	Jan Clayton*1
Old Lady on Levee	Frederica Slemons
Jimmy Craig	Charles Tate

Musical Numbers: "Cotton Blossom," Show Boat Parade and Ballyhoo; "Only Make Believe," "Ol' Man River," "Can't Help Lovin' Dat Man," "Life Upon The Wicked Stage," "No Gems, No Roses, No Gentlemen," "No Shoes," "You Are Love," Levee Dance, "At The Fair," Congress of Beauties, "Why Do I Love You?" "In Dahomey," "Bill"**, St. Agatha's Convent Service Music, Goodbye, My Lady Love Cake Walk, Magnolia's Debut 'After The Ball', "Nobody Else But Me††," Dance 1927.

A new production of the musical drama in two acts, fifteen scenes. The Action takes place on the Levee at Natchez, Mississippi; Kitchen Pantry, Auditorium, Stage, Box-Office, Foredeck and Top Deck of the 'Cotton Blossom'; and the Levee at Greenville during the eighties. The Midway Plaisance, Chicago World's Fair, 1893, a Room on Ontario Street, 1904, Rehearsal Room, St. Agatha's Convent, Trocardero Music Hall, New Year's Eve, 1905, Stern and Top Deck of 'Cotton Blossom', 1927.

Charles Fredericks and Jan Clayton

General Manager, Robert Milford
Press, Michel Mok, Mary Ward
Stage Director, Reginald Hammerstein
Stage Manager, William Hammerstein

†The libretto and score are substantially as they were when originally written in 1927—one front scene and three minor musical numbers have been eliminated.

††This number takes the place of a series of imitations of stars of the twenties performed in this spot by the original Magnolia, Norma Terris.

*1. Miss Clayton was replaced by 2. Nancy Kenyon, who was replaced by Evelyn Wick.
**Lyric for "Bill" by P. G. Wodehouse.

Buddy Ebsen—Colette Lyons—Ralph Dumke—Carol Bruce—Robert Allen

Carol Bruce sings "Bill"

Kenneth Spencer sings "Ol' Man River"

BILTMORE THEATRE

Opened Monday, January 7, 1946*
Blevins Davis and Archie Thomson present:

A JOY FOREVER

By Vincent McConnor; Staged by Reginald Denham; Designed by Stewart Chaney.

Cast of Characters
(In order of appearance)

Tina	Dorothy Sands
Frith	Charles Laffin
Benjamin Vinnicum	Guy Kibbee
Young Dan	William Nunn
Old Dan	Seth Arnold
Constance Sherman	Ottilie Kruger
Harrison Eames	Loring Smith
Archer Barrington	Nicholas Joy
Wallace	Joe Johnson
Mrs. Tillery	Frieda Altman
Guard	Rollin Bauer
Allora Eames	Natalie Schafer
Model	Charles Boaz, Jr.
Delivery Man	Fred Knight
Assistant Delivery Man	Lucian Self
Mrs. Homer W. Danforth	Lois Bolton

A Comedy in three acts. The Scene is the Studio of Benjamin Vinnicum, overlooking Fort Tryon Park in New York City.

Company Manager, Lee Holland
Press, Fred Spooner
Stage Manager, Lucien Self

*Closed January 19, 1946   (16 performances)

Guy Kibbee and Dorothy Sands

Ottilie Kruger—Natalie Schafer—Charles Boaz, Jr.

Monsieur Jourdain entertains in the drawing-room of his house in Paris

Bobby Clark as "Monsieur Jourdain"

BOOTH THEATRE

Opened Wednesday, January 9, 1946***
Michael Todd presents:

THE WOULD-BE GENTLEMAN

Adapted from Moliere's "Le Bourgeois Gentilhomme"†; Staged by John Kennedy; Scenery by Howard Bay; Costumes by Irene Sharaff; Music adapted by Jerome Moross from the original Jean Baptiste Lully score.

Cast of Characters

Music Master ....Donald Burr*1
Dancing Master ....Alex Fisher
Criquet ....Fred Werner
Nicole ....Ann Thomas
Marcel ....Rand Elliot
Baptiste ....Albert Henderson
Monsieur Jourdain ....Bobby Clark
Mademoiselle Valere ....Ruth Harrison
Singers: Constance Brigham, Mary Godwin, Lewis Pierce
Madame Jourdain ....Edith King*2
Fencing Master ....Earl MacVeigh
Philosopher ....Frederic Persson
Count Dorante ....Gene Barry*3
Lucille Jourdain ....Eleanore Whitney
Covielle ....Leonard Elliott
Cleonte ....John Heath
Tailor ....LeRoi Operti**
Raymond (tailor's apprentice)......Lester Towne
Marquise Dorimene ....June Knight
Musicians: Gregory Bemko, David Gindin, James Nassy, Eric Silberstein, Max Tartasky

A Comedy with music in two acts. The scene is the Drawing-room in Monsieur Jourdain's House in Paris—circa 1670.

General Manager, James Colligan
Company Manager, Louis Epstein
Press, Bill Doll, Morton Nathanson, Dick Williams
Stage Manager, Murray Queen

†Adaptation unaccredited.

*Played during tryout tour by 1. Rolfe Sedan, 2. Bertha Belmore, 3. Philip Bourneuf.

**Replaced by Jerome Collamore.

***Closed March 16, 1946 (77 performances)

59

CORT THEATRE

Opened Tuesday, January 15, 1946**
The Theatre Guild presents revival of:

THE WINTER'S TALE

By William Shakespeare; Directed by B. Iden Payne and Romney Brent; Settings and Costumes by Stewart Chaney; Supervised by Lawrence Langner and Theresa Helburn.

Cast of Characters

Prologue	Romney Brent
Archidamus	Guy Arbury*1
Camillo	Colin Keith-Johnston*2
Polixenes	David Powell
Leontes	Henry Daniell
Hermione	Jessie Royce Landis
Mamillius	Judson Rees*3
1st Lady	Lucille Patton
2nd Lady	Jennifer Howard
3rd Lady	Denise Flynn
1st Lord	Baldwin McGaw
Antigonus	Charles Francis
2nd Lord	Lionel Ince*4
3rd Lord	Frank Leslie
Paulina	Florence Reed
4th Lord	Jules Racine
Keeper of the Jail	Guy Arbury*5
Emilia	Genevieve Frizzell
Mariner	Maury Yaffee*6
Bear	Jo Van Fleet
Dion	Philip Huston*7
Old Shepherd	Whitford Kane
Clown	Kurt Richards
Cleomenes	Charles Atkin*8
Time	Philip Huston*9
Autolycus	Romney Brent
Florizel	Robert Duke*10
Perdita	Geraldine Stroock
Dorcas	Jo Van Fleet
Mopsa	Helen Wagner
Servant	Victor Beecroft
Dancing Ram	James Starbuck
Dancing Ewe	Lili Mann
Dancing Horsemen	{ Francis Burnell { Jules Racine

A Comedy in two acts and fifteen scenes. The Action takes place in A Corridor, A Room, A Prison Corridor, and The Court Room of King Leontes' Palace, Sicilia; a Road, A Cave and Outside a Shepherd's Cottage in Bohemia; near Leontes' Palace; and a Chapel in Paulina's House.

Company Manager, John Yorke
Press, Joseph Heidt, Howard Newman
Stage Manager, Mortimer Halpern

*Played during road tour by 1, 6. Michael Bey, 2. Edwin Cushman, 3. Maurice Covell, 4. Arnold Emmanuell, 5. Victor Beecroft, 7. Marriott Wilson, 8. Jules Racine, 9. Morty Halpern, 10. Fred Bradlee.
**Closed February 16, 1946 (39 performances)

Encircled, Florence Reed
Below, Colin Keith-Johnston, Henry Daniell, Jessie Royce Landis, Florence Reed, Robert Duke, Geraldine Stroock, David Powell

Jessie Royce Landis and Henry Daniell

ADELPHI THEATRE

Opened Monday, January 21, 1946.**
Nat Karson and Eddie Cantor present:

NELLIE BLY

Book by Joseph Quillan; Lyrics by Johnny Burke; Music by James Van Heusen; Musical Supervision, Joseph Lilley; Choreography by Edward Caton and Lee Sherman; Dialogue directed by Edgar MacGregor; Orchestra under the direction of Charles Drury; Orchestrations by Ted Royal and Elliott Jacoby; Choral Direction by Simon Rady; Designed and Lighted by Nat Karson.

Cast of Characters
(In order of appearance)

Pulitzer	Walter Armin
Bennett	Edward H. Robins
Newsboy	William O'Shay
Frank Jordan	William Gaxton
Ferry Captain	Fred Peters
Deckhand	Harold Murray
Phineas T. Fogarty	Victor Moore
First Reporter	Robert Strauss
Murphy	Artells Dickson
Wardheeler	Jack Voeth
Second Reporter	Larry Stuart
Third Reporter	Eddy Di Genova
Nellie Bly	Joy Hodges*
Battle Annie	Benay Venuata
Steward	Larry Stuart
Honeymoon Couple	{ Doris Sward { Jack Voeth
French Girl	Drucilla Strain
Grisette	Lubov Roudenko
French Dandy	Jack Whitney
French Mayor	Walter Armin
Santos Dumont	Fred Peters
Reporters	The Debonairs
Czar	Walter Armin
Russian Captain	Fred Peters
First Sheik	Robert Strauss
Second Sheik	Edward H. Robins
Third Sheik	Larry Stuart
Official	Harold Murray
Copygirl	Suzie Baker

Musical Numbers: "There's Nothing Like Travel," "All Around the World," "Fogarty the Great," "That's Class," "Nellie Bly," "May the Best Man Win," "How About a Date?" "You Never Saw That Before," L'Esposition Universalle, "Sky High," No News Today, Choral Russe, "Just My Luck," "Aladdin's Daughter," Start Dancing, "Harmony," "You May Not Love Me."

A Musical Comedy in two acts, eighteen scenes. The Action takes place around the world in the year 1889. The Slip and in front of the Ferry House at Barclay Street, New York, Battle Annie's Saloon, City Hall Square, Steamship Pier in Hoboken, The After Deck and a Stateroom of the S.S. "Augusta Victoria," at the Gates and Inside the Paris Exposition, City Room of the New York Herald, The Stratosphere, Public Square in Moscow, Street in Aden, The Pass, Somewhere in Texas.

General Manager, Irving Cooper
Company Manager, S. M. Handelsman
Press, Karl Bernstein, Martha Dreiblatt
General Stage Director, Milton Stern
Stage Manager, Hal Voeth

*Played during road tour by Marilyn Maxwell.
**Closed February 2, 1946 (16 performances)

Victor Moore and William Gaxton

Victor Moore—Joy Hodges—William Gaxton

61

Louis Calhern as Justice Holmes

Dorothy Gish as Fanny Holmes

Justice Holmes (Louis Calhern) and Mrs. Holmes (Dorothy Gish) welcome Mr. Holmes' former secretaries, who come to congratulate him upon his eightieth birthday

ROYALE THEATRE

Opened Tuesday, January 22, 1946†
Arthur Hopkins presents:

THE MAGNIFICENT YANKEE

By Emmet Lavery*; Setting and Costumes by
Woodman Thompson; Directed by Mr. Hopkins.

Cast of Characters

Dixon, a real estate broker............Mason Curry
Mr. Justice Holmes ....Louis Calhern
Fanny Dixwell Holmes..............Dorothy Gish***
Henry Adams ....Fleming Ward
Copeland, a secretary ....Christopher Marvin
Mason, a secretary ....Nicholas Saunders
Mary, housekeeper ....Eleanor Swayne
Mr. Palmer of "The Transcript"
....William Roerick
Owen Wister ....Sherling Oliver
Northrop, a secretary ....Philip Truex
Hamilton, a secretary ....Robert Healy
Mr. Justice Brandeis ....Edgar Barrier**
Mapes, a secretary ....Grey Stafford
Rogers, a secretary ....Edward Hudson
Jackson, a former secretary.......Edwin Whitner
Halloran, a former secretary......Bruce Bradford

A Biographical Drama in three acts, seven
scenes, based on incidents from the career and
private life of Justice Oliver Wendell Holmes.
The action covering the period from December,
1902, to March, 1933, takes place in the Library of Justice Holmes, in Washington, D. C.

Company Manager, Max Siegel
Press, Richard Maney, Anne Woll
Stage Manager, Paul Porter

*The author is indebted to Mr. Francis Biddle
for use of certain material from Mr. Biddle's
biography, "Mr. Justice Holmes."

**Replaced by Richard Bowler.
***Alternate, Sylvia Fields
†Closed June 8, 1946   (159 performances)

Dorothy Gish and Louis Calhern

Louis Calhern—Fleming Ward—Edgar Barrier—Eleanor Swayne—Dorothy Gish and Sherling Oliver

EMPIRE THEATRE

Opening Wednesday, January 23, 1946
The Theatre Guild and John C. Wilson
present:

O MISTRESS MINE*

By Terence Rattigan; Settings by Robert
Davison; Miss Fontanne's dresses by Moly-
neaux; Directed by Mr. Lunt.

Cast of Characters
(In order of appearance)

Olivia Brown ....Lynn Fontanne
Polton ....Margery Maude
Miss Dell ....Esther Mitchell
Sir John Fletcher ....Alfred Lunt
Michael Brown ....Dick Van Patten
Diana Fletcher ....Ann Lee
Miss Wentworth ....Marie Paxton

A Comedy in three acts. Time: London,
1944. Scenes: A House in Westminster and a
Flat in Baron's Court.

General Manager, C. Edwin Knill
Company Manager, Lawrence Farrell
Press, Joseph Heidt, Howard Newman
Stage Managers, Charva Chester,
Charles Bowden

*Presented last season in London and for the
troops in France under the title of "Love in
Idleness."

Alfred Lunt

Lynn Fontanne as "Olivia Brown"

Miss Lynn Fontanne

Alfred Lunt and Dick Van Patten

Dick Van Patten—Lynn Fontanne—Alfred Lunt—Ann Lee

Judy Holliday

Encircled, Gary Merrill and Judy Holliday

LYCEUM THEATRE
Opening Monday, February 4, 1946
Max Gordon presents:

BORN YESTERDAY

By Garson Kanin; Staged by the author; Setting by Donald Oenslager; Customes supervised by Ruth Kanin Aronson.

Cast of Characters
(In order of appearance)

Helen ....Ellen Hall
Paul Verrall ....Gary Merrill**
Eddie Brock ....Frank Otto*1
Bellhop ....William Harmon
Bellhop ....Rex King*2
Harry Brock ....Paul Douglas
The Assistant Manager..........Carroll Ashburn
Billie Dawn ....Judy Holliday***
Ed Devery ....Otto Hulett
Barber ....Ted Mayer
Manicurist ....Mary Laslo
Bootblack ....Parris Morgan
Senator Norval Hedges ....Larry Oliver
Mrs. Hedges ....Mona Bruns
Waiter ....C. L. Burke

A Comedy in three acts. The scene: Grand Suite of exclusive Washington, D. C., Hotel, 1945.

General Manager, Ben A. Boyar
Press, Nat N. Dorfman
Stage Manager, David M. Pardoll

*Replaced by 1. Harry M. Cooke, 2. James Daly

**Played by Richard E. Davis during tryout.

***Miss Holliday replaced Jean Arthur, who left the production during its tryout tour.

Frank Otto, Larry Oliver, Paul Douglas, Gary Merrill, Otto Hulett and Judy Holliday

Paul Douglas loses to Judy Holliday at gin rummy

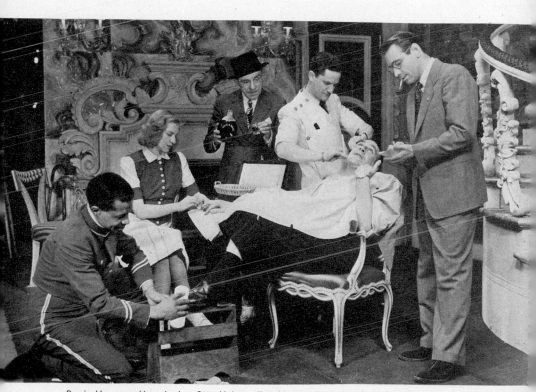

Parris Morgan—Mary Laslo—Otto Hulett—Ted Mayer—Paul Douglas—Gary Merrill

Lulu Mae Hubbard—Robert Keith—
John Hudson

GOLDEN THEATRE
Opened Monday, February 4, 1946*
Michael Todd presents:

JANUARY THAW

Adapted by William Roos from the novel of
the same title by Bellamy Partridge; Staged by
Ezra Stone; Setting by Watson Barratt.

Cast of Characters
(In order of speaking)

Frieda ....Norma Lehn
Herbert Gage ....Robert Keith
Sarah Gage ....Lorna Lynn
Paul Gage ....Charles Nevil
Marge Gage ....Lulu Mae Hubbard
Barbara Gage ....Natalie Thompson
George Husted ....John Hudson
Jonathan Rockwood ....Charles Middleton
Mathilda Rockwood ....Helen Carew
Mr. Loomis ....John McGovern
Uncle Walter ....Charles Burrows
Matt Rockwood ....Irving Morrow
Carson ....Henry Jones
Melvin Gorley ....Paul Weiss

A Comedy in three acts. The Scene is the
Living-room of an old house in Connecticut
into which the Gage Family have just moved,
after restoring it to its Colonial State.

General Manager, James Colligan
Company Manager, Richard Highley
Press, Bill Doll, Morton Nathanson,
and Dick Williams
Stage Manager, John Scott

*Closed March 16, 1946   (48 performances)

Robert Keith—Natalie Thompson—Lulu Mae Hubbard—Charles Middleton—Charles Nevil—
Lorna Lynn—Helen Carew

Jimsey Somers and Walter Huston

BILTMORE THEATRE

Opened Tuesday, February 5, 1946**
Jed Harris in association with Watler
Huston presents:

APPLE OF HIS EYE

By Kenyon Nicholson and Charles Robinson;
Setting by Raymond Sovey; Directed by Mr.
Harris

Cast of Characters
(In order of appearance)

Stella Springer ....Doro Merande
Foss Springer ....Arthur Hunnicutt *1
Lily Tobin ....Mary James
Tude Bowers ....Roy Fant
Sam Stover ....Walter Huston
Nina Stover ....Mary Wickes
Carol Ann Stover ....Jimsey Somers*2
Ott Tobin ....Joseph Sweeney
Nettie Bowers ....Claire Woodbury
Glen Stover ....Tom Ewell*3

A Rural Comedy in two acts. The Action
takes place several years ago at Sam Stover's
Maple Lawn Farm, Highland Township, Montgomery County, Indiana.

General Manager, Ben Stein
Company Manager, James S. Miller
Press, Dick Weaver
Stage Manager, Herman Shapiro

*Replacements: 1. Maurice Manson, 2. Car-
roll Daniels, 3. Ross Elliott.

**Closed May 18, 1946   (118 performances)

Mary Wickes—Jimsey Somers—Mary James—Walter Huston

PLYMOUTH THEATRE

Opened Wednesday, February 6, 1946**
Michael Myerberg presents:

LUTE SONG

By Sidney Howard and Will Irwin (from the famous Chinese play, "Pi-Pa-Ki"); Music by Raymond Scott; Lyrics by Bernard Hanighen; Directed by John Houseman; Choreography by Yeichi Nimura; Musical Director, Eugene Kusmiak; Orchestrations by Raymond Scott; Miss Martin's Costumes by Valentina; Scenery, Costumes and Lighting by Robert Edmond Jones.

Cast of Characters
(In order of appearance)

The Manager	}.......Clarence Derwent
The Honorable Tschang	
Tsai-Yong (Son)	..............Yul Brynner
Tsai (Father)	.........................Augustin Duncan
Madame Tsai (Mother)	.........Mildred Dunnock
Tchao-Ou-Niang (Wife)	.................Mary Martin†
Prince Nieou (Imperial Preceptor)	
	McKay Morris
Princess Nieou, His Daughter	.........Helen Craig
Si-Tchun, A Lady in Waiting	.........Nancy Davis
Waiting Women	{ Pamela Wilde
	{ Sydelle Sylovna
Hand Maidens	{ Blanche Zohar
	{ Mary Ann Reeve
Youen-Kong (Steward)	...............Rex O'Malley
A Marriage Broker	......................Diane De Brett
A Messenger	...........................Jack Amoroso
The Imperial Chamberlain	............Ralph Clanton*
The Food Commissioner	...............Gene Galvin
First Clerk	.....................................Max Leavitt
Second Clerk	....................................Bob Turner
First Applicant	.................Tom Emlyn Williams
Second Applicant	.........................Michael Blair
Imperial Guards	{ John Robert Lloyd
	{ John High
Imperial Attendants	{ Gordon Showalter
	{ Ronald Fletcher
The Genie	...............................Ralph Clanton*
The White Tiger	...........................Lisa Maslova
The Ape	....Lisan Kay
Phoenix Birds	{ Lisa Maslova
	{ Lisan Kay
Li Wang	....Max Leavitt
Priest of Amida Buddha	
	Tom Emlyn Williams
A Bonze	....Gene Galvin
Two Lesser Bonzes	{ Joseph Camiolo
	{ Leslie Rheinfeld
A Rich Man	....Bob Turner
A Merchant	....John High
A Little Boy	...................................Donald Rose
The Lion	{ Walter Stane
	{ Alberto Vecchio
Children	{ Mary Ann Reeve
	{ Blanche Zohar
	{ Teddy Rose
A Secretary	....................................Michael Blair

Musical Numbers: "Mountain High, Valley Low," North Road, Imperial March, "Monkey See, Monkey Do," "Where You Are," Marriage Music, "Willow Tree," Beggars' Music, "Vision Song," Chinese Market Place, "Bitter Harvest," Dirge Song, Genie Music, Phoenix Dance, Lion Dance, "Lute Song."

A Love Story with music in three acts, seventeen scenes. The Action takes place in the House of Tsai, a Public Granary, The Market Place—Street of the Hair Buyers, and a Burial Place in the Village of Tchin-Lieou; The North Road leading to, and a Street in the Capital; The Gate to the Palace of the Voice of Jade; The Gardens, a Room, and the Blue Pavilion of the Palace of the Prince Nieou; The Temple of Amidha Buddha.

General Manager, Matilda Stanton
Company Manager, J. Charles Gilbert
Press, Richard Maney, Anne Woll
Stage Manager, Jose Vega
†Played by Dolly Haas during last week.
*Replaced by George Cotton
**Closed June 8, 1946   (142 performances)

Mary Martin and Yul Brynner

Helen Craig and Mary Martin

Foreground, Yul Brynner and Mary Martin
Background, Helen Craig and Ralph Clanton

Mildred Dunnock—Augustin Duncan—Clarence Derwent—Mary Martin—Yul Brynner

ADELPHI THEATRE

Opened Wednesday, February 13, 1946*
A. P. Waxman presents:

THE DUCHESS MISBEHAVES**

Music by Dr. Frank Black; Book and Lyrics by Gladys Shelley; Additional Dialogue by Joe Bigelow; Staged by Martin Manulis; Musical Numbers and Dances staged by George Tapps; Production supervised by Chet O'Brien; Designed by A. A. Ostrander; Costumes by Willa Kim; Lighting by Carlton Winckler; Orchestrations by Don Walker; Vocal arrangements by Clay Warnick; Orchestra under direction of Charles Sanford.

Cast of Characters
(In order of appearance)

In Carlton's Department Store

Woman	Grace Hayle
Franchot	Buddy Ferraro
1st Sister	Elena Boyd
2nd Sister	Mildred Boyd
3rd Sister	Edith Boyd
Butterfly	Penny Edwards
Paul	Larry Douglas
Fitzgerald	James MacColl
Woonsocket	Joey Faye***
1st Girl	Gail Adams
2nd Girl	Ethel Madson
Miss Kiester	Paula Laurence
Crystal Shalimar	Audrey Christie
Reporter	Al Downing
Neville Goldglitter	Philip Tonge

In Spain

Pablo	Larry Douglas
Amber	Grace Hayle
Goya	Joey Faye***
Model	Joanne Jaap
Roberto	James MacColl
Duchess of Alba	Audrey Christie
Mariposa	Penny Edwards
Barber	Paul Marten
Manicurist	Joanne Jaap
Tailor	Ken Martin
Ass't Tailor	Bernie Williams
Messenger	Buddy Ferraro
1st Student	Victor Clark
2nd Student	Jess Randolph
Duke of Alba	Philip Tonge
Ladies in Waiting	The Boyd Triplets
Queen of Spain	Paula Laurence
A Model	Norma Kohane
Matador	George Tapps
Jose	Al Downing
Dancer	Mata Monteria
The Woman	Jean Handzlik
Her Man	George Tapps

Musical Numbers: "Art," "My Only Romance," "Broadminded," "I Hate Myself in the Morning," "Men," "Couldn't Be More in Love," Dance of the Matador†, "Ole' Ole'," "Katie Did in Madrid," "Morning in Madrid," "Lost," "Honeymoon Is Over," "Nuts," "Fair Weather Friends," "The Nightmare."

A Musical Comedy in two acts, eight scenes, with a present day prologue and epilogue. The action takes place in the Art Section of Carlton's Department Store, Goya's Studio in Spain, a Street in Madrid, Outside the Fiesta Grounds, Public Square in Madrid, and a Side Street.

General Manager, Ben A. Boyar
Company Manager, Joseph N. Grossman
Press, Michael Goldreyer
General Stage Director, Frank W. Shea
Stage Manager, Alfred Morse

*Closed February 16, 1946 (5 performances)

**Built around the incident of the Duchess of Alba being painted in the nude by Goya. Other than this fact, the only thing historically accurate in the book was the use of a few 18th Century names.

***Played during tryout tour by James Gleason.
†Manuel De Falla's "Ritual Fire Dance."

72

Penny Edwards and Larry Douglas

Joanne Jaap—Paul Marten—
Joey Faye—Audrey Christie

Katharine Cornell as Antigone

CORT THEATRE

Opened Monday, February 18, 1946*
Katharine Cornell in association with Gilbert Miller presents:

ANTIGONE

Adapted by Lewis Galantiere from the French play by Jean Anouilh**; Staged by Guthrie McClintic; Setting by Raymond Sovey; Costumes by Valentina.

Cast of Characters
(In order of speaking)

Chorus	Horace Braham
Antigone	Katharine Cornell
Nurse	Bertha Belmore
Ismene	Ruth Matteson
Haemon	Wesley Addy
Creon	Cedric Hardwicke
First Guard	George Mathews
Second Guard	David J. Stewart
Third Guard	Michael Higgins
Messenger	Oliver Cliff
Page	Albert Biondo
Eurydice	Merle Maddern***

A Tragedy in one act, presented in a modernized form adapted from the classical Greek style.

General Manager, Gertrude Macy
Company Manager, William Tisdale
Press Representative, Francis Robinson
Stage Manager, James Neilson

*Closed May 4, 1946   (64 performances)

**M. Anouilh's play was written and produced in Paris in 1943 under Nazi occupation. By making Creon a most eloquent dictator, Anouilh was able to receive the sanction of a German censor, and still present "Antigone," symbolizing patriotic France rejecting the German order.

***Replaced by Eveline Vaughan.

Wesley Addy   Katharine Cornell

Cedric Hardwicke—Katharine Cornell—
Ruth Matteson

Katharine Cornell   Bertha Belmore

74

Ossie Davis and Laura Bowman

MARTIN BECK THEATRE

Opened Thursday, February 21, 1946*
Herman Shumlin presents:

JEB

By Robert Ardrey; Staged by Mr. Shumlin;
Scenery and Lighting by Jo Mielziner; Costumes
by Patricia Montgomery; Production Associate,
David Merrick.

Cast of Characters
(In order of appearance)

Solly ....Morris McKenney
Don ....Charles Holland
Cynthie ....Carolyn Hill Stewart
Hazy Johnson ....Wardell Saunders
Jeb Turner ....Ossie Davis
Bush ....P. Jay Sidney
Flabber ....Percy Verwayen
Simpson ....G. Harry Bolden
Mr Touhy ....W. J. Hackett
Amanda Turner ....Laura Bowman
Rachel ....Reri Grist
Libby George ....Ruby Dee
Libe ....Rudolph Whitaker
Jefferson ....Christopher Bennett
Julian ....Maurice Ellis
Paul Devoure ....Santos Ortega
Mrs. Devoure..........................Grace McTarnahan
Charles Bard ....Frank M. Thomas
Dr. Hazelton ....Edwin Cushman
Mr. Gibney ....Grover Burgess
Joseph ....Milton Shirah
Mr. Dowd ....Edward Forbes
Another White Man ....Owen Hewitt

A Drama on racial tolerance in two acts,
seven scenes: The Elite Cafe, in the Negro Section of a Northern City; Amanda Turner's
Kitchen, the Devoure Back Parlor, the Time-
keeper's Shed at the Sugar Mill and behind Dr.
Hazelton's Church, in a small Louisiana Town.

Company Manager, Madeline Healy
Press, Richard Maney, Anne Woll
Stage Manager, Henri Caubisens

*Closed February 28, 1946   (9 performances)

Morris McKenney—P. Jay Sidney—Percy Verwayen—Ossie Davis—Carolyn Stewart—Charles Holland—
Wardell Saunders—W. J. Hackett

Ann Shepherd—Marlon Brando—Richard Waring—
Virginia Gilmore—David Manners

BELASCO THEATRE

Opened Wednesday, February 27, 1946**
Harold Clurman and Elia Kazan in association with the Playwrights' Company
present:*

TRUCKLINE CAFE

By Maxwell Anderson; Directed by Harold
Clurman; Setting by Boris Aronson; Costumes
by Millia Davenport.

Cast of Characters
(In order of appearance)

Toby	Frank Overton
Kip	Ralph Theadore
Stew	John Sweet
Maurice	Kevin McCarthy
Min	June Walker
Wing Commander Hern	David Manners
Anne	Virginia Gilmore
Stag	Karl Malden
Angie	Irene Dailey
Celeste	Joanne Tree
Patrolman Gray	Robert Simon
Evvie Garrett	Joann Dolan
Hutch	Kenneth Tobey
Matt	Louis A. Florence
June	Jutta Wolf
Sissie	Leila Ernst
Tory McRae	Ann Shepherd
Sage McRae	Marlon Brando
Man With a Pail	Lou Gilbert
The Breadman	Peter Hobbs
Janet	Peggy Meredith
Mildred	June March
Bimi	Richard Paul
Tuffy Garrett	Eugene Steiner
First Man	Solen Hayes
First Woman	Lorraine Kirby
Mort	Richard Waring
Second Man	Joseph Adams
Second Woman	Rose Steiner
First Girl	Ann Morgan
Second Girl	Gloria Stroock

A Drama in three acts... The Scene is the
Interior of a Diner Cafe on the Ocean High-
way between Los Angeles and San Francisco

General Manager, Walter Fried
Press, James D. Proctor, Lewis Harmon
Stage Manager, James Gelb

*After receiving an adverse critical barrage
from the press, the producers gave vent to
their feelings in newspaper ads, which
stated that the critics were "not qualified
. . . . either by their training or by their
taste," and the author dubbed them "Jukes
Family of Journalism."

**Closed March 9, 1946. (13 performances)

MARTIN BECK THEATRE

Opened Wednesday, March 6, 1946*
Courtney Burr presents:

LITTLE BROWN JUG

By Marie Baumer; Directed by Gerald Savory;
Settings and Lighting by Frederick Fox.

Cast of Characters
(In order of appearance)

Irene Haskell ....Katharine Alexander
Henry Barlow ....Ronald Alexander
Carol Barlow ....Marjorie Lord
Ira ....Percy Kilbride
Lydia ....Frieda Altman
Michael Andrews ....Arthur Franz
Norman Barlow ....Arthur Margetson

A Murder Melodrama in three acts. The
Time is late March, 1945. The Action takes
place in Henry Barlow's combined Lodge and
Boat House in Maine and Irene Haskell's House
in Connecticut.

General Manager, Edward Choate
Manager, Allan Attwater
Press, Marian Byram
Stage Manager, William Atlee

*Closed March 9, 1946 (5 performances)

Percy Kilbride
Encircled, Katharine Alexander

Percy Kilbride—Marjorie Lord—Katharine Alexander

ADELPHI THEATRE

(Moved to the BROADHURST THEATRE,
May 20, 1946)
Opening Thursday, March 7, 1946.
Stanley Gilkey and Barbara Payne present:

THREE TO MAKE READY

Sketches and Lyrics by Nancy Hamilton;
Music by Morgan Lewis; Production devised
and staged by John Murray Anderson; Sketches
directed by Margaret Webster; Dances and Musical Numbers staged by Robert Sidney; Designed by Donald Oenslager; Costumes by
Audre; Vocal Arrangements by Joe Moon; Orchestrations by Russell Bennett, Charles L.
Cooke, Elliott Jacoby, Ted Royal, Hans Spialek
and Walter Paul; Orchestra directed by Ray M.
Kavanaugh.

Featuring

Ray Bolger	Brenda Forbes
Rose Inghram	Gordon MacRae
Bibi Osterwald	Harold Lang
Jane Deering	Garry Davis
Althea Elder	Joe Jonson
Meg Mundy	Carleton Carpenter
Mary Alice Bingham	Martin Kraft
Mary McDonnell	Jack Purcell
Edythia Turnell	Irwin Charles
Candace Montgomery	Jimmy Venable
Iris Linde	Jim Elsegood

and
Arthur Godfrey†

Musical Numbers:†† "It's a Nice Night for It,"
"There's Something on My Program," "Tell Me
the Story," "The Old Soft Shoe," "Barnaby
Beach," "Kenosha Canoe," "If It's Love," "A
Lovely Lazy Kind of Day," "And Why Not I?"
Finale.
Sketches: Post Mortem, The Shoe on the Other
Foot, The Russian Lesson, Cold Water Flat,
Wisconsin or Kenosha Canoe,* The Story of the
Opera,** The Sad Sack.***

A Musical Revue in two acts and twenty
scenes.
Company Manager, Warren Munsell, Jr.
Press, Sol Jacobson
Production and General Stage Manager,
Francis Spencer

†Was forced to leave the show due to com-
plete physical exhaustion.
††The number "Hot December" was added to
the show to replace Mr. Godfrey's material.
*A take-off on "An American Tragedy" done
in the style of "Oklahoma."
**From "One for the Money."
***Based on the character created by Sgt.
George Baker.

Ray Bolger.

"The Old Soft Shoe"

Brenda Forbes sings
"And Why Not I?"

Harold Lang and Jane Deering dance
"There's Something On My Program"

"A Lovely Lazy Kind of Day"

Ray Bolger as the Scarecrow

Bambi Osterwald as the Milkmaid

Philip Bourneuf—Francis J. Felton—Judith Parrish

BELASCO THEATRE

Opened Tuesday, March 19, 1946*
Rowland Stebbins† presents:

FLAMINGO ROAD

By Robert and Sally Wilder; Adapted from Mr. Wilder's book of the same name; Staged by Jose Ruben; Settings by Watson Barratt; Costumes by Emeline Roche; Lighting by Leo Kerz.

Cast of Characters
(In order of appearance)

Boatright ....Olvester Polk
Titus Semple ....Francis J. Felton
Fielding Carlisle ....Lauren Gilbert
Henry Veech ....Frank McNellis
"Doc" Watterson ....Will Geer**
Dan Curtis ....Philip Bourneuf
Ulee Jackson ....Paul Ford
Tate Hadley ....Bernard Randall
Lute-Mae Saunders ....Doris Rich
Goldie ....Martha Jensen
Another "Lute-Mae" Girl ....Sally Carthage
Lane Ballou ....Judith Parrish
Burrell Lassen ....Tom Morrison
"Red" ....Marcella Markham
Matron ....Hazele Burgess
Virgie ....Evelyn Davis
Grocery Boy ....Mahlon Naill

A Melodrama on political corruption in three acts, six scenes: The Front Porch of the Palmer House, a Small Hotel in Florida, the Yard of the Women's Prison Farm, a Room at Lute-Mae Saunders', and the Living-room at 32 Flamingo Road.

Production Supervisor, Miriam Doyle
General Manager, Charles Stewart
Company Manager, Louis Cline
Press, Leo Freedman
Stage Manager, George W. Smith

*Closed March 23, 1946   (7 performances)
**Replaced by Ralph Riggs after second performance.
†Produced in the past under title, Laurence Rivers Inc.

Hazele Burgess—Sally Carthage—Olvester Polk—Judith Parrish—Will Geer—
Francis J. Felton—Frank McNellis—Mahlon Naill

Susan Douglas, Dennis King, Russell Collins, John M. O'Connor, Wolfe Barzell—seated, and circus performers

Stella Adler, John Abbott, Dennis King, and Susan Douglas—seated

BOOTH THEATRE

Opened Wednesday, March 20, 1946**
The Theatre Guild presents a revival of:

HE WHO GETS SLAPPED

By Leonid Andreyev; English Version by Judith Guthrie; Staged by Tyrone Guthrie; Settings and Costumes by Motley; Supervised by Theresa Helburn and Lawrence Langner.

Cast of Characters
(In order of appearance)

Tilly ....Bobby Barry
Polly ....John M. O'Connor
Count Mancini ....John Abbott*1
Papa Briquet ....Wolfe Barzell
Zinaida ....Stella Adler
Funny ....Dennis King*2
Jim Jackson ....Russell Collins*3
Consuela ....Susan Douglas*4
Alfred Bezano ....Jerome Thor
A Gentleman ....Tom Rutherford*5
Baron Regnard ....Reinhold Schunzel
Housekeeper ....Edith Shayne
Ringmaster ....Arthur Foran
1st Jockey ....George Cory
2nd Jockey ....Tony Albert
3rd Jockey ....Ellis Eringer
Thomas ....Ernest Sarracino
Equestrienne ....Cynthia Blake
Tap Dancing Trio ....Phil Sheridan
                     Jack Orton, Leatta Miller.
Strong Man ....Paul Alberts.
Dancers........Cynthia Carline, Letitia Fay Sydna
              Scott, Jackie Jones, Elsbeth Fuller.
Clowns........Michael Wyler, Joseph Singer, Carl
              Specht, Douglas Hudelson.
Jugglers................Frank de Silva, Robin Taylor.
Waiter ....Frank de Silva

A Tragedy in two acts. The Action takes place Back Stage of a Small Circus in a City in France, about 1919.

Company Manager, John Yorke
Press, Joseph Heidt, Howard Newman
Stage Manager, Jus Addiss

*Played during road tour by 1. John Wengraf, 2. John Abbott, 3. Augustus Smith, 4. Beatrice Pearson, 5. Norman Stuart.

**Closed April 27, 1946.   (46 performances)

81

Bert Lytell—Ellis Baker—Oscar Karlweis

GOLDEN THEATRE
Opened Friday, March 22, 1946*
William Cahn presents:

I LIKE IT HERE

By A. B. Shiffrin; Directed by Charles K. Freeman; Setting by Ralph Alswang.

Cast of Characters
(In order of appearance)

Mr. Smedley ....Seth Arnold
Captain Leroux ....John Effrat
Laura Merriweather ....Mardi Bryant**
Matilda Merriweather ....Beverly Bayne
Sebastian Merriweather ....Bert Lytell
Brad Monroe ....William Terry
Willie Kringle ....Oscar Karlweis
David Bellow ....Donald Randolph
Saphronia Lawrence ....Ellis Baker

A Comedy in three acts. The Action takes place in the New England Home of the Merriweathers.

General Manager, Irving Pincus
Press, Ivan Black, Lenny Traube
Stage Manager, John Effrat

*Closed May 4, 1946   (51 performances)
**Replaced by Sherry Bennett.

William Terry—Mardi Bryant—Beverly Bayne—Bert Lytell—Oscar Karlweis

Elizabeth
Ross
as
"Bernadette"

BELASCO THEATRE

Opened Tuesday, March 26, 1946th
Victor Payne Jennings and Frank McCoy
present:

THE SONG OF BERNADETTE

Dramatized by Jean and Walter Kerr from
Franz Werfel's novel of the same name; Di-
rected by Walter Kerr; Settings by Willis
Knighton; Production Equipment Designed by
Joseph Brown.

Cast of Characters

Sister Marie Theresa Vauzous	Jean Mann
Jeanne Abadie	Christina Soulias
Bernadette Soubirous	Elizabeth Ross
Marie Soubirous	Pamela Rivers
Dean Peyramale	Keinert Wolff
Louise Soubirous	Marjorie Hurtubise
Soubirous	Whit Vernon
Croisine Bouhouhorts	Mimi Norton

Louis Bouriette	Anthony Messuri
Bernarde Casterot	Gertrude Kinnell
Madame Sajou	Cavada Humphrey
Antoine Nicalau	Bruce Hall
Mayor Lacade	Michael Vallon
Jacomet	Richard Karlan
Dr. Dozous	Francis Compton
Celeste	Octavia Kenmore
Madame Pernet	Kay Macdonald
Mother Josephine	Ruth Gregory
Schoolgirl	Jane Thomas

A Drama of Religious Faith in three acts, ten
scenes. Time: Lourdes, France, 1858. Action
takes place in a Schoolroom, the Grotto of Mas-
sabielle, the Cachot, home of the Soubirous,
the Office of Mayor Lacade, Dean Peyramale's
Garden, and the Convent at Nevers.

Company Manager, Joseph Roth
Press, Ray Payton
Stage Manager, John Lynds
*Closed March 27, 1946 (3 performances)

CHANIN AUDITORIUM

Opened Tuesday, March 27, 1946**
Gustav Blum presents:

WALK HARD†

By Abram Hill, based on the novel "Walk Hard—Talk Loud" by Len Zinberg; Directed by Gustav Blum; Settings and Lighting by John Wenger.

Cast of Characters
(In order of appearance)

Bobby ....Richard Kraft
Mack Jeffris ....Leonard Yorr
Andy Whitman ....Maxwell Glanville
Mr. Berry ....Fred C. Carter
Lou Foster ....Joseph Kamm
Happy ....Howard Augusta
Mickey ....Stephen Elliott
Larry Batcheller ....Mickey Walker*
Becky ....Jacqueline Andre
Charlie ....Maurice Lisby
Susie ....Lulu Mae Ward
Ruth Lawson ....Dorothy Carter
Bartender ....John O. Hewitt
Sadie ....Jean Normandy
Dorothy ....Miriam Pullen
George, The Bellhop ....Leslie Jones
Hotel Clerk ....Richard Kraft
Lady Friend ....Fiona O'Shiel
Reporter ....Edward Kreisler
Announcer ....Richard Kraft

A Drama in three acts, eight scenes. The Action takes place on a Street Corner, Lou Foster's Office, The Whitman Home, A Jersey Tavern, A Hotel Lobby and The Ringside.

General Manager, Gilbert Weiss
Company Manager, George Zorn
Press, Marjorie Barkentin, Michael O'Shea
Stage Manager, Lulu Mae Ward

†Tried out last season by The American Negro Theatre.

*Former middle-weight boxing champ.
**Closed March 31, 1946   (7 performances)

Maxwell Glanville and Dorothy Carter

Mickey Walker—Jean Normandy

Leonard Yorr—Mickey Walker—Fiona O'Shiel—Maxwell Glanville

MARTIN BECK THEATRE

Opened Saturday, March 30, 1946✻.
Edward Gross presents:

ST. LOUIS WOMAN

Music by Harold Arlen; Lyrics by Johnny Mercer; Book by Arna Bontemps and Countee Cullen (Based on the novel, "God Sends Sunday," by Arna Bontemps); Production directed by Rouben Mamoulian; Costumes and Settings by Lemuel Ayers; Dances by Charles Walters; Musical Director, Leon Leonardi.

Cast of Characters
(In order of speaking)

Badfoot ....Robert Pope
Little Augie ....Harold Nicholas
Barney ✻..Fayard Nicholas
Lila ....June Hawkins
Slim ....Louis Sharp
Butterfly ....Pearl Bailey
Della Green ....Ruby Hill
Biglow Brown ....Rex Ingram
Ragsdale ....Elwood Smith
Pembroke ....Merritt Smith
Jasper ....Charles Welch
The Hostess ....Maude Russell
Drum Major ....J. Mardo Brown
Mississippi ....Milton J. Williams
Cake Walk Couples:
    Betty Nichols and Smalls Boykins
    Rita Garrett and Theodore Allen
    Dorothea Green and Milton Wood
    Royce Wallace and Lonny Reed
    Gwendolyn Hale and Norman DeJoie
    Enid Williams and George Thomas
Dandy Dave ....Frank Green
Leah ....Juanita Hall
Jackie ....Joseph Eady
Celestine ....Yvonne Coleman
Piggie ....Herbert Coleman
Joshua ....Lorenzo Fuller
Mr. Hopkins ....Milton Wood
Preacher ....Creighton Thompson
Waiter ....Carrington Lewis

Musical Numbers: "Li'l Augie Is a Natural Man," "Any Place I Hang My Hat Is Home," "I Feel My Luck Comin' Down," "True Love," "Legalize My Name," Cake Walk Your Lady, "Come Rain or Come Shine," "Chinquapin Bush," "We Shall Meet to Part, No Never," "Lullaby," "Sleep Peaceful," "Leavin' Time," "I Wonder What Became of Me," "A Woman's Prerogative," "Ridin' on the Moon," "Least That's My Opinion," "Racin' Form," "Come On, Li'l Augie."

A Musical Play in three acts, twelve scenes. The Action takes place in St. Louis, 1898: A Stable, Biglow's Bar, Outside Barney's Room, A Ballroom, Augie's and Della's Home, The Alley, Funeral Parlor, Street Corner Close to the Race Track.

Manager, Rube Bernstein
Press, Phyllis Perlman
Production Assistant, Nelson Gross
Stage Managers, Frank Hall, Ed Brinkman
✻Closed July 6, 1946   (113 performances)

Harold Nicholas

Pearl Bailey sings, "Legalize My Name" to Fayard Nicholas

85

Little Augie Wins the Race

Ruby Hill and Harold Nicholas

Rex Ingram and June Hawkins

CORT THEATRE

Opened Wednesday Matinee, April 3, 1946*

Katharine Cornell in association with Gilbert Miller presents a revival of:

CANDIDA†

By Bernard Shaw; Staged by Guthrie McClintic; Setting by Woodman Thompson.

Cast of Characters
(In order of speaking)

Miss Proserpine Garnett ....Mildred Natwick
James Mavor Morell ....Wesley Addy
Alexander Mill ....Oliver Cliff
Mr. Burgess ....Cedric Hardwicke
Candida ....Katharine Cornell
Eugene Marchbanks.....................Marlon Brando

A Play in three acts. The scene is the Sitting-room of St. Dominic's Parsonage in the Northeast Suburb of London.

General Manager, Gertrude Macy
Company Manager, William Tisdale
Press, Lorella Val-Mery
Stage Manager, James Neilson

†Alternated in repertory with "Antigone."
*Closed May 2, 1946   (24 performances)

Katharine Cornell as "Candida"

Marlon Brando and Katharine Cornell

87

BELASCO THEATRE

Opened Wednesday, April 17, 1946**
Kermit Bloomgarden presents:

WOMAN BITES DOG

By Bella and Samuel Spewack; Staged by
Coby Ruskin; Settings by Howard Bay; Costumes by Mary Grant.

Cast of Characters
(In order of appearance)

Amanda Merkle	Eda Heinemann
Tony Flynn	Frank Lovejoy
Betsy Lous Eric	Himself
Commander Southworth*	Taylor Holmes
Sims	E. G. Marshall
Wilson	Harold Grau
Betty Lord	Mercedes McCambridge
Major Southworth	Royal Beal
Lizzie Southworth	Ann Shoemaker
Hopkins	Kirk Douglas
1st Attorney	Richard Clark
2nd Attorney	Arthur Russell
Slim	Dudley Sadler
Waiter	Sam Bonnell
Valet	Russell Morrison
Breckenridge	Robert Le Sueur
Maurice Crash	Maury Tuckerman
Sokonovski	Boris Kogan
Lee	John Shellie
Mayor Stevens	Ed Nannery
Dean West	Roger Quinlan

A Comedy in three acts. The Action takes place in the Office of the Publisher of The Herald, and the Living-room of Commander Southworth's Suite at the Royal Hotel at the present time.

General Manager, Max Allentuck
Press, James D. Proctor, Lewis Harmon
Stage Manager, Richard Beckhard

*Although the program carried the note: "The characters in the play are fictional, of course," many reviewers found a similiarity between The Patterson-McCormick Publishing Family, owners of the Chicago Tribune-New York Daily News—Washington Times Herald, and the Southworths.

**Closed April 20, 1946 (5 performances).

Taylor Holmes—Frank Lovejoy

Ann Shoemaker—Royal Beal—Kirk Douglas—Taylor Holmes

Betty Garrett singing "South America, Take It Away"
Her Partners—Alan Manson—Chandler Cowles—George Hall—Harry Clark

89

NATIONAL THEATRE

Opening Thursday, April 18, 1946.
Melvyn Douglas and Herman Levin present:

CALL ME MISTER

Music and Lyrics by Harold Rome; Sketches by Arnold Auerbach, The Sketches, "Once Over Lightly" and "Off We Go," written in collaboration with Arnold B. Horwitt; Directed by Robert H. Gordon; Dances by John Wray; Musical Direction by Lehman Engel; Scenery by Lester Polakov; Costumes by Grace Houston.

Featuring

Betty Garrett	Jules Munshin
Betty Lou Holland	Bill Callahan
Paula Bane	Danny Scholl
Maria Karnilova	David Nillo

Lawrence Winters

Robert Baird	Joan Bartels
Harry Clark	Joe Calvan
Chandler Cowles	Fred Danieli
Virginia Davis	Alex Dunaeff
Bettye Durrence	Ruth Feist
Shellie Filkins	Kate Friedlich
Ward Garner	Darcy Gardener
Betty Gilpatrick	George Hall
Bruce Howard	George Irving
Tommy Knox	Henry Lawrence
Sid Lawson	Betty Lorraine
Rae MacGregor	Howard Malone
Alan Manson	William Mende
Marjorie Oldroyd	Doris Parker
Patricia Penso	Paula Purnell
Roy Ross	Evelyn Shaw
Edward Silkman	Kevin Smith
Alvis Tinnin	Eugene Tobin

Glen Turnbull

Musical Numbers: "The Jodie Chant," "Goin' Home Train," "Along With Me," "Surplus Blues," "The Drug Store Song," "The Red Ball Express," "Military Life," "Call Me Mister," "Yuletide, Park Avenue," "When We Meet Again," "The Face on the Dime," "A Home of Our Own," "His Old Man," "South America, Take It Away," "The Senators' Song."

Sketches: Welcome Home, The Army Way, Off We Go, Yuletide, Park Avenue, Once Over Lightly, A Home of Our Own, South Wind.

A Musical Revue in two acts, twenty-three scenes.

General Manager, Phil Adler
Press, Bernard Simon, Dorothy Ross
Stage Manager, B. D. Kranz

Danny Scholl and Paula Bane

Bill Callahan

Alan Manson—Jules Munshin—George Hall

First Act Finale of "Call Me Mister"

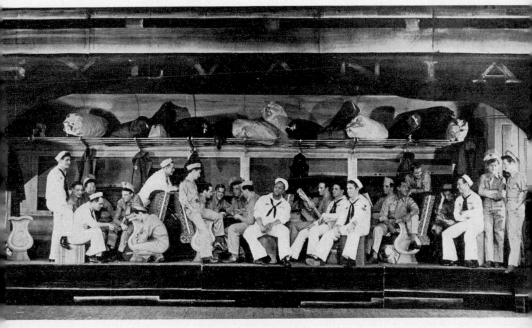

"Goin' Home Train"

BELASCO THEATRE

Opening Tuesday, April 30, 1946*
Richard Krakeur and David Shay present:

THIS, TOO, SHALL PASS

By Don Appell; Staged by the oouthor; Setting by Raymond Sovey.

Cast of Characters
(In order of appearance)

Janet Alexander ....Jan Sterling
Martha Alexander ....Kathryn Givney
Dr. Steven Alexander ....Ralph Morgan
Mac Sorrell ....Sam Wanamaker
Buddy Alexander ....Walter Starkey

A Drama on racial tolerance in three acts.
The scene is the Home of Dr. Steven Alexander
in a small Midwestern Town at the present time.

Company Manager; Lee K. Holland
Press, Karl Bernstein, Martha Dreiblatt
Stage Manager, Joseph Olney
*Closed June 22, 1946   (63 performances)

Jan Sterling—Sam Wanamaker—Ralph Morgan
Encircled, Kathryn Givney—Walter Starkey

Kathryn Givney—Walter Starkey—Jan Sterling—Sam Wanamaker—Ralph Morgan

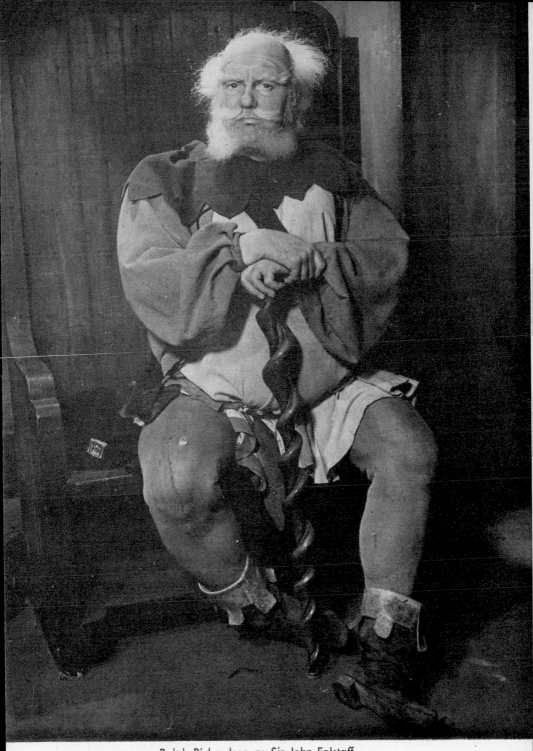

Ralph Richardson as Sir John Falstaff

Laurence Olivier   Michael Warre   Laurence Olivier   Margaret Leighton

CENTURY THEATRE

Opened Monday, May 6, 1946.*
Theatre Incorporated presents the Old Vic
Theatre Company:

HENRY IV, PART I

By William Shakespeare; Staged by John Burrell; Music by Herbert Menges; Costumes by
Roger Furse; Scenery by Gower Parks; Lighting
by John Sullivan; Fights arranged by Peter Copley; Orchestra directed by Herbert Menges.

Cast of Characters

King Henry IV . ...Nicholas Hannen
Henry, Prince of Wales ....Michael Warre
John of Lancaster ....Robin Lloyd
Earl of Westmoreland ....Peter Copley
Earl of Warwick ....Kenneth Edwards
Sir Walter Blunt ....Cecil Winter
Earl of Worcester ....George Relph
Earl of Northumberland ....Miles Malleson
Henry Percy (Hotspur)...........Laurence Olivier
Lord Mortimer, Earl of March........David Kentish
Owen Glendower ....Harry Andrews
Archibald, Earl of Douglas...........William Monk
Sir Richard Vernon ....Frank Duncan
Sir John Falstaff ....Ralph Richardson
Bardolph ....Michael Raghan
Poins ....Sidney Tafler
Peto ....George Rose
Mistress Quickly ....Ena Burrill
Lady Percy, Wife to Hotspur..Margaret Leighton
Lady Mortimer, Daughter to Glendower,
                              Diana Maddox
Servant to Hotspur ....Joseph James
A Traveler ....Frank Duncan
Another Traveler ....William Squire
Francis, a Winedrawer ....John Garley
Vintner of the Boar's Head......Kenneth Edwards
Sheriff ....William Monk

The first part of the English Chronicle is presented in three parts. It covers the end of the
reign of King Henry IV, through the death of
Hotspur, to the rise of Prince Hal.

*Closed June 13, 1946 (played 18 performances
in Repertory).

Ralph Richardson—Laurence Olivier

94

Ralph Richardson and Laurence Olivier

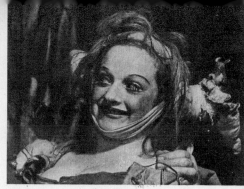

Joyce Redman

CENTURY THEATRE

Opened Monday, May 13, 1946*
Theatre Incorporated presents the Old Vic
Theatre Company:

HENRY IV, PART II

By William Shakespeare; Staged by John Burrell; Music by Herbert Menges; Costumes by Roger Furse; Scenery by Gower Parks; Lighting by John Sullivan; Orchestra directed by Herbert Menges.

Cast of Characters

Rumour, The Presenter ....Nicolette Bernard
King Henry IV ....Nicholas Hannen
Henry, Prince of Wales (Afterwards
  King Henry V) ....Michael Warre
Prince John of Lancaster ....Robin Lloyd
Thomas, Duke of Clarence ....George Rose
Prince Humphrey of Gloucester.......John Garley
Earl of Warwick ....Kenneth Edwards
Earle of Westmoreland ....Peter Copley
The Lord Chief Justice ....Cecil Winter
His Servant ....Max Brent
Fang ....Frank Duncan
Snare ....Joseph James
Gower ....Kenneth Edwards
Earl of Northumberland ....Miles Malleson
Lady Northumberland ....Byrony Chapman
Lady Percy ....Margaret Leighton
Travers ....Robin Lloyd
Morton ....Peter Copley
Scroop, Archbishop of York.........Harry Andrews
Lord Mowbray ....William Squire
Lord Hastings ....David Kentish
Lord Bardolph ....George Rose
Sir John Coleville ....Sidney Tafler
Sir John Falstaff ....Ralph Richardson
His Page ....Brian Parker
Mistress Quickly ....Ena Burrill
Bardolph ....Michael Raghan
Poins ....Sidney Tafler
Peto ....George Rose
Doll Tearsheet ....Joyce Redman
Pistol ....George Relph
Francis, a Winedrawer ....John Garley
Another Winedrawer ....Robin Lloyd
Justice Shallow ....Laurence Olivier
Justice Silence ....Miles Malleson
Davy, Servant to Shallow ....William Monk
Mouldy ....George Rose
Wart ....John Garley
Shadow ....Frank Duncan
Feeble ....David Kentish
Bullcalf ....Joseph James
Lords, Attendants, Soldiers, Citizens: Eleanora
    Barrie, Byrony Chapman, Julie Harris, Dee
    Sparks, Jane Wenham, Lawrence Carr,
    Rudolph Cavell, George Cooper, Will Davis,
    Frank Duncan, Carl James, Elmer Lehr,
    Bernard Pollack, John Reilly, Paul Riley,
    Sandy Roe, William Squire, Al Studer, Alvin
    Sullum, Richard Wendley.

The concluding half of the King Henry Cycle is presented in three parts and covers the death of Henry IV, the crowning of Prince Hal, and the banishment of Falstaff.

*Closed June 13, 1946 (played 9 performances in Repertory).

Ralph Richardson and Joyce Redman

CORT THEATRE

Opening Wednesday, May 8, 1946.
Canada Lee and Mark Marvin in association with George McLain present:

ON WHITMAN AVENUE

By Maxine Wood; Directed by Margo Jones; Setting and Lighting by Donald Oenslager; Lullaby composed by Paul Bowles.

Cast of Characters
(In order of appearance)

Johnnie Tilden ....Martin Miller
Kate Tilden ....Ernestine Barrier
Ed Tilden ....Will Geer
Owen Bennett ....Richard Williams
Gramp Bennett ....Augustus Smith
Wini Bennett ....Vivienne Baber
Bernie Lund ....Kenneth Terry
Aurie Anderson ....Hilda Vaughn
Cora Bennett ....Abbie Mitchell
Toni Tilden ....Perry Wilson
David Bennett ....Canada Lee
Jeff Hall ....Philip Clarke
Belle Hall ....Betty Greene Little
Walter Lund ....Robert Simon
Ellen Lund ....Jean Cleveland
Wilbur Reed ....Stephen Roberts
Edna Reed ....Joanna Albus

A Drama on racial prejudice in two acts, four scenes. The Action takes place in the Tildens' Home in Lawndale, a suburban development in the Midwest, September, 1945.

Company Manager, Charles Mulligan
Press, Bernard Simon, June Greenwall
Stage Manager, Harry Altner

Perry Wilson and Canada Lee

Ernestine Barrier, Canada Lee, Will Geer, Perry Wilson, on upper porch Augustus Smith

CENTURY THEATRE

Opened Tuesday, May 1, 1946.＊
Theatre Incorporated presents the Old Vic
Theatre Company:

UNCLE VANYA
Scenes from Country Life

By Anton Chekhov, from the Russian by Constance Garnett; Staged by John Burrell; scenery and costumes by Tanya Moiseiwitsch; lighting by John Sullivan; orchestra directed by Herbert Menges.

Cast of Characters
(In order of appearance)

Marina (The Family Nurse) ....Ena Burrill
Astrov (A Doctor) ....Laurence Olivier
Voynitsky ("Uncle Vanya")....Ralph Richardson
The Professor ....Nicholas Hannen
Yelena (The Professor's Second Wife),
　　　　　　　　　　　　　Margaret Leighton
Sonya (The Professor's Daughter by His
　First Wife, Vanya's Sister) ....Joyce Redman
Telyegin ("Waffles") ....George Relph
Marya Voynitsky (Vanya's Mother)
　　　　　　　　　　　　　Byrony Chapman
Yefim (A Peasant Servant).........William Monk

A Drama in three acts, four scenes. Outside the house, a room and Uncle Vanya's room in the house on the Professor's Estate in Southern Russia at the end of the Nineteenth Century.

Closed June 14, 1946 (played 8 performances in Repertory).

Margaret Leighton—Laurence Olivier

Insert, Laurence Olivier—Ralph Richardson—
Joyce Redman

Ralph Richardson—Laurence Olivier—Margaret Leighton—Byrony Chapman—
George Ralph—Joyce Redman

97

BOOTH THEATRE

Opening Wednesday, May 15, 1946.
John Clein presents:

SWAN SONG

By Ben Hecht and Charles MacArthur, based
on a story by Ramon Romero and Harriett Hinsdale;† Staged by Joseph Pevney; Setting and
Lighting by Ralph Alswang. "Dance of the Buf-
faloes" music written by Lou Cooper.

Cast of Characters
(In order of appearance)

Louise Kubin	Marianne Stewart
Titogh	Ivan Simpson
Eric Moore	Scott McKay*
Stella Hemingway	Mary Servoss
Victor Remezoff	Michael Dalmatoff
Stanislaus Kubin	Theo Goetz
Vera Novak	Jacqueline Horner**
Leo Pollard	David Ellin
Katya	Kasia Orzazewski
Sister Agatha	Leni Stengel
Max Vonzell	Harry Sothern
Gustav Wexler	Louis Sorin
Oscar Mutzenbauer	Rand Elliot
Ruth Trefon	Barbara Perry
Dr. Corbett	Owen Coll
Captain Bartow	Arthur L. Sachs
Nurse	Mary Jones

A Murder Melodrama in three acts, four
scenes. The Action takes place in the Long
Island Home of Stanislaus Kubin at the present time.

General Manager, Irving Cooper
Company Manager, Joe Roth
Press, Dick Weaver
Stage Managers, Ben Ross Berenberg,
Mae Cooper

†See notes on "Crescendo" page 129.
 *Made former stage appearances under name
   of Carl Gose.
**Miss Horner is an accomplished pianist and
  plays many numbers in this production.

David Ellin and Jacqueline Horner

Jacqueline Horner—Theo Goetz—Louis Sorin—Harry Sothern—Kasia Orzazewski—
Michael Dalmatoff—Ivan Simpson—Owen Coll—David Ellin—Rand Elliott—Barbara
Perry. Seated on sofa, Mary Servoss—Marianne Stewart—Scott McKay.

Ethel Merman as Annie Oakley

IMPERIAL THEATRE

Opening May 16, 1946*
Richard Rodgers and Oscar Hammerstein II
present:

ANNIE GET YOUR GUN

Music and Lyrics by Irving Berlin; Book by
Herbert and Dorothy Fields; Directed by Joshua
Logan; Sets and Lighting by Jo Mielziner;
Dances by Helen Tamiris; Costumes by Lucinda
Ballard; Orchestra Directed by Jay S. Blackton.

Cast of Characters
(In order of appearance)

Little Boy ....Warren Berlinger
Little Girl ....Mary Ellen Glass
Charlie Davenport ....Marty May
Iron Tail ....Daniel Nagrin
Yellow Foot ....Walter John
Mac (Property Man) ....Cliff Dunstan
Cowboys.............. { Rob Taylor, Bernard Griffin,
                        Jack Pierce
Cowgirls ....Mary Grey, Franca Baldwin
Foster Wilson ....Art Barnett
Coolie ....Beau Tilden
Dolly Tate ....Lea Penman
Winnie Tate ....Betty Anne Nyman
Tommy Keeler ....Kenny Bowers
Frank Butler ....Ray Middleton
Girl With Bouquet ....Katrina Van Oss
Annie Oakley ....Ethel Merman
Minnie (Annie's Sister) ....Nancy Jean Raab
Jessie (Another Sister) ....Camilla De Witt
Nellie (Another Sister) ....Marlene Cameron
Little Jake (Her Brother)............Clifford Sales
Harry ....Don Liberto
Mary ....Ellen Hanley
Col. Wm. F. Cody (Buffalo Bill)
                                        William O'Neal
Mrs. Little Horse ....Alma Ross
Mrs. Black Tooth ....Elizabeth Malone
Mrs. Yellow Foot ....Nellie Ranson
Trainman ....John Garth III
Waiter ....Leon Bibb
Porter ....Clyde Turner
Riding Mistress ....Lubov Roudenko
Major Gordon Lillie (Pawnee Bill)
                                         George Lipton
Chief Sitting Bull ....Harry Bellaver
Mabel ....Mary Woodley
Louise ....Ostrid Lind
Nancy ....Dorothy Richards
Timothy Gardner ....Jack Byron
Andy Turner ....Earl Sauvain
Clyde Smith ....Victor Clarke
John ....Rob Taylor
Freddie ....Robert Dixon
The Wild Horse (Ceremonial Dancer)
                                          Daniel Nagrin
Pawnee's Messenger ....Milton Watson
Major Domo ....John Garth III
1st Waiter ....Clyde Turner
2nd Waiter ....Leon Bibb
Mr. Schuyler Adams ....Don Liberto
Mrs. Schuyler Adams ....Dorothy Richards
Dr. Percy Ferguson ....Bernard Griffin
Mrs. Percy Ferguson ....Marietta Vore
Debutante ....Ruth Vrana
Mr. Ernest Henderson ....Art Barnett
Mrs. Ernest Henderson ....Truly Barbara
Sylvia Potter-Porter ....Marjorie Crossland
Mr. Clay ....Rob Taylor
Mr. Lockwood ....Fred Rivett
Girl in Pink ....Marietta Vore
Girl in White ....Mary Grey

Musical Numbers: "Buffalo Bill," "I'm a Bad,
Bad Man," "Doin' What Comes Naturally,"
"The Girl That I Marry," "You Can't Get a
Man With a Gun," "Show Business," "They Say
It's Wonderful," "Moonshine Lullaby," "I'll
Share It All With You," "Ballyhoo," "My De-
fenses Are Down," "Wild Horse Ceremonial
Dance, "I'm an Indian Too," "Adoption Dance,
"Lost in His Arms," "Who Do You Love, I
Hope?" "Sun in the Morning," "Anything You
Can Do."

*The Production was scheduled to open on
April 25, but due to a backstage structural de-
fect the opening had to be postponed.

Ray Middleton and Ethel Merman

Clifford Sales and Ethel Merman

A Musical Comedy in two acts, nine scenes:
Wilson House, a summer hotel on the outskirts
of Cincinnati, Ohio; Pullman Parlor in an Over-
land Steam Train; Fair Grounds at Minneapolis,
Minn.; Arena and Dressing-room of the Big
Tent; Deck of a Cattle Boat; Ballroom of the
Hotel Brevoort; Aboard the Governor's Island
Ferry; Governor's Island, near the Fort.

General Manager, Morris Jacobs
Company Manager, Maurice Winters
Press, Michel Mok, Abner D. Kilpstein
General Stage Manager, Charles Atkin
Stage Manager, John Sola

Harry Bellaver and Ethel Merman

Marty May—Kenny Bowers—Betty Anne Nyman

Marty May—Lea Penman—Ethel Merman—Kenny Bowers—Betty Anne Nyman

Ena Burrill—Laurence Olivier—Miles Malleson

Ralph Richardson—Laurence Olivier

CENTURY THEATRE

Opened Monday, May 20, 1946*
Theatre Incorporated presents the Old Vic
Theatre Company: in the double bill of
"Oedipus" and "The Critic":

OEDIPUS

By Sophocles, English version by W. B. Yeats;
staged by Michel Saint Denis; music by Anthony
Hopkins; costumes by Marie-Helene Daste;
scenery by John Piper; lighting by John Sullivan;
orchestra conducted by Herbert Menges.

Cast of Characters

Oedipus ....Laurence Olivier
A Priest ....Cecil Winter
Creon ....Harry Andrews
Tiresias ....Ralph Richardson
Boy ....Rudolph Cavell
Jocasta ....Ena Burrill
Attendants to Jocasta..................Joyce Redman,
      Margaret Leighton, Nicolette Bernard
First Messenger ....Miles Malleson
Herdsman ....George Relph
Second Messenger ....Michael Warre
Antigone ....Jane Wenham
Ismene ....Dee Sparks
Chorus Leader ....Nicholas Hannen
Chorus of Theban Elders: Max Brent, George
      Cooper, Peter Copley, Frank Duncan, Ken-
      neth Edwards, John Garley, Joseph James,
      David Kentish, Robin Lloyd, William Monk,
      Michael Raghan, George Rose, William
      Squire, Sydney Tafler.
Attendants, Guards, Priests, Servants, Crowd:
      Eleanora Barrie, Byrony Chapman, Julie
      Harris, Diana Maddox, Jane Wenham, Law-
      rence Carr, Will Davis, Carl James, Elmer
      Lehr, Brian Parker, Barnard Pollack, John
      Reilly, Paul Riley, Sandy Roe, Al Studer,
      Alvin Sullum, Richard Wendley.

A Tragedy in one act. The action takes place
in front of the palace of King Oedipus.
*Closed June 15, 1946 (played 15 performances
in Repertory).

Laurence Olivier as Oedipus

THE CRITIC
or, A Tragedy Rehearsed

By Richard Brinsley Sheridan; Staged by Miles Malleson; Scenery and Costumes by Tanya Moiseiwitsch; Lighting by John Sullivan; fight arranged by Peter Copley; Orchestra conducted by Herbert Menges.

Cast of Characters
(In order of appearance)

Mr. Dangle	George Relph
Mrs. Dangle	Margaret Leighton
Servant	Robin Lloyd
Mr. Sneer	Peter Copley
Sir Fretful Plagiary	Miles Malleson
Mr. Puff	Laurence Olivier
First Scene Shifter	William Squire
Under Prompter	John Garley
First Sentinel	Frank Duncan
Second Sentinel	George Cooper
Sir Christopher Hatton	George Rose
Sir Walter Raleigh	Michael Warre
Earl of Leicester	Michael Raghan
Governor of Tilbury	Nicholas Hannen
Master of the Horse	Kenneth Edwards
Tilburina	Nicolette Bernard
Confidant	Joyce Redman
Whiskerandos	Sydney Tafler
Second Scene Shifter	Max Brent
Beefeater	William Monk
Lord Burleigh	Ralph Richardson
First Niece	Diana Maddox
Second Niece	Jane Wenham
Thames	Kenneth Edwards
First Bank	Robin Lloyd
Second Bank	Joseph James
Neptune	George Cooper

A Comedy in one act, two scenes: Mr. Dangle's House and the Drury Lane Theatre, 1779.

Managing Director, Richard Aldrich
General Manager, Laurence Evans
Company Manager, Edward Choate
Press, William Fields, Walter Alford
Stage Director, John Sullivan
Stage Managers, David Kentish
Diana Boddington

Ralph Richardson   Laurence Olivier

George Relph—Laurence Olivier—Peter Copley

Laurence Olivier—Peter Copley—George Relph—Joyce Redman—Nicolette Bernard

ADELPHI THEATRE

Opened Friday, May 31, 1946*
Orson Welles presents a Mercury production:

AROUND THE WORLD
In Eighty Days

Music and Lyrics by Cole Porter; Adapted by Mr. Welles from the novel by Jules Verne; Choreography by Nelson Barclift; Settings by Robert Davison; Costumes by Alvin Colt; Circus arranged by Barbette; Musical Director, Harry Levant; Staged by Mr. Welles.

Cast of Characters
(In order of appearance)

A Bank Robber ....Brainerd Duffield
A Police Inspector ....Guy Spaull
Dick Fix ....Orson Welles
London Bobbies ....⎰ Nathan Baker
                                  ⎱ Jack Pitchon
                                  ⎱ Myron Speth
                                  ⎱ Gordon West
A Lady ....Genevieve Sauris
Mr. Phileas Fogg ....Arthur Margetson
Avery Jevity ....Stefan Schnabel
Molly Muggins ....Julie Warren
Passepartout ....Larry Laurence
Mr. Benjamin Cruett-Spew......Brainerd Duffield
Mr. Ralph Runcible ....Guy Spaull
Sir Charles Mandiboy ....Bernard Savage
Lord Upditch ....Billy Howell
A Scrvingman ....Bruce Cartwright
Another Serving Man ....Gregory McDougall
A Station Attendant ....Billy Howell
Meerahlah ....Dorothy Bird
Two Dancing Fellas ....⎰ Lucas Aco
                            ⎱ Myron Speth
The British Consul, in Suez .....Bernard Savage
An Arab Spy ....Stefan Schnabel
A Second Arab Spy ....Brainerd Duffield
Snake Charmers ....⎰ Eddy Di Genova
                              ⎱ Victor Savidge
                              ⎱ Stanley Turner
A Fakir ....Lucas Aco
Maurice Goodpile ....Guy Spaull
A Sikh ....Spencer James
Mrs. Aouda ....Mary Healy
A High Priest ....Arthur Cohen
Various Sinister Chinese ....⎰ Phil King,
                                 ⎱ Billy Howell,
                                 ⎱ Lucas Aco,
                                 ⎱ Nathan Baker
Lee Toy ....Jackie Cezanne
Two Daughters of Joy ....⎰ Lee Morrison
                             ⎱ Nancy Newton
Mr. Oka Saka ....Brainerd Duffield
Circus Artists:
The Foot Jugglers ....The Three Kansawa
The Rolling Globe Lady ....Adelaide Corsi
The Contortionist ....Miss Lu
The Hand Balancer ....Ishikawa
The Aerialists ⎰ Mary Broussard, Lee Vincent,
               ⎱ Patricia Leith, Virginia Morris
Assistants ....⎰ Billy Howell,
                             ⎱ Lucas Aco,
                             ⎱ Gregory McDougall,
                             ⎱ Myron Speth
The Slide for Life ....Ray Goody
Roustabouts ....Jack Pitchon, Tony Montell
Clowns:
Mother ....Stefan Schnabel
Father ....Nathan Baker
Child ....Bernie Pisarski
Bride ....Cliff Chapman
Groom ....Larry Laurence
Minister ....Arthur Cohen
Policeman ....Jack Cassidy
Monkey Man ....Eddy Di Genova
Kimona Man ....Allan Lowell
Firemen.......................⎰ Bruce Cartwright
                             ⎱ Gordon West
Dragon ....Daniel DePaolo
An Attendant ....Stanley Turner
A Bartender ....Eddy Di Genova

Mexican Dancers ....⎰ Dorothy Bird
                              ⎱ Bruce Cartwright
Lola ....Victoria Cordova
Sol ....Brainerd Duffield
Sam ....Billy Howell
Jim ....James Aco
Jake ....Spencer James
A Medicine Man of the Ojibiway.Stefan Schnabel
Other Medicine Men ....⎰ George Spelvin
                             ⎱ Billy Howell
Jail Guard ....Allan Lowell

Musical Numbers: "Look What I Found," "There He Goes, Mr. Phileas Fogg," "Meerahlah," Suttee Procession, "Sea Chantey," "Should I Tell You I Love You?", "Pipe Dreaming," Oka Saka Circus, "If You Smile at Me," "Wherever They Fly The Flag of Old England," "The Marine's Hymn."

A Musical Extravaganza in two acts, thirty-four scenes including motion pictures. The Action takes place around the world in 1872.

Synopsis of Scenes: Act 1.—Scene 1—Movies. Scene 2—Interior of Jevity's Bank, London, England. Scene 3—Movies. Scene 4—Hyde Park. Scene 5—A London Street. Scene 6—Mr. Fogg's Flat in London. Scene 7—A Street Before the Whist Club. Scene 8—The Card Room of the Whist Club. Scene 9—Fogg's Flat. Scene 10—The Charing Cross Railroad Station. Scene 11—Suez, Egypt. Scene 12—The End of Railway Tracks in British India. Scene 13—The Great Indian Forest. Scene 14—The Pagoda of Pilagi. Scene 15—A Jungle Encampment in the Himalayas. Scene 16—Aboard the S.S. Tankadere on the China Sea. Scene 17—Movies. Scene 18—A Street of Evil Repute in Hong-Kong. Scene 19—Interior of an Opium Hell in the Same City. Scene 20—The Oka Saka Circus, Yokohama, Japan. Act II.—Scene 1—Movies. Scene 2—Lola's, a Low Place in Lower California. Scene 3—The Railroad Station in San Francisco. Scene 4—Movies. Scene 5—A Passenger Car on the Central Pacific Railway—Somewhere in the Rocky Mountains. Scene 6—The Perilous Pass at Medicine Bow. Scene 7—A Water Stop on the Banks of the Republican River. Scene 8—The Peak of Bald Mountain. Scene 9—The Harbor, Liverpool, England. Scene 10—The Gaol in Liverpool. Scene 11—A Cell in the Liverpool Gaol. Scene 12—A Street in London. Scene 13—Outside the London Whist Club. Scene 14—Grand Tableau.

Executive Director, Richard Wilson
General Manager, Hugo Schaaf
Press, Frank Goodman
General Stage Manager, Henri Caubisens
*Closed August 3, 1946   (74 performances)

Orson Welles and Stefan Schnabel

Julie Warren   Larry Laurence

Arthur Margetson—Orson Welles—Mary Healy—Larry Laurence

Ruth Hammond—Lily Cahill—Pamela Gillespie

EMPIRE THEATRE

(Moved to BIJOU THEATRE, September 9, 1945)
Opened Wednesday, November 8, 1939.
Oscar Serlin presents:

LIFE WITH FATHER

By Clarence Day, made into a play by Howard Lindsay and Russel Crouse; Staged by Bretaigne Windust; Setting and Costumes by Stewart Chaney.

Cast of Characters
(In order of appearance)

Annie	Mary McNamee
Vinnie	Lily Cahill
Clarence	Harvey Collins
John	Raymond Moorhead*1
Whitney	David Garden or John Grinnell
Harlan	Paul Wells or David Anderson
Father	Wallis Clark
Margaret	Dorothy Bernard
Cousin Cora	Ruth Hammond
Mary Skinner	Gertrude Beach*2
The Rev. D. Lloyd	Richard Sterling
Delia	Jacquelin Daniels
Nora	Elaine Ivans
Dr. Humphreys	A. H. Van Buren
Dr. Sommers	Charles Collier
Maggie	Margaret Randall*3

A Comedy in three acts, six scenes. The entire action takes place in the morning room of the Day House on Madison Avenue. The time is late in the 1880's.

General Manager, Harry D. Kline
Press, Harry Forwood
Stage Manager, Charles Collier

*Replacements: 1. Robert Donnelly, 2. Pamela Gillespie, 3. Ruth McArthur.

Harvey Collins   Pamela Gillespie   Wallis Clark   Lily Cahill

ST. JAMES THEATRE

Opening Wednesday, March 31, 1943.
The Theatre Guild presents:

OKLAHOMA!

Based on the play, "Green Grow the Lilacs," by Lynn Riggs; Music by Richard Rodgers; Book and Lyrics by Oscar Hammerstein 2nd; Directed by Rouben Mamoulian; Dances by Agnes de Mille; Settings by Lemuel Ayers; Costumes by Miles White; Supervised by Lawrence Langner and Theresa Helburn.

Cast of Characters

Aunt Eller	Ruth Weston
Curly	Harold Keel
Laurey	Betty Jane Watson
Ike Skidmore	Barry Kelly*1
Fred	Allen Sharp
Slim	Herbert Rissman
Will Parker	James Parnell
Jud Fry	Richard Rober*2
Ado Annie Carnes	Bonita Primrose
Ali Hakim	Joseph Buloff
Gertie Cummings	Vivienne Allen
Ellen	Dania Krupska
Kate	Mae Muth
Sylvie	Beatrice Lynn
Armina	Irene Larson*3
Aggie	Ruth Harte
Andrew Carnes	Florenz Ames
Cord Elam	Owen Martin
Jess	Vladimir Kostenko
Chalmers	John Butler*4
Joe	Lloyd Cole*5
Sam	Remi Martel

Musical Numbers: Oh, What a Beautiful Mornin'; The Surrey With the Fringe on Top; Kansas City; I Can't Say No; Many a New Day; It's a Scandal! It's an Outrage!; People Will Say; Pore Jud; Lonely Room; Out of My Dreams; The Farmer and the Cowman; All er Nothin'; Oklahoma.

A Musical Play in two acts, six scenes. The action takes place in Indian Territory (now Oklahoma) just after the turn of the Century: The front yard, The Smoke House, A Grove, and the Back Porch on Laurey's Farm; The Skidmore Ranch and Kitchen Porch.

Company Manager, Max A. Meyer
Press, Joseph Heidt, Peggy Phillips
Stage Managers, Jerome Whyte,
Ted Hammerstein

*Replacements: 1. Joseph Meyer, 2. Bruce Hamilton, 3. Phyllis Gehrig, 4. Tom Avera, 5. Stokely Gray.

Ruth Weston   Harold Keel

Bonita Primrose   Betty Jane Watson   Harold Keel   Joseph Buloff

John Beal—Vicki Cummings

Martha Scott—John Beal

Martha Scott—John Beal—Vicki Cummings

MOROSCO THEATRE

Opened Wednesday, December 5, 1943*
Alfred De Liagre, Jr., presents:

THE VOICE OF THE TURTLE

By John van Druten; Staged by Mr. van
Druten; Setting by Stewart Chaney.

Cast of Characters
(In order of appearance)

Sally Middleton ....Martha Scott
Olive Lashbrooke ....Vicki Cummings
Bill Page ....John Beal

A Comedy in three acts. The action takes
place over a weekend in the early spring of
1945 in an apartment in the East Sixties, near
Third Avenue, New York City.

Company Manager, Samuel Schwartz
Press, Jean Dalrymple, Philip Bloom
Stage Manager, Edwin Gordon

*Vacationed from June 30, 1945 to August 27,
1945.

Irra Petina—Lawrence Brooks—Kirsten Kenyon

IMPERIAL THEATRE

(Moved to BROADWAY THEATRE, April 15, 1946).
Opening Monday, August 21, 1944.
Edwin Lester presents:

SONG OF NORWAY

Music from Edvard Grieg; Musical Adaptation and Lyrics by Robert Wright and George Forrest; Book by Milton Lazarus (from a Play by Homer Curran); Musical Direction by Arthur Kay; Choreography and Singing Ensembles Staged by George Balanchine; Designed by Lemuel Ayers; Settings Supervised by Carl Kent; Book Direction by Charles K. Freeman; Costumes by Robert Davison.

Cast of Characters

Rikard Nordraak ....Robert Shafer
Sigrid ....Janet Hamer
Einar ....John Henson
Eric ....William Carroll*1
Gunnar ....Gerald Matthews*2
Grima ....Grace Carroll*3
Helga ....Diane Woods*4
Nina Hagerup ....Helena Bliss*5
Edvard Grieg ....Lawrence Brooks
Father Grieg ....Walter Kingsford
Father Nordraak ....Philip White
Mother Grieg ....Ivy Scott
Freddy ....Richard Reed
Inn Keeper ....Lewis Bolyard
Count Peppi Le Loup ....Sig Arno
Louisa Giovanni ....Irra Petina
Members of the Faculty .... { Ewing Mitchell / Audrey Guard / Paul DePoyster
Frau Professor Norden ....Margaret Ritter
Elvera ....Sharon Randall
Hedwig ....Karen Lund
Greta ....Gwen Jones
Margareta ....Kaye Connor
Hilda ....Elizabeth Bockoven
Miss Anders ....Sonja Orlova
Henrik Ibsen ....Dudley Clements

Tito ....Richard Reed
Waitresses at Tito's .... { Gloria Stone / Jeanne Jones
Maestro Pisoni ....Robert Bernard
Butler ....Cameron Grant
Adelina ....Dorothie Littefield
Signora Eleanora ....Barbara Boudwin
Children .... { Sylvia Allen*3 / Shannon Randolph*1
The Maiden Norway ....Olga Suarez
The Minstrel ....Roland Guerard
Dancing Peasants, Employees at Tito's. The Ballet of the Teatro Reale, and Characters of the Fantasy by the Artist Personnel of the Ballet Russe de Monte Carlo, Sergei J. Denham, Director.
Singing Peasants, Guests and Facultiy at Copenhagen and Guests at the Villa Pincio.
By the Singing Ensemble of the Los Angeles and San Francisco Civic Light Opera.

Musical Numbers: The Legend; Hill of Dreams; In the Holiday Spirit; Freddy and His Fiddle; Now; Strange Music; Midsummer's Eve; March of the Trollgers; Hymn of Betrothal; Papillon; Bon Vivant; Three Loves; Down Your Tea; Nordraak's Farewell; Chocolate Pas des Trois; Waltz Eternal; Peer Gynt; I Love You; At Christmastime; The Song of Norway.

An Operetta based on the life and music of Grieg in two acts, seven scenes. The action takes place at the hill of the Trolls; A square on the outskirts of Bergen, Norway; Reception Room of the Royal Conservatory, Copenhagen; Tito's Chocolate Shop and the Ballroom of Villa Pincio, Rome; Grieg's home Troldhaugen. Time: Around 1860.

Company Manager, R. Victor Leighton
Production Manager, Peter Bronte
Press, C. P. Greneker, Ben Kornzweig
Stage Manager, Dan Brennan

*Replacements: 1. Michael Guerard, 2. Alexander Goudovitch, 3. Sharon Randall, 4. Gloria Stone, 5. Kirsten Kenyon.

Valerie Black and Claire Jay

MANSFIELD THEATRE

Opening Wednesday Evening, August 30, 1944.

John Wildberg presents Harry Wagstaff Gribble's Production of:

ANNA LUCASTA

By Philip Yordan; Settings by Frederick Fox; Costumes by Paul Dupont.

Cast of Characters

Katie	Edith Whiteman
Stella	Rosetta LeNoire*1
Theresa	Georgia Burke*2
Stanley	John Proctor*3
Frank	Warren Coleman
Joe	Frank Silvera
Eddie	Monte Hawley
Noah	Alvin Childress*4
Blanche	Alice Childress*5
Officer	William Dil'ard
Anna	Valerie Black
Danny	Lance Taylor
Lester	Duke Williams*6
Rudolf	Charles Swain

The Play is in three acts and two sets: the Lucasta living-room, Pennsylvania; and Noah's bar, Brooklyn. Time: early 1941.

Company Manager, Harry Lee
Press, Ivan Black
Stage Manager, Walter Thompson Ash
*Alternates: 1. Inge Hardison, 2. Georgette Harvey, 3. Roy Allen, 4. Slim Thompson, 5. Claire Jay, 6. Gerard Beverly.

"Mr. Lucasta" comes to Noah's Bar in Brooklyn to ask his daughter "Anna" to come home

Richard Bishop—Tony Miller

Joan Tetzel—Mady Christians—Nancy Marquand—

Mady Christians and Josephine Brown

MUSIC BOX THEATRE

Opened Thursday, October 19, 1944.†
Richard Rodgers and Oscar Hammerstein 2nd present:

I REMEMBER MAMA

By John Van Druten; Adapted from Kathryn Forbes' "Mama's Bank Account"; Staged by the Author; Designed and Lighted by George Jenkins; Costumes by Lucinda Ballard.

Cast of Characters

Katrin ....Joan Tetzel**
Mama ....Mady Christians
Papa ....Richard Bishop
Dagmar ....Carolyn Hummel
Christine ....Nancy Marquand*1
Mr. Hyde ....Oswald Marshall
Nels ....Marlon Brando*2
Aunt Trina ....Adrienne Gessner
Aunt Sigrid ....Ellen Mahar
Aunt Jenny ....Ruth Gates
Uncle Chris ....Oscar Homolka
A Woman ....Dorothy Elder
Mr. Thorkelson ....Bruno Wick
Dr. Johnson ....William Pringle
Arne ....Robert Antoine
A Nurse ....Lois Holmes
Another Nurse ....Lujah Fonnesbeck*3
Soda Clerk ....Frank Babcock
Madeline ....Cora Smith*4
Dorothy Schiller ....Ottilie Kruger*5
Florence Dana Morhead...........Josephine Brown
Bellboy ....Herbert Kenwith

A Comedy Drama in two acts. The action passes in and around the Hansens' home on Steiner Street, San Francisco, some years ago. An attic study; the kitchen; Aunt Jenny's Kitchen; Corridor, room and waiting room of a hospital; the pantry; a Soda Parlor; room at the High School; Mrs. Semple's boarding house; a telephone booth; in a room and on the porch of the Halverson Ranch house; in the park; Lobby of the Fairmont Hotel.

General Manager, Morris Jacobs
Company Manager, Maurice Winters
Press, Michel Mok, Mary Ward
Stage Manager, Edward Mendelsohn

*Replacements: 1. Celia Babcock, 2. Tony Miller, 3. Ruth Sever, 4. Olive Stacey, 5. Margaret Garland.
**Frances Heflin substituted during Miss Tetzel's absence.
†Closed June 29, 1946 (713 performances)

48TH STREET THEATRE

Opening Wednesday Evening, November 1, 1944.

Brock Pemberton presents:

HARVEY

By Mary Chase; Directed by Antoinette Perry; Settings by John Root.

Cast of Characters
(Order in which they speak)

Myrtle Mae Simmons ....Jane Van Duser
Veta Louise Simmons ....Josephine Hull
Elwood P. Dowd ....Frank Fay
Miss Johnson ....Eloise Sheldon
Mrs. Ethel Chauvenet ....Frederica Going
Ruth Kelly, R.N. ....Janet Tyler
Marvin Wilson ....Jesse White
Lyman Sanderson, M.D. ....Tom Seidel
William R. Chumley, M.D. ....,Fred Irving Lewis
Betty Chumley ....Dora Clement
Judge Omar Gaffney ....John Kirk
E. J. Lofgren ....Robert Gist

The Play is in three acts, five scenes. The action takes place in a city in the Far West in the library of the Old Dowd Family Mansion and the reception room of Chumley's Rest.

General Manager and Press Representative, Thomas Kilpatrick

Company Manager, Clarence Taylor

Stage Manager, Bradford Hatton

Frank Fay and Josephine Hull

Fred Irving Lewis—Jesse White—Jane Van Duser—Josephine Hull—John Kirk

Michael Road—Augusta Dabney

HENRY MILLER THEATRE

Opened Wednesday Evening, December 13, 1944***

Joseph M. Hyman and Bernard Hart present:

DEAR RUTH

By Norman Krasna; Directed by Moss Hart; Setting by Frederick Fox.

Cast of Characters
(In order of appearance)

Dora ....Pauline Myers
Mrs. Edith Wilkins ....Helen MacKellar
Miriam Wilkins ....Lenore Lonergan*1
Judge Harry Wilkins ....Howard Smith**
Ruth Wilkins ....Augusta Dabney
Lt. William Seawright ....Michael Road
Albert Kummer ....Bartlett Robinson
Martha Seawright ....Kay Coulter*2
Sgt. Chuck Vincent ....Anthony Carr
Harold ....Otis Bigelow*3

A Play in two acts. Setting is the living-room of the Wilkins home, Kew Gardens, Long Island. Late Summer, 1944.

Manager, Al Goldin
Press Representatives, Michel Mok and Mary Ward
Stage Manager, Don Hershey

*Replacements: 1. Rosemary Rice, 2. Mary Kay Jones, 3. Sterling Mace.

**During Mr. Smith's absence Louis Hector substituted.

***Closed July 27, 1946   (680 performances)

Howard Smith—Bartlett Robinson—Augusta Dabney   Michael Road—Helen MacKellar—Howard Smith

THE PLAYHOUSE

Opened Saturday, March 31, 1945*
Eddie Dowling and Louis J. Singer present:

THE GLASS MENAGERIE

By Tennessee Williams; Setting designed and
lighted by Jo Mielziner; Original music composed by Paul Bowles; Staged by Eddie Dowling
and Margo Jones.

Cast of Characters

The Mother ....Laurette Taylor
Her Son ....Eddie Dowling
Her Daughter ....Julie Haydon
The Gentleman Caller ....Anthony Ross

A Play in two parts. The action takes place
in an Alley in St. Louis. Time: Now and the
past.

General Manager, Alex Yokel
Company Manager, James Hughes
Press Representative, Harry Davies
Stage Manager, Tom Ward

*Closed August 3, 1946   (563 performances)

Eddie Dowling   Laurette Taylor

Anthony Ross   Julie Haydon

Laurette Taylor   Eddie Dowling

115

MAJESTIC THEATRE

Opening Thursday, April 19, 1945.
Theatre Guild presents:

CAROUSEL

Based on Ferenc Molnar's "Liliom"; as adapted by Benjamin F. Glazer; Music by Richard Rodgers; Book and Lyrics by Oscar Hammerstein 2nd; Directed by Rouben Mamoulian; Dances by Agnes de Mille; Settings by Jo Mielziner; Costumes by Miles White; Production supervised by Lawrence Langner and Theresa Helburn; Musical Director, Joseph Littau; Orchestrations by Don Walker.

Cast of Characters
(In order of appearance)

Carrie Pipperidge ....Jean Darling
Julie Jordan ....Jan Clayton *1
Mrs. Mullin ....Jean Casto**1
Billy Bigelow ....John Raitt
Bessie ....Mimi Strongin
Juggler ....Lew Foldes*2
1st Policeman ....Robert Byrn
David Bascombe ....Franklyn Fox
Nettie Fowler ....Christine Johnson**2
June Girl ....Pearl Lang
Enoch Snow ....Eric Mattson
Jigger Craigin ....Murvyn Vye
Hannah ....Annabelle Lyon
Boatswain ....Peter Birch
Arminy ....Connie Baxter
Penny ....Marilyn Merkt
Jennie ....Joan Keenan
Virginia ....Ginna Moise
Susan ....Suzanne Tafel
Jonathan ....Richard H. Gordon*3
2nd Policeman ....Lawrence Evers
Captain ....Blake Ritter
Heavenly Friend (Brother Joshua) ....Jay Velie
Starkeeper ....Russel Collins*4
Louise ....Bambi Linn
Carnival Boy ....Robert Pagent
Enoch Snow, Jr. ....Ralph Linn
Principal ....Lester Freedman*5

Musical Numbers: Carousel Waltz; "You're a Queer One, Julie Jordan"; "When I Marry Mr. Snow"; "If I Loved You"; "June Is Bustin' Out All Over"; "When the Children Are Asleep"; "Blow High, Blow Low"; Billy Bigelow's soliloquy; "This Was a Real Nice Clam Bake"; "Geraniums in the Winder"; "There's Nothin' So Bad for a Woman"; "What's the Use of Wonderin'?"; "You'll Never Walk Alone"; "The Highest Judge of All."

A Musical Play in a prelude, two acts, and nine scenes. An amusement park, a tree-lined path, Nettie Fowler's Spa, an Island across the bay, and the Waterfront on the New England Coast, 1873; Up There; a beach, outside Julie's cottage and a school house, 1888.

Company Manager, John H. Potter
Press, Joseph Heidt, Peggy Phillips
General Stage Manager, Andy Anderson
Stage Manager, Paul Crabtree

*Replacements: 1. Iva Withers, 2. Walter Hull, 3. Louis Freed, 4. Calvin Thomas, 5. Robert Byrn.

**Alternates: 1. Effie Afton, 2. Mimi Cabanne.

Bambi Linn   John Raitt

Jean Darling   Murvyn Vye

3rd. Scene: The Informer.

Wife	Else Basserman
Husband	Albert Basserman
Boy	Werner Friedman
Maid	Margaret Bell

3rd. Part
1st. Scene: The Box.

Woman	Eda Reiss-Merin
Young Woman	Margaret Bell
Young Worker	Robert Carricart
Boy	Eugene Granof
Girl	Iris Swarzman
S.A. Men	Ludwig Roth
	William Malten

2nd. Scene: The Sermon on the Mount.

Dying Man	Dwight Marfield
Wife	Elizabeth Neumann
Son	Klaus Kolmar
Pastor	Paul Andor

3rd. Scene: The Plebiscite.

The Woman	Hestor Sondergard
The Worker	Lothar Rewalt
Young Worker	Shepard Menken
Narrator	Maurice Ellis
Ballad Singer	Robert Penn

Assistant Director, George George
Stage Managers, Edward Greer, Myra Seld

AS YOU LIKE IT

A Modernized Version of William Shakespeare's comedy in three acts, seven scenes; Produced by Beverly Bush and John Burgess; from an original idea by Mr. Burgess; Staged by Miss Bush; Settings by Charles Elson; Music under direction of George L. Headley. Opened at the President Theatre, Tuesday, July 3, 1945. (7 performances.)

Cast of Characters

Rosalind	Margretta Ramsey
Celia	Marian Hall
Touchstone	Norman Budd
Madame LeBeay	Gertrude Kinnell
Duke Frederick	Edward Kreisler
Orlando	John Burgess
Adam	Ted Field
Phoebe	Nancy Headley
Sylvius	David Rogers
Oliver	Scott Kennedy
Duke Senior	Leon Forbes
Wife	Marcena Woerner
Jacques	George L. Headley
Audrey	Beverly Bush
William	Stanley Jennings

The Action takes place in the Courtyard of Duke Frederick, a Bedroom in the Palace, Courtyard of Oliver's House, and The Forest of Arden.

Company Manager, Paul Groll
Press, Michael Goldreyer
Stage Manager, Stanley Jennings

OEDIPUS REX

A Reading of the Greek Tragedy by Sophocles; English Version by William Butler Yeats; Produced by the Readers Theatre, Inc. (James Light, Joel W. Schenker, Henry G. Alsberg); Directed by James Light; Narrator's Text by Henry B. Alsberg and Eugene O'Neill, Jr. At the Majestic Theatre, Sunday, December 16, 1945. (2 performances.)

Cast of Characters

Narrator	Eugene O'Neill, Jr.
Oedipus	Frederic Tozere
Jocasta	Blanche Yurka
Creon	William Adams
Tiresias	Henry Irvine
Priest	Martin Wolfson
First Messenger	Robert Harris
Second Messenger	Frederic Downs
Herdsman	Art Smith
Chorus Leader	Bram Nossen
Chorus	William Hughes

Company Manager, M. Eleanor Fitzgerald
Press, Marjorie Barkentin

HOME IS THE HUNTER

A Drama in two acts, four scenes, by Samuel M. Kootz; Produced by The American Negro Theatre; Directed by Abram Hill; Setting by Irene Bresadola; Supervised by Walter Graves. Opened at the ANT Playhouse, Harlem, Thursday, December 20, 1945. (18 performances)

Cast of Characters

Dawson Drake, Sr.	Evelio Grillo
Rusty Saunders	Maxwell Glanville
Ann Drake	Clarice Taylor
Dawson Drake, Jr.	Elwood Smith

The Action takes place in the Living-room of the Drake Residence in an Industrial town in the U.S.A. at the present time.

Company Manager, Letitia Toole
Business Manager, Jefferson Davis, Jr.
Press, Jack Hamilton, Gail Wadro
Stage Manager, Howard Augusta

THE MAYOR OF ZALEMEA

A Reading of the drama in three acts, thirteen scenes, by Pedro Calderon De La Barca; English version by Edward Fitzgerald; Produced by the Readers Theatre, Inc.; Directed by James Light. At The Majestic Theatre, Sunday, January 27, 1946. (2 performances.)

Cast of Characters

Narrator	Eugene O'Neill, Jr.
Rebolledo, a soldier	Philip Robinson
Chispa, his mistress	Amelia Romano
A Soldier	Will Davis
Don Alvaro, a captain	Jack Manning
A Sergeant	Marriott Wilson
Don Mendo, poor Hidalgo	Robert Gardet
Nuno, his servant	Leonard Cimino
Isabel, daughter of Crespo....	Ellen Andrews
Pedro Crespo, a farmer	Herbert Berghof
Juan, his son	Philip Gordon
Don Lope de Figueroa	Gregory Morton
Notary	Will Davis
King Philip II	Frederic Downs

Company Manager, M. Eleanor Fitzgerald
Press, Marjorie Barkentin

ON STRIVERS' ROW

A Comedy in three acts, four scenes, by Abram Hill; Produced by The American Negro Theatre; Directed by the Author; Setting by Charles Sebree. Opened at the ANT Playhouse, Harlem, Thursday, February 28, 1946. (26 performances)

Cast of Characters

Dolly Van Striven	Dorothy Carter
Sophie	Isabell Sanford
Professor Hennypest	Draynard Clinton
Tillie Petunia	Letitia Toole
Chuck	Oliver Pitcher
Cobina Van Striven	Javotte Sutton
Mrs. Pace	Hattie King-Reavis
Oscar Van Striven	Stanley Greene
Lily Livingston	Verneda La Selle
Louise Davis	Hilda Haynes
Dr. Leon Davis	Charles Henderson
Rowena	Courtenaye Olden
Ed Tucker	Austin Briggs-Hall
A Reporter	Vivian Dogan
Ruby Jackson	Jacqueline Andre
Beulah	Sally Alexander
Joe Smothers	Fred Carter

The Scene is the Van Striven Residence on Harlem's exclusive Strivers' Row, New York City.

Business Manager, Jefferson Davis
Press, Jack Hamilton, Evelio Grillo
Stage Manager, George Lewis

PLAYS AT THE NEW YORK CITY CENTER

The Theatre Guild presents the Margaret Webster production of:

OTHELLO

By William Shakespeare; Designed and Lighted by Robert Edmond Jones; Music Composed by Tom Bennett; Associate Producer, John Haggott; Supervised by Lawrence Langner and Theresa Helburn. Opened at City Center Tuesday, May 22, 1945. Closed June 10, 1945 (24 performances.)

Cast of Characters

Roderigo ....Don Keefer
Iago ....Jose Ferrer
Brabantio ....Francis Compton
Othello ....Paul Robeson
Cassio ....Ralph Clanton
Duke ....Louis Lytton
Lodovico ....Philip Huston
1st Senator ....Ronald Bishop
2nd Senator ....Ted Yaryan
3rd Senator ....Francis Letton
A Messenger ....Stockman Barner
Desdemona ....Uta Hagen
Montano ....Angus Cairns
1st Soldier at Cyprus ....Jay Brassfield
2nd Soldier at Cyprus ....Ronald Bishop
3rd Soldier at Cyprus ....William Browder
Emilia ....Edith King
Bianca ....Nan McFarland
Gratiano ....Louis Lytton

Senators, Soldiers, Servants and Citizens: Barbara Anderson, Virginia Mattis, John Granger, Leonard Klein, Robert Leser, Robinson Stone, William Sandy, Daniel Cullitan.

A Tragedy in two acts, eight scenes; a Street in Venice; The Council Chamber; A Seaport; A Castle and a Street in Cyprus; A Room and a Bedroom in the Castle.

Company Manager, John Yorke
Press, Howard Newman
Stage Manager, Drexel Layton

Paul Robeson as "Othello"

Canada Lee as "Caliban"

Cheryl Crawford presents the Margaret Webster production of:

THE TEMPEST

By William Shakespeare; original music by David Diamond; Settings and Costumes by Motley; Lighting by Moe Hack; Based on a production idea by Eva Le Gallienne; Orchestra directed by Drago Jovanovich. Opened at the City Center Monday, November 12, 1945. Closed December 1, 1945. (25 performances.)

Cast of Characters

Ship-Master ....Beaumont Bruestle
Boatswain ....Angus Cairns
Alonso, King of Naples ....Bram Nossen
Gonzalo ....Robert Harrison
Antonio, brother to Prospero ......Joseph Hardy
Sebastion, brother to Alonzo..Eugene Stuckmann
Prospero ....Arnold Moss
Miranda ....Diana Sinclair
Ariel ....Vera Zorina
Caliban ....Canada Lee
Ferdinand ....Albert Hachmeister
Adrian ....Jack Bostic
Trinculo ....Wallace Acton
Stephano ....Benny Baker
Master of Ceremonies) Spirits..) Bernard Miller
Dancer   )   ) Peggy Allardice
Mariners, Shapes and Spirits: Peggy Allardice, Beaumont Bruestle, Angus Cairns, Cebert La Vine, Bernard Miller, Thomas Vize.

A Fantasy in a Prologue and two parts. The Action takes place on a Ship at Sea, and On An Island.

Company Manager, James Miller
Press, Howard Newman
Production Manager, Moe Hack
Stage Manager, Thelma Chandler

Richard Camp

Frank McCoy presents:

LITTLE WOMEN

Adapted by Marian De Forest from Louisa M. Alcott's story; Staged by Mr. McCoy. Opened at the City Center Sunday Matinee, December 23, 1945. Closed January 5, 1946. (16 performances.)

Cast of Characters

Jo ....Margaret Hayes
Meg ....Gloria Stroock
Amy ....Billie Lou Watt
Beth ....Dortha Duckworth
Mrs. March ....Velma Royton
Hannah ....Georgia Harvey
Brooke ....Clark Williams
Laurie ....Richard Camp
Aunt March ....Grace Mills
Mr. March ....David Lewis
Mr. Laurence ....Harrison Dowd
Professor Bhaer ....Jack Lorenz

A Comedy Drama in four acts. The Action takes place in the Sitting Room of the March Home in a small town in New England in the years 1863 and 1864.

Company Manager, Ray Payton
Press, Jean Dalrymple, Marian Graham

Billie Lou Watt

Russell Lewis and Howard Young present:

THE DESERT SONG

Book and Lyrics by Otto Harbach, Oscar Hammerstein II and Frank Mandel; Music by Sigmund Romberg; Directed by Sterling Halloway; Ballets by Aida Broadbent; Orchestra Directed by Waldemar Guterson; Scenery by Boris Aronson. Opened at the City Center, Tuesday, January 8, 1946. Closed February 16, 1946. (46 performances.)

Cast of Characters

Mindar ....Edward Wellman
Sid El Kar ....Richard Charles
Ahmed ....Kelth Gingles
Omar ....Jack Saunders
Hassi ....Thayer Roberts
Pierre Birabeau ....Walter Cassel*1
Benjamin Kidd ....Jack Goode
Sentinel ....William Bower
Captain Paul Fontaine ....Wilton Clary
Sergeant La Verne ....Joseph Claudio
Sergeant De Boussac ....Antonio Rovano
Azuri Clarissa*2
Edith ....Tamara Page
Susan ....Sherry O'Neil
Mardi ....Barbara Bailey
Florette ....Betina Orth
Yvonne ....Maria Taweel
Margot Bonvalet ....Dorothy Sandlin
General Birabeau ....Lester Matthews
Clementina ....Jean Bartel
Harem Guard ....Richard Hughes
Ali Ben Ali ....George Burnson
Nogi ....Louis DeMagnus
Riff Runner ....Paul Ruth

Musical Numbers: "The Riff Song," "Margot," "I'll Be A Bouyant Girl," "French Military Marching Song," "Romance," "Then You Will Know," "I Want A Kiss," "Tropics," "The Desert Song," Morocco Dance of Marriage, "My Little Castagnet," "Song of the Brass Key," Spanish Dance, "One Good Boy Gone Wrong," "Eastern and Western Love," "Let Love Go," "One Flower in Your Garden," "One Alone," "The Saber Song," "Farewell."

A Musical Comedy in two acts, eight scenes. The Action takes place in North Africa, 1925: Hiding Place of the Red Shadow in the Riff Mountains, General Birabeau's Villa, Garden outside the Villa, Desert Retreat of Ali Ben Ali, Corridor to the Bath, Room of the Silken Couch and Edge of the Desert.

Company Manager, Emmett Callahan
Press, Helen Hoerle
Stage Director, Michael Jeffrey

*Replacements: 1. Harry Stockwell, 2. Iris Whitney.

Clarissa as "Azuri"

Muriel Smith

Elton Warren—LeVern Hutcherson

Billy Rose presents:

CARMEN JONES*

By Oscar Hammerstein II (based on Meilhac and Halevy's adaptation of Prosper Merimee's "Carmen"); Music by Georges Bizet; Staging, Lighting and Color schemes by Hassard Short; Libretto directed by Charles Friedman; New Orchestral Arrangements by Robert Russell Bennett; Settings by Howard Bay; Costumes by Raoul Pene Du Bois; Choreography by Eugene Loring; Choral Direction by Robert Shaw; Orchestra conducted by David Mordecai. Opened at the City Center Sunday, April 7, 1946. Closed May 4, 1946. (32 performances.)

Cast of Characters

Corporal Morrell	Robert Clarke
Foreman	George Willis
Cindy Lou	{ Elton J. Warren or Coreania Hayman†
Sergeant Brown	Jack Carr
Joe	{ Napoleon Reed or Le Vern Hutcherson†
Carmen	Muriel Smith or Urylee Leonardos†
Sally	Sibol Cain
T-Bone	Edward Roche
Tough Kid	James May
Drummer	Oliver Coleman
Bartender	Andrew J. Taylor
Waiter	Edward Christopher
Myrt	Ruth Crumpton
Frankie	Theresa Merritte
Rum	John Bubbles
Dink	Ford Buck
Boy	Bill O'Neil
Girl	Erona Harris
Husky Miller	Glenn Bryant
Soldiers	{ Robert Clarke, Randall Steplight, George Willis, Elijah Hodges
Mr. Higgins	Jack Carr
Miss Higgins	Fredye Marshall
Photographer	Harold Taylor
Card Players	{ Fredye Marshall, Doris Brown, Sibol Cain,
Waiter	Richard de Vaultier
Dancing Girl	Audrey Vanterpool
Poncho	Frank Palmer
Dancing Boxers	{ Sheldon B. Hoskins Randolph Sawyer
Bullet Head	George Willis
Referee	George Spelvin

Musical Numbers: "Lift 'Em Up and Put 'Em Down," "Honey Gal O' Mine," "Good Luck, Mr Flyin' Man," "Dat's Love," "You Talk Just Like My Maw," "Carmen Jones Is Goin' To Jail," "Dere's A Cafe on the Corner," "Beat Out Dat Rhythm on a Drum," "Stan' Up and Fight," "Whizzin' Away Along de Track," "Dis Flower," "If You Would Only Come Away," "De Cards Don't Lie," "Dat Ol' Boy," "Poncho De Panther From Brazil," Ballet Divertissement, "My Joe," Get Yer Program for de Big Fight," "Dat's Our Man."

A Musical Comedy in two acts, five scenes Outside a Parachute Factory; a Nearby Roadside; Billy Pastor's Cafe; Terrace of the Meadowlawn Country Club, Southside of Chicago Outside of Sport Stadium.

Company Manager, Harold Goldberg
Press, Ned Alvord
Stage Director, Roger Gerry
Stage Manager, David Morton

†Owing to the vocal exactions of these parts they are played alternately by the artists.

*Mr. Hammerstein has adhered, as closely a possible, to the original form of "Carmen. All the melodies—with a few minor exceptio —are sung in their accustomed order.

Eden Burrows, Steve Carter, Pauline Bradshaw, Al Penalosa and Carl Low
in a scene from "The Letter"

THE EQUITY-LIBRARY THEATRE

By GEORGE FREEDLEY

The third season of the Equity-Library Theatre was concluded in the first week of June, 1946, after a successful presentation of forty-eight productions. This was somewhat more than half the total of all Broadway stage presentations and made ELT the most prolific single producer in New York. This organization operates through special dispensation of Actors' Equity Association and The New York Public Library and is manned by an executive secretary, Anne Gerlette, and with co-chairmen, Sam Jaffe (Equity) and George Freedley (Library). John Golden, through the John Golden Theatre Fund, pays the secretary's salary and provides the modest budget for the various productions.

The fiftieth anniversary of Oscar Wilde's "The Importance of Being Earnest" was marked with the presentation of this comedy at the Hudson Park Branch beginning November 7. Also during November, the unforgettable "Rain" was staged at the George Bruce Branch, Pinero's "The Enchanted Cottage" at Fort Washington, Raphaelson's "Jason" at Hudson Park, Odets' "Golden Boy" at Hamilton Grange, and Noel Coward's "Hay Fever" at George Bruce. December brought Heijermans' "The Good Hope" to Hudson Park for its third local professional production; Massinger's "A New Way to Pay Old Debts" was seen in the same branch library for its first Manhattan production in sixty years; a stylized production of "The Drunkard" was seen at George Bruce and Coward's "Blithe Spirit" at Fort Washington.

Nineteen forty-six dawned with "The Green Bay Tree" at Hudson Park and was followed in quick succession by "Springtime for Henry" at George Bruce, "Night Must Fall" at Fort Washington, Maugham's "The Letter" at Hudson Park, Priestley's "Dangerous Corner" at Fort Washington, Coward's "Tonight at 8:30" at Hudson Park and finally Goethe's "Faust" in an extraordinarily fine presentation by John Reich at George Bruce. The February offerings included "Outward Bound" at Hudson Park with a mixed cast of whites and Negroes, Coward's "The Vortex" at Fort Washington, "Those Endearing Young Charms" at Hudson Park and two plays of Ibsen, "Ghosts" at Fort Washington and "A Doll's House" at George Bruce. During March, "Candlelight" was seen at Hamilton Grange and Totheroh's "Live Life Again" and Tennessee Williams' "This Property Condemned" at Hudson Park, Sidney Howard's "The Silver Cord" at George Bruce, Ardrey's "Thunder Rock" at Fort Washington, Anderson's "High Tor" at Hamilton Grange, a bill of Chekhov one-act plays at Hudson Park and Maugham's "Theatre" at George Bruce.

Goldoni's "The Servant of Two Masters" was the first April offering at Hamilton Grange. Following it were "Coquette" at Hudson Park, "Waiting for Lefty" at Fort Washington, Machiavelli's "Mandragola" at George Bruce, "The Last Mile" at Fort Washington, Molnár's "The Lawyer" at Hudson Park (first American presentation), "Blind Alley" at George Bruce, "The Hasty Heart" at Fort Washington, "Othello" at Hudson Park (where hundreds were turned away at each performance) and "Family Portrait" at Hamilton Grange.

May brought O'Neill's "Anna Christie" to George Bruce, "The Cherry Orchard" to Fort Washington, "The Animal Kingdom" to Hamilton Grange, Cocteau's "The Infernal Machine" to George Bruce, "One-Man Show" to Hudson Park, Dryden's "All For Love" to Fort Washington (first New York presentation since 1797), "The World We Make" to Hudson Park and Moliere's "The Physician in Spite of Himself" (first professional production in English in New York) to George Bruce. The final production of the year came the first week in June, due to booking difficulties, in Mady Christians' production of "The Affairs of Anatol" with Tonio Selwart in the title role at George Bruce.

It is easy to see that Noel Coward was the favorite author with four plays to his credit. He was closely followed by Somerset Maugham (in derived as well as his own plays) with three. Ibsen was represented twice as were Priestley and Clifford Odets. Such unfamiliar names to the Broadway scene as Dryden, Goldoni, Moliere, Cocteau, Schnitzler and Machiavelli were seen in the Equity-Library Theatre productions. It was ELT's most successful season.

Joel Marston, Roland Von Weber, Susan Roy, Joel Thomas, June Morgan and Marion Sweet
in Dryden's "All For Love"

PLAYS THAT OPENED OUT OF TOWN
BUT DID NOT ARRIVE ON BROADWAY

SUDS IN YOUR EYES*

Revival of a comedy in three acts. Dramatized by Jack Kirkland from Mary Lasswell's book of the same title; Produced by Louis O. Macloon; Staged by John Kerr. Opened at the Curran Theatre, San Francisco, Monday, September 3, 1945.**

Cast of Characters

Chinatown ....Robert Cabal
Buyer ....Robert Marvin
Mrs. Feeley ....June Evans
Mr. Fitzgerald ....Lewis Corbitt
Miss Tinkham ....Maudie Prickett
Shipyard Worker ....John Herkimer
Conchita ....Georgia Skinner
Mr. Reynolds ....Victor Dial
Mrs. Rasmussen ....Irene Seidner
Mrs. Rasmussen's Daughter ....Ellen Mills
Kate Logan ....Jan Erhard
Mrs. Ferguson ....Lottie Loeffler
Mr. Wilson ....Drake Smith
Mac ....Gene Settle
June Miller ....Beatrice Hassel
Danny Feeley ....Wally Pindell
Policeman ....George Spelvin
Ormond Hansen ....Robert Tobin
Pinky Kennedy ....Dave York

The Action takes place in Mrs. Feeley's Junk Yard on the Waterfront in San Diego, California at the present time.

Company Manager, Charles Williams
Press, George "Lefty" Miller
Stage Manager, Beatrice Hassel

*Tried out at the Pasadena Playhouse.

**Closed Great Northern Theatre, Chicago, February 16, 1946.

FOREVER IS NOW

A Comedy in three acts by Adele Longmire; Produced by Gertrude Macy; Directed by Robert Ross; Single Setting by Raymond Sovey. Opened at Playhouse Theatre, Wilmington, Friday, September 7, 1945.*

Cast of Characters

Murphy ....Edmon Ryan
Joe Bridger ....Richard Wilder
Allan Flythe ....Douglas Dick
Carrot O'Neill ....George Botbyl
Viola Gregory ....Vivienne Segal
Arthur Saphire ....Leonard Carey
Darby Jones ....Eleanor Lynn
Bill Henderson ....Walter Starkey

Action takes place in an Italian Villa in the process of being converted into a Rest Club for American officers.

Company Manager, Edgar Runkle
Press, Francis Robinson, Lorella Val-Mery
Stage Manager, Lucian Self

*Closed Shubert Theatre, Philadelphia, September 15, 1945.

EMILY

A Drama in three acts by John Colton and Robert Harris; Produced by Messrs. Shubert in association with Albert De Courville; Directed by Mr. De Courville; Single Setting by Edward Gilbert. Opened at Walnut Street Theatre, Philadelphia, Saturday, September 8, 1945.*

Cast of Characters

Valerie Ambruster ....Mary Best
Emily Wingate ....Simone Simon
Mrs. Wingate ....Leonore Harris
Mrs. Hecker ....Margaret Wycherly
Camilla (maid) ....Sara Andrews
Wallace (butler) ....Lester Austen
Owen Wingate ....Weldon Hayburn
Lisa Jessup ....Marta Linden
Paul Jessup ....Ralph Forbes
Lorry Wingate ....John Campbell

Action takes place in Emily Wingate's Bedroom in the old Wingate Mansion in Philadelphia.

Company Manager, Harry Shapiro
Press, Claude Greneker, Ben Kornzweig
Production Associate, John Holden
Stage Manager, A. Martial Copbern

*Closed September 15, 1946.

Roger Pryor   Kay Francis

WINDY HILL

A Comedy in three acts by Patsy Ruth Miller; Produced by Ruth Chatterton in association with J. J. Leventhal; Staged by Miss Chatterton; Setting by Edward Gilbert. Opened at Shubert Theatre, New Haven, Thursday, September 20, 1945.*

Cast of Characters

Lola La Paz ....Eileen Heckart
Buck McGrew ....Donald McClelland
Steve Kinney ....Lawrence Fletcher
Ethel Kinney ....Ruth Conley
Peter Grayson ....Roger Pryor
Arabella ....Eulabelle Moore
Antonia Conners ....Kay Francis
Matt Bromley ....Grant Gordon
Dr. Young ....Earle Mayo
A Cab Driver ....James Hagan

Time: 1945. Place: Living-room of Peter Grayson's House in Nyack, New York.

Company Manager, William Croucher
Press, Joe Phillips
Stage Manager, James Hagan

*Closed Harris Theatre, Chicago, May 25, 1946.

MR. COOPER'S LEFT HAND

A Comedy in three acts by Clifford Goldsmith; Produced by George Abbott and Richard Myers; Staged by Mr. Abbott; Setting by John Root. Opened at Wilbur Theatre, Boston, Tuesday, September 25, 1945.*

Cast of Characters

Mr. Cooper ....Stuart Erwin
Mrs. Cooper ....Katharine Alexander
Ellen Cooper ....Lorna Lynn
Marjorie Cooper ....Bethel Leslie
Amy ....Edmonia Nolley
Mr. Sullivan ....Paul Ford
Daphne ....Carol Petersen
Sailor ....Cy Howard
Watkins ....Willfred Stratton
Aunt Susan ....Frieda Altman
Lee ....Richard Sanford
Kirkpatrick ....Kenneth Tobey
Smith ....Roger Quinlan
Larkin ....Douglas Jones

The Scene is the Cooper Living-room.

General Manager, Charles Harris
Company Manager, Louis Kaliski
Press, Phyllis Perlman
Stage Manager, Robert Griffith

*Closed October 6, 1945.

SPRING IN BRAZIL

A Musical Comedy in two acts; fifteen scenes, by Philip Rapp; Produced by Monte Proser in association with the Messrs. Shubert; Staged by John Murray Anderson; Music and Lyrics by Robert Wright and George Forrest; Dances by Margery Fielding; Ballet and Native Dances by Esther Junger; Costumes by Ted Shore and Mary Schenck; Settings by Howard Bay; Musical Director, Anthony R. Morelli; Orchestral and Choral arrangements by Arthur Kay. Opened at Shubert Theatre, Boston, Monday, October 1, 1945.**

Cast of Characters

High Priest of Arupa ....Roger Obardieno
Roland Peoples ....Gene Blakeley
Justin Lake ....Ray Arnette
Amazon Queen ....Christine Ayers*1
John Randall ....Kent Edwards
Col. Roland Peoples ....Joseph Macaulay
Bill McEvoy ....Jack McCauley
Rafferty ....Jack Kerr
Tamamint ....Harry Klein
Addison ....Jay Brennan
Patterson ....Charles Hart
Watterson ....Harold Crane
Katie Warren ....Rose Marie*2
Clump ....William Quentmayer
Lucius Sneed ....John Cherry*3
Hon. Justin Lake ....Morton J. Stevens
Walter Gribble Jr. ....Milton Berle
Dancing Guest ....Dee Turnello
Martin Graham ....Don Roberts
Samuel Prouty ....Silas Engum
Anya Veranda ....Bernice Parks*4
Divine Delight ....Rita Angel
Robert Harkness ....Gene Blakeley*5
Pilot ....Danny Hoctor
Beniamino ....Don Arres*6
Police Officer ....Randolph Symonette*7
Pablo ....Russo de Pandeiro
Pedro ....Gordon Gains
Pancho ....Walter Gonsalves
Fazendoros ....James Riley
Fazendoros ....Talley Beatty
Fazendoros ....Laverne French
Walter's Guide ....Wilson W. Woodbeck
Jongo ....Ray Long
Lana ....Joe Burns
Tapirape Chief ....Roger Obardieno

Musical Numbers: "Fernando," "Our Day," "Little Ol' Boy," "Chi-ni-qui-chi," "Riot in Rio," "Spring in Brazil," "Frenetica," "Samba at Daybreak," "The Bean of the Coffee Tree," "New Worlds," "Rough, Rugged and Robust," "Arupan Ballet," and "Carnival in Rio."

The Action takes place in the Trophy Room of the Magellan Society, Walter's Workroom, The Map Room, The Ramp at La Guardia Airport, Abroad the Pan-Andean Clipper, The Casino in Rio de Janeiro, A Coffee Plantation in Leopoldina, Brazil, Among the Coffee Trees, A Pool in the Matto Grosso, On the Jungle Trail, Arupa, and at The Carnival in Rio.

Company Manager, Jack Small
Press, C. P. Greneker, Lewis Harmon
Stage Manager, William Smythe

*Replacements: 1. Dorothy De Winter, 2. Mary Healy, 3. Harry Sothern, 4. Marion Colby, 5. Jack Collins, 6. Dean Campbell, and 7. Howard Hoffman.

**Closed at Great Northern Theatre, Chicago, January 12, 1946.

CAVIAR TO THE GENERAL

A Comedy in three acts by George S. George and Eugenie Leontovich; Produced by Theron Bamberger and Robert Henderson; Directed by Mr. Henderson; Setting by Stewart Chaney. Opened at Playhouse Theatre, Wilmington, Thursday, October 18, 1945.*

Cast of Characters

Joshua ....John Marriott
Ivan ....Nicholas Saunders
Captain Petroff ....Alexander Asro
Bartlett ....Lyle Bettger
Rita Allison ....Leila Ernst
James Carter Allison ....Sidney Blackmer
Pat Thurber ....Marty May
Tanya ....Eugenie Leontovich
Captain Sokoloff ....Lonya Kalbouss
Lt. Sonya Jefferson Davis ....Maude Russell
Major Babych ....Boris Yaroslavsky
Guards ....{ George Jason
{ Brant Gorman

The Play takes place in the Government House at Yakutsk, Siberia, September, 1945.

Company Manager, Chandos Sweet
Press, Leo Freedman
Stage Manager, Paul Porter

*Closed Locust Theatre, Philadelphia, October 27, 1945.

THE LAST HOUSE ON THE LEFT

A Farce-Comedy in three acts, six scenes by Jean Carmen and Irish Owen; Produced by Violla Rubber; Directed by Mr. Owen; Setting by Watson Barratt. Opened at Bushnell Memorial, Hartford, Friday, November 2, 1945.*

Cast of Characters

1st Little Man ....Liam Dunn
2nd Little Man ....Joe Jones
Sandra ....Jacqueline Paige
Dr. Gregory Walters ....Graham Velsey
George Wilson ....James Coyle
Joe Doyle ....John O'Connor
Michael Candless.........................Rodman Bruce
"Telly" Lawrence................. George Blackwood
Judge Harper........................Charles Henderson
Jerry Whistler................................ Bruce Adams
Jean Carroll.................................Jean Carmen
Mary Moriarity.......................Grania O'Malley
King Christopher........................Gene Barry
Rudolf ....Walter Palm
Grocery Boy................................Alvin Allen
Mrs. George Wilson.......................Wauna Paul
Stefan ....Donald Moors
Dimitri ....Gabriel Cosmo

The entire Action is laid in the Living-room of "Last House on the Left."

General Manager, Charles Stewart
Company Manager, Louis Cline
Press, Leo Freedman
Stage Manager, Guy Monypenny

*Closed Wilbur Theatre, Boston, November 10, 1945.

THE PASSING SHOW†

A Musical Review in two acts, fourteen scenes; Produced by Messrs. Shubert; Staged by Russell Mack; Dances by Carl Randall and Joe Crosby; Ballets by Mme. Kamarova; Lyrics and Music by Ross Thomas, Will Morrissey, Irving Actman, Eugene Burton and Dana Slawson; Scenery by Watson Barratt; Costumes by Stage Costumes, Inc. and Mme. Veronica; Orchestra under direction of Alfred Evans. Opened at Bushnell Memorial, Hartford, Friday, November 9, 1945.**

Featuring*

Willie Howard	Sue Ryan
Bobby Morris	Richard Buckley
John Masters and Rowena Rollins	
Bob Russell	Betty Luster
Ruth Clayton	Mimi Kellerman
Gil Johnson	Ruth Davis
Sylvia Russell	Dan Harding
Diana Marsh	Al Kelly
Al Klein	Matthew Smith
Patricia Flynn	Fred Catuniu
Virginia Stanton	Barbara Leonard

Musical Numbers: "Passing Show," "Could You Use A New Friend," "Then There's Romance," "A Song Is Born," "You're My Kind Of Ugly," Chinese Ballet, "The Avenue Of Americas," "Along The South American Coast Line," "The Girl From Oklahoma Meets The Boy From Carousel," "It Seems Like Yesterday," "White Rhapsody," "Back In The Kitchen Again," "Living In A Brand New Day."

Skits: Bobby Socks Convention, Two Cups of Coffee, You Are The Jury, Doughnuts, Lonely Hearts, Pantomimic Illusion, His First Case, Kid's First Fight.

Company Manager, George Oshrin
Press, Al Butler
Stage Manager, Guy Palmerton
†16th. Edition, since the 1st. in 1912.
*After the opening, Myrtill and Pacaud joined the show with the number, Rhapsody in Diamonds.
**Closed at Erlanger Theatre, Chicago, February 17, 1946.

Patricia Fargo   Ethel Barrymore

THE JOYOUS SEASON

Revival of a Drama in three acts by Philip Barry; Produced by Arthur Hopkins; Designed by Robert Edmond Jones; Directed by Mr. Hopkins. Opened at Lyric Theatre, Bridgeport, Friday, November 9, 1945.*

Cast of Characters

Teresa Farley Battle	Mary Welch
Francis Battle	Craig Kelly

Martin Farley	Hugh Franklin
Patrick	William J. McCarthy
Hugh Farley	Don Keefer
Ross Farley	Ty Perry
Monica Farley	Patricia Fargo
John Farley	Frank Conroy
Edith Choate Farley	Elizabeth Dewing
Christina Farley	Ethel Barrymore
Sr. Aloysius	Olive Dunbar
Nora	Lida Kane

The Action takes place one Christmas during the late '30s in the Living-room of the Farley's House on Beacon Street, Boston.

Company Manager, Tom Powers
Press, Tom Kane
Stage Managers, Edward A. McHugh, Kenneth Dobbs
*Closed at Selwyn Theatre, Chicago, March 23, 1946.

OF ALL PEOPLE

A Comedy in three acts, five scenes by Ralph Spence; Produced by Monte Proser and Walter Batchelor; Directed by Edward Padula; Setting by Stewart Chaney. Opened at Town Hall, Toledo, Thursday, November 29, 1945.*

Cast of Characters

Joseph	Reginald Mason
Oliver	Harold Grau
Daisy	Gloria Story
Stella	Emily Lawrence
Mr. Sugarman	John Harmon
Elkins	Tom Ewell
Miss Targo	Jayne Fortner
Edgar Brinker	Millard Mitchell
Julius	Walter Catlett
Mike McGuire	Bruce McFarlane
Sebastian	Bert Wheeler
Miss Carroll	Frances Charles
The Sugarman Girls	Patti Morgan / Elsie Hanover / Helen Seamon / Emily Jewell / Billie Boze
Alex	James Walker
Senator Marsh	Taylor Holmes
Danny	Arthur B. Allen
General Hathaway	John Leslie
Mr. Corwin	Donald Foster
FBI Men	Frank Malet / Charles Baker
Democratic Husband	Charles Bond
Democratic Wife	Jane Rentfor
Republican Husband	McGreggor Gibb
Republican Wife	Marian Weeks
Briggs	Brian Connaught

The Action takes place in The Drawing Room of Halcyon Hall, a stately old Mansion in Washington, D. C.; Anybody's Radio anywhere; Two American Homes; and a Newsreel Theatre.

General Manager, Eddie Lewis
Press, Wolfe Kaufman
Stage Manager, John Effrat
*Closed Ford's Theatre, Baltimore, December 22, 1945.

MURDER WITHOUT CRIME†

A melodrama in two acts by J. Leo Thompson; Produced by Theodore C. Ruskin; Staged by Hale McKeen; Setting by Raymond Sovey. Opened at Lyric Theatre, Bridgeport, Friday, November 30, 1945.*

Cast of Characters

Stephan	Tom Rutherfurd
Grena, his mistress	Sonia Sorel
Matthew, his friend	John Carradine
Jan, Stephan's wife	Lilian Harvey

The Action takes place in Stephan's Flat in Matthew's House in Mayfair.

General Manager, Ben F. Stein
Company Manager, James M. McKechnie
Press, Samuel J. Friedman, James P. Davis
Stage Managers, Lucia Victor, Viola Kruener
*Closed at Copley Theatre, Boston, December 15, 1945.
†Revival

A GIFT FOR THE BRIDE

A Comedy in three acts, six scenes, with music; Produced by Jules J. Leventhal in association with the Shuberts; Adapted by Rowland Leigh from the Hungarian Comedy by Andrew Solt and S. Bekeffi; Directed by Rowland Leigh and Andrew Solt; Music by Jean Schwartz; Lyrics by Rowland Leigh; "See You In The Morning" words and music by Jay Rogers; Scenery, Lighting and Costumes by Watson Barratt. Opened at Park Theatre, Youngstown, Saturday, December 1, 1945.*

Cast of Characters

Head Waiter	Roy Johnson
Henriette	Lee Truehill**
Albert	Michael Steele
Fernande Poncelet	Louise Rainer
Alexander Poncelet	Wells Richardson
Edmond Cognerel	Stapleton Kent
Adrienne Cognerel	Kay Du Bois
Maid	Fay Sappington
Jean	Earl McDonald
Joseph	Forrest Taylor Jr.
Alice Villeneuve	Ruth Amos
Jules Villeneuve	Marion Green
Pierre Villeneuve	Paul Kaye
Madeline Montel	Hazele Burgess
Philip Montel	Cyrus Staehle
Gabriella Castel	Jean Cleveland
Count Leon Castel	Bert Bertram
Baron Clitescu	George Jason
Yvonne De La Motte	Adrienne Bayan
Madame De La Motte	Claire Evans
Masked Lady	Peggy Pakenham
Larry Barton	Jay Rogers
Doctor Andre	Leonard Bach
Madame Andre	Lona Foster
Lili Pascal	Gloria Humphreys

Musical Numbers: "Charm," "All the Time," "Home From Home," and "See You in The Morning."

The Action takes places in present day Paris; The Bridal Suite at the Ritz Hotel, Edmond Cognerel's Bedroom, Pierre's Study and Reception Room of the Villeneuve Home, and Terrace of the Cafe Colobri, Montmarte.

Company Manager, Harold Hevia
Press, Lee Kugel
Stage Manager, Forrest Taylor Jr.

*Closed at Royal Alexandra Theatre, Toronto, January 12, 1946.
**Replaced by Cyrilla Dorn.

"Fridolin"   Miriam Hopkins

ST. LAZARE'S PHARMACY

A Drama in three acts by Miklos Laszio, Adapted by Eddie Dowling; Produced by Eddie Dowling and Louis J. Singer; Designed and Lighted by Jo Mielziner; Staged by Mr. Dowling; Associate Director, Wesley McKee. Opened His Majesty's Theatre, Montreal, Thursday, December 6, 1945.*

Cast of Characters

An Old Woman } Therese }	Miriam Hopkins
Michel } Albert }	Gratien Gelinas†
Jean Jr. } Jean Sr. }	Herbert Berghof
Marie Rose	Lucienne Letondal
Louise	Huguette Oligny
Popinot } Grave Digger }	Somer Alberg
Police Captain	Georges Alexandre
Editor	Henri Letondal
Engineer } Waiter }	Guy Mauffette
Napoleon	Harry Davis
Bus Boy	Jean Lajeunesse
Organist	Jean Pierre Masson
Choir Soloist	Judy Maas

The Action takes place in the Apothecary of the French-Canadian town of St. Lazare, Quebec, on the eve of All Souls' Day not so long ago, and a winter morning 30 years earlier.

Company Manager, Harold Jacoby
Press, Harry Davies, Maurice Turet
Stage Manager, William McFadden

*Closed at Harris Theatre, Chicago, March 2, 1946.
†Mr. Gelinas is known in the French-Canadian Theatre as "Fridolin," inventor, producer and star of the "Fridolinons" or "Fridolin Revues."

PORTRAIT IN BLACK

Melodrama in three acts, five scenes, by Ivan Goff and Ben Roberts; Produced by Leland Hayward; Directed by Robert B. Sinclair; Setting by Lee Simonson; Gowns by Hattie Carnegie. Opened at Shubert Theatre, New Haven, Thursday, December 27, 1945.

Cast of Characters

Peter Talbot	Donald Devlin
Gracie McPhee	Jean Adair
Cob O'Brien	J. Pat O'Malley
Tanis Talbot	Geraldine Fitzgerald
Rupert Marlowe	James Rennie
Winnifred Talbot	Mary Barthelmess
Dr. Philip Graham	John Howard
Blake Ritchie	Rex Williams

The Action takes place in the Living-room of the Talbot House in San Francisco at the present time.

General Manager, Herman Bernstein
Company Manager, Warren P. Munsell Jr.
Press, Richard Maney, Ted Goldsmith
Stage Manager, Eddie Dimond

*Closed at Nixon Theatre, Pittsburgh, January 12, 1946.

GEORGIA BOY

A Drama in three acts, four scenes by Jack Kirkland from the novel by Erskine Caldwell. Produced by Mr. Kirkland and Haila Stoddard. Staged by Mr. Kirkland; Setting By Frederick Fox. Opened at Copley Theatre, Boston, Saturday, December 29, 1945.*

Cast of Characters

William Stroup	Peter Griffith
Martha Stroup	Joyce Arling
Handsome Brown	Christopher Bennett Jr.
Morris Stroup	Henry Hul
Ned Stroup	Russell Collin
Garden Cherrill	Marleen Cameron
Sheriff Vergil Sanford	Arthur Foran
Jupiter Cain	Timothy Grace

Clint Gross ....Donald Hastings
Calvin Woodward ....Michael Keene
Hester Woodward ....Jacqueline Miles
Starks Rice ....Richard Jedson
Mrs. Dudley ....Sara Perry
Mr. Dudley ....Bernard Randall

The Action takes place in the Back Yard of Morris Stroup's House in a Small Town in Georgia.

General Manager, John H. Del Bondio
Press, Mike Goldreyer
Stage Manager, Shelley Hull

*Closed January 5, 1946

YOU TWINKLE ONLY ONCE

A Comedy-drama in three acts, seven scenes, by Aben Kandel; Produced by Martin Blaine; Directed by Sanford Meisner; Setting by Albert Johnson. Opened at the Shubert Theatre, New Haven, Thursday, January 3, 1946.*

Cast of Characters

Ben Munro ....Philip Loeb
Joe ....Tom Pedi
Kitty Doone ....Gladys George
Plank Metcalf ....Glenn Anders
Mrs. Doone ....Laura Pierpont
Felix ....Francisco Salvacion
Pomerantz ....John Nelson
Mr. Reynolds ....James Todd
Ruth Fenton ....Catheryn Gael
Gene Morton ....Alexander Nicol
Delcorte ....Lou Polan

The Action takes place in the Playroom of Kitty Doone's Home in Brentwood, California.

General Manager, Jesse Long
Press, James Proctor, Frank Goodman
Stage Manager, Herbert Giffin

*Closed at Wilbur Theatre, Boston, January 19, 1946.

BY APPOINTMENT ONLY

A Comedy in three acts, four scenes, by Bene Russell; Produced by David Wolper; Directed by Harold Winston; Setting by Edward Forrest. Opened at Lyric Theatre, Bridgeport, Friday, January 11, 1946.*

Cast of Characters

"Uncle Charlie" Stevens ....Taylor Holmes
Lena ....Justina Wayne
Nancy Myles ....Patricia Clark
Sophia Myles ....Nancy Sheridan
Dr. Grant Myles ....Walter N. Greaza
Bonnie Myles ....Mary Ellen Glass
Frederick ....Edwin Redding
John Roberts ....John Gerstad
Ralph Myles ....David Forrest
Danny Boyle ....Benny Baker
Ivan Alexas Daghelov ....Daniel Ocko
Mrs. Twiller ....Catharine Doucet
Drake Colby ....Lowell Judson
Mrs. Grayson ....Patricia Quinn O'Hara
Mrs. Wilk ....Debby Dare
Leila ....Eileen Herrick
Georgia ....Frances Henderson
Auctioneer ....Philip Miller
Truckman (Mac) ....Frank Richards
2nd Truckman (Steve) ....John Red Kullers
Mr. Twiller ....Edward Broadley

The Action takes place at Dr. Grant Myles' summer home in a suburb near New York City.

General Manager, John Tuerk
Company Manager, Manning Gurian
Press, Ivan Black, Stanley Seiden
Stage Manager, Harold Altner

*Closed at Copley Theatre, Boston, January 19, 1946.

CRESCENDO

A Murder Melodrama with music in two acts, four scenes by Ramon Romero and Harriet Hinsdale; Produced by John Clein; Staged by David Burton; Music by Sigmund-Romberg, Chopin, Debussy; Setting and Lighting by Ralph Alswang. Opened at Bushnell Memorial, Hartford, Friday, January 18, 1946.*

Cast of Characters

Jan Marklyn ....Howard Johnson
Marya Lubek ....Sara Anderson
Gerald Thane ....Neil Hamilton
Maestro Anton Lubek ....Ralph Morgan
Elloise Griffin ....Jacqueline Horner
Miss Isabel Fenton ....Nance O'Neil
Pola ....Elisabeth Neumann
Tony ....Tito Vuolo
Mr. Norris ....Hugh Rennie

The Action takes place in the Living-room of Maestro Lubek's Long Island Home

Company Manager, Norman Stein
Press, David Lipsky
Stage Manager, Hugh Rennie

*Closed at Shubert Theatre, Philadelphia, February 16, 1946. (See page 98).

QUESTIONABLE LADIES

A Mystery-Comedy in three acts by Margery Williams; Produced by Morris Green and Lou DuFour in association with George Rilling; Staged by Russell Mack; Setting by H. Gordon Bennett. Opened at Shubert Theatre, New Haven, Thursday, January 31, 1946.**

Cast of Characters

Ruby Dunlap ....Mary Best
Princess Jennifer D'Aviland Katharine Warren
Ammah ....Margaret Fuller
Carla Standish ....Arlene Dahl
Mrs. Jeffery Arlington Taylor, 3rd..Eve McVeagh
Audrey Charleston ....Marlo Dwyer
Mademoiselle Melanie Beaupre
                                              Bobette Christine*
Mrs. Seth Darwin ....Helene Le Berthon
Tully La Rue ....Virginia Smith
Margherita Vosselli ....Helene Arthur
Prince Michael Alexis D'Aviland
                                              Edward G. Greer

The Scene is the Reception Room of Princess D'Aviland's Town House in New York City, Late November, 1945.

Company Manager, James Kenney
Press, Charles Washburn
Stage Manager, Edward G. Greer

*Replaced by Kay Parker.

**Closed at Walnut Street Theatre, Philadelphia, February 16, 1946.

DEARLY BELOVED

A Drama in three acts, five scenes by Lula Vollmer; Produced by Howard Lang; Staged by Anthony Mann; Setting by Sam Leve; Costumes by Eaves. Opened at Newark Opera Playhouse, Newark, Thursday, February 14, 1946.*

Cast of Characters

Sid Matthews ....Edmund Glover
Pauline ....Phyllis DuBus
Bobby ....Donald Hastings
Alex Ballard ....John Connor
Rena Yates ....Mary Rolfe
Liza Yates ....Marjorie Rambeau
Eben Turner ....Richard Barrows
Arch Whitaker ....Harry Sheppard
Hessie Greeley ....Florence Sundstrom
Delia Blossom ....Claiborne Foster
Dr. Owens ....Lester Lonergan Jr.

The Action takes place in the Living-room of the Yates Farm House in the Midwest shortly after the turn of the century.

Company Manager, Irving Becker
Press, Elise Chisholm
Stage Manager, Myles Putnam

*Closed at Locust Street Theatre, Philadelphia, February 23, 1946.

ONE SHOE OFF

A Comedy in three acts by Mark Reed; Produced and Staged by George Abbott; Setting by John Root; Costumes by Lucinda Ballard; Second Act Dance devised by Emy St. Just. Opened at Nixon Theatre, Pittsburgh, Monday, February 18, 1946.*

Cast of Characters

J. Grover Wing	Edward Clarke Lilley
Grace Wing	Paula MacLean
Maggie	Carree Clarke
Lois Wing	Margaret Hayes
John Wing	Douglas Jones
Arthur Pond	Robert Sully
Marjorie Thompson	Billie Lou Watt
Waggenseller	Darren Dublin
Phillips	Don Symington
Jim Leonard	Roy Walling
Janette Leonard	June Dayton
Henry T. McCutcheon	W. O. McWatters

The Scene is the Living-room of the Wing Home in Cynthiana, a small city in Southern Ohio.

General Manager, Charles Harris
Company Manager, Joseph C. Cohne
Press, Richard Maney, Ted Goldsmith
Stage Manager, Robert Griffith

*Closed Shubert Theatre, New Haven, March 2, 1946.

SECOND GUESSER

A Comedy Farce about baseball in three acts, ten scenes, by Harold M. Sherman; Produced by Mid-West Productions Inc.; Scenery by Hugh McGowan; Technical Direction by Monte Fassnacht; Staged by Mr. Sherman. Opened at Civic Opera House, Chicago, February 18, 1946.*

Cast of Characters

Brooklyn Sportscaster	Ramsey Burch
Sam Bumpus	Al Schacht
First Bleacher Fan	Bruno VeSoto
Second Bleacher Fan	Briton Kirby
Third Bleacher Fan	Ben Roseman
A Giant Fan	Bernard Kobiella
Edwin Emerson	Edward Meekin
Nellie Bumpus	Hope Summers
Babe Ruth Bumpus	Jane Butler
Walter Johnson Bumpus	Don DeLeon
Attorney Bell	Ralph Juul
Second Baseman Miller	Bruno VeSoto
Catcher Hank Rowdy	Ernst Nobbe
Carl "Speed" Norton	Lester Podewell
Steve Haskell	Robert Hoffman
Editor Deagen	Klock Ryder
Big Jim Haggard	Briton Kirby
Slim Baker	Jay Merrick
Park Policeman	Joe Panzica
Slugger McGinty	Ben Roseman
Right Fielder Nelson	Bernard Kobiella
Left Fielder Taylor	John Sorich
Shortstop Pee Wee Russell	Ed Doring
Third Baseman Dingle	Arthur Chester
Durocher's Voice	Ernst Nobbe
Umpire's Voice	Joe Panzica

The Action takes place in Centerfield Bleacher seats at Ebbets Field, and the Living-room of the Bumpus Apartment in Brooklyn. In Niagara Falls, the Ball Club Office of the Tigers, the Bumpus Apartment, the Playing Field, Reporter's Desk in the Gazette Office, the Tigers' Dugout, the Pitcher's Mound and the Falls.

Company Manager, Harry Rosnagle
Press, Danny Newman
Stage Manager, Klock Ryder

*Closed March 2, 1946.

BETWEEN COVERS†

A Comedy in three acts by Charles Raddock; Produced by Leslye Karen; Directed by Robert Henderson*1; Setting by Perry Watkins; Costumes by Paul Du Pont. Opened at Hanna Theatre, Cleveland, Monday, February 25, 1946.**

Cast of Characters

Terry	Solveig Dahl
Edgar Crump	Bruce Adams *2
Bill Hatch	Millard Mitchell
Fudge Farrell	Jacqueline Susann*3
Nelson Parrington, Jr.	Curtis Cooksey
Mac	Edward Mullen
Joe	David Durston
Jim	Ladd Haynes
Mlle. Genevieve	Ruth Altman
J. Dean Loveridge	David Lewis
Rev. Hawkins	John Souther
Runo	William Colby
Mamie Lou Willis	Cecil Elliott
Cyrus Wheelock	Richard Temple

The Action of the play occurs in the Sanctum Sanctorum of Parrington Publishers in the Fifties, New York City, at the present time.

Company Manager, John J. Garrity, Jr.
Press, Ivan Black
Stage Manager, Lucia Victor

†Tried out last season under the title, "Merely Coincidental." Is slated to try again next season, presumably under a third title.
*During the tour, there was a re-write, restaged by 1. Edward Clarke Lilley; and the following cast replacements: 2. Roland Hogue, 3. Ruth Webb. The part of Miss Campbell was added with Lorraine McMartin playing it.

**Closed at Great Northern Theatre, Chicago, March 23, 1946.

A YOUNG AMERICAN*

A Drama in three acts by Edwin M. Bronner; Produced by Messrs. Shubert and Albert De Courville; Staged by Mr. De Courville. Opened at Great Northern Theatre, Chicago, Tuesday, February 26, 1946.**

Cast of Characters

Mrs. Hastings	Grace Mills
Jacob Geismar	Liam Dunn
Alexander Cortell	Raymond Edward Johnson
Lynn Cortell	Martha Jean
Steve Willoughby	Lyle Bettger
William Farrell	William Greaves
Sophie Baines	Sheila Guyse
Prof. Arnold Harmon	J. Rosamond Johnson

The Action takes place in the New York Penthouse Apartment of Alexander Cortell.

Business Manager, Eddie Lewis
Press, C. P. Greneker
Stage Manager, Stuart Fox

*Introduced by the Blackfriars' Guild on January 17, 1945. Rights purchased by present producers after seeing first performance.

**Closed March 9, 1946.

MISS JONES

An Autobiographical Comedy in three acts by Ruth Gordon; Produced by Max Gordon; Staged by Garson Kanin; Settings by Donald Oenslager; Costumes by Ruth Kanin Aronson. Opened at Playhouse Theatre, Wilmington, Friday, March 1, 1946.*

Cast of Characters

Clinton Jones	Victor Kilian
Annie Jones	Sawyer Smith
Ruth Gordon Jones	Barbara Leed
Katherine Follett	Betty Caulfield
Anna Witham	Janet Crew
Fred Whitmarsh	Palmer William
Mr. Bagley	Howard Ferguson
Miss Glavin	Margaret Mulle
Mr. Sparrow	Charles Kean

The Scene is the Jones' Dining-room-Sitting room at 14 Elmwood Avenue, Wollaston, Massachusetts, 1913.

General Manager, Ben A. Boyar
Company Manager, Michael Goldreyer
Press, William Fields, Walter Alford
Stage Manager, Kip Good

*Closed at National Theatre, Washington, D. C. March 23, 1946.

TWILIGHT BAR

A Drama in three acts by Arthur Koestler; Produced by George Abbott; Directed by Everett Sloane; Settings by Oliver Smith; Music by Paul Bowles; Costumes by Lucille Little. Opened at Ford's Theatre, Baltimore, Tuesday, March 12, 1946.*

Cast of Characters

Glowworm ....Luther Adler
Sam ....William Hansen
Henry Gonzales ....Philip Arthur
Lucy ....Mary Cooper
Mary ....Mercedes McCambridge
Colonel of Police ....George Baxter
Senora Gonzales ....Edith Meiser
Inspector Walker ....Robert Strauss
First Detective ....Charles Mendick
Second Detective ....Bernard Hoffman
Alpha ....John Baragray
Omega ....Lois Wheeler
Prime Minister ....Guy Arbury
Minister for Foreign Affairs ....Ernest Rowan
Minister for Enlightenment ....Harrison Dowd
Minister for Air ....Jonathan Harris
Minister for Justice ....Joseph Mann
Minister for Sabbath Gloom ....John Morny
Minister for War ....Geoffrey Lumb
Minister for Sweat and Toil ....Edgar Kent
Mr. Smith ....John Robb

The Action takes place at any time in an Island Republic. The Scenes are The Twilight Bar, The Prime Minister's Conference Room, An Open Place, and A Square in the Capital.

General Manager, Charles Harris
Company Manager, Joseph Cohne
Press, Richard Maney, Ted Goldsmith
Production Manager, Robert Griffith
Stage Manager, Emery Battis
Closed at Walnut Street Theatre, Philadelphia, March 23, 1946.

LOVE IN THE SNOW

A Musical Romance in three acts, twelve scenes; Produced by Messrs. Shubert; Book and Lyrics by Roland Leigh; Music by Ralph Benatzky; Book Directed by John Baird; Settings by Lawrence Goldwasser; Dances by Myra Finch; Costumes by Jac-Lewis; Orchestrations by Daniel Mendlsohn; Orchestra under direction of Pierre de Reeder. Opened at Bushnell Memorial, Hartford, Friday, March 15, 1946.**

Cast of Characters

Kurt Remsen ....Jay Rogers
Ingrid Siebert ....Betty Luster
Cordelia Hansen ....Nan Shanon
Leif Hansen ....Robert Pitkin
Miss Swastrom ....Charlotte Lansing
Hendrick Van Rhyn ....Robert Douglas
Princess Martha ....Nancy Donovan
Mrs. Siebert ....Ellen Love
Griselda ....Lola Kendrick
Hank ....Arthur Mack
Crown Prince Paul ....Raymond Bailey
Count Remsen ....Le Roi Operti
Caretaker ....Peter Preses
Rosella Picelli ....Allegra Varron
The Duke of Parthay ....Paul Kaye
Collette Palermo ....Rachelle Carlay
The Court Photographer ....Charles Dubin
Ballet Master ....Lee Lindsey
Dancers ....Allyn and Anthony*

Musical Numbers†: "Halfway Chalet," "When We're Together," "Love in the Snow," Interlude, "First Love," "Once in a Lifetime," "Make Up Your Mind," "Savoire Faire," "Twilight," Winter Ballet, "Party Dress," "Farewell Letter," "Collette," "Serenade," Court Ballet, "Portrait for Posterity," Ballet Rehearsal.

The Action takes place in Mythical Scandinavian Country of Olafland, 1872. The Halfway Chalet, on the way to Norseholm, Mrs. Siebert's Drawing Room, Near Halfway Chalet, Princess Martha's Boudoir, Ante Room and Ballroom of the Royal Palace, and Corridor and Green Room at the Opera House.

Company Manager, George Oshrin
Press, C. P. Greneker, George H. Atkinson
Stage Manager, Arthur Mayberry

†Also includes excerpt from "Queen of Sheba" and "La Traviata."

*Joined show after opening and were given two dance specialties.

**Closed at Forrest Theatre, Philadelphia, April 6, 1946.

Charles Coburn   Jessie Royce Landis

MERRY WIVES OF WINDSOR

A Comedy in two acts, sixteen scenes, by William Shakespeare Produced by the Theatre Guild; Directed by Romney Brent; Settings by Stewart Chaney; Supervised by Lawrence Langner and Theresa Helburn. Opened at Playhouse Theatre, Wilmington, Friday, March 15, 1946.*

Cast of Characters

Shallow, a country justice ....Baldwin McCaw
Sir Hugh Evans, a Welsh parson..Charles Francis
Slender, nephew to Shallow ....Frank Leslie
Master Page ....Robin Craven
Sir John Falstaff ....Charles Coburn
Bardolph ⎫   George Rees
Pistol   ⎬ Followers of Falstaff ....Robert Sloat
Nym   ⎭   Allen Collins
Mistress Page ....Gina Malo
Anne Page, her daughter ....Jennifer Howard
Simple ....Jules Racine
Mistress Quickly ....Wauna Paul
Rugby, servant to Dr. Caius ....Douglas Watson
Dr. Caius, a French physician ......Romney Brent
Fenton, a young gentleman ....Dorman Leonard
Host of the Carter Inn ....Lionel Ince
Mistress Ford ....Jessie Royce Landis
Master Ford ....David Powell
Robin, page to Falstaff ....Judson Rees
Servant to Ford ....Dennis Dengate
Servant to Ford ....George Morgan
Servant to Mistress Ford ....Lucille Patton

The Action takes place in Windsor, England: a public square, a street, a room in Dr. Caius' house, a field near Windsor, a field near Frogmore, a room in Ford's House, and at Herne's Oak.

Company Manager, John H. Potter
Press, Dorothy Johnson
Stage Manager, Mortimer Halpern
*Current on Road June 1, 1946.

JUDY O'CONNOR

A Comedy-drama in three acts, four scenes, by Andrew Solt and Frank Ross; Produced by Frank Ross; Settings by Frederick Fox; Costumes by Robert Knox; Lighting by Al Alloy; Staged by John Berry. Opened at Shubert Theatre, New Haven, Thursday, March 21, 1946.*

Cast of Characters

Mrs. Farago ....Olga Fabian
Judy O'Connor ....Anne Sargent
David Rice ....William Prince
Mike O'Connor ....Don DeFore

The Action takes place in the O'Connor Living-room and David's Room in the New Yorker Hotel at the present time.

General Manager, S. M. Handelsman
Press, Willard Keefe
Stage Manager, David Gray

*Closed at Copley Theatre, Boston, March 30, 1946.

SALUTE TO MURDER

A Drama in three acts by Myron C. Fagan; Produced by Bruce V. Fagan; Directed by Myron Fagan; Setting by Samuel Leve. Opened at Shubert-Lafayette Theatre, Detroit, Sunday, March 24, 1946.*

Cast of Characters

Scanlon ....Alexander Campbell
Boris Sarnoff ....Raymond Greenleaf
D. A. Dritt ....Grandon Rhodes
Gorman ....Frank Richards
Roxie Gainsborough ....Vivian Keefer
Maj. Bob Brainard ....Richard Beach
Arline Mason ....Mary Patton
Jensen ....Henry Vincent
Senator Derlin ....Edward H. Robins
Mrs. Meadow ....Nancy Cushman
J. Kerrigan Kane ....Frederic Tozere
Congressman Feltz ....Walter Kohler

The Action takes place in J. Kerrigan Kane's Penthouse Apartment.

Company Manager, Paul Vroom
Press, Charles Washburn, Tom Weatherly
Stage Manager, Lucien Self

*Closed April 6, 1946.

WEST OF THE MOON*

A Drama in three acts by Louis Bromfield and Laslo Vadnay; Produced by Alexander Ince and Albert De Courville; Directed by Mr. De Courville; Setting by Edward Gilbert. Opened at National Theatre, Washington, D. C., Monday, March 25, 1946.**

Cast of Characters

Cyrus Avery ....Edgar Stehli
Beatrice ....Mabel Bergen
Henry Avery ....Harry Worth
West ....Earl McDonald
Margaret Avery ....Anne Burr
Mrs. Thomas Avery ....Estelle Winwood
Dr. Lamar Forest ....Donald Cook
Sylvia Serruti ....Marta Linden
Dr. Onslow ....Wyrley Birch

The Scene is the Thomas Avery Living-room, Pasadena, California.

Company Manager, Edward Lewis
Press, Ben Kornzweig
Production Manager, John Holden

*Formerly known as "Agnes," "In My Father's House," "Bread of Deceit," and "And Yet So Far."
**Closed at Wilbur Theatre, Boston, April 13, 1946.

SHOOTIN' STAR

The Musical Story of Billy The Kid, in two acts, seven scenes; Produced by Max Liebman and Joseph Kipness; Book by Walter Hart, Louis Jacobs, Halsted Welles; Music by Sol Kaplan; Lyrics by Bob Russell; Choreography by Lester Horton; Settings by Frederick Fox; Costumes by Kenn Barr; Orchestrations by Hershey Kay; Musical Director, Pembroke Davenport; Staged by Halsted Welles. Opened at Shubert Theatre, New Haven, Thursday, April 4, 1946.**

Cast of Characters

Folk Singer ....Susan Reed
Beaver .... Lee Fairfax
Curley ....Marco Rosales
Hank ....Larry Stewart
Cash Claghorne ....Art Smith
Sarilla ....Margaret Irving
Windy ....Richard Gibbs
Ross Dixon ....Howard da Silva
Fancy ....Edward Andrews
Amy ....Doretta Morrow
Mr. Barry ....Everett Gammon
Soldier ....Walter Stane
Buckshot ....Elliott Sullivan
Chuck Wagner ....Rex King*1
Sheriff Brody ....James Moore
Willy ....Aldo Cadena
Spike ....Peter Gray
Lola ....Emily Earle
Billy ....David Brooks
Lorraine ....Bernice Parks
Teaser ....Sandra Grube
Paradise ....Ruth K. Hill
Velvet ....Elline Walther
Saddle Jane ....Jean Olds
Sally ....Nelle Fisher
Jerry ....Ray Harrison
Mr. Eliot ....Thom Conroy
Mr. MacDonald ....Jack MacGraw
Mr. Adams ....Howard Culler
Francis T. Corey ....Clay Clement
Olie ....Larry Anderson
Luke ....Larry Gray
Bartender ....Rex King*2
Raphael Ventura ....James Moore
Maria Ventura ....Emily Earle
Conchita ....Sonia Shaw
Pedro ....Nathan Kirkpatrick
General Wallace ....Bram Nosser

Musical Numbers: "Saga of Billy the Kid," "Footloose," "Kid Stuff," "Friendly Country," "What do I Have to Do?," "Mighty Big Dream," Party Dance, "Sometime Tomorrow," "It's a Cold Cruel World," "Music to a Dancing Birl," "Chin-Che," "Free," "Nothin'," "I'm Paying You."

The Action takes place in Lincoln, Lincoln County, New Mexico, about 1880. The Square, the Corral and Patio of the Adams-MacDonald ranch, Ross Dixon Lincoln Plaza Saloon, Home of the Venturas.

General Manager, Jack Small
Press, James D. Proctor, Lewis Harmon
Stage Manager, Eddie Dimond

*Replacements: 1. Marco Rosales, 2. Jerry Bercier.
**Closed at Shubert Theatre, Boston, April 27, 1946.

WINDY CITY

A Play with music in two acts, prologue, epilogue and nine scenes;† Produced by Richard Kollmar, Book by Philip Yordan; Music by Walter Jurman; Lyrics by Paul Francis Webster; Directed by Edward Reveaux; Choreography by Katherine Dunham; Sets and Lighting by Jo Mielziner; Costumes by Rose Bogdanoff; Vocal Arrangements by Clay Warnick; Orchestrations by Don Walker; Ballet Music by Dorothea Freitag; Musical Direction, Charles Sanford. Opened at Shubert Theatre, New Haven, Friday, April 18, 1946.**

Cast of Characters

Danny O'Brien	John Conte
Frankie Keaton	Ralph Hertz
Angel	Grace Hayle
Ruby	Joey Faye
Kitty	Norma Vaslavina
Al, a Newsboy	James Russell
Officer O'Leary	Owen Hewitt
Martin O'Brien	Loring Smith
"Gramps" O'Brien	Al Shean
Lola	Susan Miller
Patsy	Frances Williams
Louie	Robert Berry
Stony	Tom Pedi
Fats	Mickey Cochran
Sam	Jack Diamond
Gloria	Betty Jane Smith
Nina	Florence Lessing
Voice in the Juke Box	Georgetta Spelvin
Jimmy Casino	Stephen Chase
Church Janitor	Richard Taber
Anna, a Scrubwoman	Irene Hawthorne
A Beggar	Eric Victor
A Reefer Man	Jerry Ross
Musicians	{ Harry Day
	{ Hal Loman
A Stripper	Lili St. Cyr
George	John C. McCord
Burlesque Girls	{ Anna Mitten
	{ Betty Lind

Vocal Ensemble: Martha Burnett, Patricia Newaq, Elizabeth Pritchett, Shirley Sudock, Ray Bessmer, Ray Cook, Thomas Edwards, Michael Kozak.

Musical Numbers: "State Street," "Don't Ever Run Away From Love," Lady of the Evening,* "Gambler's Lullaby," The Beggar,* "As the Wind Bloweth," "It's the Better Me," "Out on a Limb," Frankie's Wife,* "Nightfall on State Street," "It's Time I Had a Break," "Mrs. O'Leary's Cow," "Where Do We Go From Here?" The Reefer Man.

The Action takes place in Chicago; the Cafe, South State Street, Room in a cheap Hotel, a Shop Window, Around the corner from the Hotel, and the Interior of a Church.

Company Manager, Leo Rose
Press, Bernard Simon, John L. Toohey
Stage Managers, Frank Coletti, David Jones
†Book completely revised after opening and Kay Stewart and Grover Burgess joined the cast.
*These dance numbers were eliminated during restaging and "The Little Girl" substituted.
**Closed Great Northern Theatre, Chicago, June 6, 1946.

Miriam Hopkins

LAURA

A Mystery Drama in three acts by Vera Caspary and George Sklar from the novel by Miss Caspary; Produced by Hunt Stromberg, Jr.; Staged by Michael Gordon; Designed by Stewart Chaney; Gown by Valentina; Production Associate, Robert Schuler. Opened at Playhouse Theatre, Wilmington, Saturday, April 19, 1946.*

Cast of Characters

Mark McPherson	Tom Neal
Danny Dorgan	Tom Walsh
Waldo Lydecker	Otto Kruger
Shelby Carpenter	Walter Coy
Bessie Clary	Camila Ashland
Mrs. Dorgan	Isabel Bonner
A Young Woman	Miriam Hopkins
Olsen	Roger Clark

The Action takes place in the Living-room of Laura Hunt's apartment in New York City.

Production Manager, Tom Elwell
General Manager, Thomas Spengler
Company Manager, Ralph Kravette
Press, Philip Stevenson
Stage Managers, Chet O'Brien, Alexander Cowley
*Current on the road, June 1, 1946.

BIGGER THAN BARNUM

A Farce in three acts by Fred Rath and Lee Sands; Produced by the authors; Directed by Edward Clarke Lilley; Setting by H. Gordon Bennett. Opened at Wilbur Theatre, Boston, Monday, April 22, 1946.*

Cast of Characters

Perly Drake	Benny Baker
Chuck Jenkins	Sid Melton
Girl Attendant	Jean Mode
Alex	Oscar Polk
Uncle Charles	Dan Evans
Claire Walker	Patricia Neal
Dominisk Pisano	Charles La Torre
Roberta Dixon	Chili Williams
Martin R. Dexter	Jack Rutherford
Stanley Ripple	Roy Johnson
Sheriff Knox	Don Roberts
"Fingers" Frawley	Harry Kingston
Sala Rombu	Lenny Ditson
and	
"Julius"	By Himself

The Action of the play takes place in an Office and Shed on the Grounds at Paradise Park, Coney Island.

Company Manager, James M. McKechnie
Press, Harry Davies, Marjorie Barkentin
Stage Manager, William Lilling
*Closed April 27, 1946.

LAMBS WILL GAMBLE

A Comedy in three acts, two sets, by Lew Lipton and Ralph Murphy from an original story by Buster Keaton; Produced by Bonfils and Somnes; Directed by Ralph Murphy; Designed, Lighted and Costumed by Frederick Fox. Opened at Shubert Theatre, New Haven, Thursday, April 25, 1946.*

Cast of Characters

Joe	William Hollenbeck
Barney	James Doody
Pancho	Ernest Sarracino
Tito	Tino Valenti
Betty	Peggy Wagner
Ed Cummings	Walter Gilbert
Doc	James O'Neill
Jimmy Leeds	Lex Lindsay
Lily King	Frances Tannehill
Richard Douglas	Eugene Stuckman
Countess de Polikoff	Helen G. Bonfils
Count de Polikoff	George Andre
Justice Somerset	Walter N. Greaza
Mrs. Somerset	Gertrude Dallas
D. B. Hartman	Jack Hartley
Claire Whiting	Sunnie O'Dea
Cabot Hawthorne	Robert Ober
Mrs. Hawthorne	Florence Beresford
Pierre	Walter Armin
Mark Trueman	Arthur Hunnicutt
Granby	Joseph Graham
Croupier	William Tregoe
Dealer	Robert Gardet

The Action takes place at the exclusive Gambling Club, "The Pyramid"—located near the famous desert winter resort — Palm Springs, California; the Entrance Hall and Dining Room; and the Gambling Room.

General Manager, Louis Cline
Press, Michael Goldreyer
Stage Manager, Charles J. Parsons
*Closed at Walnut Street Theatre, Philadelphia, May 11, 1946.

SECOND BEST BED†

A Comedy by N. Richard Nash; produced by Ruth Chatterton and John Huntington in association with J. J. Leventhal; Staged by Miss Chatterton and Mr. Nash; Setting and Costumes by Motley. Opened at Erie Theatre, Schenectady, Friday, May 3, 1946.*

Cast of Characters

Ballad Seller	Richard Dyer-Bennet
Nell	Elizabeth Eustis
Fenny	Peter Boyne
Yorick	Ralph Cullinan
Anne	Ruth Chatterton
Lewie	Ralph Forbes
Squire Simon	Richard Temple
The Beadle	Max Stamm
Will	Barry Thomson
Master Yarrow	John McKee
Farmer Legge	Jefferson Coates
Michael	Ralph Sumpter
Ben	John Gay

The entire Action takes place in the combination "Main Road" and "Parlor" in Anne Hathaway's Cottage, Shottery, parish of old Stratford-on-Avon, County of Warwickshire at the beginning of the Seventeenth Century.

Company Manager, Sam Nixon
Press, Vince McKnight
Stage Manager, Lillian Udvardy

†Title taken from the only mention made by William Shakespeare of his wife, Anne Hathaway in his last will and testament: *"Itm.: I Gyve unto my wief my second best bed."*
*Current on Road June 1, 1946.

Jose Ferrer   Leif Erickson

CYRANO DE BERGERAC

A Revival of the Brian Hooker version of the Rostand Comedy drama in five acts; Produced by Jose Ferrer; Directed by Melchor G. Ferrer; Settings and Costumes by Lemuel Ayers; Music Composed and Orchestrated by Paul Bowles; Supervised by Arthur S. Friend. Opened at Shubert Theatre, New Haven, Friday, May 17, 1946.*

Cast of Characters

Porter	Victor Beecroft
Cavalier	Robert Rockwell
Musketeer	George Oliver
A Guardsman	Charles Zanbello
Flower Girl	Phyllis Hill
A Citizen	Wallace Widdecombe
His Son	Sandy Campbell
A Cut Purse	Leonardo Cimino
A Meddler	Francis Letton
Carbon De Castel-Jaloux	Nelson Leigh
Orange Girl	Patricia Wheel
A Marquis	Robert Carroll
Brissaille	Albert Whitley
Ligniere	John O'Connor
Christian De Neuvillette	Leif Erickson
Ragueneau	Hiram Sherman
Le Bret	Francis Compton
Roxane, Nee Madeleine Robin	Ruth Ford
Her Duenna	Paula Laurence
Comte De Guiche	Ralph Clanton
Vicomte De Valvert	Dean Cetrulo
Another Cut Purse	Nick Dennis
Montfleury	Leopold Badia
Cyrano De Bergerac	Jose Ferrer
Bellerose	Howard Wierum
Jodelet	Robinson Stone
A Soubrette	Neva Patterson
A Comedienne	Barbara Joyce
Lise	Jacqueline Paige
A Capuchin	Robinson Stone
Sister Marthe	Barbara Joyce
Mother Marguerite	Jacqueline Paige
Sister Claire	Phyllis Hill
A Nun	Patricia Wheel

The Action takes place in the Hall of the Hotel Bourgogne, 1640; The Bake-shop of Ragueneau; The House of Roxane in a Little Square in Old Marais; The Post of the Company of Carbon de Castel-Jaloux, at the siege of Arras; and the Park of the Convent in Paris, 1650.

General Manager, Jules J. Leventhal
Company Manager, Charles Mulligan
Press, David Lipsky
Stage Manager, Hugh Rennie

*Current on the road June 1, 1946.

THE DANCER

A melodrama in three acts by Milton Lewis and Julian Funt; Produced by George Abbott; Staged by Everett Sloane; Music by Paul Bowles; Designed by Motley; Opened at Walnut Street Theatre, Philadelphia, Monday, May 20, 1946.

Cast of Characters

Henry Wilkins	Edgar Kent
Aubrey Stewart	Colin Keith-Johnston
The Inspector	Luis Van Rooten
Sergei Krainine	Leon Fokine
Madeline Krainine	Bethel Leslie
Catherine Krainine	Helen Flint

Action takes place in the Living-room of Aubrey Stewart's House in present day Paris.

General Manager, Charles Harris
Press, Richard Maney, Anthony Buttitta
Production Manager, Robert Griffith
Stage Manager, Emery Battis

*Current on the road June 1, 1946.

COME ON UP
("Ring Twice Tonight")

A Comedy in two acts, four scenes, and a prologue by Miles Mander, Fred Schiller and Thomas Dunphy; Produced by Select Operating Corporation; Directed by Russell Fillmore; Setting by Ernest Glover; Miss West's gowns by Peter Johnson. Opened at Oakland Auditorium, Oakland, Monday, May 20, 1946.*

Cast of Characters
(In order of appearance)

General Quantillo ....Charles La Torre
Krafft ....John Doucette
Carliss Dale ....Miss Mae West
Jeff Bentley ....Michael Ames
Lottie ....Cleo Desmond
J. W. Bentley ....Roy Gordon
Doug Wade ....Charles G. Martin
Annette ....Francesca Rotoli
Mike Annegan ....Joe McTurk
Twilby ....Harold Bostwick
Sailor ....Allan Nixon
Lou Baker, Sailor Harry (The Hipster) Gibson
Nick ....Don Harvey
Ramon Rodriguez ....Robert Tafur
Senator Carlton ....Willis Claire
Larkin ....Jon Anton
Bell Captain ....John Hampton
Ed ....Peter Dunne
Frank ....George Spelvin
General Housenborough ....Robert Long

The Prologue takes place in a private room in a penthouse above the "El Flamingo" night club in Mexico City and the four scenes in Carliss Dale's apartment, Washington, D. C., at the present time.

Company Manager, Harry Mirsky
Press, John J. Hill
Stage Manager, Charles La Torre
*Current on the road, June 1, 1946.

Harry Gibson—Mae West—Allan Nixon

CHICAGO SEASON
By WILLIAM LEONARD

The Loop experienced its busiest season since first the sound track and then the depression put the skids temporarily under the theatre. More than three dozen attractions opened between June 1, 1945 and June 1, 1946, and fourteen of them were on "pre-Broadway" tours.

This was a new phenomenon for Chicago playgoers. Philadelphia, Boston and New Haven are accustomed to being treated as try-out grounds. Chicago heretofore has been too far from Manhattan to see many marginal enterprises in their formative state, although it has entertained its quota of Theatre Guild and other firmly established productions still en route to New York.

It wasn't altogether a pleasant experience. Of the fourteen, only four—"The Winter's Tale," "The Desert Song," "A Joy Forever" and "Second Best Bed"—eventually arrived in Manhattan.

Most of the others went directly from the Loop to the warehouse. Of these, "St. Lazare's Pharmacy," "The Joyous Season" and "Windy City" came closest to making the grade. The first named was produced by Eddie Dowling and Louis J. Singer, who had premiered "The Glass Menagerie" in Chicago the preceding year, but despite a capable cast of French-Canadians and a splendid set by Joe Mielziner, its span of life did not extend more than ten weeks. "The Joyous Season" cast Ethel Barrymore as a nun, in a revival of Philip Barry's play in which Lillian Gish was starred back in 1934. "Windy City," a "play-with-music" by Philip Yordan, author of "Anna Lucasta," was set in Chicago's grimy South State Street and had many things to recommend it, but was lost in a confusion of song, dance and story.

"The Merry Wives of Windsor," second production of the Theatre Guild Shakespeare Company which had revived "The Winter's Tale" earlier in the season, went on to the West Coast, where Charles Coburn, its Falstaff, had a motion picture engagement, instead of essaying New York.

The six other "pre-Broadway" shows "Spring In Brazil," "The Passing Show," "A Young American," "Second Guesser," "Between Covers," and "Windy Hill" all collapsed without ever getting out of Cook County, although the last named managed to stay twelve weeks at the Harris on the strength of the movie magic in Kay Francis' name.

"Second Guesser," farce starring Al Schacht, a baseball player making his bow in the legitimate theatre, was the only home produced play of the season, and its two weeks in the huge Civic Opera House did not encourage its promoters to try again.

In all, 37 attractions arrived in the twelve months starting June 1, 1945. This was two fewer than in the season of 1944-45, but the number of playgoing weeks available to Chicagoans increased from 302 to 326, largest total since the '20s. There were thirteen musicals included in the total, compared with eighteen a year earlier.

Long-run champion was "Anna Lucasta," whose success vindicated John Wildberg's courage in bringing the New York cast direct to Chicago in September, 1945, while continuing the Broadway run with a second company, and likewise confirmed his judgment in leasing the Civic Theatre to the four walls for a full year. This unprecedented maneuver paid off, as the Harry Wagstaff Gribble production ran up 36 weeks by June 1.

Next longest runs were the 35 weeks of "Dear Ruth" and the 32 weeks of "The Voice of the Turtle," holdovers from the 1944-45 season.

The Majestic, dark for eleven years, was relighted on September 19 with Olsen and Johnson advertising they "will wreck this beautiful theatre" but, instead, they got it off to a great start as the Sam S. Shubert Memorial Theatre by hanging up 30 amazingly successful weeks.

Other fairly lengthy stands included "Carmen Jones," 19 weeks; "Dark of the Moon" and "Windy Hill," twelve weeks; "Good Night Ladies!" (in a return engagement), "The Two Mrs. Carrolls" and "The Late George Apley," eleven weeks; and "St. Lazare's Pharmacy" and "The Joyous Season," ten weeks.

Most exciting single week was the first one in May, when Chicago became the first city to be "dimmed out" because of the nation-wide coal strike. Forbidden to use electricity from the public utility companies, theatre managers scurried about in pursuit of generators which enabled them to set up their own lighting plants. Most of them managed to carry on, but "The Late George Apley" missed a whole week's performance at the Erlanger.

It was an exciting season as well as a crowded one, and the slight improvement in the quality of incoming attractions gave hint of better things to come in 1946-47.

Beatrice Pearson
(See page 174)

GALLERY OF EXCLUSIVE PORTRAITS OF PROMISING PERSONALITIES

Marlon Brando
(See page 148)

Barbara Bel Geddes
(See page 147)

Paul Douglas
(See page 157)

Wendell Corey
(See page 154)

Mary James
(See page 164)

Burt Lancaster
(See page 166)

Bill Callahan

(See page 150)

Patricia Marshall
(See page 170)

John Archer   Phyllis Avery   Walter Abel

BIOGRAPHIES OF POPULAR BROADWAY PLAYERS

ABBOTT, JOHN. Born in London, June 5, 1905. Made his first stage appearance in 1934 at the London Westminster Theatre in a revival of "Aurengzebe". ..A long association with the Old Vic followed. For the past few years he has been in Hollywood. The revival of "He Who Gets Slapped" marked his Broadway debut.

ABEL WALTER. Born in St. Paul, Minn., June 6, 1898. Received his stage training at the American Academy of Dramatic Arts. First N. Y. appearance at Manhattan Opera House, 1919, in "Forbidden". Made more recent N. Y. appearances in "When Ladies Meet", "Wife Insurance", "Invitation to a Murder", "Merrily We Roll Along", and "The Wingless Victory". After a long session in films, he returned to Broadway stage, 1945, in "The Mermaids Singing".

ADDY, WESLEY. His N. Y. appearances include Maurice Evans' productions of "Henry IV", "Hamlet", and "Twelfth Night", Leslie Howard's "Hamlet", Laurence Olivier's "Romeo and Juliet", and more recently "Antigone", and Katharine Cornell's 1946 revival of "Candida".

ADLER, LUTHER. Born in N. Y. C., May 4, 1903. Educated at Lewis Institute, Chicago. Made his first stage appearance in 1908 at the Thalia Theatre, Bowery, New York, as a child in the Yiddish play, "Schmendrick". His recent Broadway plays include "Night Over Taos", "Success Story", "Alien Corn", "Men in White", "Gold Eagle Guy", "Awake and Sing", "Paradise Lost", "Johnny Johnson", "Golden Boy", "Rocket to the Moon", "The Russian People", "Two on an Island", "Common Ground", "Beggars Are Coming to Town", and "Dunnigan's Daughter".

ADLER, STELLA. Born in N. Y. C., Feb. 10, 1902. Educated New York University. Received her stage training with her father, Jacob Adler, and with Maria Ouspenskaya. First stage appearance with her father in 1906 at the Garden Theatre, N. Y., in "Broken Hearts". Recent stage roles include "House of Connelly", "Success Story", "Night Over Taos", "Gentlewoman", "Gold Eagle Guy", "Awake and Sing", "Paradise Lost", and more recently "Sons and Soldiers", "Pretty Little Parlor", and the revival of "He Who Gets Slapped".

AHERNE, BRIAN. Born in King's Norton, Worcestershire, England, May 2, 1902. Educated at Malvern College. On Feb. 9, 1931, made his Broadway debut in "The Barretts of Wimpole Street". Also appeared with Katharine Cornell in "Lucrece", "Romeo and Juliet", and "Saint Joan". In 1937 he played Iago in "Othello". Between 1937 and 1945 he spent most of his time in Hollywood. Returned to Broadway for a revival of "The Barretts of Wimpole Street" and "The French Touch".

ALEXANDER, CRIS. Born in Tulsa, Okla., 1920. Only Broadway appearances: revival of "Liliom" and "Onthe Town."

ALEXANDER, KATHARINE. Born in Ft. Smith, Arkansas, 1901. Made Broadway bow in 1917 in "A Successful Calamity". Other appearances include "Little Accident", "Hotel Universe", "The Left Bank", "Letters to Lucerne", and "Little Brown Jug".

ALLEN, ROBERT. Born Mt. Vernon, N. Y., March 28, 1906. Educated N. Y. Military Academy and Dartmouth College. Spent fifteen years in movies, radio and stock companies. Appeared on Broadway in "Blessed Event", "A Few Wild Oats", "I Killed the Count", "Kiss Them for Me", and "Show Boat".

ALLEN, VERA. Born N. Y. C. Made her debut on New York stage 1925 in "The Grand Street Follies". Recent appearances include "At Home Abroad", "The Show Is On", "Susan and God", "A Woman's a Fool to Be Clever", "Glorious Morning", "The Philadelphia Story", and "Strange Fruit".

ALLGOOD, SARA. Born Dublin, Ireland, October 31, 1883. Recent N. Y. stage appearances include "Storm Over Patsy", "Shadow and Substance", and a revival of "Juno and the Paycock".

ALTMAN, FRIEDA. Born Boston, Mass., August 18, 1904. Educated at Wellesley College. Received her stage training at American Laboratory Theatre. Made her Broadway debut in "Carrie Nation", and since then has appeared in "We, the People", "Another Language", "Spring Song", "Paradise Lost", "Guest in the House", "Ah, Wilderness", "Hickory Stick", "Days to Come", "Counsellor-at-Law", "The Naked Genius", "A Joy Forever", and "Little Brown Jug".

Ellis Baker Henry Bernard Beverly Bayne

AMES, ADRIENNE. Born in Ft. Worth, Texas. Well known as a motion picture and radio actress. Made her Broadway debut in "Beggars Are Coming to Town".

AMES, MICHAEL. Born in N. Y. C., Nov. 10, 1914. Educated at Washington State College. Stage training at Pasadena Playhouse. Broadway plays: "Quiet, Please", "My Sister Eileen", "Storm Operation", "Mrs. Kimball Presents", and "That Old Devil".

ANDERS, GLENN. Born Los Angeles, California, Sept. 1, 1890. Educated at Columbia University. Made first appearance on the stage with Los Angeles stock company in 1910 as Lennox in "Macbeth". Since then he appeared in "Just Around the Corner", "Civilian Clothes", "Scrambled Wives", "The Ghost Between", "The Demi-Virgin", "Hell-Bent for Heaven", "Bewitched", "They Knew What They Wanted", "The Constant Nymph", "Murray Hill", "Strange Interlude", "Dynamo", "Farewell to Arms", "Hotel Universe", "Tomorrow and Tomorrow", "Another Language", "Love and Babies", "I Was Waiting for You", "False Dreams, Farewell", "Moor Born", "A Sleeping Clergyman", "On to Fortune", "If This Be Treason", "There's Wisdom in Women", "The Masque of Kings", "Three Waltzes", "Call It a Day", and more recently "Skylark", "Get Away, Old Man", "Career Angel", and "Soldier's Wife".

ANDERSON, JUDITH. Born in Adelaide, Australia, Feb. 10, 1898. Made her American debut in 1918 with a stock company on Fourteenth Street in N. Y. Made Broadway bow in 1923 in "Peter Weston". Since then has appeared in "Cobra", "The Dove", "Behold the Bridegroom", "Anna", "Strange Interlude", "As You Desire Me", "Mourning Becomes Electra" (on tour), "Firebird", "Conquest", "The Mask and the Face", "The Drums Begin", "Come of Age", "Divided by Three", "The Old Maid", the Queen to John Gielgud's Hamlet, "Family Portrait" and more recently Lady Macbeth to Maurice Evans' Macbeth.

ANDREWS, HARRY. Born in Tonbridge, Kent, England, November 10, 1911. Received his stage training with the Liverpool Repertory Company. Made his American debut 1936 in Gielgud's "Hamlet". Only other Broadway appearance with Old Vic's Repertory Company.

ANGLIN, MARGARET. Born Ottawa, Canada, April 3, 1876. Educated at Loretto Abbey, Toronto, and Convent of the Sacred Heart, Montreal. Made N. Y. debut 1894 in "Shenandoah". Since then her brilliant career included roles in "Mrs. Dane's Defence", "Diplomacy", "The Importance of Being Earnest", "Camille", "The Marriage of Kitty", "Frou-Frou", "The Second Mrs. Tanqueray", "The Great Divide", "The Awakening of Helena Richie", "Antigone", "Green Stockings", such Shakespearean roles as Viola, Katherine, Rosalind, and Cleopatra, "Beverly's Balance", "Iphigenia in Tauris", "Electra", "The Woman in Bronze", "Foot-Loose", "A Woman of No Importance", and more recently "Fresh Fields".

ARCHER, JOHN. Born in Osceola, Neb., May 8, 1915. Educated at Hollywood High School and U. of Southern California. Played in many motion pictures before coming to N. Y. for his stage debut in "The Odds on Mrs. Oakley". "One-Man Show", "A Place of Our Own" and "The Day Before Spring" followed.

ARCHIBALD, WILLIAM. Born March 7, in Trinidad, he came to the United States in 1937 and joined the Weidman Dance Group. His first Broadway show was "One for the Money". Since then he has appeared in "Two for the Show", "All in Fun", "Dancing in the Streets", Youman's "Ballet Revue", "Laughing Room Only", and "Concert Varieties". He also wrote the book and lyrics of "Carib Song".

ARNO, SIG. Born in Hamburg, Germany, Dec. 27, 1895. Was well known in the Berlin Theatre until Hitler came into power. He then went to Hollywood. "Song of Norway" marks his N. Y. debut.

AVERY, PHYLLIS. Born in N. Y. C. Made her Broadway bow in 1940 revival of "Charley's Aunt". Since then she has appeared in "Letters to Lucerne", "Little Darling", "Ask My Friend Sandy", "The Doughgirls", "Winged Victory", and "Brighten the Corner."

BACLANOVA, OLGA. Born in Moscow, Russia, August 19, 1899. Educated Cherniavsky Institute, Moscow. A product of the Moscow Art Theatre, she made her Broadway debut in 1925 in "Lysistrata". Subsequently appeared in "Carmencita and the Soldier", "Love and Death", and "The Fountain". In 1926 played the Nun in "The Miracle" on tour. Recent appearances include "Grand Hotel", "Twentieth Century", and "Idiot's Delight" on tour, and in New York, "$25 a Hour", "Murder at the Vanities", "Mahogany Hall", and "Claudia".

BAILEY, PEARL. Has appeared in vaudeville and many night clubs. "St. Louis Woman" marks her Broadway debut.

145

Frank Baxter

Barbara Bel Geddes

Alan Baxter

BAINTER, FAY. Born in Los Angeles, Dec. 7, 1892. Made her Broadway bow 1912 in "The Rose of Panama". After several seasons of stock at Albany, Des Moines, and Toledo, she made her first N. Y. hit in "Arms and the Girl". This was followed by "The Willow Tree", "The Kiss Burglar", "East Is West", "The Lady Cristilinda", "The Other Rose", "The Dream Girl", "The Enemy", a revival of "The Two Orphans", "First Love", "Fallen Angels", revivals of "She Stoops to Conquer", "The Beaux Stratagem", "The Admirable Crichton", and "Lysistrata". More recently she appeared in "Jealousy", "For Services Rendered", as Topsy in Players Club revival of "Uncle Tom's Cabin", "Move On, Sister", "Dodsworth", and "The Next Half Hour".

BAKER, ELLIS. Born Muskegan, Mich., Oct. 26, 1898. Educated at St. Agatha. Made stage debut at age of five in "The Point of View". Supported such stars as Grace George and Otis Skinner. Recent N. Y. appearance in "I Like It Here".

BANE, PAULA. Born in Seattle, Wash. Educated at Cornish School of Arts. Received her stage training at Seattle Repertory Playhouse. Made her Broadway debut in "Seven Lively Arts". "Call Me Mister" followed.

BANKHEAD, TALLULAH. Born in Huntsville, Ala., January 31, 1902. Made N. Y. stage debut in 1918 in "Squab Farm". This was followed by "Footloose", "39 East", "Nice People", "Everyday", "Danger", "Her Temporary Husband", and "The Exciters". In 1923 went to London, where she became the toast of the town. Her London appearances included "The Dancers", "This Marriage", "The Creaking Chair", "Fallen Angels", "The Green Hat", "Scotch Mist", "They Knew What They Wanted", "The Gold Diggers", "The Garden of Eden", "Blackmail", "Mud and Treacle", and "Her Cardboard Lover". Returning to America in 1930, she made a series of motion pictures for Paramount before reappearing on Broadway in 1933 in "Forsaking All Others". This was followed by "Dark Victory", "Something Gay", "Reflected Glory", and revivals of "Rain", "The Circle", and "Anthony and Cleopatra". Next came "The Little Foxes", "Clash by Night", "The Skin of Our Teeth", and "Foolish Notion". Her recent screen appearances include "Lifeboat" and "A Royal Scandal".

BARNARD, HENRY. Born in Birmingham, Ala., March 1, 1921. Has appeared on Broadway in "The First Million", "Theatre", "Othello", "Mr. January and Mrs. X", "The Searching Wind", "The Wind Is 90", and "Home of the Brave".

BARRY, GENE. Born in N. Y. C., June 14, 1919. Educated at New Utrecht High School. Appeared on Broadway in Revival of "New Moon", "Rosalinda", "The Merry Widow", "Catherine Was Great", and "The Would-Be Gentleman".

BARRY, JOHN. Born in Amsterdam, N. Y., June 13, 1915. Educated at Univ. of Pennsylvania, where he sang with the Mask and Wig. Spent two years with the Philadelphia Opera Co. Made Broadway debut in 1945 in "Follow the Girls".

BARRYMORE, ETHEL. Born in Philadelphia, August 15, 1879. Made N. Y. debut at the Empire Theatre, January 25, 1894, in "The Rivals". Among the many plays she has appeared in are "Captain Jinks of the Horse Marines", "Cousin Kate", "Alice Sit-by-the-Fire", "Mid-Channel", "The Twelve Pound Look", "A Slice of Life", "Tante", "The Shadow", "Our Mrs. McChesney", "The Lady of the Camellias", "The Off-Chance", "Belinda", "Declassée", "Claire de Lune", "The Laughing Lady", "A Royal Fandango", "The Constant Wife", "Scarlet Sister Mary", "The Kingdom of God", "The Love Duel", and revivals of "The Second Mrs. Tanqueray", "The School for Scandal", and "Trelawney of the Wells". Her recent Broadway engagements include "An International Incident", "Ghost of Yankee Doodle", "Whiteoaks", "Farm of Three Echoes", "The Corn Is Green", "Embezzled Heaven", and toured in "The Joyous Season". Made several early silent pictures, also "Rasputin and the Empress", "None but the Lonely Heart", and "The Circular Staircase".

BARTON, JAMES. Born Gloucester, N. J., November 1, 1890. Spent his early years in stock companies in Middle West and South. Made his first Broadway appearance in "The Passing Show of 1919". Since then appeared in "The Last Waltz", "The Rose of Stamboul", "Dew Drop Inn", "The Passing Show of 1924", "Artists and Models", "No Foolin'", "Sweet and Low", and on tour in "Burlesque". More recently he devoted a great deal of his time to "Tobacco Road".

BASEHART, RICHARD. Born in Zanesville, Ohio. Received his stage training at the Hedgerow Theatre. Broadway appearances include "Counterattack", "Othello", "Take It as It Comes", "Ramshackle Inn", "Hickory Stick", and "The Hasty Heart".

BAXTER, ALAN. Born East Cleveland, Ohio, Nov. 19, 1908. Educated Cleveland Heights public schools, Williams College, and Yale University (Dept. of Drama, 1930-32). Appeared on Broadway in "Lone Valley", "Men in White", "Gold Eagle Guy", "Black Pit", "Winged Victory", "Home of the Brave", and "The Voice of the Turtle". Has also played in many motion pictures.

146

Ralph Bellamy   John Beal   Lyle Bettger

BAXTER, FRANK. Born Bola Cynwyd, Pa., March 25, 1922. Received his stage training at Barter Theatre, Abingdon, Va., and the Neighborhood Playhouse. Has appeared on Broadway in "Janie", revival of "R.U.R.", and "Catherine Was Great".

BAYNE, BEVERLY. Born in Minneapolis, Minn., November 22, 1896. Educated at Hyde Park High School, Chicago. Was famous star in silent pictures with the old Essanay and Metro film companies. Has appeared on Broadway in "Gala Night", "Piper Paid", "Claudia", and "I Like It Here".

BEAL, JOHN. Born in Joplin, Mo., Aug. 13, 1909. Educated Joplin High School and Univ. of Pennsylvania. Studied for stage with Jasper Deeter at the Hedgerow Theatre. Made his first appearance on the N. Y. stage as a page in "Give Me Yesterday" in 1931. Subsequently appeared in "Wild Waves", "Another Language", "She Loves Me Not", "Russet Mantle", "Soliloquy", "Miss Swan Expects", and "Liberty Jones". Returned to Broadway after a session in Hollywood and the U. S. Army in "The Voice of the Turtle".

BEAL, ROYAL. Born in Brookline, Mass., and educated at Harvard. He has appeared in "Take a Chance", "Elizabeth the Queen", "All That Glitters", "Page Miss Glory", "Noah", "Boy Meets Girl", "The Lady Has a Heart", "Susanna and the Elders", "Without Love", and "Kiss and Tell." Most recent appearance in "Woman Bites Dog".

BEECHER, JANET. Born in Jefferson City, Mo., Oct. 21, 1884. Made her N. Y. debut as a walk-on in 1904 in "The Two Orphans". Among her many successes were "The Concert", "The Lottery Man", "The Purple Road", "The Great Adventure", "Fair and Warmer", "Call a Doctor", "A Bill of Divorcement", "Courage", and "Men Must Fight". In 1932 she deserted Broadway for Hollywood, where she remained twelve years, appearing in many films. Since her return played in "Slightly Scandalous" and "The Late George Apley".

BEL GEDDES, BARBARA. Born in N. Y. C., Oct. 31, 1923. Her first stage role was as a walk-on in "School for Scandal" with Ethel Barrymore at the Clinton (Conn.) Playhouse. Made her Broadway bow in "Out of the Frying Pan". Since then has appeared in "Little Darling", "Nine Girls", "Mrs. January and Mr. X", and "Deep Are the Roots".

BELLAMY, RALPH. Born in Chicago, Ill., June 17, 1904. Made his Broadway debut in 1929 in "Town Boy". This was followed by "Roadside" which led him to Hollywood, where he remained, making pictures from 1930 until 1943 when he returned to Broadway to act in "Tomorrow the World". This season found him in "State of the Union".

BELMORE, BERTHA. Born in Manchester, England, December 20, 1882. Made her debut in America in 1910 with the Ben Greet Players. Played Portia in William Faversham's production of "The Merchant of Venice". Was in "Ziegfeld Follies" of '27 and '28 and in Ziegfeld's "Show Boat". Recent appearances include "Heart of a City", "By Jupiter", "Rhapsody", and "Antigone".

BERGNER, ELISABETH. Born in Vienna, August 22, 1900. Began stage career at fourteen. Toured with a Shakespearean company in Germany and Austrian provinces. Later became one of Max Reinhardt's greatest stars. In 1934 went to England, where she starred in such films as "Catherine the Great", "Escape Me Never", "As You Like It", and "Dreaming Lips". Her Broadway appearances were in "Escape Me Never" and "The Two Mrs. Carrolls".

BERLE, MILTON. Born in New York City, July 12, 1908. Educated at the Professional Children's School. Was a child actor in silent motion pictures. New York stage appearances include "Saluta", "Life Begins at 8:40", and "Ziegfeld Follies".

BEST, PAUL. Born in Berlin, Germany, August 30, 1908. His Broadway appearances include "La Vie Parisienne", "Rosalinda", "The Merry Widow", "Firebrand of Florence", and "The Day Before Spring".

BETTGER, LYLE. Born in Philadelphia, February 13, 1915. Educated at Haverford School, Haverford, Pa. Received his stage training at American Academy of Dramatic Arts. Appeared on Broadway in "Brother Rat", "Dance Night", "The Flying Gerardos", "The Moon Is Down", "All for All", "The Eve of St. Mark", and "Oh Brother!"

BIRCH, PETER. Born in New York City, December 11, 1922. Made his debut as a dancer with the Fokine Ballet. "One Touch of Venus", "Dream With Music", and "Carousel" are his Broadway engagements to date.

BISHOP, RICHARD. Born in Hartford, Conn., April 27, 1898. Educated at the Hartford Public School. Broadway plays include "Missouri Legend", "An International Incident", "Sweet Mystery of Life", "One Good Year", "Where Do We Go From Here?" "Key Largo", and "I Remember Mama".

147

Anita Bolster   Ray Bolger   Mary Boylan

BLACKMERE, SIDNEY. Born in Salisbury, N. C., July 13, 1894. Educated at Warrenton High School and Univ. of North Carolina. Made Broadway debut in 1917 in "The Morris Dance". Other plays include "Not So Long Ago", "The Mountain Man", "The Love Child", "The Moon-Flower", "Quarantine", "The Carolinian", "Love in a Mist", "The Springboard", "Mima", "Chicken Every Sunday", and "Round Trip".

BLAKELY, GENE. Born Osceola, Iowa, June 8, 1922. Educated at Univ. of Wisconsin. Toured in "The Eve of St. Mark" and "Janie". Made his Broadway debut in "Brighten the Corner".

BLISS, HELENA. Born in St. Louis, Mo., Dec. 31, 1919. Educated at Hosmer Hall and Washington University. Plays on Broadway: "Very Warm for May", "Du Barry Was a Lady", and "Song of Norway".

BOLAND, MARY. Born in Philadelphia, Jan. 28, 1885. Educated at Sacred Convent in Detroit. Received her stage training in stock. Was John Drew's leading lady in "Inconstant George", "Smith", "The Single Man", "The Perplexed Husban", "The Will", "The Tyranny of Tears", and "Much Ado About Nothing". Her important appearances on Broadway include "My Lady's Dress", "Clarence", "The Torch Bearers", "Meet the Wife", "Cradle Snatchers", "Women Go On Forever", "Ada Beats the Drum", "The Vinegar Tree", and more recently "Jubilee", and the Theatre Guild revival of "The Rivals".

BOLGER, RAY. Born in Dorchester, Mass., January 10, 1906. Made Broadway bow in 1926 in "The Merry World". Followed by "A Night in Paris", "The Passing Show of 1926" (on tour), "Heads Up", "George White's Scandals of 1931", "Life Begins at 8:40", "On Your Toes", "Keep Off the Grass", and "Three to Make Ready".

BOLSTER, ANITA. Born in Glenlohane, Ireland, August 28, 1900. Received her stage training at the Abbey Theatre, Dublin. Made her Broadway bow in 1939 in "Where There's a Will". "Lady in Waiting" followed, and a session in Hollywood. Returned to Broadway for "Pygmalion".

BOOTH, SHIRLEY. Born in N. Y. C. Broadway plays include "Bye, Bye, Baby", "Laff That Off", "The War Song", "Too Many Heroes", "Three Men on a Horse", "Excursion", "The Philadelphia Story", "My Sister Eileen", and "Hollywood Pinafore".

BOURNEUF, PHILIP. Has appeared on Broadway in "Dead End", "Two Bouquets", "On the Rocks", "One for the Money", "Native Son", "The Rivals",

"Moon Vine", "Winged Victory" and "Flamingo Road".

BOWERS, KENNY. Born in Jersey City, N. J., March 10, 1923. Educated at Jersey City Grammar and Junior High. Has appeared on Broadway in "Best Foot Forward" and "Annie Get Your Gun".

BOYD, SYDNEY. Born in Glasgow, Scotland, Feb. 25, 1901. Educated at Battle Creek High School. Has appeared in vaudeville, minstrel, night clubs, and radio. "Are You With It?" marked his Broadway debut.

BOYLAN, MARY. Born in Plattsburg, N. Y. Educated at Mount Holyoke College. Received stage training at Barter Theatre. Made Broadway bow 1938 in "Dance Night". This was followed by "Susanna and the Elders", "The Walrus and the Carpenter", the revival of "Our Town" and "Live Life Again".

BRAHAM, HORACE. Born London, July 29, 1896. Educated City of London School. Made N. Y. debut 1914 as Lentulus in "Androcles and the Lion". His N. Y. appearances include "The Shatter'd Lamp", "Too Many Boats", the Le Gallienne revival of "L'Aiglon", "Journey to Jerusalem", and "Antigone".

BRANDO, MARLON. Born in Bangkok, Siam, April 3, 1924. Served his apprenticeship at the New School of Social Research. Made Broadway debut Oct. 19, 1944, in "I Remember Mama". This season saw him in "Truckline Cafe" and as Marchbanks in the Cornell revival of "Candida".

BRENT, ROMNEY. Born in Saltillo, Mexico, January 26, 1902. Made his New York debut in 1922 in "He Who Gets Slapped". Played in "The Simpleton of the Unexpected Isles" and revivals of "Ghosts" and "Bird in Hand". Returned to Broadway for "The Deep Mrs. Sykes", after serving 2 years as a Captain in the Canadian army. Appeared this season in "The Winter's Tale".

BRIAN, DONALD. Born St. John's, Newfoundland, Feb. 17, 1877. Made first N. Y. appearance 1899 in "On the Wabash". His important appearances on Broadway include "Little Johnny Jones", "Forty-five Minutes from Broadway", "The Merry Widow", "The Dollar Princess", "The Siren", "The Marriage Market", "The Girl from Utah", "Sybil", "Her Regiment", "The Girl Behind the Gun", "Buddies" and more recently "Fly Away Home" and "Very Warm for May".

BRIGGS, BUNNY. Born in N. Y. C., Feb. 26, 1923. Made his Broadway debut in "Are You With It?"

Eric Brotherson   Betty Bruce   Lawrence Brooks

BRISSON, CARL. Born Copenhagen, Denmark, Dec. 24, 1895. Only N. Y. legitimate appearance in 1936 in "Forbidden Melody". Recently had great success as a night club entertainer.

BROOKE, RALPH. Born N. Y. C., May 22, 1920. Educated at Columbia. Studied acting with Max Reinhardt. Appeared on Broadway in the Olivier-Leigh production of "Romeo and Juliet", "All in Favor", and "A Sound of Hunting".

BROOKS, DAVID. Born in Portland, Ore., Sept. 24, 1917. Educated at U. of Washington. Won a scholarship at the Curtis Institute. Sang baritone roles with the Philadelphia Opera Company. Made his first Broadway appearance in "Bloomer Girl".

BROOKS, LAWRENCE. Born in Westbrook, Maine, Aug. 7, 1915. Educated at Westbrook High School. Received his stage training with the Portland Maine Players. Made first appearance on Broadway in "Song of Norway."

BROTHERSON, ERIC. Born in Chicago, Ill., May 10, 1911. Educated Univ. of Wisconsin. Made his Broadway debut 1937 in "Between the Devil". Other appearances include "Set to Music", "Lady in the Dark", and "My Dear Public".

BROWN, JOE E. Born Holgate, Ohio, July 28, 1892. Started theatrical career as a child actor, and for a time was a professional baseball player. Later appeared in road companies of "Listen Lester", and made first N. Y. C. appearance in 1920 in "Jim Jam Jems". Also appeared in "The Greenwich Village Follies", "Betty Lee", "Captain Jinks", "Twinkle, Twinkle", "Elmer the Great", "Square Crooks", and "Shore Leave". Since 1928 appeared frequently in the films. In current season returned to stage and played in road company of "Harvey".

BRUCE, BETTY. Born in N. Y. C., May 2, 1921. Educated at the Professional Children's School. As a child, danced in the Metropolitan Opera ballets. Appeared on Broadway in "Boys from Syracuse", "Keep Off the Grass", "High Kickers", "Something for the Boys", and "Up in Central Park".

BRUCE, CAROL. Played bits in "Nice Going" and George White's "Scandals". Made more recent appearances in "Louisiana Purchase" and "Show Boat".

BRUNS, MONA. Born Nov. 26, in St. Louis, Mo., and educated at St. Mary's Convent, Belleville. Made her debut on Broadway 1918 in "Chin-Chin". More recently has appeared in "Wednesday's Child", "Chicken Every Sunday", and "Born Yesterday".

BRYANT, JOHN. Born Dixon, Ill., Aug. 10, 1916. Educated at Northwestern University. Received training at Goodman Theatre, Chicago. Evans' G. I. "Hamlet" marked his N. Y. debut.

BRYANT, MARDI. Born in Milwaukee, Wis., March 4, 1924. Educated at Downer Seminary, Milwaukee, and Lawrence College. Appeared in summer stock and radio before making N. Y. debut in "I Like It Here".

BRYANT, NANA. Born in Cincinnati, Ohio. Appeared in N. Y. in "The Firebrand", "The Wild Rose", "The Circus Princess", "A Connecticut Yankee", "The First Apple", and more recently "Marriage Is for Single People".

BUKA, DONALD. Born in Cleveland, Ohio, 1921. Discovered by the Lunts while he was a drama student at Carnegie Tech. Toured a full season with the Lunts, then played a minor role in the Maurice Evans-Helen Hayes production of "Twelfth Night". Replaced Richard Waring in the role of Morgan Evans opposite Ethel Barrymore in "The Corn Is Green". Broadway appearances include "Bright Boy", "Helen Goes to Troy", "Sophie", and "Live Life Again."

BULOFF, JOSEPH. Born in Russia in 1901. Made N. Y. debut in "Don't Look Now". Other Broadway appearances: "Call Me Ziggy", "To Quito and Back", "The Man From Cairo", "Morning Star", "Spring Again", "My Sister Eileen", and "Oklahoma".

BURKE, BILLIE. Born Washington, D. C., Aug. 7, 1885. First stage appearance was in England in 1903 in "The School Girl". Made N. Y. debut opposite John Drew in "My Wife" in 1907. First starred in "Love Watches", and later played in "Mrs. Dot", "The Runaway", "The Mind-the-Paint Girl", "The Amazons", "The Land of Promise", "Jerry", "The Intimate Strangers", "Rose Briar", "The Marquise", "The Happy Husband", "Family Affairs", and "The Truth Game". First appeared in silent films in 1916, and since 1936 has appeared in many pictures. Seen on Broadway more recently in "This Rock" and "Mrs. January and Mr. X".

BURKE, GEORGIA. Born in Atlanta, Ga., Feb. 27, 1908. Educated at Claflin University of Orangeburg, S. C. Began her stage career in Lew Leslie's first edition of "Blackbirds". Appearances followed in "Five-Star Final", "Savage Rhythm", "In Abraham's Bosom", "Old Man Satan", "They Shall Not Die", "Mamba's Daughter", "Cabin in the Sky", "No Time for Comedy", "Sun Field", "Decision", and "Anna Lucasta".

Donald Buka   Mardi Bryant   Bill Callahan

BURKE, MAURICE. Born in Hartford, Conn., April 13, 1902. Made Broadway appearances in "Ladies of Creation", "Helena's Boys", "The Marquise", "Kiss the Boys Goodbye", "In Time to Come", "The Doughgirls", and "Up in Central Park".

BURKE, WALTER. Well known to radio audiences for his work in "Dr. Christian". Appeared on N. Y. stage in "The Eve of St. Mark", "The World's Full of Girls", "Sadie Thompson", and "Up in Central Park".

BURR, ANNE. Born in Boston, Mass., June 10, 1920. First N. Y. appearance was in "Plan M". This was followed by "Native Son", "Dark Eyes", "Lovers and Friends", "While the Sun Shines", and "The Hasty Heart".

BURRY, SOLEN. Born in Russia, Sept. 10, 1902. Has appeared on Broadway in "Having Wonderful Time", "The World We Make", "Arsenic and Old Lace", "Cafe Crown", "Native Son", and "Devils Galore".

BUSLEY, JESSIE. Born Albany, N. Y., March 10, 1869. First appeared with R. B. Mantell's company and made her first N. Y. success in "The Bells of Haslemere" in 1894. Later she played in "Charley's Aunt", "The New Boy", "The Sporting Duchess", "Hearts Are Trumps", "The Girl With the Green Eyes", "Little Mary", "Mice and Men", "The Admirable Crichton", "Mrs. Leffingwell's Boots", "The Painful Predicament of Sherlock Holmes". For a time she was seen in vaudeville, and later appeared in "In the Bishop's Carriage", "Beverly of Graustark", "Old Heidelberg", "Half a Husband", "Pollyanna", "A Young Man's Fancy", "Daisy Mayme", "The Bride the Sun Shines On", and "Alien Corn". More recently has appeared in "The Great Waltz", "First Lady", "The Women", "The Birds Stop Singing", "Over 21", and "The Rich Full Life".

BUTLER, JOHN. Born in Greenwood, Miss., Sept. 29, 1920. Educated at Univ. of Mississippi. Studied dancing with Eugene Loring and Martha Graham. Appeared on Broadway in "On the Town", "Hollywood Pinafore", and "Oklahoma".

BUTTERWORTH, CHARLES. Born South Bend, Ind., July 26, 1896. Studied at Notre Dame University and made stage debut in vaudeville in 1924. First N. Y. appearance was in 1926 in "Americana", and later he played in "Allez-Oop", "Good Boy", "Sweet Adeline", and "Flying Colors". Since 1936 has been active in films and radio. Recently returned to Broadway in "Count Me In" and "Brighten the Corner".

BYRON, PAUL. Born N. Y. C., Sept. 12, 1888. Made his Broadway debut 1919 in "Abraham Lincoln". Recently has appeared in "The Sap from Syracuse", "Prologue to Glory", "Ten Little Indians", and "Devils Galore".

CAHILL, LILY. Born in Texas, 1891. She made first stage appearance in 1909 in support of Mr. Leslie Carter in "Vasta Hearne". Later appeared in "Two Women", "The Concert", "Joseph and His Brethren", "Under Cover", "The Melody of Youth", "Rosamond", "Over Here", "The Purple Mask", "Opportunity", "So This Is London", "Lovely Lady", "Caprice", "The Tyrant", "As Husbands Go", "Chrysalis", "Alien Corn", "Women Kind", "And Be My Love", "Reunion in Vienna", "Rain From Heaven", "First Lady", and "Life With Father".

CALHERN, LOUIS. Born N. Y. C., Feb. 19, 189_. Appeared first as a child actor, and in 1914 went into stock. Played with Margaret Anglin and served in First World War. Reappeared in N. Y. C. 1922 in "The White Peacock", and later appeared in "The Czarina", "Roger Bloomer", "The Song and Dance Man", "Cobra", "In a Garden", "Hedda Gabler", "The Woman Disputed", "Up the Line", "A Distant Drum", "The Love Duel", "The Tyrant", "Give Me Yesterday", "Brief Moment", "Dinner at Eight", "Birthday", "Agatha Calling", "Hell Freezes Over", and "Robin Landing". More recently he has appeared in "Life With Father", "The Great Big Doorstep", "Jacobowsky and the Colonel", and "The Magnificent Yankee".

CALLAHAN, BILL. Born in N. Y. C., August 2_, 1926. Educated at Barnard School for Boys, Fordham Prep School and Fordham University. Made his Broadway debut January 7, 1943, in "Something for the Boys". Appearances in "Mexican Hayride" and "Call Me Mister" followed.

CAMP, RICHARD. Born in Perry, Iowa, April 1_, 1923. Educated at Univ. of Iowa and Drake University. Appeared on Broadway in "Junior Miss", "Three's a Family", "Men to the Sea", "Little Women", and "This Too Shall Pass".

CAMPBELL, SANDY. Born N. Y. C., April 22, 192_. Educated at Kent School and Princeton. Played "Life With Father" and "Othello" on the road. "The Rugged Path" marked his Broadway debut.

CANNON, MAUREEN. Born in Chicago, Ill., December 3, 1926. Only Broadway appearances made in "Best Foot Forward" and "Up in Central Park". Sang the leading roles in "Irene", "No, No, Nanette", and "Hit the Deck" with the St. Louis Municipal Opera Company.

Frances Carson   Anthony Carr   Rosita Cosio

CANTOR, EDDIE. Born N. Y. C., January 13, 1893. Made first stage appearance in vaudeville in 1907, and later appeared in "Not Likely", "Canary Cottage", "The Midnight Revue", "The Ziegfeld Follies" 1917-19, "Broadway Brevities of 1920", "Make It Snappy", "Follies" of 1927, "Kid Boots", "Whoopee", and more recently "Banjo Eyes". In recent years has devoted most of his time to radio.

CARR, ANTHONY. Born in Reading, Pa., Feb. 6, 1924. Educated at Albright College. Received his stage training in summer stock. Made his Broadway debut in "Dear Ruth", June 1, 1945.

CARROLL, LEO G. Born in Weedon, England, 1892. Made stage debut 1911 as a walk-on in "Prisoner of Zenda". Came to America twenty years ago and made his N. Y. debut with Noel Coward in "The Vortex". Since then appeared in "The Constant Nymph", "The Perfect Alibi", "The Green Bay Tree", "Petticoat Fever", "The Masque of Kings", "The Two Bouquets", "Angel Street", and "The Late George Apley".

CARSON, FRANCES. Born in Philadelphia, April 1, 1895. Received her stage training in stock in Ottawa. Made N. Y. debut in 1914 in "Poor Little Thing". Then played leads in "The Bad Man", "The White Feather", and "The Hottentot". Went to London where she had great success for the past twenty years. Returned to the Broadway scene in 1944 in "Slightly Scandalous" and "The Visitor".

CHARLES, ZACHARY A. Born in N. Y. C. Made debut on Broadway Oct. 7, 1943, in "One Touch of Venus". Other N. Y. appearances include "Pick-Up Girl", "Live Life Again", and "Skydrift".

CHASE, ILKA. Born in New York City, 1900. First N. Y. stage role in "The Red Falcon". Among the other plays in which she has appeared are "Shall We Join the Ladies?" "Antonia", "Embers", "The Happy Husband", "The Animal Kingdom", "Forsaking All Others", "Days Without End", "While Parents Sleep", "Wife Insurance", "Small Miracle", "Revenge With Music", "Keep Off the Grass", "Beverly Hills", "The Women", and "In Bed We Cry".

CHASE, STEPHEN. Born in Huntington, Long Island, N. Y., April 11, 1902. Educated at Loomis School, Windsor, Conn. Until 1941 appeared on stage as Alden Chase. Among his many appearances include "Wooden Kimono", "The Silver Cord", "Zeppelin", "People on the Hill", "Reflected Glory", "Uncle Harry", and "Strange Fruit".

CHATTERTON, RUTH. Born N. Y. C., Dec. 24, 1893. Made first appearance on stage in stock in Washington in 1909. N. Y. debut in 1911 in "The Great Name", and since then she has appeared in "Standing Pat", "The Rainbow", "Daddy Long Legs", "Frederic Le Maitre", "Come Out of the Kitchen", "A Bit O' Love", "Perkins", "A Marriage of Convenience", "Moonlight and Honeysuckle", "Mary Rose", "La Tendresse", "The Changelings", "The Magnolia Lady", "The Little Minister", "The Man With the Load of Mischief", and "The Devil's Plum Tree". After a long session in Hollywood, returned to stage in "West of Broadway" on the road. "Leave Her to Heaven" marked her return to Broadway. This was followed by a long tour of "Private Lives". "Second Best Bed" was her most recent appearance in N. Y.

CHISHOLM, ROBERT. Born Melbourne, Australia, April 18, 1898. Received his stage training at Royal Academy of Music, London. Made his Broadway debut in "Golden Dawn". Since then New Yorkers have seen him in "Sweet Adeline", "Luana", "Nina Rosa", "The Two Bouquets", "Higher and Higher", "Knights of Song", "Without Love", the revivals of "A Connecticut Yankee" and "The Merry Widow". "On the Town" and "Billion Dollar Baby" were his latest appearances.

CHRISTI, VITO. Born in Philadelphia, Dec. 28, 1924. Educated at Central School for Boys, Philadelphia. Received his stage training with Neighborhood Players and in stock at Plymouth, Mass. Made first Broadway appearance in "Hickory Stick", followed by "Pick-Up Girl", "The Tempest", and "The Rugged Path".

CHRISTIANS, MADY. Born Vienna, Austria, January 19, 1900. Before coming to this country achieved fame in many of Max Reinhardt's productions. Made her N. Y. stage debut in "The Divine Drudge". Since then has appeared in Orson Welles' production of "Heartbreak House", Maurice Evans' productions of "Hamlet" and "Henry IV", "The Lady Who Came to Stay", "Watch on the Rhine", and "I Remember Mama".

CHRISTIE, AUDREY. Born in Chicago, Ill., June 27, 1911. Educated at Yates Grammar School and Lake View High School of that city. Her Broadway plays number "Follow Thru", "Sweet and Low", "Sailor Beware", "Sons of Guns", "The Women", "I Married an Angel", "Banjo Eyes", "Without Love", "The Voice of the Turtle", and "The Duchess Misbehaves".

CLAIRE, INA. Born Washington, D. C., Oct. 15, 1895. Educated Holy Cross Academy. First stage appearance was in vaudeville in 1907. Later appeared in "Jumping Jupiter", "The Quaker Girl", "The Honeymoon Express", "Lady Luxury", "The Follies" of 1915 and 1916, "Polly With a Past",

Zachary A. Charles   Audrey Christie   Vito Christi

"The Gold Diggers", "Bluebeard's Eighth Wife", "The Awful Truth", "Grounds for Divorce", "The Last of Mrs. Cheyney", "Our Betters", "Biography", "Ode to Liberty", "Love Is Not So Simple", "Barchester Towers", "Once Is Enough", and "The Talley Method".

CLANTON, RALPH. Born in Fresno, Calif., September 11, 1914. Received his stage training at the Pasadena Community Playhouse. Made Broadway appearances in "Victory Belles", Evans' production of "Macbeth", George Colouris' production of "Richard III", "A Strange Play", "Othello" with Paul Robeson, and "Lute Song".

CLARISSA. Born in Colorado, June, 1924. Appeared on Broadway in "Three Waltzes", "Something for the Boys", and a revival of "The Desert Song".

CLARK, BOBBY. Born in Springfield, Ohio, June 16, 1888. With his partner, Paul McCullough, appeared for years in vaudeville. Made his first N. Y. appearance at Madison Square Garden with Ringling Bros. Circus in 1905. New Yorkers have also seen him in "The Music Box Revue" (1922), "The Ramblers", "Strike Up the Band", "Here Goes the Bride", "Walk a Little Faster", "Thumbs Up", and, more recently, "Ziegfeld Follies", "Streets of Paris", the Players' revival of "Love for Love",

"All Men Are Alike", the Theatre Guild's revival of "The Rivals", "Star and Garter", "Mexican Hayride", and "The Would-Be Gentleman".

CLARK, WALLIS. Received his stage training with the Sarah Thorne Stock Company in England where he was born March 2, 1888. His N. Y. appearances include "Justice", "Jane Clegg", "Peter Ibbetson", "The Betrothal", "The Light of the World", "Dulcy", "The Exile", "Tweedles", "The Laughing Lady", "White Cargo", "Zeppelin", the last Gillette revival of "Sherlock Holmes", and more recently "Suspect" and "Life With Father".

CLARKE, PHILIP. Born in London, England, Aug. 4, 1904. Educated at Cathedral St. John the Divine. Received his stage training touring with the Ben Greet Players. Made his Broadway debut 1912 in "Joseph and His Brethren". Recent N. Y. appearances include, "Macbeth", "Native Son", and "On Whitman Avenue".

CLAYTON, JAN. Born in New Mexico, she turned to Hollywood where she has appeared in stock. "Carousel" marked her Broadway debut. This season she appeared in the revival of "Show Boat".

CLEVELAND, JEAN. Born in Fayetteville, N. Y., Aug. 6, 1903. Made Broadway bow January 1, 1918, in "Cohan's Revue". Other plays include

Stephen Chase   Clarissa   Wallis Clark

Helen Craig

Montgomery Clift

Katharine Cornell

"Shubert's Gaieties", "My Fair Ladies", "House of Fear", and more recently, "Mexican Hayride" and "Devils Galore".

CLIFF, OLIVER. Born in Sebring, Ohio, June 4, 1918. Educated at Los Angeles City College. Appeared on Broadway in the Olivier-Leigh production of "Romeo and Juliet", "Othello", "Jacobowsky and the Colonel", "Ten Little Indians", "Antigone", and Miss Cornell's 1946 revival of "Candida".

CLIFT, MONTGOMERY. Born in Omaha, Neb., October 17, 1920. Made his N. Y. stage bow in "Fly Away Home". Since then has appeared in "Jubilee", "Yr. Obedient Husband", "Dame Nature", "The Mother", "There Shall Be No Night", "Mexican Mural", "Skin of Our Teeth", "Our Town" (City Center revival), "The Searching Wind", "Foxhole in the Parlor", and "You Touched Me".

COBURN, CHARLES. Born Macon, Georgia, June 19, 1877. First played stock in Chicago and made N. Y. C. debut in 1901 in "Up York State". Later he toured in "The Christian", after which he organized the Coburn Shakespearean Players, which he maintained for many years, and with which he played many roles. He also played in "The Coming of Mrs. Patrick", "The Yellow Jacket", "The Imaginary Invalid", "The Better 'Ole", "French

Leave", "The Bronx Express", "So This Is London", "The Farmer's Wife", "Trelawney of the Wells", "The Right Age to Marry", "Old Bill", "M.P.", "The Tavern", "Falstaff", "The Plutocrat", "The First Legion", "The County Chairman", and "Sun Kissed". Recently toured with "Merry Wives of Windsor".

COCA, IMOGENE. Born in Philadelphia, November 18, 1908. Began her N. Y. career in the chorus of "When You Smile". Other appearances include "Garrick Gaieties", "Flying Colors", "New Faces", "Fools Rush In", "Who's Who", "Folies Bergere", "Straw Hat Revue", "All in Fun", and "Concert Varieties".

COLLINGE, PATRICIA. Born in Dublin, Ireland, September 20, 1894. Made her debut in England and her first N. Y. C. appearance was in 1908 in "The Queen of the Moulin Rouge". Later she played in "The Girl and the Wizard", "The Blue Bird", "The Thunderbolt", "Everywoman", "The New Henrietta", "Billy", "He Comes Up Smiling", "The Show Shop", "A Regular Business Man", "Pollyanna", "Tillie", "Golden Days", "Just Suppose", "Tarnish", "The Dark Angel", "Venus", "The Lady With the Lamp", "Another Language", "Autumn Crocus", "To See Ourselves", and "The Little Foxes".

Blanche Collins

John Compton

Ronnie Cunningham

Mason Curry   Lili Darvas   Jean Darling

COLLINS, BLANCHE. Born N. Y. C., May 12, 1918. Educated at Columbia University. Appearances on Broadway include "Scarlet Sister Mary", "Strike Me Pink", "The Cradle Will Rock", and Maurice Evans' G.I. version of "Hamlet".

COLLINS, CHARLES. Born in Oklahoma. Made his N. Y. debut with his father-in-law, Fred Stone in "Ripples". Since then has played in "As Thousands Cheer", "Say When", "Sea Legs", "Hooray for What", and the revival of "The Red Mill".

COLLINS, RUSSELL. Born in Indianapolis, Ind., October 6, 1897. Educated at Indiana State University and Carnegie Tech Drama School. The Cleveland Playhouse was the scene of his stage training. On Broadway has had important roles in "Men in White", "Gold Eagle Guy", "Waiting for Lefty", "Johnny Johnson", "Star Wagon", "Here Come the Clowns", "Mornings at Seven", "The Heavenly Express", "The Moon Is Down", revival of "Juno and the Paycock", "In Time to Come", "Carousel", and the revival of "He Who Gets Slapped".

COLMAN, BOOTH. Born in Portland, Ore., March 8, 1923. Educated Univ. of Washington. Received stage training at Showboat and Penthouse Theatres, Seattle. Made debut on Broadway in "The Assassin". Maurice Evans' G.I. "Hamlet" followed.

COMDEN, BETTY. Born in Brooklyn and educated at Brooklyn Ethical Culture School, Erasmus Hall, and N. Y. U. Spent five years with The Revuers, a night club act. "On the Town" marked her N. Y. stage debut.

COMPTON, JOHN. Born in Lynchburg, Tenn., June 21, 1923. Educated at Washington University. Received stage training with little theatre groups. "The Ryan Girl" marked his Broadway debut.

CONKLIN, PEGGY. Born Dobbs Ferry, N. Y., 1912. First N. Y. C. appearance in 1929 in "The Little Show". Later she was seen in "His Majesty's Car", "Purity", "Old Man Murphy", "Hot Money", "Mademoiselle", "The Party's Over", "The Ghost Writer", "The Pursuit of Happiness", "The Petrified Forest", "Co-Respondent Unknown", "Yes, My Darling Daughter", "Miss Swan Expects", "Casey Jones", "Mr. and Mrs. North", "Alice In Arms", and "Feathers in a Gale".

CONROY, FRANK. Born in Derby, Eng., October 14, 1890. Made his first professional appearance at the Spa Theatre, Scarborough, 1908, as the second murderer in "Macbeth". Made his N. Y. debut at the Bandbox Theatre in 1915 in "Helena's Husband". Other plays include "The Bad Man", "The

Constant Wife", and more recently, "On Borrowed Time", "The Little Foxes", "For Keeps", and "One Man Show."

COOK, DONALD. Born in Portland, Ore., September 26, 1901. Educated at Portland Grade and High Schools. Dramatic training at the Kansas City Community Theatre. Plays on Broadway: "N. Y. Exchange", "Paris Bound", "Rebound", "Wine of Choice", "American Landscape", "Skylark", "Claudia", and "Foolish Notion".

COOPER, ANTHONY KEMBLE. Born London, Eng., Feb. 6, 1908. Is a descendant of the Kembles, one of England's oldest acting families. Made his first N. Y. appearance in 1925 in "Lass O' Laughter". Since then has played in "The School for Scandal", "His Majesty's Car", "The Command to Love", "Quiet Please", "Anne of England", "Hay Fever", "Mary of Scotland", "Age 26", "Sheppey", and "Ten Little Indians".

COOPER, DULCIE. Born in San Francisco, Nov. 3, 1907. Educated Hollywood High School and Columbia University. Appeared in N. Y. in "Happily Ever After", "Peter Flies High", "Courage", "The Little Spitfire", "Married and How", "Three's a Family", and "Brighten the Corner".

COOPER, GLADYS. Born Lewisham, Eng., Dec. 18, 1888. After a distinguished career on the British stage, made her N. Y. C. debut in 1934 in "The Shining Hour", and since then has appeared on Broadway in "Othello", "Macbeth", "Call It A Day", "White Christmas", and "Close Quarters".

COOPER, MELVILLE. Born in Birmingham, Eng., Oct. 15, 1896. Made his Broadway debut in "Laburnum Grove". Since then had leading roles in "Jubilee", "The Merry Widow", "While the Sun Shines", "Firebrand of Florence", and the recent revival of "Pygmalion".

CORBETT, LEONORA. Born London, Eng., June 28, 1908. Made her British debut in 1927. Only N. Y. appearance to date was "Blithe Spirit" in 1941.

COREY, WENDELL. Born Dracut, Mass., March 20, 1914. Made his Broadway debut May 26, 1942 in "Comes the Revelation". Since then New Yorkers have seen him in "The Life Of Reilly", "Strip for Action", "The First Million", "It's Up to You", "Jackpot", "Manhattan Nocturne", "But Not Goodbye", "The Wind Is Ninety", and "Dream Girl".

CORNELL, KATHARINE. Born Berlin, Germany, Feb. 16, 1898. Made her N. Y. debut November 13, 1916 with the Washington Square Players in

154

Susan Douglas   Milton Douglas   Katherine Dunham

Bushido". Plays since then include "Nice People", "A Bill of Divorcement", "Will Shakespeare", "The Enchanted Cottage", "Casanova", "The Way Things Happen", "The Outsider", "Tiger Cats", "Candida", "The Green Hat", "The Letter", "The Age of Innocence", "Dishonored Lady", "The Barretts of Wimpole Street", "Lucrece", "Alien Corn", "Romeo and Juliet", "Flowers of the Forest", "St. Joan", "The Wingless Victory", "Herod and Miriamne", "No Time For Comedy", "The Doctor's Dilemma", "The Three Sisters", "Lovers and Friends", and "Antigone".

COSIO, ROSITA. Born in Puerto Rico, Dec. 11, 1933. Educated Professional Children's School. Made her Broadway debut in "Skydrift".

COSSART, ERNEST. Born Cheltenham, Eng., Sept. 24, 1876. First appeared on the English stage in 1896, and made his N. Y. C. debut in 1910 in "The Girls From Gottenburg". Has played in "Mrs. Dot", "Love Among the Lions", "Marrying Money", "Androcles and the Lion", and many other plays. Recent appearances include "Reunion in Vienna", "The Mask and the Face", "Accent On Youth", "Madame Bovary", and "Devils Galore".

COTTER, JAYNE. Born in WuChang, China, Sept. 27, 1923. Educated at St. Margaret's School. Has appeared on Broadway in "Spring Again", "Another Love Story", "The Odds on Mrs. Oakley", "Many Happy Returns", and "Kiss Them for Me".

COTTON, FRED AYRES. Born in Central City, Neb. Educated Hastings College and Columbia University. Stage training in stock at Elitch's Gardens Theatre, Denver, Colo. Played on Broadway in "Swing Your Lady", "Tide Rising", "The Brown Danube", "Winged Victory", and "State of the Union".

COULOURIS, GEORGE. Born Manchester, Eng., Oct. 1, 1903. Appeared first in N. Y. C. in "The Novice and the Duke" in 1929. Later he played in "The Apple Cart", "The Late Christopher Bean", "Best Sellers", "Mary of Scotland", "Valley Forge", "Blind Alley", "St. Joan", "Ten Million Ghosts", "Julius Ceasar", "The Shoemaker's Holiday", "Madame Capet", "The White Steed", and "Richard II".

COWL, JANE. Born Boston, Mass., Dec. 14, 1890. Made her debut in 1903 in "Sweet Kitty Bellairs". Among her most successful roles were "Within the Law", "Common Clay", "Lilac Time", "Smilin' Through", "Romeo and Juliet", and "The Road to Rome". Her more recent plays were "Rain From Heaven", "First Lady", "The Merchant of Yonkers", and "Old Acquaintance".

COWLES, CHANDLER. Born in New Haven, Conn., Sept. 29, 1917. Educated at Yale. Received stage training at Bennington Theatre School and Dramatic Worskshop of the New School. Made his Broadway debut April 18, 1946 in "Call Me Mister".

CRAIG, HELEN. Born in San Antonio, Tex., May 13, 1914. Educated at Scarborough School, N. Y. Received her stage training at Hedgerow Repertory Theatre. Made her debut on Broadway January 16, 1936 in "Russet Mantle". Other plays on Broadway include "New Faces", "Julius Caesar", "Soliloquy", "Family Portrait", "The Unconquered", "Johnny Belinda", "As You Like It", and "Lute Song".

CRANDALL, EDWARD. Born in Brooklyn, March 2, 1904. Educated at Hackley School, Tarrytown, and Oxford University, England. Plays on Broadway: "Young Woodley", "The Play's the Thing", "Heavy Traffic", "Our Betters", "Lady of the Orchids", "Give Me Yesterday", "Absent Father", "A Party", "Small Miracle", and "Kiss Them For Me".

CUMMINGS, CONSTANCE. Born in Seattle, Wash., May 15, 1910. Was a chorus girl in "The Little Show". Other N. Y. engagements include "Treasure Girl", "This Man's Town", "June Moon", "Accent On Youth", "Young Madame Conti", "Madame Bovary", "If I Were You", and "One Man Show".

CUMMINGS, VICKI. Has appeared on Broadway in "The Time, the Place, the Girl", "Sunny River", "Mrs. Kimball Presents", "Lady in Danger", and "The Voice of the Turtle".

CUNNINGHAM, RONNIE. Born in Washington, D. C., Nov. 3, 1923. Educated at Academy-of-the-Immaculate Conception. Plays on Broadway include "Banjo Eyes", "Lady Says Yes", and "Marinka".

CURRY, MASON. Born in Halifax, N. S., Canada, June 28, 1908. Educated at Music Acadia University. Appeared on Broadway in "Ramshackle Inn", and "The Magnificent Yankee".

DA COSTA, MORTON. Born in Philadelphia, March 7, 1914. Educated Temple University. Appeared on Broadway in "The Skin of Our Teeth", "It's a Gift", "Stovepipe Hat", and Evans' G.I. "Hamlet".

DAILEY, JACK. Born in Fall River, Mass., Aug. 31, 1883. Made his Broadway bow in 1926 in "The Noose". Appeared in "Hot Cha", the original "Show Boat" (1927), and the 1932 and 1946 revivals of "Show Boat".

Judith Evelyn   David Ellin   Nanette Fabray

DALE, MARGARET. Born in Philadelphia, March 6, 1880. Made stage debut at Girard Avenue Theatre of that city in 1897. Was leading lady to such famous stars as John Drew, E. H. Sothern, Henry Miller, William H. Crane, and George Arliss. More recently has appeared in "Dinner at Eight", "Tovarich", "Lady in the Dark", and "The Late George Apley".

DALYA, JACQUELINE. Born N. Y. C., Aug. 3, 1919. Has appeared in many motion pictures. "The French Touch" marked her Broadway debut.

DANIELL, HENRY. Born London, March 5, 1894. First appeared on the stage in England in 1913, and in N. Y. C. in 1921 in "Claire de Lune". After that he alternated acting in both countries and his most outstanding work here has been in "Serena Blandish", and "Kind Lady". More recently he has appeared in "Murder Without Crime", "Lovers and Friends", and "The Winter's Tale".

DANIELS, DANNY. Born in Albany, N. Y., Oct. 25, 1924. Appeared on Broadway in "Best Foot Forward", "Count Me In", and "Billion Dollar Baby".

DARLING, JEAN. Born in Santa Monica, Calif., August 23, 1925. Was the little girl with the golden curls in "Our Gang" comedies some years ago. Made her Broadway debut in "Count Me In". Since then has appeared in "Marianna", and "Carousel".

DARVAS, LILI. Born in Budapest, Hungary, and is the wife of Ferenc Molnar. Discovered by Max Reinhardt, she played in many of his famous productions. Made her first English-speaking appearance in America in "Criminals" at the New School. "Soldier's Wife" marked her Broadway debut. She was seen last in Evans' G.I. "Hamlet".

DAVIS, EVELYN. Born in N. Y. C., October 31, 1906. Began her stage career in "Run, Lil' Children". Since then New Yorkers have seen her in "Two on an Island", "Vickie", "The Perfect Marriage", and "Flamingo Road".

DAVIS, NANCY. Born in N. Y. C., July 6, 1921. Educated at Smith College. Played at Summer Theatres in Oconomowoc, Wisc., and Bass Rock, Mass. Made her Broadway bow February 6, 1946 in "Lute Song".

DAVIS, RICHARD. Born in Boston, Mass. Made his first stage appearance in "Siege". After a session in Hollywood and the Army, returned to Broadway in "Kiss Them For Me".

DEE, FRANCES. Born in Los Angeles, Calif., November 26, 1907. Has appeared in many motion pictures. "The Secret Room" marked her first appearance on N. Y. stage.

DEERING, OLIVE. Made her N. Y. debut in "Girls in Uniform". Since then has appeared in "Growing Pains", "Picnic", "Daughters of Atreus", "The Eternal Road", "Winged Victory", and "Skydrift".

DE NEERGAARD, BEATRICE. Born in Baltimore, Md., December 7, 1910. Made Broadway debut in "John Gabriel Borkman" (1926). Was with Civic Repertory Theatre from 1926 to 1933. More recent appearances were made in "Squaring the Circle", Nazimova's revival of "Ghosts", "Arms For Venus", "Letters to Lucerne", "Land of Fame", and "Live Life Again."

DERWENT, CLARENCE. Born in London, March 23, 1884. Appeared on the English stage for fifteen years before making his American debut. New Yorkers have seen him in Ziegfeld's production, "The Three Musketeers", "Serena Blandish", "Topaze", "Mary of Scotland", "The Doctor's Dilemma", "The Pirate", "Lady in Danger", and "Lute Song". Recently elected President of Actors' Equity Association.

DEW, EDWARD. Born in Sumner, Wash., January 29, 1909. Educated at Pomona College. Appeared in many motion pictures. Made his Broadway debut in the revival of "The Red Mill".

DIGGES, DUDLEY. Born in Dublin, Ireland, 1880. Has appeared in many plays, among which are "John Ferguson", "Jane Clegg", "The Guardsman", "Ned McCobb's Daughter", "Marco Millions", "Pygmalion", "Liliom", "The Doctor's Dilemma", "Major Barbara", "The Brothers Karamazov", "Juarez and Maximilian", "A Month in the Country", "The Masque of Kings", "On Borrowed Time", Cornell's revival of "Candida", "Listen, Professor!", and "The Searching Wind".

DIXON, JEAN. Born in Waterbury, Conn., July 14, 1905, and attended St. Margaret's School. Her many Broadway engagements include "Golden Days", "To the Ladies", "The Wooden Kimono", "Behold the Bridegroom", "Heavy Traffic", "June Moon", "Once in a Lifetime", "Dangerous Corner", "Heat Lightning", "George Washington Slept Here", and "The Deep Mrs. Sykes".

DOBSON, JAMES. Born in Greenville, Tenn. Made Broadway bow 1943 in "Life With Father". Also appeared in "Love on Leave", "The Day Will Come", "The Firebrand of Florence", and "The Wind is Ninety".

DOUCET, CATHARINE. Born Richmond, Va. Broadway appearances include "The Devil in the Cheese", "The Royal Family", "The Perfect Alibi", "Dynamo", "Camel Through a Needle's Eye", "Topaze", "As Husbands Go", "When Ladies Meet", "Last Stop", and "Oh Brother!"

156

Melchor Ferrer   Arlene Francis   Eddie Foy Jr.

DOUGLAS, KIRK. Made his initial Broadway appearance as a singing Western Union boy in "Spring Again". Since then has had roles in "Kiss and Tell", Cornell's revival of "The Three Sisters", "Alice In Arms", "The Wind Is Ninety", and "Woman Bites Dog".

DOUGLAS, MARGARET. Born in Dallas, Tex. Broadway roles: "Russet Mantle", "The Women", "Out From Under", "Yesterday's Magic", "Eight O'Clock Tuesday", "The Damask Cheek", and "Bloomer Girl".

DOUGLAS, MILTON. Born in N. Y. C., December 7, 1901. Received his stage training in vaudeville, burlesque and nite clubs. Apppeared on Broadway in "Texas Guinan's Padlocks", "Summer Wines", and "Follow the Girls".

DOUGLAS, PAUL. Was better known as a sports announcer on radio until his outstanding success in "Born Yesterday". Only other N. Y. stage appearance made in "Double Dummy" in 1935.

DOUGLAS, SUSAN. Born in Czechoslovakia in 1926. Educated in her native country and England. Appeared extensively on radio until her Broadway debut March 20, 1946 in "He Who Gets Slapped".

DOWLING, EDDIE. Born Woonsocket, R. I., December 9, 1895. Broadway audiences have seen him in "She Took a Chance", "Ziegfeld Follies" (1919), "The Magic Melody", "The Girl in the Spotlight" "Hello America", "The Fall Guy", "Sally, Irene and Mary", "Honeymoon Lane", "Sidewalks of New York", "The Rainbow Man", "Thumbs Up", "Here Come the Clowns", "The Time of Your Life", "Hello Out There", "Magic", and "The Glass Menagerie".

DOWNING, JOE. Born N. Y. C., June 26, 1904. Appeared on Broadway in "Garrick Gaieties", "Farewell to Arms", "Shooting Star", "Heat Lightning", "Page Miss Glory", "Ceiling Zero", "Dead End", and "Ramshackle Inn".

DOWNS, JOHNNY. Born in Brooklyn, N. Y. Was one of the original kids in "Our Gang" comedies. Appeared on Broadway in "Strike Me Pink", "Growing Pains", and "Are You With It?"

DRAKE, ALFRED. Born in Brooklyn, N. Y., 1914. Has appeared on Broadway in "White Horse Inn", "Babes in Arms", "The Two Bouquets", "Straw Hat Revue", "One For the Money", "Two For the Show", "Out of the Frying Pan", "As You Like It", "Yesterday's Magic", "Oklahoma", and "Sing Out, Sweet Land".

DULO, JANE. Born in Baltimore, Md., October 13, 1918. As Jane Dillon appeared in N. Y. nite clubs. "Are You With It?" marks her Broadway debut.

DUNCAN, AUGUSTIN. Born San Francisco, Calif., April 17, 1873. Made his first N. Y. C. appearance with Richard Mansfield in "Henry V" in 1900. He has had a long career both here and in England, and has produced and staged plays as well as acted in them. He appeared this Season in "Lute Song".

DUNHAM, KATHERINE. Born in Chicago, June 22, 1912. Graduate of the Univ. of Chicago. Appeared on Broadway in "Cabin In The Sky", "Tropical Revue", and "Carib Song".

DUNNOCK, MILDRED. Born in Baltimore, Md., and educated at Goucher College and Columbia University. She was Queen Margaret in George Coulouris' revival of "Richard III" and more recently played in "Only the Heart", "Foolish Notion" and "Lute Song".

DUPREE, MINNIE. Born in San Francisco, Calif., January 19, 1875. Her long and varied stage career began in 1887. Her first big success was scored in "The Road to Yesterday". More recent engagements include "The Charm School", "The Old Soak", "The Eldest", "Arsenic and Old Lace", "Dark Eyes", and "Last Stop".

EBSEN, BUDDY. Educated at Rollins College, Fla. First N. Y. job in chorus of "Whoopee". Since then has appeared in "Flying Colors", "The Ziegfeld Follies of 1936", "Yokel Boy", the Chicago company of "Good Night Ladies", and the revival of "Show Boat".

EDEN, TONY. Born in N. Y. C., March 31, 1927. Educated at Fairfax Hall, Va., and Ethical Culture, N. Y. Plays on Broadway: "Up in Central Park", "Dark of the Moon", and "Devils Galore".

EDNEY, FLORENCE. Born in London, England, June 2, 1879. First N. Y. stage appearance in 1906 in "The Price of Money", and since then has appeared in many plays, both here and in England. Recently she has appeared in "Waterloo Bridge", "Topaze", "Twentieth Century", "Barchester Towers", and "Angel Street".

EFFRAT, JOHN. Graduate of Ohio State Univ. Appeared on Broadway in "Autumn Hill", "The American Way", "Holy Night", and "I Like It Here".

EGGERTH, MARTA. Born in Budapest, Hungary, 1915 Broadway appearances were in "Higher and Higher" and "Polonaise".

Russell Hardie   Margaret Hayes   George Hall

ELLERBE, HARRY. Born in Columbia, S. C., Jan. 13, 1905. Made his initial Broadway appearance in "Philip Goes Forth". Other roles followed in "Thoroughbred", "Strange Orchestra", "The Man on Stilts", "The Mad Hopes", the Nazimova revivals of "Ghosts" and "Hedda Gabler", "Outward Bound", "Whiteoaks", and "Sleep, My Pretty One".

ELLIN, DAVID. Born in Montreal, Canada, Jan. 10, 1925. Received theatrical training at the American Academy of Dramatic Arts. "Swan Song" marked his Broadway debut.

ELLIOTT, CECIL. Born New Bedford, Ill., Oct. 25, 1900. Educated at Dixon College. Made Broadway debut in "One Touch of Venus". Since then was seen in "A Boy Who Lived Twice".

ELLIOTT, JAMES. Born N. Y. C., Jan. 15, 1924. Plays on Broadway as an actor: "Junior Miss", "Men to the Sea", and "Love's Old Sweet Song". Has the title of the youngest producer on Broadway, where he has presented "Arlene", "The First Million", and "Too Hot for Maneuvers".

EVANS, MAURICE. Born Dorchester, Dorset, England, June 3, 1901. Made first professional appearance in England in 1926 in "The Orestia" of Aeschylus. First N. Y. appearance was as Romeo in Katharine Cornell's "Romeo and Juliet" in 1935. Since then has appeared in "Saint Joan", "St. Helena", "Richard II", "Henry IV, Part I", "Hamlet", "Twelfth Night", "Macbeth", and his G. I. version of "Hamlet".

EVANS, WILBUR. Born in Philadelphia, 1905. Educated at the Curtis Institute of Music. Made his stage debut at the Curran Theatre, San Francisco, in 1930 in "Bambina". Was in the Carnegie Hall productions of "The Merry Widow" and "New Moon". Also sang in the New Opera Co. production of "La Vie Parisienne". His most recent roles were in "Mexican Hayride" and "Up in Central Park".

EVELYN, JUDITH. Born in Seneca, S. D., March 20, 1913. Made her Broadway debut in "Angel Street". Also appeared in "The Overtons" and "The Rich Full Life".

EVEREST, BARBARA. Born in London, June 9, 1890. First appeared in England in 1912 in "The Voysey Inheritance", and had a long and successful career in that country. Made her American debut in "Anne of England", and since then appeared in "Sheppey".

FABRAY, NANETTE. Began her career with Fanchon and Marco unit in vaudeville. Has appeared on Broadway in "Meet the People", "Let's Face It", "By Jupiter", "Jackpot", and "Bloomer Girl".

FAY, FRANK. Born in San Francisco, Nov. 17, 1897. Made his stage debut at seven in "Babes in Toyland". Was also a child actor with Rose Stahl in "The Chorus Lady". Later he appeared with Sir Henry Irving and E. H. Sothern in Shakespearian roles. In the golden days of vaudeville he was one of the most popular headliners at the Palace. Starred in "Jim Jam Jems", "Frank Fay's Fables", and the recent vaudeville show, "Laugh Time". "Harvey" marks his first straight play since his child actor days.

FELLOWS, EDITH. Veteran of almost 500 movies. Appeared on road in "Janie", and made her Broadway debut in "Marinka".

FERGUSON, ELSIE. Born N. Y. C., Aug. 19, 1883. First appearance was in the chorus of "The Belle of New York" in 1900. Among her outstanding successes are "Such a Little Queen", "The Strange Woman", "Outcast", and "Sacred and Profane Love". More recently she has appeared in "The House of Women", "Scarlet Pages", and "Outrageous Fortune".

FERRER, JOSE. Born in Puerto Rico, 1909. Educated at Princeton. Plays on Broadway: "Spring Dance", "Brother Rat", "How to Get Tough About It", "Missouri Legend", "Mamba's Daughter", "Key Largo", a revival of "Charley's Aunt", "Vickie", and "Othello". More recently he played "Cyrano de Bergerac" on the road.

FERRER, MELCHOR. Educated at Princeton. Played on Broadway in revival of "Kind Lady", and "Strange Fruit".

FIELD, BETTY. Born Boston, Mass., Feb. 8, 1918. Studied at the American Academy of Dramatic Art, but her first role was in London in 1934 in "She Loves Me Not". In N. Y. she has appeared in "Page Miss Glory", "Three Men on a Horse", "Room Service", "Angel Island", "If I Were You", "What a Life", "The Primrose Path", "Two on an Island", and "Flight to the West". More recently she has been seen in "A New Life", "Voice of the Turtle", and "Dream Girl".

FIELD, ROBERT. Born in Attleboro, Mass., March 25, 1916. Educated at Deerfield Academy and Tufts College. Made his Broadway bow in 1937 in "Babes in Arms". Other N. Y. engagements include "Knickerbocker Holiday", "Higher and Higher", "The Merry Widow", the title role in revival of "Robin Hood", and "The Day Before Spring".

FLETCHER, LAWRENCE. Born in Canton, Ohio, March 5, 1902, and educated at Howe School, Howe, Ind. Started his footlight career with the Stuart

Robert Healy   Herbert Heyes   Gordon Heath

Walker Company in Canton, Ohio. Broadway appearances include "Another Language", "Subway Express", "Sailor Beware", "Boy Meets Girl", "Spring Again", Orson Welles' "Julius Caesar", "Janie", "Hickory Stick", "The Man Who Had All the Luck", "Signature", "Too Hot for Maneuvers", and "The Rugged Path".

FONTANNE, LYNN. Born in London, 1887. She made first stage appearance in "Alice Sit by the Fire" with Ellen Terry in 1905. First seen in N. Y. in 1910 in "Mr. Preedy and the Countess". Among her more important plays are "Dulcy", "The Guardsman", "The Goat Song", "At Mrs. Beam's", "The Second Man", "Strange Interlude", "Caprice", "Elizabeth the Queen", "Reunion in Vienna", "Design for Living", "Idiot's Delight", "Amphytrion 38", a revival of "The Sea Gull". More recently she appeared in "There Shall Be No Night", "The Pirate", and "O Mistress Mine".

FORBES, BRENDA. Born in London, England. Made her American debut with Katharine Cornell in "The Barretts of Wimpole Street". Since then she has appeared in "Candida", "Lucrece", "Flowers of the Forest", "Pride and Prejudice", "Storm Over Patsy", "Heartbreak House", "One for the Money", "Two for the Show", "Yesterday's Magic", "The Morning Star", "Suds in Your Eye", and "Three to Make Ready".

FORBES, EDWARD. Born May 28, 1889 in Chicago. Made Broadway debut in 1918 with Sir Herbert Tree in "Henry VIII". More recently he has been seen in "False Dreams, Farewell", "Cue for Passion", "The Willow and I", "Sons and Soldiers", and "Jeb".

FORBES, RALPH. Born in London, England, Sept. 30, 1902. Made his Broadway debut in 1924 in "Havoc". Since then has had leading roles in "The Man With the Load of Mischief", "Stronger Than Love", the revivals of "The Doctor's Dilemma", and "A Kiss for Cinderella", "A Highland Fling", "The Visitor", and "Second Best Bed". He has also played in over fifty films.

FORD, PAUL. Born in Baltimore, Md., Nov. 2, 1901. Educated at Dartmouth. Made Broadway debut in "Decision" on Feb. 4, 1944. Since then appeared in "Lower North", "Kiss Them for Me", and "Flamingo Road".

FOY, JR., EDDIE. Born in New Rochelle, N. Y., Feb. 4, 1905. Educated at St. Gabriel's School. Appeared on Broadway in "Smiles", "Show Girl", "Ripples", "Cat and the Fiddle", "At Home Abroad", "Orchids Preferred", and the revival of "The Red Mill".

FRANCINE, ANNE. Born Philadelphia, Pa. Well known as a night club entertainer. Made her Broadway debut in "Marriage Is for Single People".

FRANCIS, ARLENE. Born in Boston, Mass., made her N. Y. bow in Orson Welles' production of "Horse Eats Hat", and again was a member of his Mercury company in "Danton's Death". Made other appearances in "All That Glitters", "Journey to Jerusalem", "The Doughgirls", "The Overtons", and "The French Touch". Has her own radio program, "Blind Date".

FRANCIS, KAY. Born in Oklahoma City, Okla., Jan. 13, 1899. Made her N. Y. debut at Booth Theatre, Nov. 9, 1925, as Player Queen in modern dress version of "Hamlet". Since then she appeared in "Crime", "Venus", and "Elmer the Great" before commencing her film career in 1930. Returned to stage in 1945 and has been touring all season in "Windy Hill".

FRANKLIN, WILLIAM. Born Shaw, Miss., Aug. 18, 1906. Educated at the Chicago Conservatory of Music. Played on Broadway in the original "Swing Mikado", "Porgy and Bess", and "Carib Song".

FRANZ, EDUARD. Born in Milwaukee, Wis., Oct. 31, 1902. His first N. Y. performance was with the Provincetown Players in "The Saint". Broadway audiences have seen him recently in "Miss Swan Expects", "Farm of Three Echoes", "The Russian People", "Cafe Crown", "Outrageous Fortune", "The Cherry Orchard", "Embezzled Heaven", "The Stranger", and "Home of the Brave".

FREDERICKS, CHARLES. Born in Jackson, Miss. Received musical training at Musical College, Chicago. "Show Boat" marks his Broadway debut.

FREED, BERT. Born in N. Y. C., Nov. 3, 1919. Educated at Penn State. Appeared on Broadway in "Johnny 2x4", "Strip for Action", "Counterattack", "One Touch of Venus", "Firebrand of Florence", "Kiss Them for Me", and "The Day Before Spring".

GARDEN, DAVID. Born in Chicago, Ill., Nov. 7, 1932. Educated at Children's Professional School. Appeared on Broadway in "Kiss and Tell" and "Life With Father".

GARRETT, BETTY. Born in St. Joseph, Mo., May 23, 1919. Received her education at the Annie Wright Seminary, Tacoma, Wash., and her stage training at the Neighborhood Playhouse, N. Y. Made appearance on Broadway in "Of Thee We Sing", "Let Freedom Ring", "Something for the Boys", "Jackpot", "Laffing Room Only", and "Call Me Mister".

Michael Higgins   Ruby Hill   Betty Lou Holland

GAXTON, WILLIAM. Born San Francisco, Dec. 2, 1893. Educated at the Univ. of Calif. Made his first Broadway appearance in the second "Music Box Revue". Since then has played leading roles in "Betty Lee", "Miss Happiness", "All for You", and the original version of "A Connecticut Yankee". Teamed up with Victor Moore and starred with him in "Of Thee I Sing", "Let 'Em Eat Cake", "Anything Goes", "Leave It to Me", "Louisiana Purchase", "Hollywood Pinafore", and "Nellie Bly".

GEAR, LUELLA. Born in N. Y. C., Sept. 5, 1897. Made her Broadway debut in 1917 in "Love O' Mike". Since then has acted in "The Gold Diggers", "Elsie", "Poppy", "Queen High", "The Optimist", "Ups A-Daisy", "The Gay Divorcee", "Life Begins at 8.40", "On Your Toes", "Crazy With the Heat", "The Streets of Paris", "Count Me In", and "That Old Devil".

GEER, WILL. Born March 9, 1902, in Frankfort, Ind. Educated at Univ. of Chicago and Columbia University. His most recent appearances on Broadway include "Tobacco Road", "Abe Lincoln in Illinois", "The Cradle Will Rock", "Of Mice and Men", "Sophie", "Flamingo Road" and "On Whitman Avenue".

GEORGE, GRACE. Born N. Y. C., Dec. 25, 1879. Training at American Academy of Dramatic Arts. N. Y. debut, Standard Theatre, June 23, 1894, as a schoolgirl in "The New Boy". Among her famous roles are "Under Southern Skies", "Clothes", "Divorcons", "Sauce for the Goose", "The Truth", "The New York Idea", "Major Barbara", "Captain Brassbound's Conversion", "The 'Ruined' Lady", "The First Mrs. Fraser", "Mademoiselle", and more recently "Kind Lady", "Matrimony Pfd.", "Spring Again", and a revival of "The Circle".

GIBSON, DON. Born Waynesburg, Pa., March 25, 1917. Educated at Univ. of Washington, Seattle. Made his N. Y. debut in "Catherine Was Great", and since has played in "Sleep, My Pretty One", "Many Happy Returns", "Clover Ring", and "Oh, Brother!"

GILBERT, MERCEDES. Born July 26, in Jacksonville, Fla. Made her Broadway debut in 1923 in "The Lace Petticoat". Recent appearances include "The Green Pastures", "Mulatto", "The Little Foxes", "Morning Star", "The Male Animal", "The Searching Wind" and "Carib Song".

GILMORE, VIRGINIA. Born in El Monte, Calif., July 26, 1919. Made her Broadway debut, 1943, in "Those Endearing Young Charms". Since then had leading roles in "The World's Full of Girls", "Dear Ruth", and "Truckline Cafe".

GILLMORE, MARGALO. Born London, May 31, 1897. Studied for the stage at American Academy of Dramatic Arts, and made first N. Y. appearance in 1917 in "The Scrap of Paper". Appeared in "The Famous Mrs. Fair", "He Who Gets Slapped", "Outward Bound", "The Green Hat", "Berkeley Square", "The Barretts of Wimpole Street", "Flowers of the Forest", and "Valley Forge". More recently she has played in "The Women", "No Time for Comedy" and "State of the Union".

GISH, DOROTHY. Born Massillon, Ohio, March 11, 1898. Made her first stage appearance as a child actress in 1903 in "East Lynne". After an eminent career in the films she returned to the stage in 1928 in "Young Love". Since then she has appeared in "The Inspector-General", "Getting Married", "The Streets of New York", "The Pillars of Society", "The Bride the Sun Shines On", "Foreign Affairs", "Mainly for Lovers", "Brittle Heaven", "Missouri Legend", "Life With Father", "The Great Big Doorstep", and "The Magnificent Yankee".

GISH, LILLIAN. Born Springfield, Ohio, Oct. 14, 1896. First appeared on stage as a child of six, and in 1913 was seen in "The Good Little Devil". After a long and successful film career she returned to the N. Y. stage in 1930 in "Uncle Vanya". Since then she has played in "Camille", "Nine Pine Street", "The Joyous Season", "Within the Gates", "Hamlet", "The Star Wagon", "Dear Octopus", "Life With Father", and "Mr. Sycamore".

GIVNEY, KATHRYN. Born in Rhinelander, Wis. Has appeared in N. Y. in "The Behavior of Mrs. Crane", "Lost Horizons", "Fulton of Oak Falls", "If This Be Treason", "Little Dark Horse", "Somewhere in France", "Flowers of the Forest", "Among the Married", "Wallflower", "Good Night Ladies", "The Happiest Days" and "This, Too, Shall Pass".

GLASER, VAUGHAN. His recent appearances on Broadway include "Many Mansions", "What a Life", and "A Boy Who Lived Twice".

GOODNER, CAROL. Born in N. Y. C., 1904. Has appeared on Broadway in "They Walk Alone", "Let's Face It", "Blithe Spirit", "The Man Who Came to Dinner", "The Wookey", "The Family", "Lovers and Friends", and "Deep Are the Roots".

GORDON, RUTH. Born in Wollaston, Mass., Oct. 30, 1896. Educated at Quincy High School, and received her dramatic training at American Academy of Dramatic Arts. Made her stage debut at the Empire Theatre, N. Y. C., with Maude Adams in "Peter Pan" in 1915. Since then has played in "Seventeen", "Fall of Eve", "Saturday's Children",

Edward Hudson   Joy Hodges   Philip Huston

"Here Today", "Ethan Frome", "The Country Wife", "Serena Blandish", "A Doll's House", "The Strings, My Lord, Are False", and "Over 21".

GOUGH, LLOYD. Has appeared on Broadway in "Yellow Jack", "The Ghost of Yankee Doodle", "Shadow and Substance", "My Dear Children", "Tanyard Street", "Golden Wings", "Heart of a City", and "Deep Are the Roots".

GRAY, DOLORES. Born in Holywood, Calif., June 7, 1924. Made her Broadway debut in "Seven Lively Arts", followed by "Are You With It?"

GREAZA, WALTER. Born St. Paul, Minn., 1900. Educated at Univ. of Minnesota. In 1927 made his N. Y. bow in "Love in the Tropics". Since then he has played in "Remote Control", "Wednesday's Child", "Ceiling Zero", "To Quito and Back", "Room Service", "A New Life", "Wallflower", "The Visitor", and "The Overtons".

GREEN, MITZI. Born N. Y. C., Oct. 22, 1920. Made N. Y. debut in 1927 in vaudeville at Keith and Proctor's. First appearance on N. Y. legitimate stage in "Babes in Arms" in 1937 after a successful film career as a child star. This season starred in "Billion Dollar Baby".

GREGG, PETER. Born in Pittsburgh, Pa., Nov. 19, 1913. Educated at Carnegie Tech. Made Broadway debut in "Cue for Passion". Other Broadway plays include "Flight to the West", "Mr. Big", "The Doughgirls", and "The Assassin".

GWENN, EDMUND. Born London, Sept. 28, 1875. First appeared on stage in England in 1895 and had long career in that country. In 1935 he made Broadway bow in "Laburnum Grove". Since then as been seen in "The Wookey", "Sheppey", and "You Touched Me".

HACKETT, RAYMOND. Born N. Y. C., July 15, 1902. First appeared on the stage as a child actor in 1907. He made his grown-up debut in "The Copperhead" in 1918 and since then has appeared in "Cradle Snatchers", "The Trial of Mary Dugan", "Piper Paid", "Up Pops the Devil", "Nine Pine Street", and "Storm Over Patsy".

HAJOS, MITZI. Born Budapest, Hungary, April 27, 1891. Among her famous starring roles are "Sari", "Pom-Pom", "Head Over Heels", "Lady Billy", "The Magic Ring", "Naughty Riquette", and "The Madcap". More recently she appeared in "You Can't Take It With You" and "Mr. Big".

HALEY, JACK. Born Boston, Mass. First N. Y. stage appearance at Century Roof, May 21, 1924, in "Round the Town". Since then appeared in "Gay Paree", "Good News", "Follow Thru", "Free for All", "Take a Chance", and more recently "Higher and Higher".

HALL, GEORGE. Born in Toronto, Canada, Nov. 19, 1916. Received his stage training at the Neighborhood Playhouse. Formerly a member of the Martha Graham dance group, he made his Broadway debut in "Call Me Mister".

HAMILTON, NEIL. Born in Lynn, Mass., Sept. 9, 1897. Educated at West Haven High School, Conn. After modelling for many prominent artists, he began his stage career in 1919. Appeared on the road in "The Better 'Ole" with the Coburns, "The 'Ruined' Lady" with Grace George, "Artist's Life" with Peggy Wood and had a season with the Toledo stock company in 1921 and the Cecil Spooner Stock Co. in Brooklyn in 1922. That year D. W. Griffith discovered him and he played the lead in his first motion picture, "The White Rose". From 1922 until 1944 appeared in motion pictures. Returned to the stage for "Many Happy Returns" and "The Deep Mrs. Sykes". Recently he played "State of the Union" on the road.

HAMPDEN, WALTER. Born Brooklyn, June 30, 1879. Educated at Brooklyn Polytechnic Institute and Harvard. Made his stage debut in 1901 as a walk-on in F. R. Benson's Shakespearian company. Since then has appeared in most of Shakespeare's and Ibsen's plays, also "Caponsacchi" and "Cyrano de Bergerac". More recently he had roles in "Seven Keys to Baldpate", "The Heel of Achilles", "The Rivals", "The Strings, My Lord, Are False", "The Patriots", and "And Be My Love".

HANNEN, NICHOLAS. Born London, May 1, 1881. Studied for the stage under Rosina Filippi and made English debut in 1910. First appeared in N. Y. in 1915 in "The Doctor's Dilemma", and in 1905 played here in "Accent on Youth". Returned to N. Y. stage for the 1946 Old Vic engagement.

HARDIE, RUSSELL. Born in Griffin Mills, N. Y., May 20, 1906. Educated at St. Mary's College. After training with the Buffalo Stock Company, made his Broadway bow in "The Criminal Code". Since then has appeared in "Pagan Lady", "The Constant Sinner", "Happy Landing", "Remember the Day", "Sun Kissed", "Society Girl", "Saint Wench", "Roosty", "The Ghost of Yankee Doodle", "Primrose Path", "Under This Roof", "Snafu", and "Foxhole in the Parlor". On road he was in "The Doughgirls" and "My Sister Eileen". Recently he played in "Home of the Brave".

Ruth Hussey

Cedric Hardwicke

Frieda Inescort

HARDWICKE, SIR CEDRIC. Born in Lye, England, Feb. 19, 1893. Recent N. Y. appearances include "Promise", "The Amazing Dr. Clitterhouse", "Shadow and Substance", and "Antigone" and the 1946 revival of "Candida".

HARE, WILL. Born in Elkins, W. Va., March 30, 1919. Received his stage training with the American Actors' Theatre. His N. Y. appearances include "The Eternal Road", "The Moon Is Down", "Suds in Your Eyes", "Only the Heart", and "The Visitor".

HARRIGAN, WILLIAM. Born in N. Y. C., March 27, 1893. Educated at N. Y. Military Academy. Among the many plays he has been featured in are "The Acquittal", "Polly Preferred", "The Dove", "The Great God Brown", "Moon in the Yellow River", "Criminal at Large", "Paths of Glory", "Portrait of Gilbert", "Among Those Sailing", "Roosty", "The Happiest Days", "In Time to Come", "Pick-Up Girl", and the Chicago company of "Dear Ruth".

HART, RICHARD. Born April 14, 1915, in Providence, R. I., and educated at Brown Univ. His first stage experience was gained at the summer theatre at Tiverton, R. I. His only Broadway plays to date: "Pillar to Post" and "Dark of the Moon".

HAVOC, JUNE. Was a member of Anna Pavlowa's ballet troupe at three, and a veteran of Mack Sennett and Hal Roach comedies before she was six. For many years she was known as "Baby June, the Darling of Vaudeville". Her first Broadway show was "Forbidden Melody". This was followed by "Pal Joey", "Mexican Hayride", and "Sadie Thompson". More recently has been seen in "The Ryan Girl" and "Dunnigan's Daughter".

HAYDON, JULIE. Born in Oak Park, Ill., June 10, 1910. Educated at the Gordon School for Girls in Hollywood. New Yorkers have seen her in "Bright Star", "Shadow and Substance", "Time of Your Life", "Magic", "Hello Out There", and "The Glass Menagerie".

HAYES, HELEN. Born in Washington, D. C., Oct. 10, 1900. Educated at Sacred Heart Convent, Washington. Made her first appearance on the stage in her native city at the National Theatre in 1908 in "The Babes in the Wood". The following year made her N. Y. debut with Lew Fields in "Old Dutch". As a child actress played in "The Summer Widowers", "The Never Homes", "The Prodigal Husband", "Pollyanna", (on tour), "Penrod", "Dear Brutus", and "Clarence". Her first real grown-up role was in "Bab". This was followed by "The Wren", "Golden Days", "To the Ladies", "We Moderns", "Dancing Mothers", "Quarantine", "Caesar and Cleopatra", "Young Blood", "What Every Woman Knows", and "Coquette". More recently she has appeared in

"Mary of Scotland", "Victoria Regina", "Ladies and Gentlemen", "Twelfth Night", "Candle in the Wind", and "Harriet".

HAYES, MARGARET. Born in Baltimore, Md. Engagements in two Broadway plays, "I Must Love Somemone" and "Bright Rebel", preceded Hollywood, where she made several pictures. Returned to N. Y. stage in "Many Happy Returns", and was last seen in "Little Women".

HEALY, MARY. Born in New Orleans, La., and educated at St. Mary's Parochial School and Redemptorist High School of her native city. Broadway engagements: "Count Me In", "Common Ground", and "Around the World".

HEALY, ROBERT. Born Jan. 19, 1922 in Kane, Pa. Educated at Carnegie Tech. He played summer stock in Middlebury, Vt., and during the war wrote, directed, and produced six full length G.I. productions. Made Broadway bow in "The Magnificent Yankee".

HEATH, GORDON. Born in N. Y. C., Sept. 20, 1918. Educated at City College and Hampden Institute. Received stage training with American Negro Theatre. "Deep Are the Roots" marks his Broadway debut.

HEMING, VIOLET. Born Leeds, England, Jan. 27, 1895. Educated at Malvern House School. All her acting has been in this country. She made her stage debut as Wendy in Frohman's children's company of "Peter Pan". Among her N. Y. plays are "Three Faces East", "Spring Cleaning", "This Thing Called Love", "Ladies All", a revival of "The Jest", "The Rivals", and "Trelawney of the Wells", "Love for Love", "Yes, My Darling Daughter", "Beverly Hills", and "And Be My Love".

HEPBURN, KATHARINE. Born Hartford, Conn., Nov. 9, 1909. Educated at Bryn Mawr College. N. Y. debut made Sept. 12, 1928, at Martin Beck Theatre in "Night Hostess", under the name Katherine Burns. This was followed by "These Days", "A Month in the Country", "Art and Mrs. Bottle", "The Warrior's Husband", "The Lake", "The Philadelphia Story", and "Without Love".

HERBERT, HUGH. Born in Binghampton, N. Y., Aug. 10, 1887. Educated at Cornell Univ. After an extensive career in Hollywood, returned to Broadway in "Oh, Brother!"

HEWITT, JOHN Q. Born in New Haven, Conn., Nov. 28, 1881. Among his many appearances on Broadway are "The Yellow Ticket", "The Little Rebel", "The Spider", "The Fall Guy", "Once in a Lifetime", and more recently "Live Life Again".

Dorothy Jarnac   Bill Johnson   Mary James

EYES, HERBERT. Born in Vader, W. N., Aug. 3, 889. Among his many appearances on Broadway re "Blind Youth", "Main Street", "The Wooden imono", and more recently "Happily Ever After" nd "State of the Union".

IGGINS, MICHAEL. Born in Brooklyn, N. Y., Jan. 0, 1921. Educated at Manhattan College. Made s Broadway debut with Miss Cornell in "An-gone".

ILL, RUBY. Born in Danville, Va., 1922. Made er Broadway debut March 30, 1946, in "St. Louis /oman".

HODGES, JOY. Born Jan. 29, in Des Moines, wa. Made her Broadway debut in "I'd Rather Be ight". Since then played in "Best Foot Forward", Something for the Boys", "Dream With Music", The Odds on Mrs. Oakley", and "Nellie Bly".

HOFFMAN, JANE. Born July 24, in Seattle, /ash. Educated Univ. of Calif. Appeared on roadway in "'Tis of Thee", "Crazy With the eat", "Something for the Boys", "One Touch of enus", "Calico Wedding", and "The Mermaids nging".

HOFMANN, ELSBETH. Born in Ellensburg, Wash. an. 15, 1918. Graduate of the Univ. of Wash. ade her Broadway debut in "Skydrift".

HOLLAND, BETTY LOU. Born in N. Y. C., Dec. 25, 926. Educated at St. Agatha and Spence High chool. Received her stage training at American cademy of Dramatic Arts. Made her Broadway ow April 18, 1946, in "Call Me Mister".

HOLLIDAY, JUDY. Born in the Bronx, N. Y. Spent everal years with the Revuers, a night club act. ppeared in the films, "Something for the Boys" nd "Winged Victory". Made her Broadway debut "Kiss Them for Me", and has since been seen "Born Yesterday".

HOLM, CELESTE. Born in N. Y. C., and was edu-ated in schools in Holland and France. Her New ork engagements include roles in "Time of Your ife", "Papa Is All", "Return of the Vagabond", Eight O'Clock Tuesday", "The Damask Cheek", Oklahoma", and "Bloomer Girl".

HOLMAN, LIBBY. Born Cincinnati, Ohio, and edu-ated at Univ. of Cincinnati. First N. Y. appearance June 8, 1925, in "Garrick Gaieties". Since then ppeared in "Greenwich Village Follies" (1926), Marry-Go-Round", "Americana", "Rainbow", "Ned ayburn's Gambols", "The Little Show", "Three's Crowd", "Revenge with Music," "You Never now", and "Mexican Mural".

HOLMAN, SANDRA. Born N. Y. C., July 14, 1928. Has appeared on Broadway in "Junior Miss" and "The Rich Full Life".

HOLMES, TAYLOR. Born Newark, N. J., May 16, 1878. Made first stage appearance in vaudeville in 1899. Among his outstanding plays were "The Midnight Sons", "The Commuters", "Marriage a la Carte", "The Million", "The Third Party", "His Majesty, Bunker Bean", "The Hotel Mouse", "Happy-Go-Lucky", "The Great Necker", "The Sap", "Your Uncle Dudley", "Salt Water", "That's Gratitude", "Riddle Me This", "Big Hearted Her-bert", and "Say When". In 1936 he toured as Jeeter Lester in "Tobacco Road", and more re-cently has appeared in "I'd Rather Be Right", "Marinka", and "Woman Bites Dog".

HOMOLKA, OSCAR. Born Vienna, Aug. 12, 1898, and graduated from the Vienna Royal Academy. On the Continent he starred in "The Emperor Jones", "Loyalties", "The Doctor's Dilemma", and "King Lear". In London he was first seen support-ing Flora Robson in "Close Quarters". He made his American debut in 1937 in the motion picture, "Ebbtide". New York first saw him on the stage in "Grey Farms", which was followed by "The Inno-cent Voyage" and "I Remember Mama".

HOPKINS, MIRIAM. Born Bainbridge, Ga., Oct. 18, 1902. Educated at Goddard Seminary, Vt., and Syracuse Univ. Made her stage bow in the chorus of the first "Music Box Revue". Other N. Y. ap-pearances include "Garrick Gaieties", "Excess Bag-gage", "The Camel Through the Needle's Eye", "Lysistrata", "Knife in the Wall", and "The Home Towners". For years she has spent most of her time in Hollywood, although she came back to N. Y. to star in "Jezebel" and "The Perfect Marriage". She also took over the role of Sabina in "The Skin of Our Teeth" when Tallulah Bankhead left the show, and played in "St. Lazare's Pharmacy" on road.

HOWARD, JACK. Born in Bay City, Mich., June 26, 1889. Has appeared recently on Broadway in George Jessel's "High Kickers" and "Up in Cen-tral Park".

HOWARD, WILLIE. Born N. Y. C., 1883. First stage appearance was in 1897 as a boy soprano in vaudeville. In 1903 he joined his brother Eugene in a vaudeville act and they played together for many years, appearing in various editions of "The Passing Show", "The Whirl of the World", and "The Show of Wonders". Later he was seen in "Sky High", "George White's Scandals", "Ballyhoo of 1932", "Ziegfeld Follies of 1934", "The Show Is On", and "My Dear Public".

George Keane Jane Kean Whitford Kane

HUDSON, EDWARD. Born in Johnstown, Pa., Jan. 9, 1924. Educated at Penn State, and had stage training at the American Academy of Dramatic Arts. Appeared on Broadway in "Junior Miss" and "The Magnificent Yankee".

HULL, HENRY. Born Louisville, Ky., Oct. 3, 1890. Among his many Broadway plays are "The Man Who Came Back", "39 East", "The Cat and the Canary", "Lulu Belle", "Ivory Door", "Michael and Mary", "Springtime for Henry", "The Youngest", "Tobacco Road", "Masque of Kings", "Plumes in the Dust", and "Foolish Notion".

HULL, JOSEPHINE. Born in Newton, Mass., Jan. 3, 1886. Educated at Radcliffe College. Made her professional debut in the Copley Square Stock Company of Boston. Among the many plays she has appeared in are "Fata Morgana", "Craig's Wife", "March Hares", "A Thousand Summers", "Fresh Fields", "Night in the House", "American Dream", "An International Incident" "You Can't Take It With You", "Arsenic and Old Lace", and "Harvey".

HUMPHREYS, CECIL. Born July 21, 1883. First appeared on the stage in England in 1904. First N. Y. appearance was in 1924 in "Parasites". More recently he has been seen in "Tovarich", "Victoria Regina", "The Merchant of Venice", the revival of "The Circle", Katina Paxinou's revival of "Hedda Gabler", Katharine Cornell's revival of "The Doctor's Dilemma", "The Patriots", and the Gertrude Lawrence revival of "Pygmalion".

HUNNICUTT, ARTHUR. Born in Gravelly, Ark. New Yorkers have seen him recently in "Love's Old Sweet Song", "Time of Your Life", "Lower North", "Dark Hammock", "Too Hot for Maneuvers", "Beggars Are Coming to Town", and "Apple of His Eye".

HUSSEY, RUTH. Born Oct. 30, in Providence, R. I. Educated at Pembrook College and Univ. of Mich. Appeared in many motion pictures before making her Broadway bow in "State of the Union".

HUSTON, PHILIP. Born in Goshen, Va., March 14, 1910. Educated at Blair Academy, Blairstown, N. J. Made his Broadway bow in 1934 in "Strange Orchestra". Since then he has played in "Whatever Possessed Her", "Window Shopping", Maurice Evans' "Macbeth" and "Twelfth Night", "Othello", "Catherine Was Great", "The Tempest", "School for Brides", "Make Yourself at Home", and "The Winter's Tale".

HUSTON, WALTER. Born Toronto, Canada, April 6, 1884. First N. Y. appearance in 1905 in "In Convict's Stripes". Spent considerable time in vaudeville. Among the many plays in which he has appeared are "Mr. Pitt", "Desire Under the Elms",

"Kongo", "The Barker", "Elmer the Great", "The Commodore Marries", and "Dodsworth". More recently he has played in "Othello", "Knickerbocke Holiday", "Love's Old Sweet Song", and "Apple o His Eye."

INESCORT, FRIEDA. Born in Hitchin, Scotland, i 1905. Made her American debut in 1922 in "Th Truth About Blayds". Many Broadway hits fol lowed, among them "Trelawney of the Wells" "Springtime for Henry", "You and I", "Love in Mist", "Pygmalion", "Major Barbara", "Escape "When Ladies Meet", "False Dream, Farewell", an she played Portia in George Arliss' production o "The Merchant of Venice". Spent ten years i Hollywood and returned to Broadway to appear i "Soldier's Wife" and "The Mermaids Singing".

INGHRAM, ROSE. Born in Pelmyra, Mo., and edu cated at Univ. of Mich. Appeared on Broadway i "By Jupiter", "Polonaise", and "Three to Mak Ready".

INGRAM, REX. Born Oct. 20, 1896, aboard a Mis sissippi river boat. Educated at Aburn Militar Academy. First N. Y. appearance in 1934 in "Theo dora the Queen", and during the same year ap peared in "Stevedore". More recently he was see in "Marching Song", "Haiti", "Sing Out the News" "Cabin in the Sky", and "St. Louis Woman".

IVANS, ELAINE. Born in Brooklyn, N. Y., Feb. 10 1900. Appeared on Broadway in "Mrs. Partridg Presents", "The Love Habit", "Headquarters", "Jus Life", "Crime Marches On", and "Life Wit Father".

JAFFE, SAM. Born N. Y. C., March 8, 1898. Stag debut in 1915 in "The Clod". Has appeared i "Samson and Delilah", "The God of Vengeance" "The Maine Line", "Izzy", "The Jazz Singer" "Grand Hotel", "The Eternal Road", "A Doll' House", "The Gentle People", and more recentl in "Thank You, Svoboda".

JAMES, MARY. Born in Washington, D. C., and educated at Sweet Briar College. Received stag training at Neighborhood Playhouse. Made he Broadway debut in "Apple of His Eye".

JANIS, CONRAD. Began his career in 1940 in Buf falo in "Tom Sawyer". Has played in "Ah, Wilder ness", "Junior Miss", "Dark of the Moon", an "The Next Half Hour".

JARNAC, DOROTHY. Born Sacramento, Calif., an educated at Sacramento High School. Made debu on Broadway in "Bloomer Girl".

Paula Laurence   Harold Lang   Gertrude Lawrence

JOHNSON, BILL. Born in Baltimore, Md., and educated at Univ. of Md. Appeared on Broadway in "Two for the Show", "All in Fun", "Banjo Eyes", "Something for the Boys", and "The Day Before Spring".

JOHNSON, CHIC (HAROLD J.). Born in Chicago, Ill., in 1891. Met and teamed up with Ole Olsen in 1914 and since then have played in nearly every town in the United States, as well as in England and Australia. Practically unknown to Broadway in 1938, they brought in their explosive "Hellzapoppin" and settled down for a three-year run. They followed this with "Sons O' Fun" and "Laffing Room Only".

JOHNSON, KAY. Born Mt. Vernon, N. Y. Studied for the stage at the American Academy of Dramatic Arts, and first played in N. Y. C. in "Go West, Young Man" in 1923. She was also seen in "Beggar on Horseback", "The Morning After", "All Dressed Up", "One of the Family", "No Trespassing", "A Free Soul", and more recently "State of the Union".

JONES, HAZEL. Born Oct. 17 in England. Made her Broadway debut in revival of "Pygmalion".

JORY, VICTOR. Born in Dawson City, Alaska, Nov. 3, 1902. Educated at Pasadena High School and Univ. of Calif. Began his stage career with a Vancouver stock company and went from there to the Pasadena Community Playhouse. He went to Hollywood in 1932, where he appeared in numerous films. Made his Broadway debut in "The Two Mrs. Carrolls". More recently he was seen in "The Perfect Marriage" and "Therese".

JOY, NICHOLAS. Born in Paris, France. Received his early theatrical training in England. Made his American debut at the age of twenty in "A Butterfly on the Wheel". Since then made notable appearances in "Wings Over Europe", "Topaze", "Rain", "End of Summer", "Ode to Liberty", "The Bride the Sun Shines On", "Music in the Air", "The Cat and the Fiddle", "Yes, My Darling Daughter", "The Philadelphia Story", "This Rock", "Mrs. January and Mr. X", "Ten Little Indians", and "A Joy Forever".

KANE, WHITFORD. Born in Larne, Ireland, Jan. 30, 1881. Made his stage debut in Belfast in 1903 in "Ticket-of-Leave Man". His first London appearance was in 1910 in "Justice", and his Broadway bow was made in 1912 in "The Drone". Since then he has become one of America's most dependable character actors. Among the many plays he has appeared in are "Hindle Wakes", "The First Legend", "The Doctor's Dilemma" (the Cornell revival), "Excursion", "The Moon Is Down", "Boyd's

Shop", "St. Helena", "Yellow Jack", "Tiger, Tiger", "The Pidgeon", "The Shoemaker's Holiday", "A Passenger to Bali", the First Gravedigger in both the Barrymore and Evans productions of "Hamlet", "Lifeline", "Land of Fame", "Thank You, Svoboda", "Career Angel", "If a Body", "It's a Gift", and "The Winter's Tale".

KARLAN, RICHARD. Born in Brooklyn, N. Y., April 24, 1919. Educated at Brooklyn College. Made Broadway bow in "Brother Cain". Other appearances include "Johnny on the Spot", "Comes the Revelation", "The Army play by Play", and "The Song of Bernadette".

KARLWEIS, OSCAR. Born in Austria. Made his Broadway debut in "Cue for Passion". Since then has appeared in "Rosalinda", "Jacobowsky and the Colonel", and "I Like It Here".

KEAN, JANE. Has appeared on Broadway in "Early to Bed", "The Girl from Nantucket", and "Are You With It?"

KEANE, GEORGE. Born in Springfield, Mass., April 26, 1917. Educated at C. C. N. Y. Received his stage training at the Maverick Playhouse, Woodstock, N. Y. Made debut on Broadway in 1938 in Maurice Evans' "Hamlet". Also appeared with Evans in "Henry IV", "Richard II", and "Twelfth Night". Other plays include "The Moon Is Down" and "Lifeline".

KEITH, ROBERT. Born Fowler, Ind., Feb. 10, 1898. First N. Y. appearance in 1921 in "The Triumph of X". Has appeared in "New Brooms", "The Great God Brown", "Gentle Grafters", "Beyond the Horizon", "Fog", "Under Glass", "Peace on Earth", "Yellow Jack", "Goodbye, Please", "The Children's Hour", "Othello", "Work Is for Horses", "Tortilla Flat", "The Good", and "The Romantic Mr. Dickens". More recently he was seen in "Ladies and Gentlemen", "Spring Again", "Kiss and Tell", and "January Thaw".

KEITH-JOHNSON, COLIN. Born London, Oct. 8, 1896. First stage appearance was made in 1917 in London. N. Y. debut in "Journey's End" in 1929. He has also been seen in this country in "Hamlet", "The Warrior's Husband", "Dangerous Corner", "Noah", "Pride and Prejudice", and more recently in Miss Cornell's revival of "The Doctor's Dilemma", "The Winter's Tale", and "The Dancer".

KELLY, PAUL. Born Brooklyn, N. Y., Aug. 8, 1899. Appeared on stage as a child actor, and had varied experience in stock before he first appeared on Broadway in "Seventeen" in 1918. Also appeared in "Penrod", "Honors Are Even", "Up the Ladder", "Whispering Wires", "Chains", "The Lady Killer",

Strelsa Leeds   Sam Levene   Norma Lehn

"Nerves", "Houses of Sand", "The Sea Woman", "Find Daddy", "The Nine-Fifteen Revue", "Bad Girl", "Hobo", "Just to Remind You", "Adam Had Two Sons", and "The Great Magoo". After a long session in Hollywood, returned to N. Y. stage in "The Beggars Are Coming to Town".

KIEPURA, JAN. Born in Sosnowicz, Poland. Sang in opera in Vienna, Paris, Berlin, Cologne, Buenos Aires, and New York. Made his Broadway debut in the New Opera Company's production of "The Merry Widow". Recently he appeared in "Polonaise".

KILBRIDE, PERCY. Born in San Francisco, Calif. Appeared on Broadway in "Lily Turner", "Post Road", "Three Men on a Horse", "George Washington Slept Here", "Cuckoos on the Hearth", and more recently in "Little Brown Jug".

KING, DENNIS. Born in Coventry, England, Nov. 2, 1897. Made his stage debut in 1916 with the Birmingham Repertory Company. His N. Y. bow was made in 1921 in "Claire de Lune". Played Mercutio in the Jane Cowl production of "Romeo and Juliet", and also was with Miss Cowl in "Anthony and Cleopatra". Other appearances include "The Vagabond King", "The Three Musketeers", "Frederika", "I Married an Angel", the Ruth Gordon revival of "A Doll's House", Katharine Cornell's revival of "The Three Sisters", the Chicago company of "Blithe Spirit", and "The Searching Wind". Recently he has appeared in "Dunnigan's Daughter" and the revival of "He Who Gets Slapped".

KING, EDITH. Recently has appeared in the Theatre Guild productions of "The Taming of the Shrew", "The Sea Gull", "Amphytrion 38", "Battle of Angels", "Hope for a Harvest", "Othello", and "The Would-Be Gentleman".

KINGSFORD, WALTER. Born in England, Sept. 20, 1881. Recently New Yorkers have seen him in "The Criminal Code", "The Pursuit of Happiness", and "Song of Norway".

KIRKLAND, ALEXANDER. Born in Mexico City, Sept. 15, 1903. Educated at Taft School and the Univ. of Virginia. Had his stage training with Jasper Deeter. Plays on Broadway include "Wings Over Europe", "The Devil to Pay", "Men in White", "Gold Eagle Guy", "The Case of Clyde Griffiths", "Till the Day I Die", "Many Mansions", the revival of "Outward Bound", "Junior Miss", and "Lady in Danger".

KNIGHT, JUNE. Born Hollywood, Calif., Jan. 22, 1911. Began her career as a dancer and first played in N. Y. in 1929 in "Fifty Million Frenchmen". She has also been seen in "Girl Crazy", "The Nine

O'Clock Revue", "Hot Cha!" "Take a Chance" "Jubilee", and more recently in "The Overtons' and "The Would-Be Gentleman".

KRAFT, MARTIN. Born in Baltimore, Md., July 17 1919. Educated at Baltimore Polytechnic Institute Has appeared on Broadway in "Polonaise" and "Three to Make Ready".

KROEGER, BERRY. Born in San Antonio, Texas Oct. 16, 1912. Educated at Univ. of Calif. Received stage training at Pasadena Playhouse. Appeared on Broadway in "The World's Full of Girls" "The Tempest", and "Therese".

KRUGER, OTTILIE. Born in N. Y. C., Nov. 20 1926. Educated at Marlborough School for Girls Played on Broadway in "I Remember Mama" and "A Joy Forever".

KRUGER, OTTO. Born Toledo, Ohio, Sept. 6, 1885 Educated at Univ. of Mich. and Columbia. First N. Y. appearance, after experience in stock and vaudeville, was in "The Natural Law" in 1915 Among the many plays in which he has appeared are "Young America", "Seven Chances", "Captain Kidd, Jr.", "The Gypsy Trail", "Adam and Eva" "The Meanest Man in the World", "To the Ladies" "The Nervous Wreck", "The Royal Family", "Karl and Anna", "The Game of Life and Death", and more recently "The Moon Is Down".

LAFFIN, CHARLES. Born Ellswodth, Me., Jan. 19 1922. Educated at Ellsworth High and Cushine Academy. Received stage training at Leland Power Dramatic School, Boston, Mass. Appeared on Broad way in "Wallflower" and "A Joy Forever".

LAHR, BERT. Born N. Y. C., Aug. 13, 1895, and first played in vaudeville and burlesque. First N. Y appearance was in "Delmar's Revels". He has also appeared in "Hold Everything", "Flying High" "Hot-Cha", "George White's Music Hall Varieties" "Life Begins at 8.40", "George White's Scandals' "The Show Is On", "Du Barry Was a Lady", an "Seven Lively Arts".

LANCASTER, BURT. Born in N. Y. C., Nov. 2 1913. Educated De Witt Clinton High School an N. Y. University. Spent five years with circuse and two years in vaudeville and fairs as an acroba Returned from 26 months overseas in the Army t make his Broadway debut in "A Sound of Hunting".

LANDIS, JESSIE ROYCE. Born Chicago, Nov. 25 1904. Made N. Y. debut in 1926 revival of "Th Honor of the Family". Among the many plays i which she has appeared are "The Furies", "Th Command Performance", "Solid South", "Marriag for Three", "Merrily We Roll Along", "Love Fron

Lenore Lonergan John Lund Ellen Love

Stranger", "Miss Quis", "Where There's a Will", Brown Danube", "Love's Old Sweet Song", "Papa , All", "Kiss and Tell" "A Winter's Tale", and The Merry Wives of Windsor" on the road.

ANG, CHARLES. Born in N. Y. C., Feb. 15, 1915. eceived stage training at American Academy of ramatic Arts. Made Broadway bow in "Pastoral". nce then has appeared in "The World's Full of irls", "Down to Miami", "The Overtons", and any motion pictures.

ANG, HAROLD. Born Daly City, Calif., Dec. 21, 920. Appeared with the Ballet Russe de Monte arlo and the Ballet Theatre before making his roadway bow in "Mr. Strauss Goes to Boston". Three to Make Ready" followed.

ARRIMORE, FRANCINE. Born Verdun, France, ug. 22, 1898. Made N. Y. debut as a child actress "A Fool There Was" in 1910. Among the plays which she has appeared are "Over Night", "Some aby" "Fair and Warmer", "Here Comes the ride", "Parlor, Bedroom and Bath", "Scandal" Nice People", "Nobody's Business", "Chicago", d "Let Us Be Gay". More recently she has played "Brief Moment", "Shooting Star", and "Spring ng".

AURENCE, LARRY. Born in Milan, Italy, March 3, 920. Studied at La Scala de Milano Conservatory Music. Has appeared on Broadway in "Holly-ood Pinafore", "Nellie Bly", and "Around the orld".

AURENCE, PAULA. Began her stage career with son Welles in his productions, "Horse Eats Hat" d "Doctor Faustus". Since then, besides becoming e of New York's most popular night club enter iners, she has appeared in "Junior Miss", "Some-ing for the Boys", and "One Touch of Venus".

AWRENCE, GERTRUDE. Born London, July 4, 1898. lucated at the Convent of the Sacred Heart, reatham. She studied dancing under Mme. Espi-sa and acting under Italia Contin. First stage pearance was as a child dancer in the pantomime "Dick Whittington". First stage appearance in Y. was in "Charlot's Revue" in 1924. She has so played in "Oh, Kay!" "Treasure Girl", "Candle-ght", "The International Revue", and "Private ves". More recently she has appeared in "Tonight 8:30", "Susan and God", "Skylark", "Lady the Dark", and a revival of "Pygmalion".

AVITT, CHARLES (formerly MAX). Born Utica, Y., June 17, 1905. Educated at N. Y. U. and merican Laboratory Theatre School. Was with the

Stuart Walker Company. New Yorkers have seen him in "Goat Song", "Volpone", "Left Bank", and more recently "Family Portrait", Hayes-Evans' pro-duction of "Twelfth Night", "Catherine Was Great", and "Lute Song".

LEDERER, FRANCIS. Born Karlin, Prague, Nov. 6, 1906. He studied for the stage in both Prague and Berlin, and appeared extensively on the Continent and England before his N. Y. debut in 1932 in "Autumn Crocus". In 1939 he replaced Lawrence Olivier in "No Time for Comedy".

LEE, CANADA. Born in N. Y. C., March 2, 1907. Received his education at Public School No. 5. Had his stage training with the WPA Negro Fed-eral Theatre Unit. New Yorkers have seen him in "Macbeth", "Haiti", "Stevedore", "Mamba's Daughters", "Native Son", "South Pacific", "Anna Lucasta", "The Tempest", and "On Whitman Avenue".

LEE, WILLIAM A. Born in Clatskanie, Ore., March 12, 1890. Has played in stock, vaudeville and radio. His recent appearances on the N. Y. stage were in "Mexican Hayride" and "Dream Girl".

LEEDS, STRELSA. Born in Philadelphia, Dec. 3, 1920. Educated at Ogontz School for Girls. Re-ceived stage training at Hedgerow Theatre and American Academy of Dramatic Arts. Appeared in "Junior Miss" on the road and on Broadway in "The Boy Who Lived Twice".

LE GALLIENNE, EVA. Born in London on Jan. 11, 1899, and studied for the stage at the Royal Academy of Dramatic Art. Her first N. Y. ap-pearance was in 1915 in Mrs. Boltay's Daughters". Among the many plays in which she has appeared are "Bunny", "The Melody of Youth", "Mr. Laza-rus", "Liliom", "The Swan", and "The Master Builder". In 1926 she started the Civic Repertory Company. Among the plays in this repertory were "Saturday Night", "Three Sisters", "The Master Builder", "John Gabriel Borkman", "La Locan-diera", "Twelfth Night", "The Good Hope", "Hedda Gabler", "The Cherry Orchard", "Peter Pan", "The Sea Gull", "The Living Corpse", and "Alice In Wonderland". This company was dis-banded in 1933. More recently she has appeared in a revival, "L'Aiglon" "Prelude In Exile", "Ma-dame Capet", "Uncle Harry", a revival of "The Cherry Orchard", and "Therese".

LEHN, NORMA. Born March 26 in York, Pa. Re-ceived stage training at American Academy of Dramatic Arts. Appeared on Broadway in "Best Foot Forward", and "January Thaw".

167

Helen MacKellar

Jack Manning

Irene Manning

LEIGHTON, MARGARET. Born in Barnt Green, Warwickshire, England, Feb. 26, 1922. Educated at Church of England College. Received stage training at Repertory Theatre, Birmingham. Made her Broadway debut on May 6, 1946 with the Old Vic Company.

LEVENE, SAM. Born in N. Y. C., 1907. A graduate of American Academy of Dramatic Arts, he has appeared on Broadway in "Dinner at Eight", "Three Men On A Horse", "Room Service", "Margin For Error", and more recently "A Sound of Hunting".

LEVEY, ETHEL. Born San Francisco, Nov. 22, 1881. Made her first stage appearance in 1897 in San Francisco, and later appeared at Koster and Bial's with Weber and Fields. From 1901 to 1907 she was associated with all the productions of George M. Cohan, playing in such shows as "Little Johnny Jones" and "George Washington, Jr.". After this, she spent many years on the English stage. More recent Broadway appearances include "Sunny River", and "Marinka".

LILLIE, BEATRICE. Born in Toronto, Canada, May 29, 1898. Made her stage debut in England in 1914 in a revue, "Not Likely". Her Broadway bow was made January 9, 1924, in "Charlot's Revue". Since then New Yorkers have seen her in a second edition of "Charlot's Revue", "Oh Please", "She's My Baby", "This Year of Grace", "Walk A Little Faster", "The Show Is On", "Set To Music", and "Seven Lively Arts".

LINDEN, ERIC. Born N. Y. C., Sept. 15, 1909. Educated at Columbia University. His first N. Y. stage appearance was in "Marco Millions" in 1928. He also played in "One Way Street", "You Never Can Tell" and "Ladies' Money". Since 1931 he has appeared in many motion pictures. Returned to the stage for "Trio" on the West Coast.

LINN, BAMBI. Born in Brooklyn, N. Y., April 26, 1926. Educated at the Professional Children's School. A student of Agnes de Mille's, she has appeared on Broadway in "Oklahoma" and "Carousel".

LOEB, PHILIP. Born Philadelphia, 1894. Received his stage training at the American Academy of Dramatic Arts. His New York appearances include "Processional", "June Moon", "The Band Wagon", "Let 'Em Eat Cake", "Room Service", "My Sister Eileen", "Over 21" and "Common Ground".

LONERGAN, LENORE. Born in Ohio, June 2, 1928. Educated at Blessed Sacrament Seminary and Dominican Convent. Plays on Broadway include, "Be-

yond the Blue", "Fields Beyond", "Mother Lode", "Crime Marches On", "The Philadelphia Story", "Junior Miss", "Dear Ruth" and "Brighten t' Corner".

LONG, AVON. Baltimore, Md. Had scholarship Boston Conservatory of Music. Appeared on Broadway in "Porgy and Bess", "Very Warm For May", "Memphis Bound" and "Carib Song".

LORD, PAULINE. Born Hanford, Calif., Aug. 1890. Made her first stage appearance in sto in San Francisco and first played in N. Y. with N Goodwin's Company in 1905. Her first hit w "The Talker" in 1912, and since then she has a peared in "On Trial", "Under Pressure", "O There", "The Deluge", "April", "Our Pleasa Sins", "Night Lodging", "Samson and Delilah "Anna Christie", "They Knew What They Wantec "Mariners", "Spellbound", "Distant Drums". Mc recently she appeared in "The Late Christoph Bean", "Ethan Frome", "Eight O'Clock Tuesday "Suspect", "The Walrus and the Carpenter" a "Sleep, My Pretty One".

LORING KAY. Born Jefferson City, Mo., Jan. 1913. Attended American Academy of Drama Arts. New Yorkers have seen her in "Three M On a Horse", "Having Wonderful Time", "What Life", "Spring Again", "Ask My Friend Sandy" a "The Rugged Path".

LOVE, ELLEN. Born in Boston, Mass, December Educated at Horace Mann School and Vassar C lege. Began Theatre Apprenticeship with the J ney Players, Winter and Summer Stock. Broadw debut was "Cape Cod Follies" in 1930. Oth appearances included "Farewell Summer", "Tell F Pretty Maiden", "Cue For Passion", "Oklahom and "Sing Out Sweet Land."

LOWE, EDMUND. Born San Jose, Calif., March 1892. He was educated at the Santa Clara Univ sity and made his first stage appearance in S Francisco in 1911. Made his N. Y. debut in 1918 "The Brat". He also appeared in "The Walk-Off", "Roads of Destiny", "The Son-Daughter", "T Right to Strike", a revival of "Trilby" and "Des Sands". He made innumerable motion pictur Recently he returned to Broadway in "The Ry Girl".

LUND, JOHN. Born in Rochester, N. Y., Feb. 1913. Began his stage career in the Railrc Pageant at the New York World's Fair. He und studied Alfred Drake in the revival of "As You L It" in 1941. In 1942 he appeared on Broadway "New Faces" and since then he has been in "Ea To Bed" and "The Hasty Heart".

168

Lucille Marsh   E. G. Marshall   Helen Marcy

NT, ALFRED. Born Milwaukee, Wisc., 1893. ucated at Carroll College and Harvard. He made s first stage appearance in stock in Boston in 13, and in 1914 he toured with Margaret glin, appearing in various roles. Following this, supported Lily Langtry in a vaudeville playlet lled "Ashes". In 1919 he made his first big hit "Clarence". Among the plays which followed s were, "The Intimate Strangers", "Banco", weet Nell of Old Drury", "Outward Bound", "The ardsman", "Arms and the Man", "The Goat ng", "At Mrs. Beam's", "Juarez and Maximilian", led McCobb's Daughter", "The Brothers Kara- azov", "The Second Man", "The Doctor's Dilem- a", "Marco Millions", "Volpone", "Caprice", lizabeth the Queen", "Reunion in Vienna", "De- n For Living", "Idiot's Delight", "The Taming of e Shrew", "Amphytrion 38", "The Sea Gull", here Shall Be No Night", "The Pirate" and "O stress Mine".

TELL, BERT. Born in N. Y. C., 1890. Made his oadway bow in 1914 with Marie Dressler in "A x Up". "If" and "Mary's Ankle" followed, then had a long career in motion pictures. Returned the stage in "Brothers". More recent appear- ces on Broadway include, "The First Legion", argin For Error", "Lady in the Dark", "The Wind 90" and "I Like It Here".

cDONALD, DONALD. Born Denison, Texas, rch 13, 1898. Studied for the stage at the merican Academy of Dramatic Arts, and first ap- ared in stock in Ottawa. Made N. Y. debut in 13 in "When Dreams Come True". Among the ys in which he has appeared are "Have A Heart", tting Gertie's Garter", "Jack and Jill", "Proces- nal", "Love 'Em and Leave 'Em", "White Wings", e Second Man", "Paris Bound", "The Left nk", "Forsaking All Others", "Little Shot", "On ge", and more recently "Deep Are The Roots".

cKELLAR, HELEN. Born in Detroit, Feb. 13, 5. First appeared on N. Y. stage in 1916 in ven Chances". Appeared in "A Tailor-Made n", "The Unknown Purple", "The Storm", "Be- d the Horizon", and "The Mud Turtle". After ong session in Hollywood, returned to Broadway 'Dear Ruth".

cMAHON, ALINE. Born in McKeesport, Pa., y 3, 1899. Educated at Barnard College, and de N. Y. debut in 1921 in "The Madras House". peared in "The Green Ring", "The Exciters", nnie Comes Home", "The Grand Street Follies", yond the Horizon", "Spread Eagle", "Maya", "Once in a Lifetime". More recently appeared Heavenly Express" and "The Eve of St. Mark".

MADDERN, MERLE. Born in San Francisco, Nov. 3, 1887. Educated at Berkeley Univ. Made Broadway bow 1909 with her aunt, Mrs. Fiske, in "Salvation Nell". Recent appearances include Cornell's pro- duction of "Romeo and Juliet", "L'Aiglon", "Deci- sion", "A New Life", "Down to Miami", and "Antigone".

MALDEN, KARL. Born in Gary, Ind. Appeared on Broadway in "Golden Boy", "Key Largo", "Flight to the West", "Missouri Legend", "Uncle Harry", "Counterattack", "Sons and Soldiers", "Winged Victory", "The Assassin" and "Truckline Cafe".

MALLAH, VIVIAN. Born N. Y. C., Jan. 16, 1924. Stage training received at Bliss Hayden in Holly- wood. "Marriage Is For Single People" marked her Broadway debut.

MALTEN, WILLIAM. Born Aug. 9, 1902, and studied for the stage under Max Reinhardt. Made Broadway debut in 1941 in "Candle in The Wind". Has appeared in "Russian People", "Thank You, Svoboda", "Private Life of the Master Race", "The Assassin", and "The French Touch".

MANNERS, DAVID. Born in Halifax, Nova Scotia, April 30, 1900. Educated at Trinity School, N. Y., and Univ. of Toronto. Received stage training at Hart House Repertory Theatre, Toronto. Made Broadway debut in "Dancing Mothers". After a long session in Hollywood, returned to Broadway in "Truckline Cafe".

MANNING, IRENE. Born in Cincinnati, Ohio, 1916. Educated at Eastman School of Music. Sang with St. Louis Municipal Opera Co. and Civic Light Opera Co. of Los Angeles, after which she appeared in films. Made Broadway debut in "The Day Before Spring".

MANNING, JACK. Born June 3 in Cincinnati, Ohio. Graduate of Univ. of Cincinnati. Has played on the Broadway stage in "The Great Big Doorstep", "Junior Miss", "Hamlet", "Othello", "The Streets Are Guarded", and "The Mermaids Singing".

MARCH, FREDERIC. Born in Racine, Wisc., Aug. 31, 1897. Educated at Univ. of Wisc. On the road played in "Tarnish", "Zeno", "A Knife in the Wall", and the Theatre Guild productions of "The Guardsman", "The Silver Cord", "Arms and the Man", and "Mr. Pim Passes By". His Broadway debut was made in Belasco's production of "De- burau". In 1932 while appearing on the West Coast in "The Royal Family", he received picture offers and remained in Hollywood for ten years. Recent appearances in New York include "Yr. Obedient Husband", "The American Way", "Hope for a Harvest", "The Skin of Our Teeth", and A Bell for Adano".

Gordon McDonald   Scott McKay   Fania Marinoff

MARCY, HELEN. Born June 3, 1920 in Worcester, Mass. Studied for the theatre at Yale Drama School. Has appeared on Broadway in "In Bed We Cry", and "Dream Girl".

MARFIELD, DWIGHT. Born in Cincinnati, and educated at Harvard and Princeton Graduate College. Theatrical training in stock, before Broadway debut in "Texas Town". Also appeared in "The Playboy of Newark", "The Private Life of the Master Race", and "The Day Before Spring".

MARGETSON, ARTHUR. Born in London, England, April 27, 1887. Made his first appearance in America in "The Passing Show of 1922". Since then New Yorkers have seen him in "Little Miss Bluebeard", "Paris", "Charley's Aunt", "Theatre", "Another Love Story", "Lovers and Friends", "Life With Father", and "Around The World".

MARINOFF, FANIA. Born Odessa, Russia, March 20, 1890. Made first stage appearance at age of eight in stock in Denver. During her early career she supported such famous players as Henrietta Crosman, Mrs. Patrick Campbell, and Arnold Daly. Among the many plays in which she has appeared are "The Man On The Box", "The House Next Door", "The Hero", "The Charlatan", "The Love Habit", and "Tarnish". More recently she appeared in revivals of "The Streets of New York", "The Pillars of Society", "Anthony and Cleopatra", and in "The Bride The Sun Shines On", "Christopher Comes Across", "Judgment Day", and "Times Have Changed".

MARKEY, ENID. Was a star in silent films before becoming a Broadway actress for A. H. Woods in "Up In Mabel's Room". Her more recent appearances on the N. Y. stage include "Barnum Was Right", "The Women", "Mornings at Seven", "Ah, Wilderness!", "Mr. Sycamore", "Run, Sheep, Run", "Beverly Hills", "Last Stop", and "Snafu".

MARSH, LUCILLE. Born in Chicago, Ill., Aug. 17, 1921. Received her education at the Highland Park, Ill., Grammar and High School. Obtained her stage training at the Goodman Theatre, Chicago, and the Max Reinhardt Workshop in Hollywood. Made one picture, "Cover Girl", before making her stage debut playing the title role in the road company of "Janie". The road also saw her in "Abie's Irish Rose", and "School for Brides". First N. Y. appearance was made in the Fred Stone revival of "You Can't Take It With You".

MARSHALL, E. G. Born June 18, 1910 in Minnesota. Educated at Carlton College and Univ. of Minn. Appeared on Broadway in "Jason", "The Skin of Our Teeth", the revival of "The Petrified

Forest", "Jacobowsky and the Colonel", "Begga Are Coming to Town", and "Woman Bites Dog".

MARSHALL, PATRICIA. Born in Minneapolis, Minn. and educated there at West High School. Has appeared on Broadway in "You'll See Stars", "Sta on Ice", "Hats Off to Ice", "What's Up", and "T Day Before Spring".

MARSTON, JOEL. Born March 30, 1922 in Was ington, D. C. Received his theatrical training Pasadena Playhouse. Made Broadway bow in 19 in "Wallflower". Has appeared in "Good Mornir Corporal", "The Streets Are Guarded", and "M riage Is For Single People".

MARTIN, MARY. Born in Wetherford, Tex Dec. 1, 1914. Educated at Ward-Belmont Scho Nashville, Tenn. Her first Broadway appearan was made in "Leave It To Me", and since then s has been starred in "One Touch of Venus", a "Lute Song".

MASSEY, RAYMOND. Born in Toronto, Canad Aug. 30, 1896. Educated at Toronto Univ. a Balliol College, Oxford. Made first professior stage appearance in England in 1922. Made Broadway bow in 1931 in title role of "Hamle Since then has appeared in N. Y. in "The Shini Hour", "Ethan Frome", "Abe Lincoln in Illinoi the Cornell revival of "The Doctor's Dilemma", a the Lawrence revival of "Pygmalion".

MATHEWS, CARMEN. Born in Philadelphia, P and had theatrical training at Royal Academy Dramatic Art in London. Made Broadway debut 1938 in Maurice Evans' production of Henry I\ Was also seen with him in "Hamlet", and "Rich II". More recently she appeared in "Harrie "The Cherry Orchard", and "The Assassin".

MATTESON, RUTH. Born in San Jose, Calif. F appeared on Broadway in "Parnell", "Wingless V tory", "Barchester Towers", "One for the Mone "The Male Animal", "The Merry Widow", "T morrow the World", "In Bed We Cry", and "Ar gone".

MAUDE, MARGERY. Born April 29, 1889 in Wi bledon, Surrey, England. Made her American del in 1913 with her father, Cyril Maude, in "Grump Appeared in N. Y. in "Lady Windemere's Fa "Paganini", "The Old Foolishness", and more cently in "Plan M", "The Two Mrs. Carrolls", a "O Mistress Mine".

McCARTHY, KEVIN. Born Seattle, Wash., Feb. 1914. Educated at Georgetown Univ. and Univ. Minn. Made Broadway bow in "Abe Lincoln Illinois". Also appeared in "Flight to the Wes "Winged Victory", and "Truckline Cafe".

Pauline Myers   Donald Murphy   Mary Ellen Moylan

McCLARNEY, PAT. Born Haileyville, Okla., March 17, 1925. Graduate of Univ. of Texas. Toured three years with U. S. O. Camp Shows, and made Broadway debut in "The Girl From Nantucket".

McCLELLAND, DONALD. Born N. Y. C., Sept. 29, 1903. Made Broadway debut in "Peter Pan", with Maude Adams in 1914. Had a long and varied career on N. Y. stage. Recently appeared in "Mask and the Face", "Ah, Wilderness", "Yankee Point", and "Make Yourself at Home".

McCORMICK, MYRON. Born in Albandy, Ind., Feb. 8, 1907. His first professional engagement was with the University Players. In 1932 he made his first N. Y. stage appearance in "Carrie Nation". Since then he has played in "Goodbye Again", "Yellow Jack", "Small Miracle", "How to Get Tough About It", "Hell Freezes Over", "How Beautiful With Shoes", "Substitute for Murder", "Paths of Glory", "Winterset", "Wingless Victory", "Lily of the Valley", "The Damask Cheek", "Thunder Rock", "Storm Operation", and more recently in "Soldier's Wife", and "State of the Union".

McCRACKEN, JOAN. Born in Philadelphia, Pa., Dec. 31, 1922. Educated at West Philadelphia High School. Studied and appeared with the Catherine Littlefield Ballet. Toured with the Eugene Loring Dance Players. Appeared on Broadway in "Oklahoma", "Bloomer Girl", and "Billion Dollar Baby".

McDONALD, GORDON. Born Long Beach, Calif., May 17, 1921. Stage training in stock in Calif., where he appeared in many films. Broadway debut in "The Wind Is Ninety".

McGEE, HAROLD. Born April 16, 1899 in Schenectady, N. Y., and educated at Union College. Broadway debut in 1921 as member of the Provincetown Playhouse, where he appeared in "Inheritors", "The Hairy Ape", "The Moon of the Caribbees", "S.S. Glencairn", and many other plays. More recently he was seen in "But Not Goodbye", and "Live Life Again".

McGREW, JAMES. Born Pittsburgh, Pa., Oct. 8, 1917. Educated at Carnegie Tech Drama Dept., and worked with the Pittsburgh Playhouse. Made Broadway bow in "A Sound of Hunting".

McKAY, SCOTT (formerly CARL GOSE). Born Pleasantville, Iowa, May 28, 1917. Educated at Univ. of Colorado. Made Broadway debut in 1938 in "Good Hunting". Since then has been seen in "The American Way", "The Night Before Christmas", "Letters to Lucerne", "The Moon Is Down", "The Eve of St. Mark", "Dark Eyes", "Pillar to Post", and "Swan Song".

MEADER, GEORGE. Born July 6, 1890 in Minneapolis, and graduated from Univ. of Minn. Sang in Opera at the Metropolitan and also in Europe. Appeared on Broadway in "The Cat and the Fiddle", "Champagne Sec", "Only Girl", and with the Lunts in "Taming of the Shrew", "Idiot's Delight", "Amphytreon 38", and "The Sea Gull". More recently he appeared in the revival of "The Red Mill".

MENDELSSOHN, ELEONORA. Born in Berlin, Germany, where she had a long and distinguished career. Has appeared on N. Y. stage in "Daughters of Atreus", "Flight to the West", "The Russian People", and "The Secret Room".

MENKEN, HELEN. Born in New York, Dec. 12, 1901, she first appeared on the stage in 1906 as one of the fairies in "A Midsummer Night's Dream". As a child actress, she played with such stars as De Wolf Hopper, Eddie Foy, and Adeline Genée, after which she had considerable experience in stock. Among her Broadway successes are "Three Wise Fools", "Drifting", "Seventh Heaven", "The Captive", and "Congai". More recently she appeared in "Mary Of Scotland", "The Old Maid", and "The Laughing Woman".

MEREDITH, BURGESS. Born Nov. 16, 1909 in Cleveland, Ohio. Educated at Amherst College. First N. Y. stage appearance in 1929 as a walk-on with the Civic Repertory Company. He remained with that company until 1933, playing numerous roles. Has appeared on Broadway in "Night Over Taos", "The Three Penny Opera", "Little Ol' Boy", "She Loves Me Not", "The Barretts of Wimpole Street", "Flowers of the Forest", "Winterset", "High Tor", "The Star Wagon", and more recently in a revival of "Liliom".

MERMAN, ETHEL. Born in Astoria, L. I., N. Y., on Jan. 16, 1909. Her first stage appearance was in vaudeville with Clayton, Jackson and Durante. She scored her first Broadway hit in 1931 in "Girl Crazy". Among the musical shows in which she has appeared are "George White's Scandals", "Take a Chance", "Anything Goes", "Red, Hot, and Blue!", "Stars in Your Eyes", "Panama Hattie", and more recently in "Annie Get Your Gun".

MERRILL, GARY. Born in Hartford, Conn. Educated at Trinity College. Appeared on Broadway in "Brother Rat", "Morning Star", "See My Lawyer", "This Is The Army", "Winged Victory", and "Born Yesterday".

MILLER, MARTY. Born June 2, 1934 in N. Y. C. and attended Professional Children's School. Broadway debut in "Seven Lively Arts". Has also appeared in "Too Hot for Maneuvers", "The Wind Is Ninety", "Skydrift", and "On Whitman Avenue".

Jay Norris Mahlon Naill Laurence Olivier

MITCHELL, ESTHER. Born Newcastle, New South Wales, Australia. Made American debut in 1921 in "The Madras House" at Neighborhood Playhouse. More recently appeared on Broadway in "The Corn Is Green", "Call It A Day", "Within the Gates", "Miss Swan Expects", and "O Mistress Mine".

MOORE, VICTOR. Born in Hammonton, N. J., Feb. 24, 1876. Made his first appearance on any stage in "Babes in the Woods" at the Boston Theatre in 1893. Was with John Drew in "Rosemary" in 1896. Subsequently played in "A Romance of Coon Hollow", "The Real Widow Brown", and "The Girl From Paris". For 25 years he toured the country in a vaudeville act "Change Your Act, or Back to the Woods". This was followed by "The Talk of New York", "The Happiest Night of His Life", "Shorty McCabe", "Patsy on the Wing", "Easy Come, Easy Go", "Oh, Kay" and "Hold Everything". His recent starring roles include "Of Thee I Sing", "Let 'Em Eat Cake", "Anything Goes", "Leave It To Me", "Louisiana Purchase", "Hollywood Pinafore", and "Nellie Bly".

MORGAN, CLAUDIA. She was born in Brooklyn, N. Y., June 12, 1912, and is the daughter of Ralph Morgan. Her first Broadway role was in "Top O' The Hill". Since then she has appeared in "Wine of Choice", "Man Who Came to Dinner", "Accent on Youth", "On Stage", "Dancing Partners", "And Stars Remained", "Storm Over Patsy", "Masque of Kings", "In Clover", "Call It a Day", "Co-respondent Unknown", "The Sun Field", and "Ten Little Indians".

MORGAN, RALPH. Born in N. Y. C., July 6, 1888. Graduate of Columbia Univ. Made his N. Y. debut in 1908 in "Blue Grass". Among the many plays in which he has appeared on Broadway are "The Blue Mouse", "Under Cover", "A Full House", "Lightnin'", "The Five Million", "In Love With Love", "Cobra", "The Woman in Bronze", and "Strange Interlude". After several years in Hollywood he re-appeared on the N. Y. stage in "Fledgling", "The Moon Is Down", and "This Too Shall pass".

MORRIS, HOWARD. Born N. Y. C., Sept. 4, 1919. Made his Broadway debut in Maurice Evans full length "Hamlet". Played with Maurice Evans and Judith Anderson in Hawaii, and returned to Broadway in the G.I. "Hamlet".

MORRIS, McKAY. Born Houston, Texas, Dec. 22, 1891. Studied for the stage under David Belasco, and made N. Y. debut in 1912 in "The Governor's Lady". For several years he was with Stuart Walker's

Portmanteau Theatre Company, and later appeared on Broadway in "Aphrodite", "Rose Bernd", "Romeo and Juliet" (Ethel Barrymore production), "The Laughing Lady", "The Shanghai Gesture", "Volpone", revivals of "Ghosts" and "Hedda Gabler" with Nazimova, and in "Retreat From Folly", and "Tovarich". Most recent appearance in "Lute Song".

MOYLAN, MARY ELLEN. Born Cincinnati, Aug. 24, 1926. Studied dancing at American School of the Ballet. Broadway debut in 1942 in "Rosalinda". Since then she has danced with the Ballet Russe de Monte Carlo, and has appeared in "Song of Norway", and "The Day Before Spring".

MUNSHIN, JULES. Born N. Y. C., Feb. 22, 1915. First appeared on Broadway in "The Army Play by Play", and more recently in "Call Me Mister".

MURPHY, DONALD. Born Jan. 29, 1920 in Chicago, Ill., and educated at Florida's Rollins College. Faced his first New York audience in "The Moon Vine". Other Broadway appearances were made in "Janie", "Try and Get It", "For Keeps", "Signature", and "Common Ground".

MYERS, PAULINE. Born Nov. 9 in Georgia. Broadway debut 1933 in "Growing Pains". Has appeared in "Plumes in the Dust", "The Willow and I", "The Naked Genius", and "Dear Ruth".

MYRTIL, ODETTE. Born in Paris, June 28, 1898. Made first appearance as a violinist in Paris in 1911. Her Broadway debut was in "The Ziegfeld Follies of 1914". She has appeared on the N. Y. stage in many musical shows which include "Vogues of 1924", "The Love Song", "Countess Maritza", "White Lilacs", "Broadway Nights", "The Cat and the Fiddle", and "Roberta". Most recent appearance was in revival of "The Red Mill".

NAGEL, CONRAD. Born Keokuk, Iowa, March 16, 1897. Made his first appearance on Broadway with Alice Brady in "Forever After". Most of his acting career has been devoted to Hollywood picture making. In recent years has returned to the stage and has been seen in "The First Apple", "The Skin of Our Teeth", "Tomorrow the World", the City Center revival of "Susan and God", and "A Goose For The Gander".

NAILL, MAHLON. Born in Philadelphia, April 6, 1912. Educated at Temple Univ. Spent nine years in repertory with Hedgerow Theatre. "Flamingo Road" marked his Broadway debut.

NATWICK, MILDRED. Born Baltimore, Md., June 19, 1908. Made N. Y. debut in 1932 in "Carrie Nation". Has appeared in "Amourette", "The Wind

Kevin O'Shea   Mary Orr   Lew Parker

and the Rain", "The Distaff Side", "Night in the House", "End of Summer", "Love from a Stranger", the Cornell revival of "Candida", "The Star Wagon", "Missouri Legend", "Stars in Your Eyes", and more recently "Blithe Spirit".

NEDD, STUART. Born San Francisco, Oct 21, 1915. Graduated from the Univ. of Calif. Stage training with Pasadena Playhouse. Has appeared on Broadway in "The Assassin" and "Dream Girl".

NICHOLAS, BROS. (HAROLD and FAYARD). First appeared professionally in 1930 at Standard Theatre in Philadelphia. Appeared together on Broadway in "Blackbirds", "Ziegfeld Follies", "Babes in Arms", and most recently in "St. Louis Woman".

NIESEN, GERTRUDE. Born at sea, July 8, 1910. Educated Brooklyn and N. Y. public schools. First regular stage appearance made at Hollywood Theatre, N. Y. Dec. 13, 1934 in "Calling All Stars". "Ziegfeld Follies" (1936) came next, and more recently "Follow the Girls".

NILLO, DAVID. Born July 13, 1918 in Goldsboro, N. C. Educated at Baltimore City College. First stage appearances with Ballet Theatre and American Ballet Caravan. Made Broadway bow in "Call Me Mister".

NILSON, LOY. Born N. Y. C. May 21, 1918. Made Broadway bow in 1942 revival of "R.U.R.". Has appeared in "Suds in Your Eyes", "Make Yourself at Home", and "A Sound of Hunting".

NORRIS, JAY. Born in Albany, Georgia, on August 3, 1917. Appeared in several movies before making Broadway bow in "Strange Fruit".

NUGENT, ELLIOTT. Born in Dover, Ohio, Sept. 20, 1900, and educated at Ohio State Univ. Among the plays in which he has appeared are "Dulcy", "The Poor Nut", "Kempy", "The Wild Westcotts", "Hoosiers Abroad", "The Male Animal", "Without Love", and "The Voice of the Turtle".

OBER, ROBERT. Born Bunker Hill, Ill., March 10, 1889. Educated at Washington Univ., St. Louis. Broadway debut in "The Little Grey Lady". Has appeared in many plays among which are "You Never Can Tell", "Ready Money", "The Bat", "The Cat and the Canary", and more recently "The Moon Is Down", and "The Assassin".

O'CONNOR, UNA. Born Belfast, Ireland, Oct. 23, 1880. Studied for the stage at the Abbey Theatre School in Dublin, and made her debut in 1911 at the Abbey Theatre. During that same season she made her first appearance on Broadway in "The Shewing Up of Blanco Posnet". She re-appeared in

N. Y. in 1924 in the "The Fake", and later played here in "Autumn Fire". She is well known through her work in Hollywood. Returned to the Broadway stage in "The Ryan Girl".

OLIVIER, LAURENCE. Born Dorking, Surrey, England, May 22, 1907. Educated at St. Edward's School, Oxford, and studied for the stage under Elsie Fogerty. Made Broadway debut in 1929 in "Murder on the Second Floor". Later he was seen here in "Private Lives", "The Green Bay Tree", "No Time for Comedy", and his own production of "Romeo and Juliet". Has appeared in Hollywood with considerable success. Returned to Broadway 1946 with the Old Vic Company.

OLMSTED, REM. Born Pasadena, Calif., June 15, 1917. Studied dancing with Doris Humphreys and Charles Weidman, and with Leon Fokine. Has appeared on Broadway in "Stovepipe Hat", "Oklahoma", "Sadie Thompson", and "Polonaise".

O'MALLEY, REX. Born in London, England, Feb. 2, 1901. He received his stage training with the Birmingham Repertory Company. Among his many N. Y. appearances are "The Marquise", "Bachelor Father", "Lost Sheep", "The Apple Cart", "Wonder Bar", "The Mad Hopes", "Experience Unnecessary", "Revenge With Music", "You Never Know", "Matrimony Pfd.", "The Simpleton of the Unexpected Isles", the Lunt's production of "The Taming of the Shrew", "No More Ladies", "The Man Who Came to Dinner", the Le Gallienne revival of "The Cherry Orchard", "Devils Galore", and "Lute Song".

ORR, MARY. Born in Brooklyn, N. Y., Dec. 21, 1918. Educated at Ward-Belmont School, Nashville, Tenn. Received her stage training at the American Academy of Dramatic Arts. Played on Broadway in "Three Men On A Horse", "Bachelor Born", "Jupiter Laughs", "Wallflower", and "Dark Hammock".

O'SHEA, KEVIN. Born Chicago, Ill., May 6, 1915. Studied for the theatre with Maria Ouspenskaya. Has been seen on Broadway in "The Eternal Road", "You Never Know", "Censored", "Lorelei", and more recently in "Dream Girl".

PAGENT, ROBERT. Born in Pittsburgh, Pa., Dec. 12, 1917. Educated at the Univ. of Indiana. He received his ballet training in Paris under Egorova. Appeared with the Chicago Opera Ballet, Ballet Russe de Monte Carlo and Col. de Basil's Ballet Russe. Has appeared on Broadway in "Oklahoma", "One Touch of Venus", and "Carousel".

PARKER, LEW. Born Oct. 29, 1910 in Brooklyn. Has appeared on Broadway in "The Ramblers", "Girl Crazy", "Red, Hot, and Blue", "Heads Up", and more recently in "Are You With It".

173

George Petrie   Beatrice Pearson   Kurt Richards

PARNELL, JAMES. Born Oct. 9, 1923 in Minnesota. Studied for the theatre under Guy Bates Post. Played two years with U.S.O. Camp Shows, and made Broadway debut in "Oklahoma".

PEARSON, BEATRICE. Born in Denison, Texas, July 27, 1920. She made her Broadway debut in the revival of "Liliom". Since then she has played in "Life With Father", "Free and Equal", "Get Away Old Man", "Over 21", "The Mermaids Singing", and "The Voice of the Turtle".

PETINA, IRA. Born in Russia, she began her musical studies in Philadelphia's Curtis Institute. Three years later she was singing with the Metropolitan Opera Company. On the West Coast she appeared in "The Chocolate Soldier", "Music in the Air", "The Gypsy Baron", and "The Waltz King". In 1944 she made her Broadway debut in "Song of Norway".

PETRIE, GEORGE. Born Nov. 16, 1915 in New Haven, Conn. Educated at Univ. of Southern Calif. In 1938 he made his Broadway bow in "The Girl From Wyoming". Has appeared in "The Army Play by Play", "Jeremiah", "Pastoral", "The Night Before Christmas", "Mr. Big", "Cafe Crown", "Winged Victory", and "Brighten the Corner".

POPE, ROBERT. Born Monroe, La., July 27, 1911. Started career as leader of a quartette, and sang with various bands, and in vaudeville. Made Broadway debut in "St. Louis Woman".

POWERS, TOM. Born July 7, 1890 in Owensboro, Ky. Studied for the stage at the American Academy of Dramatic Arts. Made his Broadway debut in 1915 in "Mr. Lazarus". Among the many plays in which he has been seen on the N. Y. stage are "He", "The Apple Cart", "Strange Interlude", the Orson Welles' "Julius Caesar", and more recently in the Cornell revival of "Three Sisters", and in "Broken Journey".

RAITT, JOHN. He was born in Santa Ana, Calif., Jan. 29, 1917 and educated at Univ. of Redlands, Calif., where he received his A.B. Began his singing career with the Los Angeles Civic Light Opera Company. Sang the lead in the national company of "Oklahoma", and made his Broadway bow in "Carousel".

RAWLS, EUGENIA. Born Sept. 11, 1916 in Macon, Ga. Educated at Univ. of N. C. Appeared with Clare Tree Major's Children's Theatre, and was first seen on Broadway in "The Children's Hour". Has since appeared in "The Little Foxes", "Guest in the House", "Cry Havoc", "The Man Who Had All The Luck", and "Strange Fruit".

REDMAN, JOYCE. Born 1919 in Ireland. Studied fo[r] the theatre at the Royal Academy of Dramatic Art and made her London debut in 1935. Played [a] great variety of roles on the English stage. Firs[t] Broadway appearance was with the Old Vic Company.

REED, FLORENCE. Born in Philadelphia, Pa., Jan. 10, 1883. Made her first appearance on the stag[e] at the Fifth Avenue Theatre, N. Y. in 1901, appear[-] ing in a monologue. After several seasons of stoc[k] in New York, Providence, Worcester and Chicago she joined E. H. Sothern's Company and toured with him during the 1907-8 season. Among her many successes are "Seven Days", "The Painted Woman", "The Girl and the Pennant", "The Yellow Ticket", "A Celebrated Case", "The Wanderer", "Chu Chin Chow", "Roads of Destiny", "The Mirage", "East o[f] Suez", "The Shanghai Gesture", and Lady Macbeth in "Macbeth". Recently NewYorkers have seen her as the nurse in Cornell's production of "Romeo and Juliet", the revival of "Outward Bound", "The Flying Gerardos", "The Skin of Our Teeth", "Rebecca", and "A Winter's Tale".

REEVES-SMITH, OLIVE. Born in Surrey, England. Broadway debut in 1916 in "The Better 'Ole". Has appeared in "Three Live Ghosts", "Aloma of the South Seas", "The Constant Nymph", "Jubilee", "Party", "Richard of Bordeaux", and more recentl[y] in "Bloomer Girl".

REID, FRANCES, born in Wichita Falls, Texas; [is] the wife of actor Philip Bourneuf. Studied at the Pasadena Playhouse. Made stage debut in Wes[t] Coast company of "Tovarich." Made Broadwa[y] debut in "Where There's a Will." Followed by— "The Rivals," "Bird in Hand," "The Patriots, "Listen Professor," "A Highland Fling," and th[is] season "The Wind is Ninety" and G. I. "Hamlet."

RELPH, GEORGE. Born Northumberland, Eng., Jan. 27, 1888. First appeared on the English stage [in] 1905, and made N. Y. debut in 1911 in "Kismet". He also appeared on Broadway in "The Yellow Jacket", "The Garden of Paradise", as Romeo [in] "Romeo and Juliet"; and played a season of stoc[k] in Boston. He re-appeared on Broadway with th[e] Old Vic Company.

RENNIE, JAMES. Born in Toronto in 1890, and edu[-] cated at Collegiate Institute in that city. In 1916 h[e] made his Broadway bow in "His Bridal Night". Ha[s] appeared in "Moonlight and Honeysuckle", "Span[-] ish Love", "Shore Leave", "The Best People", "Th[e] Great Gatsby", "Young Love", "Alien Corn", an[d] "Abide With Me". More recently he was seen i[n] "One-Man Show", and on the road in "State [of] the Union".

Lubov Roudenko   Joan Roberts   Tatiana Riabouchinska

RIABOUCHINSKA, TATIANA. Born in Moscow, May 23, 1916. Studied dancing in Paris under Volinine, and first appeared in N. Y. in 1931 in "Chauve Souris". She is one of the most outstanding dancers in modern ballet. Recently she appeared in "Polonaise".

RICHARDS, KURT. Born in Philadelphia, Pa., and graduated from Penn State. Made Broadway debut in Evans' production of "Hamlet" and also appeared with Mr. Evans in "Henry IV" and "Richard II". Has also been seen in the revival of "Counsellor At Law", "Wallflower", "Sophie", and "A Winter's Tale".

RICHARDSON, RALPH. Born in Cheltenham, Goucestershire on Dec. 19, 1902. Made English debut in 1921 in "The Merchant of Venice". In 1935 he toured this country with Katherine Cornell, and was first seen on Broadway as Chorus and Mercutio in "Romeo and Juliet" in that year. He returned to N. Y. C. with the Old Vic Company.

RING, BLANCHE. Born Boston, Mass., April 24, 1877. She first appeared in support of such players as James H. Herne, Nat Goodwin, Chauncey Olcott, and James T. Powers. Among her greatest successes were "The Jewel of Asia", "The Blonde in Black", "Sergeant Brue", "About Town", "The Great White Way", "The Midnight Sons", "The Yankee Girl", and "The Wall Street Girl". More recently she has been seen in "Strike Up the Band", "Stepping Sisters", "Madame Capet", "De Lux", and "Right This Way".

RIVERS, PAMELA. Born Chicago, June 11, 1926. Made Broadway debut in "Pick-Up Girl", and has since been seen in "The Next Half Hour", and "The Song of Bernadette".

ROACHE, VIOLA. Born Norfolk, Eng., Oct. 3, 1885. Studied for the stage at the Royal Academy of Dramatic Art. First appeared on Broadway in 1914 in "Panthea". Has been seen in "A Woman Disputed", "The Bachelor Father", "The Distaff Side", "Pride and Prejudice", "Call It a Day", and more recently in "Bird in Hand", "Theatre", and "No Way Out".

ROBER, RICHARD. Born in Rochester, N .Y., May 14, 1906, he was educated at the Univ. of Rochester and Washington Univ. Received his stage training with the Lyceum Players at Rochester. He has appeared in "Berkely Square", "East of the Sun", the Maurice Evans productions of "Richard II" and "Henry IV", and the Lunt productions of "Amphytryon 38", "The Sea Gull", and "Idiot's Delight", as well as "Behind Red Lights", "Banjo Eyes", "Star and Garter", "Ramshackle Inn", "She Had to Say Yes", and "Oklahoma".

ROBERTS, JOAN. Born July 15, 1918, in N. Y. C. Made her Broadway debut in "Sunny River", and has since been seen in "Oklahoma", "Marinka", and "Are You With It?"

ROBERTSON, GUY. Born Denver, Colo., Jan. 26, 1892. Originally planned to become an engineer, and made first stage appearance in road company of "Head Over Heels". Made Broadway bow in 1919 in "See-Saw". Has appeared in "Wildflower", "Song of the Flame", "The Circus Princess", "White Lilacs", "The Street Singer", "Nina Rosa", "All the King's Horses", "White Horse Inn", and "Right This Way".

ROBESON, PAUL. Born Princeton, N. J., April 9, 1898. Educated at Rutger's and Columbia Univ. Studied for the law and was admitted to the bar, but turned to the stage and made N. Y. debut in 1921 in "Simon the Cyrenian". Appeared in "Taboo", "All God's Chillun Got Wings", "The Emperor Jones", "Black Boy", and "Porgy". He played "Show Boat" in London, and afterwards appeared in the N. Y. 1927 revival. He is also known for his international song concerts, and his work in the films. Last Broadway appearance was in "Othello".

ROBSON, FLORA. Born March 28, 1902, in South Shields, Durham, and studied for the stage at the Royal Academy of Dramatic Art. Made her English debut in 1921. Appeared on the N. Y. stage in "Ladies in Retirement" and "The Damask Cheek".

ROERICK, WILLIAM. Born N. Y. C., Dec. 17, 1912, and educated at Hamilton College. Broadway debut in 1935 in the Cornell production of "Romeo and Juliet". Has appeared in "Saint Joan", the Gielgud "Hamlet", "Our Town", "The Importance of Being Earnest", "The Land Is Bright", "Autumn Hill", "This Is the Army", and "The Magnificent Yankee".

ROGERS, EMMETT. Born Plainfield, N. J., Nov. 30, 1915. Has appeared on Broadway in "Growing Pains", "Man of Wax", "The First Legion", "Alice Takat", "Strip Girl", "Ethan Frome", "Richard II", "Henry IV", "Hamlet", "Papa Is All", and the G.I. "Hamlet".

ROSS, ANTHONY. Born in N. Y. C., 1906, he graduated from Brown Univ. in 1932. His first appearance on Broadway was in "Whistling in the Dark". He has also played in "Bury the Dead", "Arsenic and Old Lace", "This Is the Army", and "The Glass Menagerie".

175

Pamela Rivers

Ralph Richardson

Frances Reid

ROSS, ELIZABETH. Born Morristown, N. J., on Aug. 28, 1926. Studied for the theatre at Catholic University, Washington, D. C. Made Broadway debut in the leading role in "The Song of Bernadette".

ROUDENKO, LUBOV. Born in Sophia, Bulgaria, and educated in Paris. Danced with the Ballet Russe de Monte Carlo, and appeared on Broadway in "The Merry Widow" and "Nellie Bly."

SANDS, DOROTHY. Born March 5, 1900, in Cambridge, Mass. Educated at Radcliffe College. Stage training with the Neighborhood Playhouse and New York Repertory Company. Appeared in "The Grand Street Follies" of 1927, '28, '29, "Many a Slip", "The Sea Gull", "The Stairs", "All the Comforts of Home", "Papa Is All", "Tomorrow the World", and more recently "A Joy Forever".

SAUNDERS, NICHOLAS. Born in Kiev, Russia, June 2, 1914. Made Broadway bow in 1942 in "Lady in the Dark". Has appeared in "A New Life", "A Highland Fling", "Marriage Is for Single People", and "The Magnificent Yankee".

SAVO, JIMMY. Born in N. Y. C., 1895. Was a prominent figure in vaudeville for many years before his first Broadway appearance in "Vanities of

1923". Has also been seen in "Vogues of 1924", "Hassard Short's Ritz Revue", "Murray Anderson's Almanack", "Earl Carroll's Vanities", "Parade", and more recently in "The Boys From Syracuse", "Wine, Women and Song", and "What's Up".

SAXTON, LUTHER. Born in Fairfax, S. C., July 12, 1916. Educated at Springfield, Mass., High School and Clark College, Atlanta, Ga. Made his Broadway bow in "Carmen Jones".

SCHEFF, FRITZI. Born Aug. 30, 1879 in Vienna. Studied music in Frankfort, and made operatic debut in the title role of "Martha" in Munich in 1898. Later she sang at Covent Garden and the Metropolitan and among her roles were Musetta in "La Boheme", Nedda in "Pagliacci", Zerlina in "Don Giovanni", and Cherubino in "Marriage of Figaro". In 1903 she made her light opera debut in "Babette". This was followed by "The Two Roses", "Fatinitza", "Giroflé-Girofla", "Boccaccio", "Mlle. Modiste", "The Prima Donna", "The Mikado", "The Duchess" "The Love Wager", "Glorianna", "The O'Brien Girl", and "Bye-Bye Bonnie". In 1929 she appeared in a revival of "Mlle. Modiste", her greatest success. Recently she has been seen on the road in "I Am Different", "Ladies In Retirement", "Tonight Or Never", and "The Circle".

Mary Servoss

Fritzi Scheff

Dorothy Sands

Danny Scholl   Eleanor Swayne   Grey Stafford

SCHILDKRAUT, JOSEPH. Born in Vienna, March 22, 1895. Studied for the stage in Germany and at the American Academy of Dramatic Arts. Made his first N. Y. stage appearance in his father's company at the Irving Place Theatre in 1910. Made his first professional appearance in Germany in 1913 under Max Reinhardt. Reappeared on N. Y. stage in 1921 in "Pagans". Was seen on Broadway in "Liliom", "Peer Gynt", "The Firebrand", "Anatol", and was also a member of the Civic Repertory Company. More recently he was seen on Broadway in "Uncle Harry", and revival of "The Cherry Orchard".

SCHOLL, DANNY. Born July 2, 1921, in Cincinnati, Ohio. Made Broadway bow in "Call Me Mister".

SCOTT, MARTHA. Born in Jamesport, Mo., 1914, she came into prominence overnight in her first New York appearance in "Our Town". Following this success she was seen briefly in "Foreigners", after which she went to Hollywood and made several pictures. Returning to the N. Y. stage she has been seen recently in "The Willow and I", "Soldier's Wife", and "The Voice of the Turtle".

SEGAL, VIVIENNE. Born in Philadelphia in 1897. Made her Broadway debut in 1915 in "The Blue Paradise". Appeared on the N. Y. stage in "Oh! Lady, Lady!", "The Yankee Princess", "Adrienne", "Castles in the Air", "The Desert Song", "The Three Musketeers", and more recently "I Married an Angel", "Pal Joey", and the revival of "A Connecticut Yankee".

SEIDEL, TOM. Born in Indianapolis, Ind., March 11, 1917. Educated at Carnegie Institute of Technology. Received his stage training at the Pasadena Community Playhouse. Broadway appearances include "Slightly Married", "Over 21", and "Harvey".

SERGAVA, KATHARINE. Born in Russia, July 30, 1918, and educated at French College, Pulcheric. Has appeared with the Mordkin Ballet, the original Ballet Russe and The Ballet Theatre. Made her Broadway bow in "Oklahoma".

SERVOSS, MARY. Born in Chicago where she first appeared on the stage playing small parts in stock. N. Y. debut in 1906 in "Bedford's Hope". Has appeared in "Upstairs and Down", as Portia in David Warfield's "The Merchant of Venice", "Tiger Cats", "Behold the Bridegroom", "Street Scene", "Counsellor-at-Law", "Dangerous Corner", and more recently in "Tortilla Flat", "Hamlet" with Leslie Howard, "Dance Night", "Suspect", and "Swan Song".

Harry Sothern   Jan Sterling   Robert Sully

Blanche Sweet   William Skipper   Geraldine Stroock

SHANNON, EFFIE. Born Cambridge, Mass., May 13, 1867. Made first stage appearance as a child in role of Little Eva in "Uncle Tom's Cabin". Her long and illustrious career has included the following plays: "Shenanadoah", "Lady Bountiful", "The Moth and the Flame", "Taps", "Years of Discretion", "Pollyanna", "Under Orders", "Mama's Affairs", "Heartbreak House", and "The Fatal Alibi". More recently she has been seen in "The Bishop Misbehaves", "The Wingless Victory", "Barchester Towers", "Parnell", and "Jeremiah".

SHARP, HENRY. Born Feb. 19, 1889, in Riga, Latvia. Studied for the theatre at American Academy of Dramatic Arts. Appeared in stock, vaudeville, and silent pictures. Among the many plays in which he has been seen on Broadway are "A Gentleman From Mississippi", "Over Night", "Madame X", and more recently "Escape Me Never", "Morning Star", "Arsenic and Old Lace", and "The Assassin".

SIMMS, HILDA. Born in Minneapolis, Minn., she received her stage training with the Edith Bush Players and the Minneapolis Coach Players. She attended the Univ. of Minn., and after receiving her B.S. degree she came East. Shortly after her arrival in N. Y. she joined the American Negro Theatre and was given a small part in their production of "Three's a Family". "Anna Lucasta" marked her Broadway debut.

SIMPSON, IVAN. Was born in England and came to this country with E. S. Willard, playing with him for several seasons in repertory. For many years he was in George Arliss' company in "The Green Goddess", "Old English", and other Arliss successes both on the stage and screen. Recent N. Y. appearances include "Bright Boy", "Sleep, My Pretty One", the revival of "The Barretts of Wimpole Street", "The Secret Room", and "Swan Song".

SKINNER, CORNELIA OTIS. Born in Chicago, Ill., May 30, 1902, while her famous father, Otis Skinner, was playing an engagement there. She made her stage debut with her father in 1921 in "Blood and Sand". Engagements in "Will Shakespeare", "The Wild Wescotts", and "White Collars" followed. She then became her own dramatist, director, costumer, and author in a series of character sketches in which she played all the parts. As a one-woman theatre her success in these monodramas was so great that for fifteen years she played in them almost exclusively. Recently she has appeared in a revival of "Love for Love" with the Players' Club, "Theatre", and "The Searching Wind".

SKIPPER, BILL. Born Feb. 28, 1922, in Mobile, Ala. First appeared on Broadway in "Higher and Higher". Has also been seen in "Panama Hattie", "Banjo Eyes", "Star and Garter", "Tars and Spars", and more recently in "Billion Dollar Baby".

SLEEPER, MARTHA. Born Lake Bluff, Ill., June 24, 1911. Made her Broadway bow in 1929 in "Stepping Out". Has appeared in "Good Men and True", "Russet Mantle", "Save Me the Waltz", "I Must Love Someone", and more recently in "The Perfect Marriage" and "The Rugged Path".

SMILEY, RALPH. Born N. Y. C., July 24, 1916. Studied for the theatre at American Academy of Dramatic Arts. Played in stock and on the road for several seasons and made his Broadway debut in "The Assassin".

SMITH, G. ALBERT. Born March 11, 1898, in Louisville, Ky. Made Broadway debut in "Rita Coventry". Has been seen in "Coquette", "The Animal Kingdom", "Of Mice and Men", "Ceiling Zero", "The Land Is Bright" and "State of the Union".

SMITH, HOWARD. Born in Attleboro, Mass., Aug. 12, 1895. He was educated at McGill College. On Broadway he has appeared in "The Eternal Magdalene", "Miss Quiss", "Solitaire", "The Life of Riley", "Decision", and "Dear Ruth".

SMITH, MURIEL. Was born in N. Y. C., Feb. 23, 1923, and educated at Roosevelt High School and the Curtis Institute, Philadelphia. Won a contest on the Major Bowes radio hour. "Carmen Jones" marks her Broadway debut.

SMITH, QUEENIE. Born N. Y. C., Sept. 8, 1902. Was trained as a dancer from early childhood at the Metropolitan Opera House Ballet School, and in 1916 first appeared on the stage of the Metropolitan. Her musical comedy debut was in 1919 in "Roly-Roly Eyes". Has appeared on Broadway in "Just Because", "Orange Blossoms", "Helen of Troy, New York", "Sitting Pretty", "Be Yourself", "Tip Toes", and "Hit the Deck".

SOMERS, JIMSEY. Born July 4, 1937, in N. Y. C. and attends the Professional Children's School. Made Broadway debut in "Violet", and has also appeared in "Carousel" and "Apple of His Eye".

SOTHERN, HARRY. Born in London, April 26, 1883, and educated at Cheltenham College. Has been in the theatre since 1906, first appearing in support of his uncle, E. H. Sothern. Among the many plays in which he has appeared on Broadway are "Kismet", "The Three of Us", "The Constant Nymph", "Lady of the Lamp", "Art and Mrs. Bottle", "Bird in Hand", and "Lean Harvest". More recently he

William Tabbert   Ann Thomas   William Terry

was seen in "Shadow and Substance", "The Wookey", "Sheppey", "Devils Galore", and "Swan Song".

STAFFORD, GREY. Born Uxbridge, Middlesex, England, Aug. 3, 1920. Played in stock on West Coast and made N. Y. debut in "Make Yourself at Home".

STARKEY, WALTER. Born May 3, 1921, in Texas. Educated at Univ. of Texas. First Broadway appearance was in "The Mermaids Singing". Has also been seen in "This, Too, Shall Pass".

STERLING, JAN. Born N. Y. C., April 3, 1923. Educated in Paris, London, and Rio de Janeiro. Studied for the stage in Fay Compton's Dramatic School, London. Broadway debut in "Bachelor Born" was followed by roles in "When We Are Married", "Grey Farm", "This Rock", "The Rugged Path", "Dunnigan's Daughter", and "This, Too, Shall Pass".

STERLING, ROY. Born in Brooklyn, July 25, 1933. Attended Professional Children's School. Made Broadway debut in "Chicken Every Sunday" and has since been seen in "The Wind Is Ninety".

STEWART, CAROLYN HILL. Born in Keystone, W. Va. Educated at West Virginia State College and Univ. Iowa. Appeared on Broadway in "Goldie", "In Abraham's Bosom", "Wingless Victory", and more recently in "Jeb".

STEWART, DAVID J. Born Jan. 8, 1918, in Omaha, Neb. Educated at Univ. of Omaha. Studied for the stage at Neighborhood Playhouse, and made Broadway debut in "Antigone".

STICKNEY, DOROTHY. Born Dickinson, N. D., June 21, 1903. Educated at St. Catherine's College, St. Paul, Minn., and the Northwestern Dramatic School, Minneapolis. Played several seasons in stock and toured in a variety of roles before she made her Broadway debut in "The Squall" in 1926. Has appeared in "Chicago", "March Hares", revival of "The Beaux Stratagem", "The Front Page", "Philip Goes Forth", "Another Language", "On Borrowed Time", and "Life With Father".

STOCKWELL, HARRY. A native of Kansas City, Mo., he started in life as a newspaper man but switched to music when he received a scholarship at the Eastman Conservatory of Music. He has appeared on Broadway in "Broadway Nights", "As Thousands Cheer", the eighth and ninth editions of Earl Carroll's "Vanities", George White's "Scandals of 1939", "Oklahoma", "Marinka", and revival of "The Desert Song".

STODDARD, HAILA. Born Nov. 14, 1914, in Great Falls, Mont. Graduate of Univ. of Southern Calif.

Broadway debut in 1938 in "Yes, My Darling Daughter". Also appeared in "Susanna and the Elders", "The Rivals", "Moonvine", "Blithe Spirit", and "Dream Girl".

STONE, DOROTHY. Born June 3, 1905, in Brooklyn. Made her Broadway debut in 1923 in "Stepping Stones". Has appeared on the N. Y. stage in "Criss-Cross", "Three Cheers", "Show Girl", "Smiling Faces", "The Gay Divorcee", "As Thousands Cheer", "Hooray for What!" and more recently with her father in a revival of "You Can't Take It With You", and in "The Red Mill".

STONE, FRED. Born near Denver, Colo., Aug. 19, 1873. His earliest years were spent with a travelling circus. Met David Montgomery in 1894 while they were both playing in vaudeville and formed a partnership that lasted until Montgomery's death. Together they starred in "The Wizard of Oz", "The Red Mill", "The Old Town", "The Lady of the Slipper", and "Chin-Chin". Alone he starred in "Jack O' Lantern", "Tip Top", "Stepping Stones", and "Criss-Cross". In recent years Broadway has seen him in "Jayhawker", and revivals of "Lightnin'" and "You Can't Take It With You".

STONE, ROBINSON. Born in Chicago, April 25, 1919. Educated at Northwestern and Yale. Made his Broadway debut in "Janie", and has since been seen in "Othello" and "Strange Fruit".

STROOCK, GERALDINE. Born N. Y. C., Oct. 29, 1925. Studied for the theatre at Neighborhood Playhouse and American Academy. Made debut on Broadway in "Follow the Girls", and more recently was seen in "The Winter's Tale".

SULLY, ROBERT. Born N. Y. C., Nov. 20, 1918. Educated at Univ. of Penna. Appeared in several moving pictures before making his Broadway bow in "Marriage Is for Single People".

SUNDSTROM, FRANK. Studied for the stage with the Royal Dramatic Theatre, Stockholm, Sweden. On the Swedish stage he played many classic roles, as well as translations of modern American successes. "The Assassin" marks his Broadway debut.

SWAYNE, ELEANOR. Born in Minneapolis, Minn. Made her Broadway debut in "The Magnificent Yankee".

SWEET, BLANCHE. Born in Chicago, Ill. Made her Broadway debut as a child actress. She appeared with great success for many years as a star in the silent films. Returned to the N. Y. stage for "The Petrified Forest", and has also been seen in "There's Always a Breeze", "Aries Is Rising", and "Those Endearing Young Charms".

Frederic Tozere   Maidel Turner   Murvyn Vye

TABBERT, WILLIAM. Born in Chicago, Oct. 5, 1921. First Broadway appearance in "What's Up", followed by "Follow the Girls", "Seven Lively Arts", and "Billion Dollar Baby".

TAFLER, SIDNEY. Born July 31, 1916, in London. Studied for the theatre at the Royal Academy of Dramatic Art. Made debut on N. Y. stage with the Old Vic Company.

TALIAFERRO, MABEL. Born on a train nearing New York, May 21, 1889. Among the many plays in which she has appeared are "Polly of the Circus", "Mrs. Wiggs of the Cabbage Patch", "You Never Can Tell", "Claudia", "George Washington Slept Here", "Victory Belles", and more recently "Bloomer Girl".

TAYLOR, LAURETTE. Born in N. Y. C., April 1, 1887. First appeared on the stage as a child in vaudeville where she was billed "La Belle Laurette". Her N. Y. debut was in 1903 in "From Rags to Riches". After several years of stock, she returned to N. Y. and established herself as one of Broadway's foremost actresses. Among the many plays in which she appeared are "Alias Jimmy Valentine", "Seven Sisters", "The Bird of Paradise", "Peg O' My Heart", "Just as Well", "Happiness", "The Harp of Life", "Out There", "The Wooing of Eve", "One Night in Rome", "The National Anthem", "Humoroesque", "In a Garden", "The Comedienne", and "The Furies". More recently she has been seen in a revival of "Outward Bound" and "The Glass Menagerie".

TERRY, WILLIAM. Born Eugene, Ore., March 21, 1914. Educated at Univ. of Oregon, and studied for the stage at the Pasadena Community Playhouse. Made N. Y. debut in 1937 in "Straw Hat". Since then has appeared on Broadway in "Out of the Frying Pan", "Brother Cain", and "I Like It Here".

THOMAS, ANN. Born July 8, 1920, in Newport, R. I. Went to Professional Children's School and first appeared on stage as a child. Among the many plays in which she has appeared on Broadway are "Doctor's Disagree", "A New Life", "Having Wonderful Time", "The Man from Cairo", "Chicken Every Sunday", and "The Would-Be Gentleman".

THOMAS, FRANK M. Born July 13, 1890, in St. Joseph, Mo. Educated at Butler College. Made Broadway debut in 1912 in "Along Came Ruth". Among the many plays in which he has acted on the N. Y. stage are "The House of Glass", "Red Light Annie", "The National Anthem", "Remember the Day", and more recently "Chicken Every Sunday", "The Rich Full Life", and "Jeb".

THOMSON, BARRY. Born N. Y. C. but educated abroad. Studied for the stage at the Royal Academy of Dramatic Art in London. First played on Broadway in 1927 in "Immoral Isabella". Appeared with the Lunts in "The Taming of the Shrew", "Idiot's Delight", and "Amphytryon 38", and more recently appeared in "Second Best Bed".

THOR, JEROME. Born Jan. 5, 1915, in N. Y. C. Studied for the stage at the Neighborhood Playhouse. Has appeared in "The Fabulous Invalid", "The American Way", "The World We Make", "Somewhere in France", "The Doughgirls", "My Sister Eileen", "Strip for Action", "Get Away, Old Man", "Calico Wedding", "No Way Out", "The French Touch", and the revival of "He Who Gets Slapped".

TIHMAR, DAVID. Born March 18, 1918, in Blair Okla. He danced with the Ballet Russe de Monte Carlo, and has been seen on Broadway in "Oklahoma" and "Follow the Girls".

TONE, FRANCHOT. Born in Niagara Falls, N. Y., Feb. 27, 1906. Educated at Cornell Univ. where he became president of the Dramatic Club. Made his Broadway bow with Katharine Cornell in "The Age of Innocence". His next engagements found him in "Cross Roads", "Red Rust", "Hotel Universe", "Green Grow the Lilacs", and "Pagan Lady". One of the original members of the Group Theatre, he played with them in "The House of Connelly", "1931", "Night Over Taos", "Success Story", and "The Gentle People". His success in the theatre sent him to Hollywood where he appeared in many films. His most recent Broadway appearances were in "The Fifth Column" and "Hope for the Best".

TOZERE, FREDERIC. Born June 19, 1901, in Brookline, Mass. Made Broadway bow in 1924 in "Stepping Stones". Has appeared in "Journey's End", "Key Largo", "Watch on the Rhine", "Outrageous Fortune", "In Bed We Cry", "Signature", and "The Rich Full Life".

TRUEX, ERNEST. He was born in Red Hill, Mo., Sept. 19, 1890, and educated at the Whittier School, Denver, Colo. Made his first appearance on the stage in 1895, playing Little Lord Fauntleroy. Made his Broadway bow in 1908 with Lillian Russell in "Wildfire". Since then he appeared in "Rebecca of Sunnybrook Farm", "The Good Little Devil", "The Dummy", "Just Boys", "New Toys", "Annie Dear", "The Fall Guy", and "Pomeroy's Past". Hollywood occupies most of Mr. Truex's time now, though he has returned to Broadway to appear in "Lysistrata", "Whistling in the Dark", "George Washington Slept Here", and "Helen Goes to Troy".

Michael Vallon   Nancy Walker   Lou Wills Jr.

TRUEX, PHILIP. Born Boston, Mass., Sept. 20, 1911. Educated at Haverford College. Made Broadway debut in 1933 in "The World Waits". Has since appeared in "Too Much Party", "The Hook-Up", "Battleship Gertie", "Mulatto", "Richard II", "The Fabulous Invalid", "Family Portrait", "The Man Who Came to Dinner", and "This Is the Army". More recently he was seen in "The Magnificent Yankee".

TUCKER, SOPHIE. Born Boston, Mass., Jan. 13, 1884. First appeared as a singer in her father's cafe in Hartford in 1905, and shortly afterwards became well known in vaudeville. First Broadway appearance was in "The Ziegfeld Follies of 1909". Since then she appeared with outstanding success in vaudeville, and was also seen in N. Y. in "Town Topics", "Hello, Alexander", "Shubert Gaieties", "Earl Carroll's Vanities", and more recently in "Leave It to Me", and "High Kickers".

TURNER, MAIDEL. Born in Sherman, Texas. Trained for the theatre at Dramatic School of the Chicago Musical College. First stage appearance was as leading lady to Maclyn Arbuckle in "Welcome to Our City". Among the many plays in which she has appeared on Broadway are "Kick In", "The Varying Shore", "Spring Is Here", "What a Life", "By Jupiter", and more recently "Dark of the Moon", and "State of the Union".

TYNE, GEORGE. Born Philadelphia, Pa., Feb. 6, 1917. Appeared on Broadway in "Of V We Sing", "Let Freedom Ring", and more recently, "A Sound of Hunting".

VALENTINOFF, VAL. Born N. Y. C., March 23, 1919. Educated at P. S. 40, Wingate Junior High, and Commercial High. Has danced with the Monte Carlo Ballet Russe, and the St. Louis and Detroit Opera Companies. Has appeared on Broadway in "Virginia", "Sons O' Fun", and "Follow the Girls".

VALENTY, LILI. Born Aug. 17, in Lodz, Poland. Studied for the theatre under Max Reinhardt in Berlin. Made Broadway debut in "Bitter Stream" in 1936. Has since been seen in "Cue for Passion", "The Land Is Bright", "Pick-Up Girl" and "Skydrift".

VALLON, MICHAEL. Born July 21, 1897, in Dover, Minn., and educated at Univ. of Minn. Made N. Y. debut in 1926 in "Deep River". Most recent Broadway appearances were in "A Bell for Adano" and "The Song of Bernadette".

VAN PATTEN, DICK. Has appeared on Broadway in "Tapestry in Grey", "The Eternal Road", "Home, Sweet Home", "The American Way", "The Woman Brown", "The Lady Who Came to Stay", "Run Sheep Run", "The Land Is Bright", "Kiss and Tell", "Decision", "The Skin of Our Teeth", "Too Hot for Maneuvers", "The Wind Is Ninety", and "O Mistress Mine".

VAN PATTEN, JOYCE. Born March 9, 1934, Kew Gardens, L. I., N. Y. Made debut in 1941 in "Popsy", and has since been seen in "This Rock", "Tomorrow the World", "The Perfect Marriage" and "The Wind Is Ninety".

VARDEN, EVELYN. Born Vinita, Okla., 1893. Made first appearance as a child actress in films, and had considerable experience in stock. Made Broadway bow in 1910 in "The Nest Egg". Appeared in "Peg O' My Heart", "Seven Days Leave", "Alley Cat", "Russet Mantle", and "To Quito and Back". More recently New Yorkers have seen her in "Our Town", "Family Portrait", "Grey Farm", "The Family" and "Dream Girl".

VERMILYEA, HAROLD. Born N. Y. C., Oct. 10, 1889. Among the many plays in which he has appeared on Broadway are "It Pays to Advertise", "Get Rich Quick Wallingford", "The Enemy", "Sun-Up", "Loose Ankles", "The Alarm Clock", "Midnight", and "Madame Bovary". More recently he has been seen in "Jacobowsky and the Colonel" and "Deep Are the Roots".

VINCENT, ROMO. Born Dec. 23, 1909, in Chicago. He has appeared in vaudeville, movies, and night clubs. On Broadway he has appeared in "Beat the Band" and "Marinka".

VYE, MURVYN. Born Quincy, Mass., July 15, 1913. Educated at Andover and Yale. Has appeared on Broadway in the Gielgud "Hamlet", "As You Like It", "Oklahoma", "One Touch of Venus", and "Carousel".

WALKER, JUNE. Born N. Y. C., 1904. First appeared on Broadway as a chorus girl in "Hitchy-Koo" in 1918. Has been seen in "Six Cylinder Love", "The Nervous Wreck", "Processional", "Gentlemen Prefer Blondes", "The Love Nest", "The Bachelor Father", "Waterloo Bridge", "Green Grow the Lilacs", "The Farmer Takes a Wife", "For Valor", and "The Merchant of Yonkers". More recently she appeared in "Round Trip" and "Truckline Cafe".

WALKER, NANCY. Born in Philadelphia, May 10, 1921. At the age of nineteen she scored an immediate success on Broadway in "Best Foot Forward" and was sent off to Hollywood where she made the films, "Best Foot Forward," "Girl Crazy", and "Broadway Rhythm." Returning to New York she scored another success in "On The Town."

Claire Windsor

Richard Widmark

Jane White

WALLACH, ELI. Born in Brooklyn, Dec. 7, 1915. Educated at Univ. of Texas and C.C.N.Y. Studied for the theatre with the Neighborhood Playhouse, and made Broadway debut in "Skydrift".

WANAMAKER, SAM. Born in Chicago, June 14, 1919. Made Broadway bow in "Cafe Crown", and has appeared in "Counterattack", and "This, Too, Shall Pass".

WARRE, MICHAEL. Born June 18, 1922, in London, and studied for the stage at the London Mask Theatre School. Made his initial appearance on Broadway in the Old Vic Company.

WATERS, ETHEL. Born Chester, Pa., Oct. 31, 1900. Commenced her career as a cabaret singer, and made Broadway debut in 1927 in "Africana". Appeared in "Lew Leslie's Blackbirds", "Rhapsody in Black", "As Thousands Cheer", "At Home Abroad", and made an outstanding success in a straight role in "Mamba's Daughter". More recent appearances include "Cabin in the Sky" and "Blue Holiday".

WATKINS, LINDA. Born Boston, Mass., May 23, 1914. Made Broadway debut in 1926 in "The Devil in the Cheese". Has appeared in "Ivory Door", "The Wild Duck", "Hedda Gabler", "Lady From the Sea", "June Moon", "Sweet Stranger", "Say When", "Penny Wise", "I Am My Youth", and more recently in "Janie".

WATSON, LUCILLE. Born Quebec, Canada, May 27, 1879. Studied for the stage at the American Academy of Dramatic Arts, and first played in Ottawa in 1900. Made N. Y. debut in 1903 in "Hearts Aflame". Has appeared in "The Girl With the Green Eyes", "The Dictator", "The City", "Under Cover", "The Eternal Magdalene", "Heartbreak House", "You and I", "No More Ladies", "Pride and Prejudice", and "Yes, My Darling Daughter". More recently she was seen in "Dear Octopus".

WATSON, MINOR. Born in Marianna, Ark., Dec. 22, 1889. Studied for the stage at the American Academy of Dramatic Arts. Played several seasons in stock before making his Broadway bow in 1922 in "Why Men Leave Home". Has appeared in "The Magnolia Lady", "Trigger", "This Thing Called Love", "It's a Wise Child", "Reunion in Vienna", "A Divine Drudge", "End of Summerr", and most recently in "State of the Union".

WATT, BILLIE LOU. Born St. Louis, Mo., June 20, 1924. Educated at Northwestern Univ. School of Speech. Played the lead in the Chicago company of "Kiss and Tell", and made Broadway bow in "Little Women".

WEAVER, "DOODLES". Born in Los Angeles, May 11, 1914. Made N. Y. debut in 1941 in "Meet the People", and has since been seen in "Marinka".

WEBB, CLIFTON. Born in Indiana, 1891. First appeared on stage as a child actor. Studied for Grand Opera, and had a brief operatic career in Boston before appearing on the regular stage. In 1913 he first played on Broadway in "The Purple Road". Among the many plays in which he has appeared are "Dancing Around", "Nobody Home", "Very Good, Eddie", "Listen Lester", "Meet the Wife", "Sunny", "She's My Baby", "Treasure Girl", "The Little Show", "Three's a Crowd", "Flying Colors", and as "Thousands Cheer". More recently he was seen in a revival of "The Importance of Being Earnest" and "Blithe Spirit".

WEBER, WILLIAM. Born in Los Angeles, July 5, 1915. Educated at Univ. of Calif. and studied for the stage at Pasadena Playhouse. First Broadway appearance in revival of "Susan and God", and has been seen also in G.I. "Hamlet".

WEIDLER, VIRGINIA. Born Eagle Rock, Calif., March 21, 1927. First appeared in the films at age of two, and made an outstanding success in Hollywood playing children's roles. "The Rich Full Life" marked her Broadway debut.

WEISS, PAUL. Born in Brooklyn, March 24, 1933. Made Broadway debut in "January Thaw".

WELLES, ORSON. Born Kenosha, Wisc., May 6, 1915. Made his first stage appearance in 1931 at the Gate Theatre in Dublin. Returning to this country, he toured with Katharine Cornell, and made his N. Y. debut as Chorus and Tybalt in her production of "Romeo and Juliet". Before this he had organized and managed the Woodstock Theatre Festival, and in 1937 was appointed a director of the Federal Theatre Project in N. Y. During this period he produced a Negro version of "Macbeth", and produced and acted in "Dr. Faustus". In 1937, with John Houseman, he founded the Mercury Theatre, which revived such plays as "Julius Caesar", "The Shoemaker's Holiday", "Heartbreak House", and "Danton's Death". He has achieved considerable fame in both films and radio, and returned to the Broadway stage in "Around the World".

WENGRAF, JOHN. Born April 23, 1907, in Vienna. Educated in Vienna, Paris, and London. Made Broadway debut in "Candle in the Wind". More recently was seen in "The French Touch".

WEST, MAE. Born in Brooklyn, Aug. 17, 1892. Made her Broadway debut in "Folies Bergere". This was followed by appearances in "A La Broad-

Lois Wilson   Peggy Wood   Mary Wickes

way", "Vera Violetta", "The Winsome Widow", "Demi-Tasse", and "The Mimic World". It was as a writer-actress in "Sex" that she first came to the attention of New York audiences. Greater success came to her in another play of her authorship, "Diamond Lil". This led to a Hollywood contract where she made several movies. She returned to Broadway in another of her own plays, "Catherine Was Great".

WHITE, DONALD. Born in Brooklyn, June 12, 1925. Educated at Emerson College. Made his Broadway bow in "Make Yourself at Home".

WHITE, JANE. Born N. Y. C., Oct. 30, 1922. Educated at Ethical Culture School and Smith College. Had her theatre training with the New School for Social Research. Made her Broadway debut in "Strange Fruit".

WHITING, JACK. Born Philadelphia, Pa., June 22, 1901. Educated at the Univ. of Penn. Made Broadway bow in "Ziegfeld Follies of 1922". Has appeared in "Orange Blossoms", "Cinders", "Aren't We All?", "Stepping Stones", "Annie Dear", "The Ramblers", "Yes, Yes, Yvette", "She's My Baby", "Hold Everything", "Heads Up", "America's Sweetheart", "Take a Chance", "Calling All Stars", "Hooray for What", "Very Warm for May", "Hold On to Your Hats", and more recently in "The Overtons" and "The Red Mill".

WHITTY, DAME MAY. Born Liverpool, June 19, 1865. Made first stage appearance in England as a chorus girl in 1881. Her first American appearance was in 1895-6 when she toured this country with the Lyceum Company under Sir Henry Irving. In 1908 she played on Broadway in "Irene Wycherly", and did not return until 1932 when she appeared in "There's Always Juliet". She also played here in "Night Must Fall" and "Yr. Obedient Servant", and has made an eminent success in films. More recently she appeared on the N. Y. stage in "Therese".

WICKES, MARY. Born in St. Louis, Mo., and educated at Washington Univ., St. Louis First played on Broadway in "The Farmer Takes a Wife". Has appeared in "One Good Year", "Spring Dance", "Stage Door", "Hitch Your Wagon", "Father Malachy's Miracle", "Stars in Your Eyes", "Danton's Death", "The Man Who Came to Dinner", "Jackpot", "Dark Hammock", "Hollywood Pinafore", and "Apple of His Eye".

WIDDECOMBE, WALLACE. Born London, Sept. 21, 1878. First appeared on the English stage in 1896. He has been seen in this country in many plays, both on Broadway and on tour. Among them are

"Victoria Regina", "So This Is London", "The Queen's Husband", "Jane Eyre", "Sheppey" and "The Mermaids Singing".

WIDMARK, RICHARD. Born Dec. 26, 1915 in Minnesota, and educated at Lake Forest College, Ill. Has appeared on Broadway in "Kiss and Tell", "Get Away Old Man", "Trio", "Kiss Them for Me", and "Dunnigan's Daughter".

WILLARD, CATHERINE. Born in Dayton, Ohio. Made her stage debut in England with the Frank Bensen Company. Later she played leading Shakespearean roles at the Old Vic in London. Her first American engagement was with the Henry Jewett Repertory Company in Boston. On Broadway she has played in "Simon Called Peter", "The Great Gatsby", "She Had to Know", "Young Love", "The Deep Mrs. Sykes", and "You Touched Me".

WILLIAMS, REX. Born N. Y. C., May 23, 1914. In 1935 he made his Broadway bow in "If This Be Treason". Since then has appeared in "Hitch Your Wagon", "Too Many Heroes", "Knights of Song", "The Man With the Blond Hair", and "The Rugged Path".

WILLIAMS, RHYS. Born Clydach-cwm-Tawe, Wales, on Dec. 31, 1897. Made Broadway debut as an off stage singer in 1926 in "The Beaten Track". Has appeared in "Richard II", "Henry IV", "Hamlet", "The Corn Is Green", "Morning Star", "Lifeline", "Harriet", and "Chicken Every Sunday".

WILLS, LOU JR. First Broadway appearance was made in chorus of "Best Foot Forward", although he was only thirteen at the time. Since then has appeared in "One Touch of Venus", "Laffing Room Only", and "Are You With It".

WILSON, LIONEL. Born in N. Y. C., March 22, 1924, he won the Annual Barter Theater Award for being the most promising actor of the 1942 season. At nine he made his stage debut in a suburban tour of "Dodsworth." The following year he joined the Ben Greet Players and had several minor Shakespearean roles with that troupe. He interrupted his career from 1940 to 1941 while he attended New York University. He made his Broadway bow in "Janie," and followed this with "Good Morning Corporal," and "Kiss and Tell,"

WILSON, LOIS. Born Pittsburgh, Pa., June 28, 1900. Played in stock on West Coast, and was very successful as a silent picture star, appearing in over 300 films. In 1937 she made her Broadway debut in "Farewell Summer". More recently she has appeared in "Chicken Every Sunday", and "The Mermaids Singing".

183

WINDSOR, CLAIRE. Born in Cawker, Kan., April 14, 1898. Started film career in 1920, and had a long and successful career in Hollywood. First appearance on the Broadway stage was in "A Boy Who Lived Twice".

WINTERS, LAWRENCE. Born Kings Creek, S. C., Nov. 12, 1915. Educated at Howard Univ. Made N. Y. debut in 1942 in "Porgy and Bess", and more recently appeared in "Call Me Mister".

WINWOOD, ESTELLE. Born in Kent, England, Jan. 24, 1883, she studied for the stage at the Lyric Stage Academy. Made her first appearance on any stage at the Theatre Royal, Manchester, Eng., 1898 in "School". Made her American debut at the Little Theatre, N. Y. in 1916 in "Hush". Since then she has been seen in "A Successful Calamity", "Why Marry?", "Helen With The High Hand", "A Little Journey", "Molière", "Too Many Husbands", "The Tyranny of Love", "The Circle", "Madame Pierre", "Go Easy, Mabel", "The Red Poppy", "Anything Might Happen", "Spring Cleaning", "The Bucaneer", "A Weak Woman", "The Chief Thing", "Beau-Strings", "Head or Tail", "Trelawney of the Wells", "Fallen Angels", "We Never Learn", and "The Furies". More recently New Yorkers have seen her in "The Distaff Side", "I Want a Policeman", "The Importance of Being Earnest", "When We Are Married", "Ladies in Retirement", and "Ten Little Indians". Her only movie was "Quality Street", with Katharine Hepburn.

WOOD, PEGGY. Born Brooklyn, N. Y., Feb. 9, 1894. Studied singing with Mme. Calvé, and made her N. Y. debut in 1910 in "Naughty Marietta". Has appeared in "The Lady of the Slipper", "Love O' Mike", "Maytime", "Buddies", "Marjolaine", "The Clinging Vine", "The Bride", in revivals of "Candida", "Trelawney of the Wells", and as Portia

with George Arliss in "The Merchant of Venice". In London she appeared with remarkable success in "Bitter Sweet". More recently she was seen on Broadway in "Old Acquaintance", and "Blithe Spirit".

WYCHERLY, MARGARET. Born London, Eng. Oct. 26, 1881. First stage appearance was in 1898 in 'What Dreams May Come", after which she acted in stock and toured with Richard Mansfield. Among the many plays in which she has appeared are "Everyman", "Cashel Byron's Profession", "The Nazarene", "The Blue Bird", "Damaged Goods", "The Thirteenth Chair", "Jane Clegg", "Back to Methuselah", "Six Characters in Search of an Author", and "The Adding Machine". More recently she played in "Another Language", "Tobacco Road", and revivals of 'Hedda Gabler", and "Liliom".

WYNN, ED. Born Philadelphia, Nov. 9, 1886. Made first stage appearance at age of fifteen, and continued for many years in vaudeville. His first Broadway show was "The Deacon and the Lady" in 1910. Has been seen in "Ziegfeld Follies" (1914-15), "Sometime", "The Shubert Gaieties of 1919", "The Ed Wynn Carnival", "The Perfect Fool", "The Grab Bag", "Manhattan Mary", "Simple Simon", "The Laugh Parade", "Hoorah for What!", and "Laugh, Town, Laugh!"

ZORINA, VERA. Born in Germany, Jan. 2, 1918. Educated in Norway and Germany. Made first professional appearance in Berlin in Max Reinhardt's production of "A Midsummer Night's Dream". Coming to this country she toured several seasons with the Russian Ballet. Her first Broadway engagement was in "I Married an Angel". Since then she has played in "Louisiana Purchase", "Dream With Music", and "The Tempest".

PRODUCERS, DIRECTORS, DESIGNERS AND CHOREOGRAPHERS

ABBOTT, GEORGE. Producer, Director, Author, Actor. Born in Forestville, N. Y., June 25, 1887. Graduated from Rochester University and studied playwriting with Professor G. P. Baker at Harvard. Made his first appearance as an actor in "The Misleading Lady", 1913. Produced such plays as "Chicago", 1926; "Coquette", 1927; "Twentieth Century", 1932; "Small Miracle", 1934; "Three Men On A Horse", "Boy Meets Girl", 1935; "Brother Rat", 1936; "Room Service", 1937; "What A Life", 1938; "Too Many Girls", 1940; "Pal Joey", 1941; "Best Foot Forward", 1942; "Kiss and Tell", 1943; many of which he co-authored. Has also produced and directed movies.

ALDRICH, RICHARD. Producer, Manager. Born in Boston, Mass., August 17, 1903. Married to Gertrude Lawrence. Graduated from Harvard, 1925; member of Professor G. P. Baker's "47 Workshop". From 1926 to 1928 was General Manager for Richard Boleslovsky's American Laboratory Theatre. Has either produced alone or co-produced; "La Gringa", 1928; "Art and Mrs. Bottle", 1930; "Springtime for Henry", 1932; "Three Cornered Moon", 1933; "Petticoat Fever", 1935; "Fresh Fields", 1936; "My Dear Children" and "Margin for Error", 1939. Operates the Cape Playhouse, Summer Theatre in Dennis, Mass. This past season he has been Managing Director of Theatre Incorporated.

ALSWANG, RALPH. Scenic Designer. Born in Chicago, Illinois, April 12, 1916. Received training at Art Institute and Goodman Theatre in Chicago. As an apprentice, worked for leading designers including Robert Edmond Jones. First Broadway production was "Come the Revelation" in 1941. Others were "Home Of The Brave", 1945; "I Like It Here", and "Swan Song", 1946.

ANDERSON, JOHN MURRAY. Director, Producer. Born September 20, 1886, in St. Johns, Newfound-

land. Educated at Edinburgh Academy, Scotland and Lausanne University, Switzerland. Began theatre apprenticeship at Herbert Tree's School of the Theatre in London. Made New York debut as director of "Greenwich Village Follies" in 1919. Among the Musicals he has staged are: "Music Box Revue" 1924; "Dearest Enemy", 1925; "Murray Anderson's Almanac", 1929; "Ziegfeld Follies", 1933; "Life Begins at 8:40", 1934; "Jumbo", 1935; "Ziegfeld Follies", 1936; "One For The Money", 1939; "Two For The Show", 1940; "Ziegfeld Follies", 1943; "Laffing Room Only", 1944; "Three To Make Ready", 1946. Motion pictures include "The King Of Jazz" in 1930 and "Bathing Beauty", 1943. Also staged the "Aquacades" at the New York World's Fair and at the San Francisco Exposition, all the "Diamond Horseshoe" Revues in New York, and in 1942 and 1943, The Ringling Bros. Barnum & Bailey Circus.

AYRES, LEMUEL. Scenic and Costume Designer. Born in New York City, January 22, 1915. Educated at Princeton and Iowa University. Broadway Debut was the revivals of "Journey's End", and "They Knew What They Wanted", in 1939. Other plays include: "Angel Street", 1941; "The Pirate", "Lifeline", "The Willow and I", 1942; "Harriet", "Oklahoma", 1943; "Song Of Norway", "Bloomer Girl", 1944; "St. Louis Woman", 1946.

BALANCHINE, GEORGE. Choreographer. Born in Russia in 1904. Graduated from the State Dancing Academy in Leningrad. In 1925 became ballet-master for Serge de Diaghilev's Company. He introduced classic dancing to the Broadway Musical in his "Slaughter On 10th Ave.", number in "On Your Toes". Other Musicals include: "I Married An Angel", 1938; "Keep Off The Grass", "Louisianna Purchase", 1940; "Rosalinda", 1942; "Song Of Norway", 1944. Has also choreographed for American Ballet Caravan, Ballet Russe de Monte Carlo, and Ballet Theatre.

BALLARD, LUCINDA. Costume Designer. Born in New Orleans, La., April 3, 1908. Studied at Art Students League in New York, Fontainebleau and Sorbonne in Paris. Worked as Assistant to Norman Bel Geddes, Claude Bragdon and Helene Pons. Broadway debut was "As You Like It" in 1937. Other plays include: "I Remember Mama" 1944, "Show Boat", and "Annie Get Your Gun", 1946.

BARRATT, WATSON. Scenic Designer. Born in Salt Lake City, Utah, June 27, 1884. Educated at Chase School of Art in New York, and Howard Pyle Illustration School, Wilmington, Delaware. First Broadway play was Al Jolson's "Sinbad" in 1918. He is the designer of the original "Student Prince" and "Blossom Time". For nine years has been Art Director and Assistant Manager of St. Louis Municipal Outdoor Opera. A few of the hundreds of Productions he has designed settings for in NewYork are: All Winter Garden Shows from 1918 to 1928; "Scarlet Sister Mary", "Artist and Models", 1930; "Three Waltzes", 1937; "Bachelor Born", "The White Steed", 1938; "The Time of Your Life", "The Importance of Being Earnest", 1939; "Love's Old Sweet Song", 1940; "Magic" and "Hello, Out There", 1942; "Ziegfeld Follies", 1943; "Rebecca", 1945; "Flamingo Road" and "January Thaw", 1946.

BAY, HOWARD. Scenic Designer. Born in Centralia, Wash., May 3, 1912. Educated at Carnegie Institute of Technology, Westminster College, Marshall College, University of Colorado, University of Washington. Did Stock work at Bucks County, Atlanta, and Stamford. Broadway debut was "Chalk Dust", 1935. Among his fifty-seven Broadway plays are: "One Third of a Nation", 1937; "Little Foxes", 1939; "The Eve of St. Mark" and "Uncle Harry", 1942; "One Touch of Venus", "Carmen Jones", 1943; "Follow the Girls", "Ten Little Indians", "Catherine Was Great", 1944; "Up in Central Park", "Deep Are the Roots", 1945; "Show Boat", 1946.

CHANEY, STEWART. Scenic Designer. Born in Kansas City, Mo. Studied at Yale. Has been one of the busiest designers in the Theatre since he scored with his sets for "The Old Maid", during the season of 1934-35, which marked his Broadway debut. Among his hits are: "Life With Father", 1939; "Blithe Spirit", 1941; "The Voice of the Turtle", 1943; "Jacobowsky and the Colonel", "The Late George Apley", "Laffing Room Only", 1944; "The Winter's Tale", 1946.

CLURMAN, HAROLD. Producer and Director. Born September 18, 1901, in New York City. Educated at Columbia University and University of Paris. After brief career as actor, worked for Theatre Guild, Jed Harris, John Golden, Rodgers and Hart on production. In 1931 joined Lee Strasberg and Cheryl Crawford in founding Group Theatre. Become close friend of Clifford Odets and has staged all of his plays but one. Has written a book, "The Fervent Years", covering the Group's history. On Broadway has directed: "Awake and Sing"; "Waiting for Lefty"; "Golden Boy", 1937; "The Russian People", 1942. This season co-produced and directed "Truckline Cafe".

CRAWFORD, CHERYL. Producer, Manager. Born September 24, 1902, in Akron, Ohio. Graduated from Smith College, 1925. Broadway debut was as Assistant Stage Manager and bit player in "Juarez and Maximilian" in 1926. At one time was Casting Director for the Theatre Guild. Also one of the Founders and Directors of the Group Theatre. Produced "All the Living", 1928; "Family Portrait", 1939; "Porgy and Bess", revival, 1942; "One Touch of Venus" and "The Tempest", 1945. She is now a Director of the newly founded American Repertory Theatre, which will become active next season.

CROUSE, RUSSEL. Producer, Author. Born February 20, 1893, in Findlay, Ohio. Served as press agent for the Theatre Guild for five years, during which time he wrote "The Gang's All Here" and "Hold Your Horses", which were produced in 1930 and 1933, respectively. In 1934 teamed up with Howard Lindsay, on the book for the Musical, "Anything Goes". Since then they have written "Red Hot and Blue", 1936; "Hooray for What", 1937; "Life With Father", 1939; "Strip for Action", 1943;

and "State of the Union", 1945. As producers Lindsay and Crouse have been represented by "Arsenic and Old Lace", 1941, and "The Hasty Heart", 1944.

CZETTEL, LADISLAS. Costume and Fashion Designer. Born in Budapest, Hungary, on March 12, 1904. Studied at the Academy of Art in Munich; at the age of 16 went to Paris and became the only pupil of Leon Bakst. For twelve years he was head designer for Vienna State Opera. Came to America in 1936 after having designed costumes for theatres in Berlin, Vienna, Salzburg, Paris and London. Has designed many Metropolitan Opera Productions, including, "The Masked Ball", "Rosalinda", "Helen Goes to Troy" and "La Vie Parisienne" are his Broadway Plays. Costumed Movie version of Shaw's "Pygmalion".

DALRYMPLE, JEAN. Producer, Publicity Director. Born September 2, 1910, in Morristown, N. J. Is divorced from Ward Morehouse. Started in vaudeville in an act with the late Dan Jarrett. She joined John Golden's staff when he produced "Salt Water", and succeeded in establishing herself as a crack publicist. Opened her own publicity office and for the past fifteen years has been press representative for numerous Broadway Plays. "Hope for the Best", 1945, marked her debut as a producer. This was followed by "Brighten the Corner".

DAVISON, ROBERT. Scenic and Costume Designer. Born in Los Angeles, Calif., July 17, 1922. Attended Los Angeles City College. Began Broadway career designing costumes for "Song of Norway" and "Embezzled Heaven" in 1944. He designed sets for "Day Before Spring" and "O Mistress Mine", 1945; "Around the World", 1946.

DE COURVILLE, ALBERT P. Producer, Director. Born in London, March 26, 1887. Studied at Lausanne University. Was formerly a journalist, then became Assistant Director of London Hippodrome. Began producing in 1912. Wrote his memoirs—"I Tell You". He came to America and joined the Shuberts; together they presented "Ten Little Indians" in 1944, and this season, "The Wind Is Ninety", both of which he staged.

DE LIAGRE, JR., ALFRED. Producer and Director. Born in Passaic, N. J., October 6, 1904. Graduated from Yale in 1926. Began his theatrical career at the Woodstock Playhouse in 1930. Served as Assistant Stage Manager for Jane Cowl's "Twelfth Night", 1931, and Stage Manager for "Springtime for Henry", 1932. Made his Broadway debut as Director and Co-producer of "Three Cornered Moon", 1933. Other plays which he has produced and directed are: "By Your Leave", "The Pure in Heart", 1934; "Petticoat Fever", 1935; "Fresh Fields", 1936; "Yes, My Darling Daughter", 1937; "I Am My Youth", 1938; "The Walrus and the Carpenter", 1940; "Mr. and Mrs. North", 1941. The last few seasons produced "The Voice of the Turtle", 1943, and "The Mermaids Singing", 1945.

DE MILLE, AGNES. Choreographer. Born in New York City. Attended the University of California. Began as a choreographer for the Joose Ballet, The Ballet Theatre, and the Ballet Russe De Monte Carlo. In 1942, she did "Rodeo" for the Ballet Russe, which led to her being chosen in 1943 to choreograph "Oklahoma". This was followed by "One Touch of Venus", 1943; "Bloomer Girl", 1944; and "Carousel", 1945.

DENHAM, REGINALD. Director, Author. Born in London, January 10, 1894. Received Scholarship at Guildhall School of Music in London. In 1913, joined Beerbohm Tree's Company at His Majesty's Theatre, London; also acted with Benson's Shakespearean Company. Came to America in 1929 to direct production of "Rope's End", followed by "Jew Suss" and "Suspense", 1930. He then went back to London, returning again in 1940 to stage "Ladies in Retirement"; "Guest in the House", 1942; "Play With Fire", 1941; "Yesterday's Magic", 1942; "Nine Girls", "Two Mrs. Carrolls", 1943; "Wallflower", "Dark Hammock", 1944. The latter two he co-authored with Mary Orr. This past season directed "A Joy Forever".

EISELE, LOU. Costume Designer. Born February 12, 1912, in New York City. Studied at the Art Students' League, Art Institute of California, and assisted well known designers on the Circus, The Diamond Horseshoe Show, night clubs and legitimate plays. Broadway debut was "Follow the Girls", 1944. Other shows include: "The Lady Says Yes", 1945, and "Ice Capades of 1947". Has done U.S.O. Camp Shows the past few years.

ELLIOTT, JAMES S. Producer, Actor. Born in New York City, January 15, 1924. Made his debut as a producer in 1942 when he presented and directed "Arlene". Other plays include "The First Million", 1943; "Too Hot for Maneuvers", 1945.

FEIGAY, PAUL. Producer. Born in New York City, March 14, 1918. Educated at Pratt University and Yale School of Fine Arts. Received theatre apprenticeship as Assistant Stage Manager and Assistant Director for the New Opera Company. In association with Oliver Smith produced "On the Town", 1944, and "Billion Dollar Baby", in 1945.

FREEMAN, CHARLES K. Director. Born in England, July 11, 1905. Broadway plays include "Life and Death of an American"; "Morning Star", 1940; "Song of Norway", 1944; "I Like It Here", 1946. Was also co-author of "Hand in Glove", 1944.

GABEL, MARTIN. Producer, Director, Actor. Born June 19, 1912, in Philadelphia, Pa. Attended Lehigh University before entering the American Academy of Dramatic Arts. Made first appearance as an actor in 1933. Plays produced include: "Medicine Show", "Young Couple Wanted", "Charley's Aunt", 1940; "Cream in the Well", 1941; "Cafe Crown", 1942. This season he presented "The Assassin", which he also directed.

GOLDEN, JOHN. Producer. Born in New York City on June 27, 1875. Educated at New York University. Made his theatrical bow as an actor at the Harrigan Theatre in 1890. After fifty years, Mr. Golden looks back, with nostalgia, on such hits as: "Lightnin'"; Three Wise Fools"; "The First Year", 1920; "Seventh Heaven"; "The Wisdom Tooth", 1926; "Let Us Be Gay", 1928; "As Husbands Go", 1930; "When Ladies Meet", 1932; "Divine Drudge", 1933; "The Bishop Misbehaves"; "Susan and God", 1937; "Skylark", 1939; "Claudia", 1941; "Theatre", 1942; "Three Is a Family", 1943. The last few seasons has devoted his time to the annual auditions, and Equity-Library Theatre.

GORDON, MAX. Producer. Born in New York City, June 28, 1892. Began as a partner with Albert Lewis in the firm of Lewis and Gordon. His firm was associated with Sam H. Harris in production of "The Family Upstairs", "The Jazz Singer", and "Easy Come, Easy Go", 1925. Commenced independent productions in 1930 with "Three's a Crowd"; "The Band Wagon", "The Cat and the Fiddle", 1931; "Design for Living", "Roberta", 1933; "Dodsworth", "The Great Waltz", 1934; "Jubilee", 1935; "The Women", 1936; "The American Way", 1939; "The Doughgirls", 1942; "The Late George Apley", 1944; "Born Yesterday", 1946.

GORDON, MICHAEL. Director. Born on September 6, 1911, in Baltimore, Md. Received degrees from Johns Hopkins and Yale Universities. Broadway debut was "Walk a Little Faster" in 1932, as an actor. Has had extensive career as Stage and Production Manager. He turned director on "Stevedore", 1934; followed by "Sailors of Cattaro", "Black Pit", 1935; "Storm Operation", "Sophie", 1944; "Home of the Brave", 1945; and "Laura", 1946.

GRIBBLE, HARRY WAGSTAFF. Director, Author. Born March 27, 1896, in Seven Oaks, Kent, England. Educated at Emmanuel College, Cambridge. Served theatre apprenticeship as an actor and stage manager in London, English provinces, South Africa and America. Broadway debut was "Quinneys" in 1916. Among the plays he has staged are: "After Dark", 1928; "Cynara", 1931; "No More Ladies", 1934; "If This Be Treason", 1935. Has written many plays, from "Let's Beat It", 1919, to "The Man From Cairo", 1938. Produced and staged "Johnny Belinda", 1940, and staged "Anna Lucasta", 1944.

GROSS, EDWARD. Producer. Born April 20, 1897, in New York City. Attended New York University. Produced over thirty motion pictures before he turned to Broadway and "Chicken Every Sunday", 1943, and "St. Louis Woman", 1946.

HAMMERSTEIN, OSCAR, 2nd. Author, Producer. Born in New York, July 12, 1895. Graduated from Columbia University. Began Theatre career as Assistant Stage Manager of "You're in Love", 1917. "Always You", 1919, was the first musical for which he wrote the book and lyrics to be produced. In 1944, he and Richard Rodgers, after extremely successful careers as Author and Composer, respectively, turned producer, presenting "I Remember Mama", 1944; "Show Boat" and "Annie Get Your Gun", 1946. This past season Broadway saw revivals of Mr. Hammerstein's "Desert Song" (originally produced 1926), "Show Boat" (originally produced 1927) and "Carmen Jones" (originally produced 1943), as well as continued runs of "Oklahoma", 1943, and "Carousel", 1945. "I Remember Mama" and "Annie Get Your Gun", which he did not author, were also presented.

HARRIS, JED. Producer, Director. Born (Horowitz) in Newark, N. J., 1899. Attended Yale University. Has produced in New York: "Week Sisters", 1925; "Broadway", 1926; "Coquette", "The Royal Family", 1927; "The Front Page", 1928; "The Green Bay Tree", 1933; "A Doll's House", 1937; "Our Town", 1938; "Dark Eyes", 1943; "One Man Show", 1945; "Apple of His Eye" and the London production of "Our Town", 1946.

HART, BERNARD. Producer. Born April 21, 1911, in New York. Began as Production Assistant and Stage Manager. In 1944 he and **JOSEPH M. HYMAN** formed a partnership and produced "Dear Ruth", followed by "The Secret Room", 1945. Both were directed by his brother, Moss Hart.

HAYWARD, LELAND. Producer. Born in Nebraska City, Neb., September 13, 1902. Attended Princeton University. After establishing successful talent agency in Hollywood and New York, turned producer in 1944 and presented "A Bell for Adano" and this season presented the Pulitzer Prize Play, "State of the Union".

HELBURN, THERESA. Producer, Administrative Director, Playwright. Born in New York City, January 12th. Studied at Bryn Mawr, Radcliffe (Prof. Baker's 47 Workshop) and Sorbonne, Paris. Began Theatre career as Playwright with Washington Square Players. One of the original founders of the Theatre Guild, and since 1939, co-administrative Director. Has actively supervised all Guild Productions. Directed "Chrysalis", 1932, and "Mary of Scotland", 1933.

HOPKINS, ARTHUR. Producer, Director. Born in Cleveland, Ohio, October 4, 1878. His first production was "The Poor Little Rich Girl", 1912. Since then has been responsible for "A Successful Calamity", "The Jest", "Anna Christie", "The Hairy Ape", "What Price Glory?", "Burlesque", "Paris Bound", "The Petrified Forest", and many more. Author of the book, "To a Lonely Boy". This last season he produced and directed "The Magnificent Yankee" and "The Joyous Season".

HOUSEMAN, JOHN. Producer, Director. Born September 22, 1902, in Bucharest, Rumania. Attended Clifton College, England. Made his Broadway debut as director of "Four Saints in Three Acts" in 1934, followed by "Valley Forge", "Lady From the Sea", 1935. Turned Producer in 1935 and presented "Panic". Produced Negro "Macbeth", "Dr. Faustus", "Cradle Will Rock", "Horse Eats Hat" for the Federal Theatre. In 1936 staged Leslie Howard's "Hamlet". In 1937 he joined the Mercury Theatre as co-producer with Orson Welles of "Julius Caesar", "Shoemakers' Holiday", "Heartbreak House", "Danton's Death", 1937-1938; "Native Son", 1940. This season he directed "Lute Song".

HOUSTON, GRACE. Costume Designer. Born in New Bedford, Mass., October 25, 1916. Began Theatre career as a dancer with the Rockettes at

Radio City Music Hall. After serving as Assistant on "Boys and Girls Together", 1940, and "Something for the Boys", 1942. In 1943 she designed her first show, "The Two Mrs. Carrolls". "What's Up", 1943; "Hats Off to Ice", 1944; "Up in Central Park", "Live Life Again", 1945; and "Call Me Mister", 1946.

JOHNSON, ALBERT. Scenic Designer. Born February 1, 1910, La Crosse, Wis. Debut on Broadway was "The Criminal Code", 1929. Broadway shows include: "Three's a Crowd"; "The Band Wagon"; "Life Begins at Eight Forty"; "The Great Waltz"; "Jumbo"; "As Thousands Cheer", 1933; "Leave It to Me", 1939; "Skin of Our Teeth", 1942; "Sing Out, Sweet Land", 1944; and "Live Life Again", 1945. Last season produced and designed "Bonanza".

JONES, ROBERT EDMOND. Scenic Designer. Born in Milton, N. H., December 12, 1887. Graduated from Harvard. Began designing in 1911. Has designed such productions as "Man Who Married a Dumb Wife", 1915; "The Jest"; "Desire Under the Elms"; "Mourning Becomes Electra", 1931; "Ah, Wilderness"; "Mary of Scotland", 1933; "Sea Gull", 1938; "Without Love", 1942; "Helen Goes to Troy", 1944, and "Lute Song", 1946.

KANIN, GARSON. Director and Playwright. Born November 24, 1912, in Rochester, N. Y. Studied at the American Academy of Dramatic Arts. Began Theatre career as Assistant to George Abbott. Broadway debut was as understudy to Burgess Meredith in "Little Ol' Boy", 1933. Turned from acting to directing and from Broadway to Hollywood in 1938. Broadway plays he has directed: "Hitch Your Wagon", "Too Many Heroes", 1937; "The Rugged Path", 1945. Wrote and directed "Born Yesterday", 1946.

KAZAN, ELIA. Director, Actor. Born September 7, 1909, in Constantinople, Turkey. Received A.B. at Williams In 1930 and had two years' graduate work at Yale Drama School. Began theatre work as an apprentice with the Group Theatre in 1932. In 1933 made his debut as an Actor in "Chrysalis". This was followed by appearances in many Group Theatre Plays. In 1938, interrupted his acting career to direct "Casey Jones". 1941 found him staging "Cafe Crown" and "Skin of Our Teeth" and turning all his time to directing. "Harriet", "One Touch of Venus", 1942; "Jacobowsky and the Colonel", 1943; "Deep Are the Roots", 1945. Motion pictures include "Tree Grows in Brooklyn", 1944, and "Sea of Grass", 1946.

KOLLMAR, RICHARD TOMPKINS. Producer. Born December 31, 1910, in Ridgewood, N. J. Educated at Tusculum College and Yale University. Married to Dorothy Kilgallen. Broadway debut was as Juvenile lead in "Knickerbocker Holiday". Appeared in many musicals, and in 1942 co-produced "By Jupiter"; "Early to Bed", 1943; "Dream With Music", 1944; "Are You With It?" 1945; and "Windy City", 1946.

LANGNER, LAWRENCE. Producer. Administrative Director and Author. Born in Swansea, Wales. Married to Armina Marshall. Attended Burbeck College, London, and Polytechnic Institute. Began Theatre work with J. Bannister Howard in London and the Washington Square Players in New York. Has actively supervised all plays produced by the Theatre Guild, of which he is one of the original directors. Authored "The Family Exit", 1932, and other one-act plays. "Pursuit of Happiness", 1933, and "The School for Husbands", which he also directed; "Susanna and the Elders", 1941. Founded and operates Westport Country Playhouse.

LEVE, SAMUEL. Scenic Designer. Born near Pinsk, Russia-Poland. Attended Yale University. Began Theatre career in Summer Theatres. Broadway debut was Mercury Theatre Productions of "Julius Caesar" and "Shoemakers' Holiday", 1937. Other plays include: "Big Blow" for Federal Theatre, 1939; "Medicine Show", 1939; "Beautiful People", 1940; Maurice Evans, "Macbeth", 1941; "Beat the Band", 1942; "Mr. Sycamore", 1943; "Wallflower", 1944, and "A Sound of Hunting", 1946.

LINDSAY, HOWARD. Producer, Author, Actor. Born in Waterford, N. Y., March 29, 1899. Attended Harvard before he enrolled at the American Academy of Dramatic Arts. Married to Dorothy Stickney. Began as an Actor in 1909. His first success as an Actor and Director came in 1920 with "Dulcy". Entered the ranks of Producers in 1935 with "A Slight Case of Murder", which he co-authored with Damon Runyon, followed by "Arsenic and Old Lace", 1941, and "The Hasty Heart", 1944.

LOGAN, JOSHUA. Director. Has staged many plays and musicals, including: "On Borrowed Time", "I Married an Angel", "Knickerbocker Holiday", 1938; "Mornings at Seven", 1939; "Two for the Show", "Higher and Higher", "Charley's Aunt", 1940. And this season "Annie Get Your Gun".

MACY, GERTRUDE M. Producer, Manager. Born October 8, 1904, in Pasadena, Calif. Attended Bryn Mawr College. Began as Assistant Stage Manager, then Stage Manager and finally General Manager for Katharine Cornell, a position she still holds. Produced the revue, "One for the Money", 1939; "Two for the Show", 1940; and "Forever Is Now", 1945.

MAMOULIAN, ROUBEN. Director. Born in Tiflis, Caucasus, Russia, October 8, 1898. Studied at Lycée Montaigne, Paris, and Moscow University. His first Broadway Production was "Porgy" for the Theatre Guild in 1927. "Marco Williams", 1927; "Wings Over Europe", 1928; "A Month in the Country", 1930; "Porgy and Bess", 1935; "Oklahoma", 1943; "Sadie Thompson", 1944; "Carousel", 1945; "St. Louis Woman", 1946. Has done a great deal of work in Hollywood.

McCLINTIC, GUTHRIE. Producer, Director. Born in Seattle, Wash., August 6, 1893. Attended University of Washington and American Academy of Dramatic Arts. Married to Katharine Cornell. Began in 1913 as Assistant Stage Manager. 1914 saw him serving in the triple capacity of Stage Manager, Casting Director and Actor in Winthrop Ames' production of "The Truth". In 1921 he became a Producer on his own. He then staged and produced "The Dover Road", 1921; "Mrs. Partridge Presents", 1925; "The Shanghai Gesture", 1926. Directed "Saturday's Children", 1927; "The Barretts of Wimpole Street", 1931; "Criminal at Large", 1932; "Alien Corn", 1933; "Yellow Jack" and "Romeo and Juliet", 1934; "The Old Maid", "Winterset", and "Parnell", 1935; "Key Largo", 1939; "Mamba's Daughters", 1940; "The Morning Star", which introduced Gregory Peck to Broadway, 1942; "The Three Sisters", 1942. Recent Productions are revival of "The Barretts", "You Touched Me", 1945; "Antigone", revival of "Candida", 1946.

MIELZINER, JO. Scenic Designer. Born March 19, 1901, in Paris, France. Studied at the National Academy of Design, Pennsylvania Academy of Fine Arts, Philadelphia, and the Art Students' League. As a scenic Artist, he made his Broadway debut as the designer of the Lunts' production of "The Guardsman" in 1924. "Strange Interlude", 1927; "The Barretts of Wimpole Street", 1931; "Dodsworth", 1932; Cornell "Romeo and Juliet", 1934; "Winterset", 1935; "Ethan Frome", "Saint Joan", Gielgud "Hamlet"; "On Your Toes", 1936; "Abe Lincoln in Illinois"; "Knickerbocker Holiday", 1938; "Pal Joey", 1940; "Watch on the Rhine", 1941; "The Glass Menagerie", 1944; "Carousel", "The Rugged Path", "Dream Girl", 1945; "Annie Get Your Gun", 1946.

MILLER, GILBERT HERON. Producer. Born July 3, 1884, in New York. Son of Henry Miller. Educated at De LaSalle Institute, New York, Freres des Ecoles Chretiennes-Passy, Paris; Muller-Gelenick Realschule, Dresden; Bedford County School, Bedford, England. Began in the theatre as Stock Actor, Stage Manager and Company Manager. In 1922 he presented Doris Keane in "The Czarina", his debut as a Broadway Producer. Other plays include: "The Swan", 1923; "The Play's the Thing", 1926; "Journey's End", 1929; "Berkeley Square", 1929; "Petticoat Influence", 1930; "The Good Fairy", 1931; "The Animal Kingdom", 1932; "The Late Christopher Bean", 1932; "The Petrified Forest", 1934; "Victoria Regina", 1935; "Tovarich", 1936; "Ladies in Retirement", 1940; and "Harriet", 1943.

MOTLEY—Trade name for **ELIZABETH MONT-GOMERY, PERCY AND SOPHIA HARRIS.** Scenic and Costume Designers. A British firm that is represented in London by the Harris Sisters, and in America by Elizabeth Montgomery. Miss Montgomery was born February 15, 1909. First Broadway Production was Olivier-Leigh "Romeo and Juliet", 1940. "The Doctor's Dilemma", 1941; "Lovers and Friends", 1943; "The Cherry Orchard", "A Bell for Adano", 1944; "The Tempest", "Hope for the Best", "You Touched Me", 1945; "Skydrift", "He Who Gets Slapped", 1946. Also did Costumes for "Pygmalion" and "Carib Song", 1946.

MYERS, RICHARD. Producer. Born March 25, 1901, in Philadelphia, Pa. Claims his Broadway debut was as the composer of the Song, "Lulu Belle", in a David Belasco Production. Has co-produced such productions as: "Margin for Error", 1939; "My Dear Children", 1940; "Sons and Soldiers", 1943; "Calico Wedding", 1945.

OENSLAGER, DONALD. Scenic Designer. Born Harrisburg, Pa., March 7, 1902. Graduated from Harvard, 1923 (worked with Baker's 47 Workshop). First Broadway Production was "A Bit o' Love", in 1925. "Good News", 1927; "Follow Thru", 1928; "Girl Crazy", 1930; "Whistling in the Dark", 1932; "Anything Goes", "Gold Eagle Guy", 1934; "I'd Rather Be Right", "Of Mice and Men", 1937; "The Circle", 1938; "The Man Who Came to Dinner", "Skylark", "Margin for Error", 1939; "The American Way", 1940; "My Sister Eileen", "Claudia", 1941. This season's Productions: "Pygmalion", "Three to Make Ready", and "Born Yesterday".

PEMBERTON, BROCK. Producer. Born Leavenworth, Kan., December 14, 1885. Attended the College of Emporia, and graduated from the University of Kansas. Served as General Manager for Arthur Hopkins from 1917 to 1920. On August 16, 1920, he made his debut on Broadway as a Producer with "Enter Madame". In the past twenty-five years he has produced: "Miss LuLu Bett", 1920; "Six Characters in Search of an Author", 1922; "White Desert", 1923; "The Living Mask", "Mister Pitt", 1924; "Goin' Home", 1928; "Strictly Dishonorable", 1929; "Personal Appearance", 1934; "Ceiling Zero", 1935; "Kiss the Boys Goodbye", 1938; "Janie", 1942, and "Harvey", 1944.

PLAYWRIGHTS' COMPANY. Founded in 1938 by Maxwell Anderson, S. N. Behrman, Sidney Howard, Elmer Rice, Robert E. Sherwood and John F. Wharton. Banded together to present their own plays; broke this policy once, when they produced Sidney Kingsley's "The Patriots". This year finds them less two members, due to the death of Mr. Howard and the resignation of Mr. Behrman, and augmented by Kurt Weill. Their initial offering was "Abe Lincoln in Illinois", followed by "Knickerbocker Holiday" and "American Landscape", in 1938. "No Time for Comedy", "Key Largo", 1939; "Two on an Island", "There Shall Be No Night", "Journey to Jerusalem", "Flight to the West", 1940; "The Talley Method", "Candle in the Wind", 1941; "The Eve of St. Mark", "The Pirate", 1942; "The Patriots", "A New Life", 1943; "Storm Operation", 1944; "The Rugged Path" and "Dream Girl", 1945.

ROBBINS, JEROME. Choreographer. Born, New York, N. Y., October 11, 1918. Attended New York University which he left to take up Dancing. Worked with the Dance Centre, Theatre Workshop, W.P.A. Classes and Summer Theatres. Danced in such Musicals as "Great Lady", "Stars in Your Eyes", and "Keep Off the Grass". Made his debut as Choreographer for the Ballet Theatre with "Fancy Free". Made his Broadway debut as Choreographer of "On the Town", 1944; "Concert Varieties", "Billion Dollar Baby", 1945.

RODGERS, RICHARD. Producer, Composer. Born June 28, 1902, in New York City. Studied at Columbia University, where he met the late Lorenz Hart. They teamed up and wrote "Garrick Gaieties", in 1925, and followed it with many hits. Collaborated with Oscar Hammerstein II, in 1943, on "Oklahoma" and "Carousel" in 1945. In 1944 they turned producers and presented "I Remember Mama" and "Annie Get Your Gun", 1946.

ROOT, JOHN. Scenic Designer. Has designed the settings for "Kiss the Boys Goodbye", 1938; "Janie", 1942; "Kiss and Tell", "Counterattack", 1943; "Snafu" and "Harvey", 1944.

ROSE, BILLY (William Samuel Rosenberg). Producer. Born in Bronx, New York, on September 6, 1899. Divorced from Fanny Brice. Married to Eleanor Holm. At 18 was shorthand king of the world, averaging 350 words a minute. Entered the world of Arts as a song writer, authoring such hits as "Barney Google", "Mmmmm, Would You Like to Take a Walk?", "Don't Bring Lulu" and others. In 1931 he made his debut as a Broadway Producer with the revue, "Sweet and Low"; it was not a hit. He changed the name to "Billy Rose's Crazy Quilt", cut it down to tabloid size, and sent it on the vaudeville circuit; it became a smash hit. Produced the "Casa Mañana" show at the Ft. Worth Centennial, and the "Aquacade" Shows at the Golden Gate International Exposition, San Francisco, and the New York World's Fair. Is owner of the successful "Diamond Horseshoe", Manhattan Night Club. Other Broadway productions: "The Great Magoo", 1932; "Jumbo", 1935; "Clash by Night", 1941; "Carmen Jones", 1942; "Seven Lively Arts", 1944; "Concert Varieties", 1945.

SABINSON, LEE. Producer. Born New York City, November 11, 1911. Attended City College of New York. Made his debut as Broadway Producer with "Counterattack", 1943. Followed by "Trio", 1944; "Home of the Brave", 1945.

SERLIN, OSCAR. Producer, Director, Author. Born Ualowka (Grodnow), Russia, January 30, 1901. Educated at De Paul Academy and University in Chicago, Ill. Began career by writing vaudeville and musical comedy acts, and working in New York as stage manager and assistant director. In 1929 co-produced nd managed "The Guinea Pig", and produced "Broken Dishes". Other plays produced include: "Lost Sheep", 1930; "Life With Father", 1939; "The King's Maid" (also adapted and directed), 1941; "The Moon Is Down", 1942; "Strip for Action", 1942; "The Family", 1943; "Beggars Are Coming to Town", 1945.

SHARAFF, IRENE. Costume Designer. Born in Boston, Mass. Studied at Art Students' League and New York School of Fine and Allied Arts. Began her Theatrical Career as assistant to Aline Bernstein at Eva Le Gallienne's Civic Repertory Theatre. It was here that she gained prominence for her settings and costumes for "Alice in Wonderland", in 1932. She made her uptown debut as designer of the costumes for "As Thousands Cheer" in 1933. Has done the costumes for: "Idiot's Delight", 1936; "Virginia", "I'd Rather Be Right", 1937; "The American Way", 1939; "Lady in the Dark", 1941; "Star and Garter", 1942; G.I. "Hamlet", "Billion Dollar Baby", 1945; "Would-Be Gentleman", 1946.

SHORT, HASSARD. Director, Actor. Born in Edlington, Lincolnshire, England, on October 15, 1877. Educated at Charterhouse School. Made his debut as an actor in "Cheer, Boys, Cheer" at the Drury Lane Theatre, London, playing opposite Fannie Ward. After a very successful career in London, he was brought to this country by Charles Frohman in 1901. He continued his career as an actor until 1920, when he retired from acting and turned to directing. Among the productions he has staged are: "Her Family Tree", with Nora Bayes, 1920; "The Music Box Revues" of 1921, '22, '23; "Sunny", 1925; "The Band Wagon", 1931; "Roberta", "Wild Violets", "As Thousands Cheer", 1933; "The Great Waltz", 1934; "Jubilee", 1935; "Three Waltzes", 1937; "The American Way", "The Hot Mikado", 1939; "Lady in the Dark", 1941; "Carmen Jones", 1943; "Mexican Hayride", 1944; "Marinka", 1945; and "Show Boat", 1946.

SHUBERT, LEE, born in Syracuse, N. Y., March 15, 1875.

SHUBERT, J. J., born in Syracuse, N. Y., August 15, 1880.

SHUBERT, MESSRS., Theatre Managers and Producers. A Corporation formed by the late **Sam S. Shubert.** Began by operating a stock company in Syracuse, and sending small companies cn tour.

Moved to New York in 1900 and took over the Management of the Herald Square Theatre. When Sam Shubert met with a fatal accident in 1905, his two brothers, Lee and Jacob J. Shubert, took over what had become one of the larger theatrical interests in New York. Today as the **Select Theatre Corp.** they manage three-fourths of the legitimate houses in New York and innumerable throughout the United States. As Messrs. Shubert they produce or are financially interested in from ten to twenty productions each season.

SHUMLIN, HERMAN ELLIOTT. Producer, Director. Born December 6, 1898, in Atwood, Col. Began as reporter on a theatrical trade publication, then turned press agent. In 1927, presented his first production, "Celebrity". This was followed by "The Last Mile", 1929; "Grand Hotel", 1930; "The Children's Hour", 1934; "The Little Foxes", 1939; "The Male Animal" and "The Corn Is Green", 1940; "Watch on the Rhine", 1941; and "Jeb", 1946.

SIRCOM, ARTHUR. Director, Producer. Born in Boston, Mass., December 15, 1899. Attended Yale University. Served his apprenticeship with American Laboratory Theatre, Ben Greet Players, Jitney Players and the Boston Repertory Theatre. Some of the plays he has staged in New York are: "Men Must Fight", 1932; "A Good Woman—Poor Thing", "Give Us This Day", "All Good Americans", 1933; "Whatever Possessed Her", 1934; "Tell Me, Pretty Maiden", 1937; "Mrs. January and Mr. X", "Ramshackle Inn", "The Odds on Mrs. Oakley", 1944.

SMITH, OLIVER. Producer, Scenic Designer. Born in Hawpawn, Wis., February 13, 1918. Graduated from Pennsylvania State College. In 1941 designed settings for the Ballet Russe de Monte Carlo. Made his Broadway debut in 1942 as designer of the scenery for "Rosalinda"; followed by "Perfect Marriage", 1944. He joined Paul Feigay as co-producer and Designer of "On The Town", 1944, and "Billion Dollar Baby", 1945.

SOVEY, RAYMOND. Scenic Designer. Born 1897 in Torrington, Conn. Left Columbia University, where he was studying, to teach Art at the Maryland Institute in Baltimore. Made his Broadway debut as designer of the costumes for Walter Hampden's "George Washington". Other productions include: "Little Accident", 1928; "Strictly Dishonorable", 1929; "Strike Up the Band", "The Vinegar Tree", 1930; "The Petrified Forest", "Fly Away Home", 1935; "Tovarich", "Libel", 1936; "Yes, My Darling Daughter", "Our Town", "French Without Tears", 1937; "Ladies in Retirement", 1940; "Jason", "The Damask Cheek", 1942; "Tomorrow the World", 1943; "The Hasty Heart", 1945.

TAMIRIS, HELEN. Choreographer. Born in New York City, April 24, 1905. Made her debut as a Concert Dancer in 1927. Has had her own Company for many years. Entered the Musical Comedy field as Choreographer of "Marianne" and "Stove Pipe Hat". Represented on Broadway by "Up in Central Park", 1945; "Show Boat", and "Annie Get Your Gun", 1946.

THEATRE GUILD, THE. A producing organization founded in 1919 by some of the members of what had been the Washington Square Players. Original board of managers were Theresa Helburn, Lawrence Langner, Philip Moeller, Lee Simonson, Maurice Wertheim and Helen Westley. Its present directors are Lawrence Langner and Theresa Helburn. Since its inception it has been a subscription theatre; and today it has almost 100,000 subscribers throughout the country. On April 19, 1919, the Guild raised the curtain on its first production "Bonds of Interest". In the intervening 25 years the Guild has presented nearly a hundred and sixty productions. Its first hit was "John Ferguson", which was also presented during its initial season. Among the Guild successes are: "Liliom", 1921; "Back to Methuselah", 1922; "Peer Gynt", "Saint Joan", 1923; "The Guardsman", 1924; "Strange Interlude", 1928; "Mourning Becomes Electra", 1931; "Mary of Scotland", 1933; "Porgy and Bess", 1935; "Philadelphia Story", 1938; "Time of Your Life", 1939; "Oklahoma", 1943; "Jacobowsky and the Colonel", 1944; "Carousel", 1945.

THEATRE INCORPORATED, a non-profit, tax exempt producing unit founded in 1945. Committed to a sustained program of great plays of the past and outstanding plays of the present. Its income is devoted to building and maintaining a New York Repertory Theatre; Sideshow, a subsidiary theatre to encourage young playwrights, directors, and actors; and to the utilization of the stage as an educational force. This season, appointed Richard Aldrich, Managing Director; produced "Pygmalion"; and imported the Old Vic Theatre Company from London.

TODD, MICHAEL (Goldbogen). Producer. Born in Minneapolis, Minn., June 22, 1907. Began Theatrical career at Chicago World's Fair in 1933. Broadway debut was "Call Me Ziggy", 1936. Other shows include: "Man From Cairo", 1938; "The Hot Mikado", 1939; "Star and Garter", 1942; "Something for the Boys", "The Naked Genius", 1943; "Mexican Hayride", "Pick-Up Girl", "Catherine Was Great", 1944; "Up in Central Park", "Hamlet", "The Would-Be Gentleman", 1945, and "January Thaw", 1946.

WEBSTER, MARGARET. Director, Actress. Born in New York City, March 15, 1905. Educated in England at Queen Anne's School and London University. Became a successful actress in London before coming back to New York. Made her Broadway debut as Director of Evans' "Richard II" in 1937. Other productions which she has staged include: "Young Mr. Disraeli", 1937; full length "Hamlet", 1938; "Family Portrait", 1939; "Flare Path", 1942; "Counterattack", 1944; "Othello", 1943; "The Tempest", 1945; "Three to Make Ready", 1946.

WHARTON, CARLY (Mrs. John F.). Producer. Born in Los Angeles, Calif. In 1937 she came across a script by Dore Schady which she liked. Secured Garson Kanin to stage it, Jo Mielziner to design it and a good cast to act it, and made her debut presenting "Too Many Heroes". Has co-produced with Martin Gabel: "Young Couple Wanted", "Medicine Show", "Charley's Aunt", 1940; "Cream in the Well", 1941; "Cafe Crown", 1942; "The Assassin", 1945. Produced color movie, "La Cucaracha".

WILDBERG, JOHN J. Producer. Born in New York City, September 4, 1902. Received Doctor's Degree at Columbia in 1923. His first theatrical association was with "Hangman's Whip" in 1932. Served as counsel to the Group Theatre from 1934 to 1938. With Cheryl Crawford operated the Maplewood Theatre in New Jersey from 1940 to 1942. Made his debut as co-producer with Miss Crawford of the revival of "Porgy and Bess", 1941, and "One Touch of Venus", 1942. Produced on his own "Anna Lucasta", 1944, and "Memphis Bound", 1945.

WILSON, JOHN C. Producer, Director. Born Lawrenceville, N. J., August 19, 1899. Graduated from Yale University. First theatrical association was with the production of "Easy Virtue" in 1925. Became Noel Coward's Manager. In 1935 joined the Lunts in presenting "Point Valaine" and "The Taming of the Shrew". Other plays include: "George and Margaret", 1937; "Blithe Spirit", 1941; "Bloomer Girl", 1944; "The Day Before Spring", 1945. Helped Alfred Lunt stage "The Pirate", 1942, and directed "Foolish Notion", 1945.

WINDUST, BRETAIGNE. Director, Actor. Born Paris, France, January 20, 1906. Graduated from Princeton University, 1929. Began his career as an actor with the University Players Inc. Joined the Lunts' Company of "The Taming of the Shrew" in 1935. He was retained by them to direct "Idiot's Delight", 1936, and "Amphitryon 38", 1937. Other plays include: revival of "The Circle", 1938; "Life With Father", 1939; "Arsenic and Old Lace", 1941; "Strip for Action", 1942; "The Family", 1943; "Hasty Heart", "State of the Union", 1945.

WOLPER, DAVID. Producer. Born June 27, 1901, in New York City. Attended Brown University and Syracuse University Law College. In 1944 he produced the long run revue, "Follow the Girls", followed by "Men to the Sea" and "Glad to See You", 1944; "By Appointment Only", 1946.

FAMOUS PLAYERS OF YESTERDAY

Argentinita

George Arliss

OBITUARIES

HENRY AINLEY, 66, noted Shakespearean actor, died in London Oct. 31, 1945. His voice was considered one of the finest on the English stage. He played scores of roles both in England and America, and was seen here in "The Little Minister" with Maude Adams, "Trilby", "The Great Adventure", "The Dover Road", and "Julius Caesar".

ARGENTINITA (Encarnacion Lopez), 44, noted dancer, died in N. Y. C. on Sept. 24, 1945. She made her stage debut in Madrid at the age of 5, and became well known throughout Europe and South America. In 1930 she appeared on Broadway in Lew Leslie's "International Revue", and since then was seen frequently in concerts, and as a guest star with the Ballet Theatre.

GEORGE ARLISS, 77, eminent star of stage and screen, died in London as a result of a bronchial ailment on Feb. 5, 1946. He first appeared on the English stage in 1886, and in 1902 came to America with Mrs. Campbell in 'The Second Mrs. Tanqueray". He supported Blanche Bates in "The Darling of the Gods", and was with Mrs. Fiske in "Becky Sharp", "Leah Kleschna", "Hedda Gabler", and "The New York Idea". Appeared in "Rosmersholm", "Septimus", "Disraeli", "Paganini", "The Professor's Love Story", "Hamilton", "Out There", "The Mollusc", "The Green Goddess", "Old English", and 'The Merchant of Venice". Film versions were made from many of his stage successes, and he will also be remembered for "The House of Rothschild", "The Man Who Played God", "The Millionaire", "Richelieu", "The Iron Duke", and "Dr. Syn".

HENRY ARMETTA, noted character actor, died of a heart attack, which struck him during the performance of the revue "Opening Night" in San Diego, California, October 21, 1945. He was discovered by Raymond Hitchcock, at an early age, and given a small part in "The Yankee Counsel." He continued with his stage career until 1929; then started work in films. He appeared in such films as "The Climax," "Magnificent Obsession," and "Thank Your Lucky Stars." He also made occasional vaudeville appearances betwen pictures.

LIONEL ATWILL, 61, noted actor, died of pneumonia in Hollywood on April 22, 1946. He played many roles on the British stage before coming to this country in 1915 as Lily Langtry's leading man. Among his greatest successes were "The Lodger", "The Wild Duck", "Hedda Gabler", "A Doll's House", "Tiger! Tiger!", "Deburau", "The Outsider", and "Caesar and Cleopatra". He entered pictures in 1932, and among the many films he made were "The Silent Witness", "Nana", and "Captain Blood".

Henry Armetta

Lionel Atwill

Noah Beery

Robert Benchley

Frank Craven

Gus Edwards

NOAH BEERY, SR., 63, veteran movie badman, died in Hollywood, April 1, 1946. He was stricken with a heart attack and died in the arms of his brother, Wallace Beery. Among the many films in which he appeared were "The Vanishing American", "The Thundering Herd", and "North of 36". His most recent work, however, was on the Broadway stage in the role of Boss Tweed in "Up in Central Park".

ROBERT BENCHLEY, 56, noted wit, writer, actor and critic, died in N. Y. C. after suffering a cerebral hemorrhage on Nov. 22, 1945. Shortly after getting out of college he made a name for himself as a humorist. He was dramatic editor of the old "Life", and later of "The New Yorker". He wrote a sketch called "The Treasurer's Report" which he read on the stage in "The Music Box Revue 1923", and later published as a book. He wrote numerous articles and books and gained great popularity as a humorist. In Hollywood he appeared with great success in a series of comedy shorts, such as "How To Sleep", and he also played comedy parts in many feature pictures.

MAE BUSCH, 44, star of silent films, died in Hollywood, April 21, 1946. She appeared on the stage with Eddie Foy, but scored her greatest success in such pictures as "Foolish Wives", "The Christian", and "The Unholy Three".

FRANK CRAVEN, 70, veteran actor, playwright and director, died of a heart ailment in his home in Beverly Hills, Calif., on Sept. 1, 1945. He began his career as a child actor, and had several years experience in stock and on the road before making his first N. Y. hit in "Bought and Paid For". He also appeared in "Under Cover", "Seven Chances", "Going Up", and "Money From Home". He acted in many plays of his own authorship among which were "Too Many Cooks", "This Way Out", "The First Year", "That's Gratitude", "Spite Corner", "New Brooms". Perhaps his greatest success was in "Our Town", and his last stage appearance was in "Mrs. January and Mr. X". In addition to writing and and acting, he also directed many plays. He also appeared in a number of Hollywood films, and wrote scripts for the pictures.

GUS EDWARDS, 66, veteran song writer, actor and talent scout, died of a heart attack in Hollywood, Nov. 7, 1945. He wrote such song hits as "School Days", "Tammany", and "By The Light of the Silvery Moon", but was perhaps best known as a talent scout in the golden days of vaudeville. For many seasons his "School Days" act brought new talent to the public, and he "discovered" Eddie Cantor, George Jessel, Groucho Marx, Walter Winchell, Lila Lee and many others.

MAISIE GAY, 62, English musical comedy actress, died in London, Sept. 14, 1945. She was on the stage for over forty years. She played in more than 30 musicals among which were "The Quaker Girl", "High Jinks", "Sybil", "London Calling", "Charlot's Revue", and "This Year of Grace".

RUSSELL GLEASON, 36, actor son of James Gleason, accidentally fell to his death from window of his N. Y. hotel on Dec. 26, 1945. He appeared in several Hollywood movies, and was seen on the stage in "The Sky's the Limit".

VIRGINIA HARNED, 74, prominent stage star, died of a heart ailment in her N. Y. home on April 29, 1946. Her greatest success was in the role of "Trilby", which she created. She played opposite E. H. Sothern, her first husband, in "Hamlet", and many other plays. She also appeared in "Iris", "Camille", "Anna Karenina", and "Josephine". Her second husband was William Courtenay.

PERCY HASWELL, 74, actress and widow of George Fawcett, died in Nantucket, Mass., June 13, 1945. She appeared on the stage in "The Complex", and "The Honor of the Family". She also appeared in films.

LIONEL HOGARTH, 71, retired veteran actor, died in Amityville, L. I., April 15 ,1946. He supported Sarah Bernhardt on tour, and appeared frequently with Maude Adams and Jane Cowl. He was seen in "Richard of Bordeaux", and his last appearance was in Maurice Evans' "Richard II".

RALPH HOLMES, 30, actor son of Taylor Holmes, was found dead in his N. Y. apartment on Nov. 20, 1945. He appeared on Broadway in "Where Do We Go From Here?" "Thanks for Tomorrow", and "Stars in Your Eyes".

GLENN HUNTER, 52, noted stage juvenile, died in N. Y. C., Dec. 30, 1945. His first big part was that of Willie Baxter in "Seventeen", after which he played in "Penrod", "Clarence", "The Intimate Strangers" before scoring his greatest success in "Merton of the Movies". He made a film version of this play, and also appeared on the screen in "West of Water Tower", "The Scarecrow", and other pictures. Among his later stage plays were "Young Woodley", "Behold This Dreamer", the musical "Spring Is Here", a revival of "She Stoops to Conquer", "Waterloo Bridge", and "A Regular Guy". His last stage appearance was in 1939 in "Journey's End".

Russell Gleason

Virginia Harned

Percy Haswell

Glenn Hunter

Doris Keane

John McCormick

Philip Merivale

DORIS KEANE, 63, noted actress, died in N. Y. C. on Nov. 25, 1945. She appeared in "The Happy Marriage", "Our World", "Arsene Lupin'," "The Affairs of Anatol", "The Light O' London", and "Roxana". She achieved her greatest success in the role of Mme. Cavallini in "Romance". This play had a long run on Broadway, and ran for three years in London. She also appeared in revivals of "Romance", both here and abroad. She scored other hits in "The Czarina" and "Starlight". Her last stage appearance was in Los Angeles in 1929 in "The Pirate".

WILLIAM KENT, 59, well known actor, died in N. Y. C. on Oct. 4, 1945. He made his first success in "Ladies First", and following this appeared in "Rose Marie", "Lady Be Good", "Funny Face", "Girl Crazy" and "Ups-a-Daisy". More recently he appeared in "Revenge With Music", and last appeared on the stage in Philadelphia in 1944 in a revival of "The Merry Widow".

JEROME KERN, 60, composer of many of America's best beloved songs, died in N. Y. C. on Nov. 11, 1945, following a cerebral hemorrhage. For forty years he wrote songs that were loved by millions. He was considered the songwriter's songwriter, and his musical talent was one of the foremost in America. He studied composition in Germany and England, and his first musical show was "Mr. Wix of Wickham". In the period 1915-18 he composed the scores of 20 shows. Among his most famous scores are "The Girl From Utah", "Sally", "Sunny", "Show Boat", "Music in the Air", "Roberta" and "The Cat and the Fiddle". He also wrote music for many Hollywood pictures. Among his most celebrated songs are "Ol Man River", "Long Ago and Far Away", "All the Things You Are", "They Didn't Believe Me", "The Touch of Your Hand", "Smoke Gets in your Eyes", and "Look for the Silver Lining".

EDWARD KNOBLOCK, 71, eminent playwright, died in London, July 19, 1945. His most famous play was "Kismet". He also wrote "Marie-Odile", "Tiger-Tiger", "Milestones" (in collaboration with Arnold Bennett) and "My Lady's Dress".

LEE KOHLMAR, 73, veteran stage actor, died of a heart attack in North Hollywood, Calif., May 15, 1946. Among the many plays in which he appeared are "The Music Master", "The Yankee Girl" ,and "Partners Again".

FREDERICK LEWIS, 73, retired actor, died March 19, 1946 in Amityville, L. I. He had been a guest at the Percy Williams Home since 1940. For many years he was a principal member of the Sothern and Marlowe Repertory Company and won recognition for his portrayal of Shakespearean roles. He also appeared in "The Prisoner of Zenda" ,"The Raven", "Know Thyself", "The Battle", and made a hit as Horatio in John Barrymore's "Hamlet". He last stage appearance was in 1934 in "Come Of Age".

JOHN McCORMICK, 61, noted tenor, died in Dublin, Sept. 16, 1945. Unrivalled as a ballad singer, he charmed audiences throughout the world with his singing of such songs as "Mother Machree", and "I Hear You Calling Me". He sang in opera at the Metropolitan, but achieved his greatest fame on the concert stage. He also appeared in several moving pictures.

PHILIP MERIVALE, 59, noted English actor, died of a heart attack in Hollywood on March 13, 1946. His wife, actress Gladys Cooper, was at his bedside. He won fame playing Shakespearean roles with Ellen Terry, and first appeared in America opposite Mrs. Campbell in "Pygmalion". On Broadway he was seen in "The Swan", "The Road to Rome", "Death Takes a Holiday", "Mary of Scotland", "Othello", "Macbeth", and "Valley Forge". His last stage appearance was in 1944 in "The Duke in Darkness".

EARLE, MITCHELL, 64, retired actor, died in N. Y. C., Feb. 18, 1946. He appeared in more than 250 plays, and was seen in "Way Down East", "Strongheart", "Baby Mine", "The Dove", and in a number of plays with Leo Ditrichstein. His last stage appearance was in 1938 in "Madame Capet".

OLIVER MOROSCO, 69, stage producer and manager, was accidentally killed by a streetcar in Hollywood, Aug. 25, 1945. For many years he was one of the most successful producers on Broadway. His greatest hits were "Peg O' My Heart", and "The Bird of Paradise", and he also produced "The Cinderella Man", "Upstairs and Down", "Canary Cottage", "The Bat", "Beyond the Horizon", "Mama's Affair", "So Long Letty", and "The Unchastened Woman". In addition to being a producer, he also wrote a number of plays himself and in collaboration.

IVAN M. MOSKVIN, 72, eminent Russian actor, died in Moscow, Feb. 18, 1946. He was a member of the Moscow Art Theatre, and appeared here in "Czar Feodor Ivanovitch", "The Lower Depths", and "The Cherry Orchard". He played on the Russian stage for a period of 40 years, and also was seen in Russian films.

ELIZABETH MURRAY, 75, noted comedienne, died in Philadelphia, March 27, 1946. She appeared in "Madame Sherry", "Watch Your Step", "High Jinks", "Cohan Revue of 1918", "Good Night Paul", "Kitty's Kisses", "Love Birds", "Sidewalks of New York", and "Madame Capet". For many years she was a star in vaudeville, and she also appeared in pictures.

ALLA NAZIMOVA, 66, eminent star of stage and screen, died of a heart attack in Hollywood, July 13, 1945. Russian born, she first played here in 1905 in "The Chosen People", as a member of the Orleneff company. Her English-speaking debut was made the next year in "Hedda Gabler", followed by "A Doll's House". Later she appeared in "The Comtesse Coquette", "The Master Builder", "The Comet", "The Passion Flower", "Little Eyolf", "The Fairy Tale", "The Other Mary", "The Marionettes", "Bella Donna", "That Sort", "War Brides", "'Ception Shoals", and "The Wild Duck". Subsequently she played for several years in silent films, and was starred in such pictures as "War Brides", "Revelation", "The Red Lantern", "Eye for Eye", "The Brat", and "Salome". She returned to Broadway in "Dagmar". After this she was seen in "The Cherry Orchard", "Katerina", "A Month in the Country", "Mourning Becomes Electra", "The Good Earth", and revivals of "Ghosts" and "Hedda Gabler". During the last few years she played character roles in various films.

FISKE O'HARA, 67, Irish tenor and actor, died Aug. 2, 1945 in Hollywood where he had been conducting a vocal school. For many years he enjoyed great popularity on the road, where he toured in such light, romantic comedies as "Springtime in Mayo", "The Man from Wicklaw", "Down Limerick Way", and "Land O' Romance". More recently he was seen in "Sidewalks of New York", and appeared in the films. He collaborated with Anne Nichols on the play "Abie's Irish Rose".

LEW POLLACK, 50, popular song writer, died of a heart attack in Hollywood, Jan. 18, 1946. He began writing songs at an early age, and in 1928 went to Hollywood where he composed songs for many pictures. Among his outstanding hits were "Charmaine", "Diane", "Angela Mia", "Two Cigarettes in the Dark", and "Yiddisher Momme".

CYRIL SCOTT, 79, veteran stage actor, died in N. Y. C. on Aug. 17, 1945. During his 53 years on the stage he supported such stars as Richard Mansfield, Anna Held, Ethel Barrymore and Mrs. Fiske. His most successful role was in "The Prince Chap", and he also played in "The Circus Girl", "The Woman of It", "Paddy the Next Best Thing", "It's a Grand World", and "The Passing Present". His last stage appearance was in 1936 in "The Holmeses of Baker Street".

ARTHUR SHAW, 65, veteran stage actor, died at his home in Washington on March 22, 1946, after a long illness. He was the son of Mary Shaw, and his acting career extended over 30 years. He scored his greatest success as the property man in "The Yellow Jacket". He was also seen in "Craig's Wife", and "Torch Song".

Elizabeth Murray

Nazimova

Fiske O'Hara

Slim Summerville

Wilella Waldorf

Charles Waldron

EDWARD SHELDON, 60, well known playwright, died at his home in N. Y. C. on April 1, 1946. His first play, "Salvation Nell", was written while a student at Harvard, and produced when he was 22. Among his other plays were "The Nigger", "The Boss", and in 1913 his greatest success, "Romance", started its long run. He adapted "The Song of Songs" from the German, "The Czarina" from the Hungarian, and entirely rewrote "The Jest" of Sam Benelli for the Barrymores. In collaboration with other writers, he did "Bewitched", "The Proud Princess", "Lulu Belle", and "Dishonored Lady". Despite partial paralysis and blindness in his later years, he remained a powerful force in the theatre.

GUS SHY, 51, stage and screen comedian, died in Hollywood, June 15, 1945 after a long illness. He is best remembered for his comedy roles in "The Desert Song", "The New Moon", "Good News", and "America's Sweetheart".

SLIM SUMMERVILLE, 54, renowned movie comedian, died in his home at Laguna Beach, Calif., on Jan. 5, 1946. He was one of the original Keystone cops, and appeared in the early days with Charlie Chaplin, Marie Dressler, and Chester Conklin. He made a great hit in the silent film, "All Quiet on the Western Front", after which he played comedy roles in a great number of films. In his lengthy career he appeared in over 600 movies.

BOOTH TARKINGTON, 76, distinguished novelist and playwright, died at his home in Indianapolis on May 19, 1946. His greatest acclaim was received from his novels which included two Pulitzer prize winners: "Alice Adams" and "The Magnificent Ambersons". He dramatized "The Gentleman from Indiana", and "Monsieur Beaucaire". Among his other plays were "The Man From Home" (with Harry Leon Wilson), "Cameo Kirby", "Mister Antonio", "Clarence", "The Wren", "The Intimate Strangers" and "Tweedles".

GEORGE C. TYLER, 78, famed Broadway producer, died of a heart attack in Yonkers on March 14, 1946. In his career of forty years he managed and produced over 350 stage productions, many of which were outstanding hits. Among his successes are "The Royal Box", "The Christian", "Children of the Ghetto", "Sag Harbor", "Mrs. Wiggs of the Cabbage Patch", "Merely Mary Ann", "The Squaw Man", "Alias Jimmy Valentine", "The Garden of Allah", "Pollyanna", "Clarence", "Dulcy", "Merton of the Movies" and "The Constant Nymph". He also brought to this country the Irish Players from the Abbey Theatre, Dublin, and presented Eleonora Duse to the American public.

WILELLA WALDORF, 46, dramatic critic, died in her N. Y. home on March 12, 1946 after a long illness. She was the dramatic critic of the New York Post, and her column "Two on the Aisle" had many readers. She began by writing movie reviews, and from 1928 to 1941 was drama editor. She was made dramatic critic in 1941, and was the only woman first-string critic on a N. Y. newspaper.

CHARLES D. WALDRON, 69, veteran stage actor, died in Hollywood, March 4, 1946. His acting career had a span of 48 years, and among his plays were "The Fourth Estate", "A Bill of Divorcement", "Magda", "The Squaw Man" and "Daddy Long Legs", "The Barretts of Wimpole Street". He specialized in roles of domineering fathers, and was last seen in "Deep Are The Roots".

EMILY ANN WELLMAN, retired actress, died of heart illness in N. Y. C. March 20, 1946. Among the many plays in which she was seen are "The Prince Chap", "Elevating a Husband", "Rockbound", "The Wasp", and more recently "Miss Quis".

HERBERT A. YOST, 65, stage actor, died in N. Y. C. Oct. 24, 1945. He first played in "Overnight" when he was 17, and was on the stage for 48 years. Also under the name Barry O'Moore, he was leading man with the old Edison Film Co. His most recent appearance was in "Jacobowsky and the Colonel".

VINCENT YOUMANS, 47, well known song writer, died in Denver, April 5, 1946. He wrote the scores of a dozen or more hit shows, among which were "Two Little Girls in Blue", "No, No, Nanette", "Wildflower", "Hit the Deck" and "Great Day". "Tea for Two", "I Want to Be Happy", "Without a Song", and "Through the Years" are some of his best beloved songs.

INDEX

198

·

PHOTO CREDITS

Chris Alexander—pages 5,117; Bauer-Toland—page 96t.; Constantine—page 141; Fred Fehl—pages 19b.L., 40b.L.; Albert A. Freeman—page 12t.; Bob Golby—page 87b; Graphic House—pages 7t., 8, 10b., 14b., 15b.L., 20, 22b.L.&r., 30, 31, 32, 40t. &b.r., 42, 48, 49, 50, 56, 57t.&b.L., 75, 82, 85r., 89, 90, 91, 93, 94t.L., 95t.r., 103, 108t.b.-c.&r., 111, 120b.; Lucas-Pritchard—pages 9b.&c., 11, 12b., 19t., 26, 28, 36, 37, 62, 63, 110, 115, 125, 127; Murray Korman—page 13; Murray Lewis—page 6t.; Abraham Mandelstam—pages 9t., 57b.r., 72; Louis Melancon—pages 6b., 58b., 124, 137, 138, 139, 140, 142, 143; Frederick New— page 96b.; Pix—pages 24, 54, 55, 70, 71; Otto Rothschild — pages 22t., 23c.&b.; Schonbrunn — page 14t.; Standard — page 128; Talbot—pages 83, 88, 121t.L.&r.; Richard Tdcker—pages 18, 27, 58t., 77, 133, 134; Alfredo Valente—pages 7b., 10t., 16, 17, 43, 44, 59, 76, 92; Vandamm Studio—pages 3, 15t.&b.r., 21, 23t., 25, 29, 33, 34, 35, 38, 39, 41, 45, 46, 47, 51, 52, 53, 60, 61, 64, 65, 66, 67, 73, 74, 78, 79, 80, 81, 85b.L., 86, 87t., 99, 100, 101, 107, 108b.L., 109, 112, 113, 114, 116, 120t., 131; Richard Vickers—pages 94t.r.&b., 95t.L.&b., 97, 102, 104; Voss—page 84; Cyril Weinstein—page 123; Dick Williams —page 68.

Key (t.) top; (b.) bottom; (c.) center; (r.) right; (L) left